Jane Yardley was brought up in Essex in the 1960s. She has a PhD from a London medical school and works on clinical projects around the globe. Her first novel, *Painting Ruby Tuesday* (which was written on aeroplanes) was shortlisted for the Guildford Arts First Novel Prize. *Rainy Day Women* is her second novel. Jane's next novel *A Saucerful of Secrets* is available soon from Doubleday.

Acclaim for *Rainy Day Women*:

'Set in the early Seventies, Jane Yardley's novel features a family in terminal decline. Fifteen-year-old Jo Starkey is a fan of Cream and Leonard Cohen; her elder brother Tarquin is an avant-garde folk musician who released a number of records before becoming a recluse. Jo's twin, Timothy, is also withdrawn (although his passion is for calculus rather than chords), and as for Pater and Mater Starkey, the former is an alcoholic, the latter a workaholic, and both feature only as absences in their children's world.

There is one further complication. The family abode – the Red House – is an architectural oddity, a place full of strange quirks and autumnal sadness. It is also, according to Jo, home to a poltergeist named Clarence. Jo sets about discovering the house's secrets and inevitably ends up unearthing some shocking truths.

A mystery story, a ghost story, a rites of passage tale – Yardley's novel excels as each. *Rainy Day Women* manages to capture the strain and pain of teenagers growing up and families breaking down and yet remain up-beat, animated by humour that is sharp but unfailingly generous'
Daily Mail

'The story of Jo and Frankie, two friends marooned in an Essex village but about to taste the delights of London, has a real feeling of experience behind it . . . you'll love this step back in time'
Red

'Funny, poignant and original'
Company

'Jane Yardley's entertaining *Rainy Day Women* is a blackly comic tale of teenage weirdness'
Image

Acclaim for *Painting Ruby Tuesday*:

'When a rash of murders startles the modest Essex village of Muningstock in 1965, the local police can't seem to crack the case. This is because ten-year-old Annie Craddock keeps inadvertently stumbling through, removing or vomiting over the evidence. An emotional mass of red hair, lanky physique and vivid imagination, Annie normally spends her summer holidays larking about with her best pal Babette, playing the piano with the dazzling charismatic Mrs Clitheroe who shares her love of music . . . (they both see music as colours), and hurling herself adoringly on Ollie the rag-and-bone man's dog. When things go frighteningly awry . . . Annie finds herself questioned by the police and wrong-footed at every turn.

The story is told in the first person by the present-day Annie, whose imminent move to New York with her husband has stirred up ghosts from her past. The highly original tale moves between past and present, told with humour and poignancy by a hugely likeable heroine. Yardley effortlessly evokes the confusion and egotism of childhood . . . Now, as an adult, [Annie] finally realises the truth behind the events of that summer . . . This is an entertaining and compelling read, filled with rounded, memorable characters, and both darkly funny and moving'   *Time Out*

Also by Jane Yardley

PAINTING RUBY TUESDAY

and published by Black Swan

RAINY DAY
WOMEN

Jane Yardley

BLACK SWAN

RAINY DAY WOMEN
A BLACK SWAN BOOK: 0 552 77102 3

Originally published in Great Britain by Doubleday,
a division of Transworld Publishers

PRINTING HISTORY
Doubleday edition published 2004
Black Swan edition published 2005

1 3 5 7 9 10 8 6 4 2

Set in 11/12pt Melior by
Falcon Oast Graphic Art Ltd.

Black Swan Books are published by Transworld Publishers,
61–63 Uxbridge Road, London W5 5SA,
a division of The Random House Group Ltd,
in Australia by Random House Australia (Pty) Ltd,
20 Alfred Street, Milsons Point, Sydney, NSW 2061, Australia,
in New Zealand by Random House New Zealand Ltd,
18 Poland Road, Glenfield, Auckland 10, New Zealand
and in South Africa by Random House (Pty) Ltd,
Endulini, 5a Jubilee Road, Parktown 2193, South Africa.

Printed and bound in Great Britain by
Cox & Wyman Ltd, Reading, Berkshire.

Papers used by Transworld Publishers are natural, recyclable products
made from wood grown in sustainable forests. The manufacturing
processes conform to the environmental regulations of the
country of origin.

To Bill, Dave and Dominic of Tapp Street,
wherever

1

I wasn't worried about the staircase – this was usually safe ground. True, the estate agent had toppled down it the first time he came to us, but we blamed this on the heavy hand with which my mother had been pouring the gin. No, the staircase generally behaved itself in front of visitors. I now watched the latest pair trot enthusiastically up it, heads wobbling from side to side like toy nodding-dogs as they took in the wheeze of the stair treads, the writhing banisters with their exquisitely carved garlands and doleful patina of grime; the decrepit grandeur of our Venetian window at the turn of the stairs, its glass spattered with the dried spores of old raindrops both outside and in, where the weather had trickled through the festering woodwork.

'Superficial, all this decay,' confided the man to his wife. 'I'd expected worse, from the price.'

Beyond the house, distorted by the watery imperfections of the original window glass, our knotty old orchard glittered with snow in the crackling light of the afternoon. Snow also dribbled from Mrs's bouncing coat. I noted with a fifteen-year-old's disdain that this managed to be an unfashionable length despite the scope offered by the styles of mini, midi and maxi. My own appearance was faultless: long hair newly ironed that very morning, flowing caftan and bare feet to match. I would have blended perfectly into an ashram in Rajasthan. Unfortunately, I was ten miles east of Romford, trying to pretend I wasn't blue with cold.

There was a brief hesitation on the landing when we encountered the door of Tarquin's room, from where emanated the sound of 'I Do Like To Be Beside The Seaside' played backwards, accompanied by clanging buckets and a noise unnervingly like someone strangling a duck, which managed to slip through his sound-proofing like missiles getting under the radar. But explaining him away was something I'd grown up with.

'My brother, Tarquin Starkey. The rock musician.'

'Does he have a studio in there, then?'

'It's sound-proof, but otherwise the room will convert straight back into an ordinary bedroom the moment he moves his equipment out.'

Yes, well, we would cross that bridge when we came to it. The couple contemplated his quivering door.

'Sound-proof bedroom,' whispered the husband. 'Come in handy, eh?'

'George!'

I hitched all the bangles ringingly up my arm and considered which room would be the least hazardous to view next. Then I detected another set of noises distinct from Tarquin's – a savage electrical *zizz* redolent of mad-eyed professors and forked lightning. This was another brother's room, Timothy's, my twin, with his bank of rodent cages, their whizzy wheels harnessed to drive other wheels and cogs. Hamster power. I veered Mr and Mrs towards the bathroom and tried to quench their quizzical looks.

'Please be good enough to step this way,' I instructed loudly, using the adult patter at which I was becoming quite polished with all this practice. The estate agent had done it himself for about a month, but that was ages ago. I didn't blame him for running away. 'It's the principal bathroom. Our parents' bedroom on the third storey also has its own.'

'En suite, it says here.' The rustle of paper. I saw the heading: The Red House, Lossing Common. 'Main bathroom fifty feet by twenty-five. Must be a misprint.'

'Nope, it really is ginormous,' I said, my patter slipping.

We crossed the tired carpet of the landing with its stains of four childhoods, towards the heavy, panelled door. I twisted the handle and pushed.

It was early March, leafless spring, a bright, brittle, snow-blown Sunday. Light from the low sun stormed the bathroom through broad sash windows, smearing the unwashed glass, electrifying the porcelain and silver-plating the Victorian tiled walls. Apart from mine, this was the only bearable room in the house. My best friend Francine and I would sometimes set up nets and play badminton in here. Tennis, too, in the summer, there being no-one who was likely to notice what we smashed. On winter nights, Francine and I often lit a fire in the grate of the appropriate period feature and locked ourselves in overnight with cushions and the leaping firelight, leaving the rest of the household to fight over the en suite.

The bath itself was enamelled cast iron, complacent on dinky claws, with rusty stains under the taps like dribbles of dog pee in this morning's snow. All four walls were tiled up to the dado rail, nineteenth-century glazed ceramic in russets and chocolate browns, which drew from my brothers untiring jokes about diarrhoea. In the fizzing snowlight, they shone like melting caramel.

And here was the original fireplace, above it the mirror handed down from my grandmother's grandmother, fittingly liver-spotted and misty like an elderly lady in gossamer shawls. I quickly checked my reflection. Last night, while I was doing my regular babysitting job down the road, Francine had dropped in and we'd practised painting each other's faces. The trendy dragon on my left cheek was now a bit bleary from being slept on, though this was still no excuse for the stare I'd got from the visitors when first I'd let them in, followed by their question as to whether it was a tortoise or a centipede.

I turned back to the focal point of the bathroom: a mahogany-seated, long-chained, blue-flowered throne of a lavatory in High Victorian Gothic. I'd removed the tottering heap of medical journals (Mum and Dad), so that our view of this masterpiece was uninterrupted.

My visitors gasped. 'Well! Needs a bit of work, but – well!'

'The plumbing is nineteenth century,' I explained with an air of professional candour, 'but all in perfect working order.'

But the plumbing didn't include central heating; there was none anywhere in the house. And my parents, with an air of refusing to recognize their noses in front of their faces, insisted on blaming this for our inability to sell.

'George, I'm bowled over. First the conservatory – now this!'

'Can't use it for tea parties though, dear. Get a chance to try out the fancy khazi, do we?'

'George!'

I drew their attention to the bath taps designated *C* and *F* from the French *chaud et froid*, causing surprise to anyone who fiddled with them not knowing that the hot tap spluttered water at boiling point, and *C* didn't stand for *cold*.

'So *F* is hot?'

'No, Madge, that's what the little lady's trying to tell you. *F* is *cold.*'

'And *C* is hot,' I confirmed smiling, and with a magician's flourish I turned on the tap.

'What do you mean – real blood?'

'Well, all right, not *real* real. Just this awful yukky red stuff.'

'Oh *gross*!' said Francine.

'And pipes jolting and banging like they were about to explode. By which time Mrs had copped the glugging taps and was retching.'

'And where was Tarquin through all this?'

'*Tarquin!* I expect he was recording the banging pipes for percussion on his next album. If Mrs had actually thrown up he'd have recorded the vomiting, probably.'

We were in Francine's bedroom, where she was painting her toenails, one long milky-white leg stretched taut across to the vanity unit as though it were a ballerina's barre.

'Doesn't that hurt?' I asked, wincing at the thought of her hamstrings.

'Like a bitch. But they told us at Lucie Clayton that stretching exercises are good for posture.' Francine unpropped the leg by lifting it off the furniture with both hands, whimpering. Then up went the other one, little balls of cotton wool peeping between her toes as though she were foaming at the feet.

'The thing is,' I continued, 'it can't be just co-incidence any more.'

'How do you mean?'

'Every single appointment to view the house. I know

13

we've always had them on and off, weird mani-festations, stupid practical jokes, whatever you want to call them – but not at this rate. Every potential buyer is treated to a display of full special effects like a Hammer horror film. Whoever's doing it, it's like he's determined to stop us selling the house.'

'I thought we knew that already.'

'This one makes it statistically significant, that's the point.'

'Sadistic is right,' agreed Francine, pensively stroking the brush along her toenails. Her portfolio was open on the bed, black and white glossies of Francine pouting leggily from the studios of the Lucie Clayton modelling agency, sometimes blond (home-grown), sometimes brunette (wig, costing twenty-eight pounds).

I wasn't a blonde, neither was I wraith-like. I was big-boned. This isn't a euphemism for fat, I had big bones with knobs on, all wrists and knuckles and knees, gargantuan hands and feet, joints like spanner heads. Tarquin, in an atypically lucid statement, once observed that I had hands big enough to tackle both a Jimi Hendrix guitar solo and an arm-wrestler. My eyes were OK. I sometimes sat in front of the mirror with the rest of my face swaddled in a scarf, admiring my eyes and dreaming of plastic surgery. What really put the kibosh on my photogenic potential was that my other features were dwarfed by the one in the middle. The word *nose* was too trite for this projection, which cast shadows and preceded me into the room; it wasn't a hooter or a conk; mine was a protuberance, a proboscis, a schnozzle. The boys at school joked that if I'd had another one on the back of my head they could have used me as a pickaxe. From the portfolio on the bed, Francine's retroussé version twinkled up at me. I wandered over to the window.

The sunlight on the garden, I noted, hardened and grew cold. We cannot cage the minute within its nets of gold. My favourite poem; Louis MacNeice. I often recited it aloud – in fact, pretty well every single time the sun went in; my English teacher had put a moratorium on it. There had been a heavy snowfall in the night (he wrote one about snow too) and this had brought down overhead cables and left us without power for most of Sunday morning, playing merry havoc with the roast beef of old England. At breakfast the trees had been heavy with it, blue-white and glistening like a Christmas card, but they were bare now, stark black in the glassy afternoon light. Francine's parents, who were from Detroit and used to Emergency Snow Routes and your sump oil freezing, had sneered at it all as paltry.

'Gordon Bennett – they've come up *pink*!' exclaimed Francine, staring scandalized at her wriggling toes. I glanced at the bottle. *Frosted pink* it said clearly on the label.

'All the bottles my mom's got, and I go and swipe a *pink* pink!'

Francine, too, had been American three years ago when the family first moved here but she was now anglicized to Gordon Bennett standard, though a recent trip home had furnished the infectious Americanism 'gross', which was a particularly worthwhile expletive as it made most adults' toes curl up. And she had achieved immortality in our village by raising her middle finger at some jibing schoolboys and screaming, '*Sit on this and rotate, you motherfuckers!*', an expression that had subsequently enjoyed a bit of a vogue.

'Look, this time the goings-on can't be anyone in your family,' she told me, reaching for the nail varnish remover, 'because nobody in your family wants to muck up the house sale.'

Well, that wasn't exactly true.

'You'll all be thrilled to see the back of the place.'

15

One of us wouldn't. One of us wouldn't leave the Red House until we burned him out.

'So maybe Tarquin's right,' continued Francine.

'About the supernatural thingy, you mean?'

'Clarence.'

'All right then, Clarence. And Tarquin's Clarence is dead set against us going. Hell bent,' I added with sad appropriateness. 'But then why won't he tell us what he wants from us? It's not like we never asked him.'

'True.'

Francine rubbed at her toes with a disintegrating Kleenex; the smell of acetone rose from her feet like one of Clarence's less offensive effluvia.

'Maybe we're asking in the wrong way,' mused Francine. 'Maybe the ghost *is* trying to get a message through to us, but the whatsit's wrong.'

'Tarquin doesn't say it's a *ghost*,' I said, hiding behind pedantry. We had tried all the whatsits we knew. We had tried Ouija, planchette and simply leaving writing materials conspicuously about the place, all lined up. The Ouija sessions delivered pages of enthusiastic gibberish that looked suspiciously like our wishful-thinking fingers pushing the glass at random. The only coherent results were from the left-around writing materials, but with two brothers in the house, one fifteen and one Tarquin, we didn't need to blame the pornographic output on a poltergeist.

'Maybe Clarence is illiterate.'

'And mute?'

We had tried calling out questions (tap once for yes, twice for no) and leaving a tape recorder running all night (Tarquin's eight-track; maybe slightly over the top). Nothing. Not even the creaking of a stair, though this itself was weird, as our staircase famously creaked all night and all day like a ship's rigging in a storm. It hadn't been easy for me, this supernatural stuff. Me with all my science and an IQ of 160.

16

'Look, Frankie. Sitting here, I mean in your house, away from the architecture and atmosphere, don't you think it sounds . . . well . . . ?'

'Barmy? Then come up with something better! I hate to say this, but we're running out of time. Mom wants out in August, to give us some leeway before I start a new school. Come the autumn we'll be up in London and at this rate you won't be in any posh pad near your dad's consulting rooms, you'll still be here.'

'Maybe your parents won't get a buyer that quickly.'

'We don't have to go through all that, I told you. The Ford people take care of it.'

And even if they didn't, why would Francine's parents have trouble getting rid of this house? It was detached, with four bedrooms, lounge, dining room and study, loos upstairs and down and full central heating; it represented the epitome of luxurious living to any British family, never mind what her mother said. And blood didn't run out of the taps.

On the record player, James Taylor's album *Sweet Baby James* was coming to an end again with a hiss, but because Francine kept the plastic arm cranked across, the stylus lumbered heavily back to the beginning again. Round and round. Sometimes when I slept here we didn't even switch it off overnight, just turned the volume down a notch.

'Pity Tim won't give us the benefit of his brilliant brain.'

'Oh, thanks a bunch, Frankie.'

'You know what I mean. You're clever, Jo, but you're not a child progeny. Protégé?'

'Prodigy. Yeah, well, Timothy still swears it's Tarquin who's doing it all, setting up the hoaxes at night. You know Tim when he gets on the subject of Tarquin. Anyway, he's not as bothered about it as I am. It's all the same to Tim whether we move, he's self-contained.' I thought of his shut door, the bookcases,

17

music and hamsters. 'And as Tim doesn't volunteer to show people round the house, he misses out on Clarence's more lurid misbehaviour. Or whoever.'

'But what about the everyday stuff? It's not like this is new since the house went on the market.'

'Tim says he's never had any silly business when he's been on his own. He says Tarquin knows that he, Timmy, won't fall for it, so he saves his energy for the gullible. Meaning us.'

Francine scrutinized her fresh handiwork. Footiwork. 'Better,' she decided. Yes, it was better. Day-Glo orange. And then, 'You could check out Tim's story. Hide under his bed or something.'

'Get lost!'

'Well, at least then you'd know whether it's true. Or whether Tim just won't admit what's going on because of being a scientific genius that doesn't believe in Clarences.'

'Maths genius,' I corrected. 'It's an art, not a science. Frankie, allow me to add to your store of entirely useless information. You've heard of quantum theory?'

'Nope.'

'Yes, you have – I've been boring you to death with it for months. Well, one of the offshoots is something called the Heisenberg Uncertainty Principle. It's about how you can't measure anything that's part of a system without altering that system. Your own interaction buggers things up. And this doesn't only affect sub-atomic particles, it applies willy-nilly across the everyday, boring, mundane problems of our lives. Meaning I can hide all I like, but just by being there I shall destroy whatever might have happened if Clarence had had Timothy to himself. That is a fundamental scientific principle.'

'So this is one of the everyday, boring, mundane problems of life, is it? Trying to hold a conversation with a poltergeist?'

2

It was early evening before I trudged home from Francine's in the snow, just a hundred yards; hers was the nearest house to ours. A beautiful evening in its way, with sun streaked across the cloud on the western horizon in watery yellows like smashed eggs, the shell shining through. One of the singers at Stavering Folk Club, in hope of whom Francine kept her toes freshly varnished, did an Al Stewart song called 'Electric Los Angeles Sunset'. I wondered whether the original looked anything like this one.

Home; my mother's car was pulling out of the drive. On call again? I watched her swing expertly through the tight bend and away up the road, revealing another car sitting there – my oldest brother Geoffrey's. This one didn't live with us, thank God, or the Red House really would have been uninhabitable. He fell over his own feet, and objects came apart in his hands; he was the only person on earth who could set stainless steel on fire; if there really was a Clarence, then Geoff Starkey was his representative among the living. No other car stood on the driveway, so heaven alone knew where my father was.

As I came in through the front door, Geoffrey's wife Angela was halfway up the stairs with the baby.

'There you are, Josephine! *What on earth* have you got on your feet?'

'Gold lamé jackboots?'

'Barefoot! In the snow!'

'Shoes are really not hip, Angela, take it from me.'

'You need your head examining, you do. Someone should have a word with your mother.'

'If they can ever get hold of her, they're welcome.'

'Don't be pert!'

'Angela, you've got baby sick all down the sleeve of your blouse.'

I padded on my snowy feet across the hallway and into the kitchen, thinking this was the one room Geoffrey would not be in. Wrong. He was bent over the sink with a baffled expression and the components of a baby's feeding bottle. He waved a rubber teat at me. 'Ah, Josie!' It flew from his fingers and bounced across the quarry tiles.

'Sorry, Geoff. Homework. Got to go.'

Back to the hall, where I ran into Timothy. He jumped.

'Oh God, it's only you, Josie! I'm trying to find a safe harbour, but every door opens onto either Geoffrey or Mrs Geoff or one of the little Geoffreys.'

'What's going on, Tim – what are they doing here?'

'A family conference about their inheritance.'

'Sorry?'

'It's because of the house. In Geoff and Angela's eyes, it's as good as sold. They're after some of the profits so they can knock their *lounge* through.' He gave an affected shudder. 'Their argument is that Mum and Dad have a duty towards their grandchildren to top up Geoff and Angela's coffers, Mum and

Dad being well off, and Geoff and Angela being skint.'

'But they've tried that before. Dad told them to take a running jump. He gave them all that stuff about when we were little, and he and Mum coped with four kids on his money as a houseman, and lived on tinned beans.'

'Well, Angela's obviously sick of beans, so they're back here on the ear'ole. This time using the house sale as a new argument.'

'But *what* family conference? Dad's out and I just saw Mum disappear off in the car.'

'Dad's not out, at least not in the way you mean. He's upstairs sleeping it off.'

'Then where's his car?'

'Golf club, I suppose. He went up there for lunch. This p.m. saw the return of one driving mother and one snoring, empurpled father. I suppose the club phoned her to take him home. She gave him a fireman's lift up the stairs and now the hospital's called her back in, so that was the last we'll see of her. And pretty much the last we'll see of him.'

Timothy looked so much like me that we'd known strangers to enquire whether you can have identical twins of different sexes, a question to which I always responded with more patience than Timothy did. Once you had worked out which of us was which, his heavy bones seemed less out of place than mine, but otherwise the most striking difference between us (even the length of our hair was as similar as Tim's school would let him get away with) was the state of our acne. While my brother's face was so pimpled and pus-ridden that it frothed like a pint of bitter, mine was bathed five times a day in dish-washing detergent, as a simple de-greasing solution. Admittedly, it was not ideal; according to Francine this was not given out as a skincare tip at the Lucie Clayton modelling agency; but it did starve the spots from the outside, and anyone who doubted the efficacy only had to glance from Timothy to me for a before-and-after comparison. Mind you, from the *inside*, it felt much as though I'd been sandpapered.

'So why,' I asked Tim, 'are Geoff and Angela still here?'

'Waiting for Dad to wake up, I s'pose. Then they'll man-trap him.'

I groaned. There was a swishing sound and our mad cat Elvis tore past us up the stairs in a blaze of fur, after mice or his imagination. The air was suddenly full of mohair; we spluttered quietly and wiped our mouths.

'So, *is* the house as good as sold, Josie?' asked Tim, stuffing a crumpled, hairy handkerchief back in his pocket. 'Have the Geoffreys got wind of something about today's visitors?'

'Well, the bath filled up with blood. Naturally, the couple were totally smitten and made us an offer we couldn't refuse.'

'Oh Christ.'

'Or Antichrist, depending on your viewpoint.' Pause. 'Speaking of which. Timothy . . .'

'What?'

'You remember how Frankie and I tried séances and Ouija?'

Timothy clucked disapprovingly.

'Perhaps it needed your superior brain behind it, Tim.'

'If this is leading up to something, save your breath.'

'*Tim*.'

'Not on your nelly! Not as long as E equals mc squared, not—'

'Why won't you help?'

'Because it's *mad*! *What* poltergeist? We've got a brother upstairs who looks like the Wild Man of Borneo and locks himself in a studio seven days a week recording screeches that probably emanate from a cat he's feeding into a food mixer . . .'

'Don't be ridiculous.'

'Don't be ridiculous? Listen, Josie – while Tarquin was swanning about North America for a couple of years, did we get any of this stuff? Not a dickie-bird, we didn't. No writing on the wall in dubious body fluids, no yowling from up the chimney, no stink bombs or clouds of pantomime mist belching across the landing in the middle of the night. Not while Tarquin was several thousand miles across the Atlantic. Elementary, my dear Watson.'

Of course, Timothy had said this many times, but none of us could remember whether it fitted the facts. Tarquin was gone from the summer of 1967 until 1969, though even then he had a habit of nipping home with some pouty American girl in one hand and a suitcase full of California grass in the other. (Tarquin had been in love with the Red House since the day – also snowing – when we moved here.) But whether or not 'Clarence's' pranks were confined to any particular stretches of time, the atmosphere of the place didn't fluctuate: there had never been any let-up from its perpetual air of dank melancholy, the all-year mean, autumnal light slanting through sad glazing; despondency in every room like a fog, like a grand decaying ballroom that's seen its last ball.

'We haven't got a poltergeist,' Timothy continued, 'because they don't exist, Josie. Have you got that?'

'Look, I *know* they don't exist – but *just in case*, Timmy. Surely anything's worth a try – the situation's desperate.'

'Rubbish! It's their quagmire, not ours. Come three years this October, we'll be at university whatever happens. Just sit it out; hold your nose when the smell of sewage wafts past, and when the wailing starts stick chewing gum in your ears. At its worst, it's not much less palatable than anything else of Tarquin's.'

'But if only we could move house, and live near Dad's consulting rooms so Mum could get a proper job at one of the London hospitals, she said so, and not be on call all hours . . .'

'. . . we'd be the ideal family. Daddy would come home sober every evening for tea and we'd toast crumpets by the fire and dote on one another.'

My eyes stung.

'Josie, it was all going to change the last time we moved, remember? Mum would get a consultant's post in Stebbing and "have time for the children". Ha! That was eight years ago.'

'Yes, Mum was always like this, but Dad wasn't. He wasn't, Timmy, not when we were in Ealing. So maybe if we got away . . .'

If we got away. And managed to uproot Tarquin, and his conjoined twin the Moog synthesizer, from that studio reeking of solder and overheated wiring. And get Timothy out of here, who was retreating further from normal life by the day. In my mind I heard those sparking electrics and hamster wheels behind his ever-shut door.

'I mean, that's the whole idea, isn't it?' I argued. 'Why else did Mum and Dad put the house on the market?'

'But it's too little too late, my dear sister.'

Too late. The most harrowing words in the world. If I accepted them, then there was nothing ahead but despair, the family disintegrating with the ruthless momentum of death-watch beetle in the Red House beams. A familiar cold ache clutched at my innards. Too late, too late. I turned away and blundered up the stairs. Timothy shouted after me.

'You forgot to add that Francine Switt and family are moving to London this summer. Isn't that right?'

This also made its mark. The prospect of losing

Frankie terrified me. I would have lobbed something back, but I'd heard the catch in Timothy's voice when he talked about Mum. I wasn't the only one to ache.

On the landing, I had to dodge the out-swing of an opening bedroom door. Angela was coming through it. She had swapped the baby for a two-year-old, my nephew Angus, carrying a potty. Oh good, he'd filled it up.

'Node,' he said, pointing a chewed finger at my face. There was a wobble and a slosh.

His mother cooed at him. 'It's Auntie Josie, darling. Say it, say "Aun-tee Jo-see".'

'Jo-dee,' stated Angus with the clarity of a phonetics teacher. 'Bid node,' he added and then, to ensure I was in no doubt about the translation, he turned the pointing finger on himself and me in turn. 'An-dus,' he explained, 'Jo-dee. Bid node.'

If Timothy was right, I thought, shutting my bedroom door on the lot of them, and our practical jokes had a human author, it wasn't poor Tarquin I'd put my money on, it was Angus.

3

Los Angeles might well have had its electric sunsets, but they were a long, long way from the folk club at Stavering where Florian Smith, he of Francine's dreams, was singing one of them into the Elizabethan rafters. We were no less chock-a than any other Monday in spite of the snow, and as Francine and I arrived late it was only by stupendous luck that we'd managed to get inside to hear Florian's set. Which was just as well, since we had trudged four miles through drifted snow to hear him. The bus had given up the ghost before we even got out of Lossing Common. Of course, we were not barefoot tonight, Angela was quite wrong about us needing our heads examining: we were shod in Dr Scholl sandals. Nevertheless there had come a moment, while cutting across a field with our snow-soaked jeans and denim-coloured extremities, when I'd suggested to Francine that on Scott's Antarctic expedition this was about the point when they'd shot the ponies.

Stavering was a proper village with a village green,

cottages and a war memorial, nothing like our own Lossing, which was centreless and inchoate, tasteless accretions round a formless core; Stavering looked like England in the movies. The folk club was held every Monday evening in the Rose and Crown pub, in a tiny, slopy room under the eaves and above the bar. As a result, nobody in the bar could hear themselves think, and they were frequently rained on by our spilled beer dripping through the floorboards. The club room had one minute casement window and a wall-mounted buffalo's head that inspired Stavering's stock joke: 'He must have been going at a hell of a speed when he hit that wall.' Tonight the former was shut against the snow, so you could hardly see the latter for cigarette smoke.

Florian Smith wasn't bad looking, and wasn't unaware of it. Six foot three with a shock of red-brown hair that looked as though it never needed ironing – and no beard, an unusual trait in a folk club; taking Stavering together with our other regular club in Brentwood, there must have been enough facial hair to stuff a three-piece suite. Neither did Florian sing with one finger stuck in his ear, the better to hear himself, like most folk singers the world over. After 'Electric Los Angeles Sunset' Florian reverted to the traditional, with a rousing song about a press gang that tried their tricks on the wrong bloke, who responded by beating them up and throwing them all in the sea. His attitude appealed to me.

At the beer break Francine scrambled upright, ready to slip out after Florian and start a conversation either with him directly or, when that inevitably failed, with me, so that I could feed her lines that allowed her to say 'Gee whiz' a lot and other cod Americanisms in accents skittering between Scarlett O'Hara and Deputy Dawg; when we first started coming here a year ago, Florian's first-ever words to Francine had been: 'A chick with an American accent? Fan*tas*tic!' (On another occasion, Francine had a cold and Florian complimented her on the sexy voice. So that night, to prolong the infection, she dowsed her nightie in a cold bath and went to bed in it wet.)

'The snow is much deeper in Detroit, is that right, Frankie?' I was now gamely bawling into the cacophony.

'Well, honeypie,' drawled Francine, tilted towards Florian at an angle like a ship's figurehead, 'I do declare ah ain't seen nuttin lahk it round these perty lil homesteads.'

Florian turned from a conversation with the club secretary and smiled. 'Accents to melt the snow,' he said and turned back, guileless, unaware of the havoc he was causing a fifteen-year-old. Not that he had the faintest idea that Francine was a fifteen-year-old; inside any folk club we turned seventeen. We intended simply to carry on being seventeen until we caught up with it naturally. Meanwhile, whenever we stepped up to a bar we had to be eighteen. All this took some keeping track of. There were increasingly frequent paranoid episodes at the school bus stop, where Francine kept making us both hide from some imagined glimpse of Florian's car; in school uniform we'd be hard pushed to convince anybody we were past the age of consent, illicit eye make-up notwithstanding.

Eleven o'clock: chucking-out time. The pub car park was a slush of lumbering vehicles, their windscreen wipers whining, snowflakes dancing in the damp head-lights. I had persuaded Francine to accept any lift home that we were offered rather than wait in hope of Florian. So we ended up disposed across three pairs of unknown masculine knees in the back of a VW Beetle driven by a man we'd never set eyes on before. He was coaxing the

28

car out of the gate on skiddy tyres, effectively bat-blind behind fogged windows. There would be a lot of people on the roads tonight driving by the Braille method.

I was relieved not to be in Florian's car for once; he had a disconcerting habit of conversing with me in the back seat, where I would be trying to lower my profile and give Francine a chance. He was always wanting to talk about Tarquin, while Francine would keep up a patter about how she was once in Los Angeles watching this truly amazing electric sunset.

'That's the sister of a famous brother you've got on your lap,' he had memorably told a fellow passenger one benighted Monday. 'Jo's brother is Tarquin Starkey, as in the soundtrack score of *Night Train To New Orleans*.'

'*Yeah?*' cried the stranger. 'I got the album! I've played "Dustbin Etudes number 9" till the vinyl's practically threadbare!'

'Well, you're currently being sat upon by a former user of that very dustbin.'

This was true. The dustbin had disappeared into Tarquin's studio one Friday morning. My family's housekeeping arrangements being what they were, it had taken a call from the local pest control officer to force my parents to get a new one after Tarquin's percussion had flattened it. In the close confines of Florian Smith's Ford Escort, Francine had improvised memories of New Orleans and explained how their dustbins were called trash cans.

'D'you ever get to see him these days?' had asked the stranger on the seat beneath me.

'See him? She lives with him!' Florian had answered on my behalf. 'He has a recording studio in the house we're about to pull up at.'

'*Yeah?* You mean the guy actually lives here in *Stavering*? With his Moog synthesizer and everything?'

29

'Except it's pronounced "Moag",' said Florian, to whom I'd left the correction.

'And this isn't Stavering,' added Francine, with increasing irritation at Florian's neglect.

'Must be some house you live in!'

'Oh yes,' Francine had mumbled grimly, 'it's some house she lives in all right.'

The unknown Good Samaritan who tonight was driving us home through the snow was now asking for guidance.

'Just drop us at the first house we come to on the left,' I directed.

'Lossing,' said the driver thoughtfully. 'Isn't that where Natasha lived?'

'Natasha?'

'Beautiful girl. Stunner. Looked like Julie Christie, as I remember. She died.'

Francine and I had been rolling our eyes, but stopped on the word 'died'. Not out of respect — people who are interested in laying a ghost of unknown identity need to follow every lead.

'When was this?' I asked.

'A few years ago. Gorgeous she was. Perhaps you're both too young to remember.'

'We're seventeen actually.'

'Frankie's lived here three years, but I've been here eight. No Natashas in my time. What was her surname?'

'What'd she die of?' asked Francine at the same time.

'Surname. Now you're asking.'

'*That*'s the house we want, *now*. No, no, *here*. *That* one!'

'What'd she die of?' asked Francine again.

The Beetle skidded. The driver wrenched the wheel and we glided groggily to a halt. I'd braced myself against the passenger seat, but Francine hadn't, so she slipped off a pair of knees halfway into the well behind the driver. As we were sorting out whose limbs were whose, he swivelled round to face us in the back.

'Now that's dangerous, that is. I suspect you two girls are too young to drive a car or you'd know about braking distances from the Highway Code and how you double them in icy conditions. When you're asking a driver to stop, think ahead.'

'Highway Code,' repeated Francine, swinging her legs out of his car the way she was taught at Lucie Clayton. 'We forgot to bring a copy with us, didn't we, Jo?'

'It's all very well being sarky . . .'

'No, Starkey,' I called behind me, hopping out myself. 'Thanks. Bye.'

As my left foot met the snow it stumbled and my bare sole landed on the wooden edge of my Scholl sandal. The pain was squeezing tears from my eyes as Francine pointed to the driveway. 'You've still got Geoffrey then, the mean sod!'

'Oh *no*!'

When we'd been pleading for a lift to Stavering earlier this evening, he and Angela had apparently been in too much of a hurry to get home. And now this. Francine left me and trudged the short distance up the road to her own house. My father's car was in our garage, though not my mother's. As I slogged up to the door and fished for my key, I felt the lack of normal family life, of loving parents, felt it in a way familiar since I was seven years old – as a dark ache deep in my tummy like something trying to chew me away with its teeth.

4

'What sort of time do you call this? You've got school tomorrow, madam!'

'I thought you two said you were in a hurry to be getting home,' I reminded Angela wearily. 'That was at half-past seven.'

'Yes and it was before your mother came in and put us in the picture about the house sale. You haven't got rid of us yet, young lady; we've got some questions for you.'

'Mum? Where is she then?'

'The hospital called her back a couple of hours ago. There's been a multiple pile-up in the snow. Never mind all that – what's this about you showing round everybody who comes to view the house? You're up to your neck in this nonsense, my girl. And it's going to stop!'

'Look, Angela, I'm tired.'

In the grate, a dirty fire crackled, spitting sparks onto the rug. I stamped them out under a sandal. There was already a starry galaxy of holes, mostly due to experiments by my nephew Angus. He had a fascination for snails; his pudgy hands went foraging in the undergrowth that constituted our garden and then, depending on the season, he would either plop them into the kettle, to manifest themselves later as bubbly scum on our cups of tea, or lob them one by one into the open fire, *crack! crack! crack!* I had caught him studiously raking the things back out again with a poker, examining their scorched helices and frothing liquefaction. His mother reacted to each of Angus's crises as though it were his first, scooping him from the sizzling rug, and cooing frantic baby-talk over the burns and blisters that bejewelled the child's white skin. The snails themselves she left for our cleaning lady to clog the Hoover with.

Elvis, the cat, twitched gently in his sleep. He was curled up on one of the dust-gathering ledges that sprouted from the chimney piece near ceiling height. Brought up in a scientific household, Elvis knew that (a) heat rises, and (b) no toddler, however psychopathic, could scale an eight-foot cliff face to get at him.

'Look, I'm tired,' I told Angela again, 'and as you so rightly pointed out, I've got school tomorrow.'

'This won't take more than a minute or two,' said Geoffrey placatingly.

'It'll take as long as it takes,' snapped Angela. 'Since when have you been showing potential buyers round the house?'

'Since the estate agent stopped coming. He still sends people to us because he wants his percentage, but . . .'

'Yes, and why did he stop coming? Your mother says he got a sack of rotting fish emptied over his head. It was balanced on a pulley system hanging from the chandelier and wired to make it tip up when *you*, madam, touched the light switch!'

True. Fish everywhere. Poor Elvis went crazy.

Above us, from the direction of Timothy's room, Cream's farewell album had been pounding through the ceiling ever since I got in. Machinery, heavy rock, Timothy relished anything that pounded. Substitutes for maternal attention come in many forms.

'She also tells us that not a single person you've shown round has ever made a further enquiry. I presume they get sacks tipped over them too, plus the rest of your brothers' repertoire of practical jokes.'

'Look, Angela, I really don't see how this is your business.'

'Don't try to fob me off, my girl! This house is Geoffrey's inheritance as much as yours, and we have two children to bring up. These shenanigans are going to stop. It's always been a madhouse – Tarquin's lunatic noises screaming through the place, Timothy's madcap inventions . . .'

'What do you expect *me* to do about it?'

'Do you think I'm too stupid to realize you're at the centre of this set-up? It's obviously co-ordinated, and it's you that directs the victims into the trap. I've already given Timothy a piece of my mind.'

Which would explain the volume of his stereo. Comfort listening. Now, as Tim's name was mentioned, the music fell silent. It really was getting late.

'Look, Angela, if somebody else wants to take over, they are more than welcome.'

'Josie,' put in Geoff, 'you must see it from our point of view – our hands are tied by the kids.' Knowing Angus, this was more than likely.

'There must be stories spreading across half of Essex!' continued his wife, ignoring him. 'Your mum says one couple were assaulted by a ghostly wailing out of the kitchen cupboards. We've all suffered the ghostly wailing, Josephine, it's that godforsaken instrument of Tarquin's!'

'Josie, you have to admit, you and Tim used to help him build the things when you were kiddies.'

They were talking about the Theremin, a weird Russian invention from the 1920s. You waved your hands around its antennae and it emitted musical pitches in a cold, unearthly ululation like stalactites of ice rubbed together by a polar wind. I had a vision of us before we moved here, in our maisonette in Ealing, happily hugger-mugger amid the gas fires smelling of anaesthetic and Grandma's hand-me-down curtains; Daddy playing showy piano, me singing along and Tarquin, already a heavy lad at thirteen, building his Theremin from a hobbyist's kit while the six-year-old Timmy, who worshipped him, screwed bits of casing together at mad angles.

Every discussion of Clarence's phenomena ran up against the uncomfortable fact that Tarquin had the technology and the know-how. Horrible noises had been his speciality since Timothy and I were small and Tarquin persuaded our grandma to buy him a Grundig tape recorder. He'd filled the house with whooshing traffic noise, doors banging, jack-hammers in the street, calling it *musique concrète* after the early taped music pioneers in Paris. To be fair, it wasn't all horrible; with no motive except the entertainment of his little brother, Tarquin used to splice our recorded voices into word salads. I could picture Timothy deranged with laughter, on his back, squealing in hysteria, little feet and arms paddling in the air like a fallen clockwork toy. I'd watch, hot with pleasure, as eventually it infected Dad, another giggler, until our stuffy rooms were thick with hilarity like flocks of birds, the flapping, squealing din of laughter out of control. Now, the memory hurt like a low punch; I felt the pain of loss flood my blood and bones. I snapped at Angela.

'This house might be haunted, have you considered that?'

'Don't start! I'm not having any of Tarquin's drivel about a poltergeist—'

I shouted her down. 'If it *isn't* haunted, how come the previous owners moved out of here for a house just two hundred yards down the road? The Richardsons sold up to move just two hundred yards. Why was that? The gypsy in them?'

'We've *found* devices planted by you and your brothers, remember? That time the rocking chair exploded so Geoffrey's trousers caught fire watching *The Benny Hill Show*?'

'Look, that was different. Timmy and Geoff had this row, so . . .'

'If you children honestly don't know who's doing it and think it's a ghost, then how come you're not frightened? Answer me that, my girl! How come you've never, in all these years, shown the slightest sign of being scared?'

This was actually a good question – a rare quality in one of Angela's. For as long as we'd lived here, the pranks had been exasperating, but we'd never felt any menace. It was almost as though the high spirits cheered the place up a bit.

'Straight question, straight answer, Josephine: are you telling prospective buyers that this house is infested with poltergeists?'

'Oh, shut up, you two. Why don't you come over here the next time the estate agent sends someone round? Just come along and do it yourself, why don't you!'

'Keep your voice down,' shouted Angela. 'Your father's asleep.'

'Lucky him.' I started for the door. 'I'm going to bed.'

'You can't.'

'I bloody well am.'

'No, you can't. Angus is in your room. You'll have to have the boxroom.'

I stopped at the door. Fury, cold as a switchblade, crept across my skin. My scalp prickled. I turned. 'What?'

'In your latest caper, you and your brothers have trickled red stuff down the walls of the boxroom, remember? Poor little Angus was in a right doodah.'

'And determined to lick it off, Josie. I mean, it could be dangerous.' This was Geoffrey.

'You've put him in *my bed*? No! You can't have. Not even you!'

'It's only for one night, you selfish little madam! You shouldn't have pulled such a rotten stunt in the first place.'

I was rigid with anger. My throat burned. Something disgusting was going on in my insides. Unable to stand still any longer, I fled. At the top of the stairs I ran headlong into a vast bare chest and a dark expanse of hair.

'Hey, cool it! Cool it, Jo.'

'I can't!' I sobbed. 'There's blood running down the walls of the boxroom and I've got to sleep in there because Angela's given my bed to Angus!'

Tarquin smelled of maleness – warm, salty and astringent. Dreadlocks tickled my face. His baggy trousers, which for one wild moment I'd mistaken for conventional pyjamas, I now saw were Ali Baba pants, decorated – if that was the word – with embroidered figures in tangled and snagged silk, based on illustrations from the Kama Sutra. Tarquin's arms clamped around me to restrain my own, whose random flailing had managed to wallop him in the eye.

'Just cool it and listen! It was only red watercolour. I've washed it off the wall and lit a heater in there. Plus a couple of joss sticks to help cover up the stink of paraffin.'

'What?' My breath was coming in gulps. Music dribbled from Tarquin's door; *real* music for once –

Pink Floyd's 'Careful With That Axe, Eugene'. Pink Floyd were apparently using a Theremin on their new album. I knew because in January they'd invited Tarquin to the Abbey Road studios to give advice. He wouldn't go. I pleaded and wept but he wouldn't. Even just a year ago he would have done it, but now Tarquin never left the house. My parents' medical journals talked about a condition called agoraphobia; it sounded frighteningly like my brother.

'Everything's sorted, Jo, I promise. And they're off in the morning, Geoff and Ange, I heard them say.'

'Oh Tarquin, what's happening? *Is* it you? I won't give you away to Tim. Please tell me!'

'It was only a bit of red paint down the wall. Serves the little sod right.'

I snuffled into the aromatic skin of his chest.

'It spelled out some words. I bet the devoted parents didn't tell you that.'

'Words? What words?'

' "Bugger off home, you little horror". I tell you, I fell about!'

From the landing of the floor above us roared my father's voice.

'For Christ's sake belt up! I've got a D&C and a laparotomy in the morning!'

'Go and check out the boxroom,' murmured Tarquin, letting go the pinion on my arms. As he turned away, his waist-length hair swung like a parody of a shampoo advert. My false eyelashes must have come adrift and landed on his knotty silk; they were now bearding a couple of the indefatigably smiling women whose legs waved breezily across Tarquin's trousers. He was talking.

'You know what Churchill used to say when he hit the sack?'

'If it was about blood, toil, tears and sweat, I don't want to know.'

'He said, "Sod the lot of them!" Sod the lot of them, Jo.'

Tarquin melted back into his studio and I made my way along the sad carpet to the bleak little boxroom at the end; now that Geoffrey and Angela had reclaimed Geoff's old one, this was the only vaguely habitable spare room in a three-storey house positively sagging with spare rooms. It smelled of paraffin warmth and the soft green-scented waft of marijuana. For all his dustbins and buckets and screaming kazoos, Tarquin knew how to create a calming atmosphere.

5

'That's got to be wrong, Jo. You can't say *Morning I stand up.*'

'In German you can.'

'But it's rubbish.'

'But it's what they say for getting up.'

'But it's *rubbish.*'

We're sitting in the gallery above the school swimming pool and Francine is copying my German homework. There's a squash because we are all up here instead of down there, all claiming the excuse of a woman's cyclical respite from swimming. Our usual PE teacher keeps careful records and challenges any claim that looks suspicious, but today she's down with flu and the lesson is taken by her male counterpart. The poor man never stood a chance. *Sorry, sir, I can't swim, sir, I've got a period, sir.* There are about fifty girls in our year. Well, there must be forty of us squeezed into the gallery. Funny really – at eleven we were half-girl half-fish, and now we refuse to get our hair wet.

'And this one says "I drove with the train".'

'No, you have to say that. *Fahren* to go, instead of *gehen*. Otherwise it means you walked with the train.'

'But it's *rubbish*.'

'Yes, Frankie. You said.'

The gallery seemed to be full of legs — shiny-hosed thighs protruded from the oddly scalloped, undulating hems of our skirts. They undulated because the waistbands were rolled over and over until an ungainly fat sausage of material bulged inside our cardigans, as though we were kitted out with coils of rope round our midriffs like the Famous Five. Below the knees we were in illegal leather boots. Forced into uniform, we all rebelled, uniformly.

'Did you get off with him last night?' Jeanette was asking Lynne.

'No such luck! But Lesley finally got off with that bloke Pete, you know, the one who got off with Janice at Mary's party when you got off with Andy.'

Barbara Paige looked up from a dog-eared copy of *Last Exit to Brooklyn*. 'You lot who do German have got a new conversation teacher. Have you seen him?'

We groaned theatrically. The previous guy had been fat and clicked his heels.

'No, this one's a dish. Really.'

'I don't suppose he's up to Florian Smith's standard,' Francine told her from out of the daydream with which she'd been palliating her German homework.

'*Florian?* What sort of a handle is that?'

'He was named after the famous café in St Mark's Square, Venice.'

'So who is he?'

'Folk singer.'

'Ah, hairies,' put in Paula, on her left. 'Now you see, I go for skinheads myself.'

God, I was so unhappy. The smell of chlorine lay across the gallery like a pall, like an emanation of my distress. Beyond the reeking pool with its handful of earnest, rubber-capped swimmers, beyond the aquarium glimmer of all our plate glass, lay the playing fields in their wet green and wet snow. Seagulls, driven inland by hunger, wheeled and squawked over the monumental Hs of the rugby posts. This afternoon two hours of German awaited us with Fräulein Schneider, known to us for complicated reasons as Jim (*Schneider* is German for tailor; therefore Taylor, therefore James, therefore Jim), and for less complicated reasons as Adolf. Everything in the curriculum I could do standing on my head. I was bored senseless. The only thing I would have enjoyed was singing, but the teacher in charge of our production of *Iolanthe* said I wasn't pretty enough for Phyllis and I was far too big for a fairy.

Beyond the playing fields lay the endlessly replicated school buildings, low-lying like the land, executed in cheap plastic and badly weathered concrete. Why couldn't I go to a proper school with gnarled red bricks and bell towers? There were a couple within whacking distance of a jolly hockey stick but they were girls' schools, and my parents insisted on co-ed, never mind that Timothy, who stood in clear and desperate need of female contact, was sent to an all-boys public school. His teachers had managed to catch our parents' attention long enough to point out that he was a child prodigy. I, who was merely clever, was dispatched to the Comprehensive. And that was pretty much the last time either of them took an interest in the academic progress of either of us.

Their child prodigy had started Sellotaping his school reports to our mother's car windscreen. I just left mine lying around for a while and then Timothy would forge the parental signature and I'd take it back to school.

Now, behind me, Stephanie Sandiman was showing off. 'Of course, Mummy and Daddy are totally against censorship. Last year they plastered make-up all over me and smuggled me in to see *Oh! Calcutta!* We're at the theatre once a fortnight . . .'

They probably were, too. When Stephanie and I were at primary school, they'd taken me to pantomimes, realizing that my own parents didn't. That I scarcely had parents at all. Now, my vision dissolved in coloured water.

'Just off to the loo!' I called behind me, blind with tears, clambering over booted legs as best I could.

The changing room, too, smelled of chlorine and the boredom of wasted time. From line after line of pegs hung school scarves and hated macs, like headless scarecrows. Navy blue, navy blue, navy blue. As I slumped onto the slats of a bench, I heard the door swing.

'Jo?' Francine. 'What's up?'

'Oh, nothing. Just the Curse.'

'Crap! It was only a fortnight ago you were up in the gallery before. Anyway, I thought your dad had given you the Pill, so as to get rid of all that.'

'I never took them. I'm only fifteen, for heaven's sake!' I had asked my father for advice about problem skin. He'd come home with six months' supply of Ortho Novum.

'If you're not going to take the things, you should sell them. Plenty of girls can't get the Pill out of their doctors.'

'Oh Frankie!'

'Or you could give them to me. In case Florian . . . you know.'

We could hear echoey instructions from the pool, a hollow male voice shouting about breast stroke. Don't they think at all, these teachers? Shouting the word *breast* at fifteen-year-old girls?

'When I got in last night,' I told Francine, strangling

back the sobs in my voice, 'the walls of the spare room were running with paint.'

'Oh, not again.'

'It said, "Bugger off home, you little horror".'

'What little horror?'

'Angus. You remember Geoff and Angela were still at my place.'

'Sounds like Clarence is pretty smart, if that was aimed at Angus. Look, Jo, let's have another crack with the Ouija.'

'That's what I was thinking.'

Tears coursed lavishly down my face, my illegal mascara running in filthy black rivulets, stinging and smarting. Either of them would do, I thought, a mum or a dad. I wasn't Timothy, who had specifically pined for the approval of our absentee mother even in the Ealing days when we still had a father. To get back the dad of our Ealing days I would have given twenty points of my IQ. And by August, my only close friend would be moving away.

'Don't, Jo.'

'Sorry.' Out it poured, a dam breached, a wound torn open to gush. Two minutes of this and I would look like a panda, but I couldn't stop. Even more horribly, my chest convulsed.

'Oh Jo, it'll be all right.' Francine sat down on the slatted wood and reached towards me, but we were teenagers and would have no truck with maternal gestures. Over one shoulder I'd slung my school bag; in an inspired compromise she caressed its leather strap. 'If it doesn't work and we move to London before you do, maybe you could come live with us. Call it a temporary measure.'

'Your mom would never let me. You know she wouldn't.'

'Dad would be real happy about it. And Mom might if it was temporary.'

'Never. And anyway, I have to get Tim and Tarquin out of the house, and Mum away to a different hospital so she's got time to spend with Dad. And to spend with us,' I added wretchedly.

'Then we'll just have to evict Clarence!'

'Yes. Just that one small thing.'

We sat slumpily, miserable, on the hard-slatted bench, and I dabbed at my messy eyes. Then the door swung open again and an adult's confident heels snapped across the flooring. Mrs Matlock, deputy head.

'Girls?' She was a tall figure in a tweed suit and black gown like a bat, like something from a proper school's belfry. The gown was a tradition that surely jarred with the philosophy of comprehensive education and all that weather-beaten concrete. Francine put on her pure-as-the-driven-snow face and turned it towards the door.

'Jo's got the most awful period pains, Mrs Matlock. Has done all morning.'

'I'm sorry to hear that. Do you usually suffer, Josephine?'

'Sometimes.'

'I gave her two aspirins a couple of minutes ago, Mrs Matlock. That's why we're down here.'

'I see. Well, give them time to work. Meanwhile, I'm sorry to see you both wearing boots. We've discussed this before.'

'But you see, Mrs Matlock, I thought Jo would be better for some fresh air, so we went for a walk outside. We've just come back.'

'Indeed. Did you also think she'd feel better for wearing make-up?'

'Oh, that was just . . .'

'Josephine can answer for herself.'

'That was just me trying to disguise the effects of the tears, Mrs Matlock. Swimming is being taken by Mr Bryant and I didn't want to embarrass him.'

'How fortunate that you happened to have the make-up with you. And your own face, Francine?'

'*I*'m not wearing make-up, Mrs Matlock. Look!' Frankie spat on a handkerchief, rubbed at her blackened eyelashes, displayed the white lawn. Nothing. Hers were dyed.

'Yes, Francine, I understand. Now, you will both take those boots off and, Josephine, you will wash away your mascara. Understood?'

'Yes, Mrs Matlock.'

'And unroll your skirt waistbands. I've explained before that you look *terrible* like that. Whatever fashionable appearance it's intended to achieve, let me assure you both that it eludes you. The effect is of a bundle of rags like Little Orphan Annie.'

'Yes, Mrs Matlock.'

'What lesson do you have after lunch?'

'Double German.'

'Fräulein Schneider?'

'*Jawohl!*'

'I beg your pardon?'

'Yes, Mrs Matlock.'

'In that case, I'll make a point of dropping in to check on Josephine's . . . welfare.'

'Thank you, Mrs Matlock.'

'I hope the aspirins set to work soon.'

'Thank you, Mrs Matlock.'

She turned on her heel and tapped away from us, disappearing through the door in her subfusc like a strutting crow.

'Ratbag!' hissed Francine. 'What was she doing in here in the first place? Can she *smell* make-up and boots through a closed door, or what?'

'It wouldn't surprise me.'

Under the coat pegs, the clumpy leather of our regulation shoes (navy blue) lolled on the bench beneath the serge of those hated macs. We tugged off

46

our boots; they had left red indents, insistent and sore-looking as though they weren't fashion items we'd discarded but some instrument of torture or restraint.

'I mean, it isn't as if we'd turned up for school in our stretch lizard-skin print!' complained Francine. Her skirt flopped heavily on one side as she jerked at the hem.

My own was so extensively mangled by all the rolling that the box pleats ran amok around my hips. Obviously I couldn't walk around dressed in something that looked stupid! I'd have to cover up with a blazer all afternoon. The words 'Little Orphan Annie' teased the edges of my despair. Orphan. Fatherless and motherless. I splashed tepid water across my smudged face where the tears welled and ran. They continued to well and run, even when the swimmers came shivering back from the pool and our schoolmates thundered down from the gallery, lighting up the changing rooms with the clamour of their impatience to be gone.

6

Barbara had been right, he wasn't bad, the German conversation teacher – tall, slim, blond hair shining well below the collar. No good to Paula then. His name was Torsten. *TORSTEN* he wrote on the board and our class, assuming this was a verb, started conjugating it – *ich torste, du torstest, er torstet* – while he looked on, decidedly unnerved. Fräulein Schneider (Jim) left us alone with him for the second hour, which we therefore spent in relative happiness, standing up morning and driving with the train. All spoiled for me, of course, sitting there bare of make-up, so that any merit my eyes might have had was completely overwhelmed by the clinical curiosities of my nose and my bones.

'You know the Richardsons,' Francine said later as we waited at the bus stop in Brentwood High Street, ignoring several boys in our year who wheeled around on their Chopper bikes, trying to get her attention. One of them had been dancing his bike about with its front wheel up, like dressage. He now toppled off the seat. We watched his body skew into the kerb.

'What about the Richardsons?' I asked.

'Suppose we had a chat with Mrs and tried to get something out of her? I mean, if Tarquin's right and you're haunted, the house must already have been haunted in her day.'

'They'd never admit they'd sold a total disaster to an unsuspecting family with children.'

'*He* wouldn't. We know what a slimy sod he is. But on her own we might get something out of her. Worth a try?'

'Oh Frankie, anything's worth a try!'

It was on this note of heroic desperation that we hopped off the number 260 bus one stop early and knocked at the door of the Richardsons' place.

Mrs Richardson was a jumpy little thing, under the thumb of a husband who joined committees, a corraller of youth and ringer-up of the police about infringed bylaws. If pop music leaked from an open window anywhere in Lossing, the police got a phone call about it from Mr Richardson. I'd been reading *The Female Eunuch* by Germaine Greer; well, Mrs Richardson was exactly the sort of wife who needed a copy.

Their tiny square house had been brand new when they'd moved into it at the cold beginning of 1963. Grindingly cold, Great Britain's worst winter for more than two hundred years, snow suffocating the fields from December to March, farmers unable to reach their starving livestock, birds dropping from frozen trees, picked out of the snow by the RSPB with not a morsel of food in their crops. At Eastbourne the sea was solid for a stretch of a mile. There was pack ice on the large estuaries and twenty-five-foot drifts on Dartmoor.

In Lossing, where the low land was scattered with ponds, these had iced over. The ice wasn't as sturdy as it looked: three young boys had drowned skating on one of them just before we moved here. My age exactly. Until last night's talk of Natasha, these were the only untimely deaths we'd ever heard of in Lossing Common.

The memory of our journey from Ealing still had the clarity of a child's nightmare. Our house move had been postponed until a brief respite from the blizzards in mid-January. Daddy drove us, Mummy being elsewhere — no doubt saving lives at either the new hospital or the old, sleepless and foodless in the middle of some forty-eight-hour bout. Tarquin and Timothy had grizzled all the way to Essex, mile after interminable mile. Tarquin was leaving behind what was surely the world's first Boy Scout R&B band, in which he had led his chums in a brooding blues that he'd picked up by blagging his way into Alexis Korner's club across the road from Ealing Broadway station (from which unlikely suburban venue the British would reinvent the genre, and take it to a white America that mostly wouldn't have known what the letters R&B stood for). And Tarquin sang it all with a South Chicago accent that must have frightened the life out of the Scout Master.

Only Geoffrey, who was nearly sixteen, wasn't sorry to leave London. He'd spent much of the last ten years kicking a football against a garage door; as long as the new house had a garage he'd be satisfied. Unfortunately, it didn't. We wouldn't be seeing much of Geoffrey once we moved to Lossing Common.

I remembered our arrival; the gravel driveway crawling between uninviting gateposts; the red-brick house standing lumpen, its Georgian elegance mutilated by Victorian elaboration; angular bay windows; a thrusting conservatory. The car was all steam, our breath was steam, unwarmed by the failing heater of the dying vehicle. We scrubbed at the wet windows with our sleeves, all four children, elbows windmilling, scrambling over one another, colliding knees and shoulders, anything to get a look. Tarquin's huge feet were mangling Geoffrey's hardback of *Nineteen Eighty-Four*, with whose Big Brother my own had been frightening me for much of the journey, while my twin, who was almost as devoted to George Orwell as he was to Tarquin, kept up a drone of telescreen announcements about Hate Week. I wasn't sorry when the car wheels ground into the snowed gravel with a definitive swish.

'The house isn't half big, Dad.'

'Cor, it's huge!'

'But it doesn't look straight. It's sort of – wobbly.'

Yes, dumped and droopy, like suet sinking in a bag.

'Mummy and Daddy are going to get it all propped up, silly! All rebuilded and everything.'

This was the reason for buying the place – our father had always wanted a stonking great piece of architectural oddity to renovate.

'It's scalene,' declared Timothy. 'Lopsided and limping, like the triangle.'

'You do talk twaddle,' Geoffrey had argued, pressing his perpetually snot-running nose against the damp window, where it left a creamy streak that glinted with a green tinge in the forlorn twilight of the winter afternoon.

'Everybody out!' announced our father. 'We're home!'

The front door swung heavily open to expose a hallway or reception room, its walls prison-high, with carved plasterwork and deep coving above curly brackets. It was cold indoors, bone-deep cold and dank – the stilled chill of an untenanted house. In front of us, off centre, a staircase rose and then turned, in aristocratic disdain of its threadbare carpet and the cumbersome Victorian bay that stared, hatchet-faced, from across the room. At the turn of the stairs was a magnificent Venetian window – a triple window, its central panel wide and arched at the top, the flanking panes narrow and square-headed. Their southern light rimed the wooden rails and balustrade, all of it deeply, intricately, *impossibly* carved with a seasonal confusion of fruit and blossom. This would be a bumpy sort of banister to slide down.

My brothers thundered off through a door on our collective right, thump thump thump, haring down a hallway with snow and mud on their boots. Daddy shouted to take them off, but the boys had gone, their voices veering away and splintering into echo. Then a different voice fluted through the musty passages, rich and happy. Tarquin's.

'*Wheeeeeeee!* Come and look! Come and look! Come and look!'

I trotted towards his tones, down a gloomy passageway into a cavernous dining room with an acrid smell I would soon come to know – mice. Beyond it, Timothy and Geoffrey were lolloping towards the threshold of some further room with a lot of glass. They stood, staring at Tarquin, their mouths slightly open. He was in the conservatory; it ran along the front of the house, overlooking a tangled garden – all richly stained glass and mosaic flooring, with window ledges tiled in glazed porcelain and cluttered with majolica pots restraining vicious, spiked cacti. A handwritten note was propped against one of them: *Thought you might like to keep these little pets – our new home doesn't suit them. Yours, Amy Richardson*.

And there was Tarquin, limbs akimbo, a towering Billy Bunter in his Boy Scout uniform, all mottled puce skin and wobbly fat, the blues forgotten, laughing his head off. Timothy and Geoff continued to stare, for once looking alike in their gaping gormlessness.

'What?' demanded Geoffrey, nasal and peevish.

'What are we supposed to be looking at? It's only a greenhouse place.'

'Just feel it!' Tarquin spun on his heels, arms flung wide to encompass the ornate Victoriana. He knocked several cacti from their pots; they rolled across the shiny floor like gherkins spilled from a jar. 'Isn't this the best house you've ever seen? It's so . . . so . . .' His large face beamed at us all as we watched gawkily from the doorway. 'It's so *atmospheric*!'

'Ginger nut, dear?'

'Sorry?'

'I was asking if you'd also like a ginger nut, dear. They are home made.'

'Oh. Yes. Thank you.' My mouth was still full of cake. Rather good, too. And on the table a saucerful of jammy dodgers.

'A second cup of tea?'

Mrs Richardson poured milk and Earl Grey palely into bone china. A genteel clink as she handed it back to me, rattling the apostle spoon. She was a small, pink, irresolute woman, pleased in a panicky sort of way to have a couple of teenagers turn up in her kitchen, bubbling and pleading to pick her brains. She had ushered us in with soap-sudded hands, shaken a snowy cloth across the Formica table and snapped the blinds closed against the day. The fluorescent strip lighting flattened perspective and tinged our skin green; its raucous, synthetic illumination somehow managed to negate both the warmth and the vanilla smell of Mrs Richardson's baked bread. Nobody was ever going to spin on their heels in here and call it atmospheric.

While the first cup of tea was being poured, Francine had announced that she'd like to use the bathroom. That was some time ago now, since when I could hear the soft padding of her feet above us, up and down, up and down, accompanied by in-substantial rustlings, as though she were setting the scene for our forthcoming ghost story. What Francine was actually doing was searching the bedrooms. We knew the layout of the house because we babysat for the Richardsons' next-door neighbours. At least I did, and Frankie always came round once they'd left for the evening, because their cocktail cabinet was filled with brilliant stuff like praline liqueur and cherry brandy.

Perhaps the noises off reminded Mrs Richardson subliminally of Francine's elfin beauty and this was why she was apparently meditating on my own short-comings. 'I always think,' she said, apropos of nothing, 'that *you*'re very attractive, too. In your own way.'

I sipped at the scented tea.

'We often see you striding past on those great long legs of yours, and in such tiny skirts. It puts me in mind of the pantomime. *Jack and the Beanstalk*; Prince Charming. We used to take Algy when he was little. He did love the panto.'

Algy, the son with a name like pond scum, was the apple of his mother's eye, now living on the American West Coast, about whose kidney-shaped swimming pool many a neighbour in Lossing had been button-holed until their eyes glazed over.

Beside my elbow was Francine's cup, cooling and clouded. Squeamish Francine was never going to put that in her mouth and swallow it. As for the fruit cake – at the mere sight of a raisin she retched and talked about the bodies of dead bluebottles.

'That's your sort of appeal, dear,' Algy's mother was now telling me, patting my hand in encouragement. 'The Principal Boy in a pantomime.'

At last Francine reappeared in the kitchen, oohing enthusiastically at the proffered cake, raisins and all.

'How I wish I had a mom who baked,' she invented, wistfully, and tucked a strand of silky hair behind her ear.

Mrs Richardson wrinkled with pleasure. 'But about this local history you want to discuss, girls,' she said. 'You'd get far more sense out of my husband, you know. He's the clever one.'

'It's more like folk history,' Francine amended, crumbling her cake and making a hedge of the raisins. I started picking them off her plate. 'You've lived in Lossing Common longer than most and we thought if anyone knew . . .'

'. . . and there's nothing at Cecil Sharp House,' I added, 'not that we could find.'

'Cecil . . . ?'

'He collected folk songs, earlier this century,' I explained.

'So we wondered if you'd ever heard any yokel superstitions . . .'

'. . . that we could make something of. For the folk clubs.'

I finished Francine's raisins and drained her cold tea. Then I rose to carry the china across to the sink. Mrs Richardson waved me back down.

'I never allow my guests to wash the dishes,' she told me, gently taking the frail cups and plates from my out-sized hands. I was visited by a golden vision of guests. A house that had guests. *Who wanted to wash the dishes.*

'But you know, girls, folksy things haven't been the vogue until a few years ago. Folk singers were considered rather peculiar people – it was like saying you were a nudist. Or a vegetarian.'

'But still,' continued Francine, 'you might have heard tell of something.'

I cast her a quick look of warning. 'Heard tell' was getting carried away, in my opinion. Close on the heels of 'yokel', too.

'The thing is, Mrs Richardson,' I said, '*any* super-stitions would be useful.'

'Ghost stories, for example,' piped up Francine, inspired. 'They'd do, wouldn't they, Jo?'

'Now that would be outta sight,' I agreed.

Mrs Richardson's habitually vague smile looked even vaguer. 'Ghost stories?' she repeated, from the sink.

'Right on!'

'I'm sorry, my dears, but I'm no use to you at all. I've never heard a real ghost story in my life.'

'No?' said Francine, smoothly. 'Jo has. In the Red House.'

The china rattled.

'In *your* house, as was,' I pointed out. 'A ghostly spirit haunted the place.'

'Haunts the place,' corrected Francine. 'The Red House has a poltergeist, Mrs Richardson.'

'It does not. No.'

'So please can you tell us . . .'

'I don't hold with this sort of talk, girls.' The small round face was patched with red and white. The creased corners of her no-longer-smiling mouth retained traces of forgotten food, like rust. 'I'm a practising Christian.'

This change of tone was more sympathetic than her habitual fluster. She was suddenly a rather dignified figure. But Francine was not to be put off.

'This is so important to us, Mrs Richardson. We've got to get it exorcized, you see . . .'

'I'm sorry, girls, but I won't collude in any nonsense about the supernatural – it goes against everything I believe in. Now then, I'll tell you what we'll do. Let's set up the cine projector. Algy's sent over a new film – half an hour of him relaxing by the swimming pool!'

Which, if it was intended to punish us, was an efficacious move. As for Algy, he was certainly relaxed

56

– in suede pants and a Grateful Dead T-shirt and, judging by the state of his pupils and dodgy smile, pretty thoroughly stoned.

'I pinched her kitchen door key,' said Francine, matter-of-fact, when we'd eventually escaped and were down the road.

'You *what*?'

'We're going back for a proper rummage round. One day when she's not in.'

'Rummage for what, for heaven's sake?'

'Oh, come on, changing the subject like that! She's guilty as hell! I bet she knew all about Clarence when she sold the place to your parents. I bet there was the same stuff going down in her day, Jo.'

'But even so, there won't be anything to find by rummaging . . .'

'I already did a quick search of the bedrooms. There's nothing really fantastic lying about, like holy water and saints' bones or anything. There's one framed photo by the bed: Algy, of course. But right at the back of a drawer there's this Richardson family album and *two* kids in all the pictures. Last photo of all is a teenage girl, the spitting image of Mrs Richardson, in the uniform of Brentwood High. She have a teenage daughter to your knowledge?'

'Of course not.'

'Then it's just a guess, but I'd say dead, wouldn't you?'

7

Francine's house.

'If the Richardsons had a daughter who died, we'd know.'

'Why would we?'

'Because they're neighbours. People would have said.'

'Not if it happened before your family moved here. They wouldn't talk about it to you – you were a child of seven.'

'No, but to Mum and Dad.'

'How can you know what people around here have or haven't told your mum and dad? You only converse about once a year.'

I couldn't argue with that.

'Tarquin's right, Jo. You got a ghost.'

'Do you think this daughter might be Natasha then?'

'Nah.' Francine waved the suggestion away with her hand. 'She wasn't very pretty in the photos.'

'No, but the bloke who told us, I mean he wasn't *all* that* himself.'

'True. True.'

'Groovy he was not. So his idea of a stunner might be anything with its limbs intact and all its own teeth.'

'Good point.'

We were in Francine's bedroom, amid the Toulouse-Lautrec posters and Turkish birdcage, all minarets and white tracery, and the only shag-pile carpet I'd ever seen. Now there was a sharp knock at the door and her father opened it. He didn't come in but stood unyielding in the doorway.

'Hi, Mr Switt.'

'Good to see you, Jo, but I'm afraid I can't hear you, not above this caterwauling.'

'Oh *Dad*. We've turned it down once!'

'Well, you can turn it down again, honey.'

'Then we won't be able to hear it at all.'

'And neither will your mom and I.'

'Oh *Dad*.'

Don't Let It Bring You Down, Neil Young entreated us. If we could have arranged for the needle to play just the one James Taylor track 'Fire And Rain' continually we would never have listened to anything else ever again, but as things were, we interwove Neil Young or British folk-rock (because of Florian) plus occasionally the dejected growl of Leonard Cohen, though only when Francine's parents were out of the house as they claimed he curdled the milk.

'We are not being unreasonable, hon. This is not music. There's no tune, the words are trash and the guy can't sing! I wouldn't even care about that if it was just your own brain cells you were destroying, but it's ours also. That shriek really travels. It gets into the radiator system. I hear him as I drive home. I dream about the guy!'

'It's folk-based rock, Dad. That's the voice you sing it in.'

'Why?'

59

'You wouldn't understand. It's poetry.'

'*This?*'

'You have to hear the entire song through.'

'We've been hearing the damn song through for months! Have you two ever listened to real rock 'n' roll? Elvis Presley?'

'Sure. He's been in the charts.'

'He has, Mr Switt. "In The Ghetto" made number one. About the effects of poverty and deprivation on American black youth.'

'Good song.'

'I'm talking about the original Leiber and Stoller stuff. They had a tune, there was a lyric you could understand and the guy knew how to sing.'

'Times change.'

'And what can you *do* with this, anyhow? You can't dance to it, you can't smooch to it . . .'

'It's philosophy, Dad. All your old stuff, "Jailhouse Rock" and whatever, it was *so* self-indulgent, just about having a good time.'

'Well, may the Lord preserve us from having a good time!'

I did know a bit about Leiber and Stoller – Tarquin's teenage bands used to slip some real rock 'n' roll into their R&B, and they would practise at the Red House. This was while Tarquin was at the Royal Academy. Then he dropped out and wrote a string of bluesy hits for Dusty Springfield. They made *serious* bread. That was how he could afford two years across the Atlantic, mostly with the composer, inventor and electronics wizard Hugh Le Caine. To give you an idea, Hugh Le Caine once spent months experimenting with the musical potential of a dripping tap, some panes of glass and a hammer, so we can assume Tarquin had a happy apprenticeship. He might have stayed there for ever but the record company that signed him folded after he'd cut his first experimental album and Tarquin got signed up by EMI. One day he reappeared at our front door with a truck, inside which was a monster customized Moog synthesizer worth the price of a small house.

This, the love of my brother's life, comprised a double keyboard befitting a church organ, vast banks of patch leads (a spaghetti explosion of inputs and outputs like the switchboard of a medium-sized telephone exchange), and an entire menagerie of plug-in boxes, boards and knobs. Tarquin let himself in with his key and sort of built a stable for the thing in his bedroom.

But even then it could have been OK; it was so nearly a wonderful turn of events for us all. Walter Carlos had just had a massive hit with 'Switched-On Bach', and the Moog synthesizer was all the rage. Among Tarquin's talents, he was a virtuoso keyboard player, and he could easily have done a Walter Carlos himself, produced Moog interpretations of some other popular composer, sold a million and picked up a Grammy. But he didn't.

Well, never mind, this was also the era of progressive rock; conservatoire-trained musicians were pouring into the scene with their classics and free jazz – and electronic music. Keith Emerson was about to make the Moog famous on the rock stage. It could have been Tarquin. It wasn't. My brother had one foot in prog rock and one in the loony bin. His next album used Moog, syncopated dustbin and piano with nails hammered into the sound-board. An American art-movie director used it, the film was an unexpected box-office smash and Tarquin was a household name.

And in no time, a virtual hermit.

'. . . your mom and I do not believe you can concentrate on math with *that* playing at that volume.'

'It helps free our heads.'

'Which is exactly the kind of meaningless trash I expect to hear from someone exposed to these kind of lyrics day in, day out. Now *turn* it *down*.'

Well, we didn't turn it down, we took it round to mine. Neither did we explain to Mr Switt that the math, as he called it, didn't actually take much concentration as Francine was merely copying mine and I didn't have to concentrate at all, as the exercise she was copying was two years old. I'd already passed O level maths and was now doing A level, 'learning' the calculus that Timothy had taught me when we were both eleven. Bored to distraction, as I said.

So, back out into the snow and down the road to my house. In my bedroom, where I'd forced Angela to strip the bed and change all the linen before they'd left for home, I now plugged in the electric fire with its frayed flex and orange elements smelling like singed hair; my charcoal-painted walls, hip though they might have been, did nothing to warm the cockles of your heart on a raw March night. The flex was not merely frayed, I saw now, but tooth-marked and sticky, as though recently chewed. Angus. You'd think that gnawing electric cable would be self-limiting, but no such luck.

From Tarquin's room emanated the heavy toll of a bell. *D-o-o-o-nnngggggg* it went, resounding in dark shivers across our shabby landing. *D-o-o-o-nnngggggg*. We turned up Neil Young.

'So,' said Francine, when we were settled, 'Ouija again?'

'Suppose so. It's the most likely to yield a result.'

'Tomorrow?'

I hesitated.

'Or do you want to rootle through the Richardsons' first?'

'But what are we going to rootle *for*?'

'Stuff about the daughter. When she died. How. I mean, say she's a teenager in that photo . . .'

'Well, yeah, we know she wasn't still alive when we moved in, and the Richardsons had lived here twenty years . . .'

'And Mrs isn't *that* ancient.'

'So, if they had a teenage girl, she died while they lived in this house.'

'In which case we've nailed Clarence.'

I thought about it. 'Funny, but I can't see it being a girl. Those puerile antics.'

There was no doubt about it, the thought of an Amy Richardson type of person filling baths with blood was a hard one to credit, not to mention the time tripe and onions exploded from the lavatory cistern. And Francine's theory was founded on one passing glimpse of some photographs.

'We've got to check it out first. Maybe we should try the church – the Registry of Burials.' Where had that idea come from? Tarquin's throbbing bell. *D-o-o-o-nnngggggg.*

'Never heard of it.'

I'd heard of it, but that was all. Would a country church keep records that were accessible to the public? How could I know? My brothers and I were brought up as humanists.

'Don't Let It Bring You Down' finished, so I lifted the stylus and dropped it back at the beginning of the track again.

'Better try the vicar,' I decided.

Meanwhile, I'd already recognized that the bedroom was getting colder instead of warmer; I now saw that Elvis had slunk in and stuffed most of his right side into the open grating of the heater. The smell that I'd mistaken for singed electric elements was actually a cat on the verge of catching fire.

'Elvis!'

63

But we were violently interrupted by the slam of the front door, echoing through the house in counterpoint to Tarquin's sound effects. The needle shivered on the vinyl, further warbling Neil Young. I ran to the landing. '*Dad?*' Oh please let it be Dad, I'd hardly seen my father for days.

Behind me, Francine had sprung from the cushions and lunged at the bouncing stylus.

'Dad?'

But it wasn't; the voice yelling below us, thick with celebration, was Timothy's. 'I WON! I BEAT THE BUGGERS!'

'Tim, shush! Mum's in bed!'

'I'M THE CHAMPION OF THE WORLD, ME! *MUM?* Where's Mum, Josie? I'm a bloody genius, man!'

'I told you. Fast asleep.'

'Better wake her up then. *MUM!*'

Timothy was barrelling up the stairs, arms and legs flying about like a stage drunk. I was no stranger to the sight of men ascending this staircase blotto and they didn't do it like that; Tim was obviously putting it on. Yet his breath hit me on the stairs: booze and – oh no. There were spots of something smelly in his hair. His school shirt hung out, like Mrs Matlock's Little Orphan Annie.

'Tim, she's only been in bed a couple of hours after working all last night and all day. There's that epidemic.'

'I got to tell her I'm bloody brilliant, Josie.'

'She knows already.'

'Does she?'

'Course she does. Why don't we go back downstairs first and find something to eat?'

He gazed hopelessly at me and sank abruptly onto the staircase. I knew what was coming next – Timothy was about to lose his cool. This no longer happened with the frequency that had marred our childhood, but the possibility never entirely retreated; it lurked in the shadows around him like the fear of a recurring bad dream. Timothy's mouth opened and spittle ran down his chin.

'No, Timmy!'

'*Jo* – sie!' It was a wail. His eyes swam, the pupils wobbling like marbles behind the meniscus of tears.

'Oh God!'

'It's not . . . it's not *fair*, Jo – sie!'

The face that beseeched me, tendrils of its rank hair plastered against the pimpled forehead, was so nearly my own. It was like a mirror in a nightmare. A biblical phrase from primary school insinuated itself into my head, coaxed by Tarquin's sonorous donging: 'Through a glass, darkly.'

Francine was on the landing. 'Jesus!'

'Come on, Timmy, let's get you downstairs. One arm each,' I suggested to Francine.

'Me?'

'Before he wakes Mum.'

'Well, she's apparently slept through Tarquin's bloody bells.'

'But the violent weeping of her youngest son might penetrate. Please, Frankie. Just grab an arm and help me haul him downstairs.'

We got no help from Timothy himself, who sort of collapsed against us, threatening to unbalance Francine's light frame and pitch her through the Venetian window, but eventually we induced him back into the hall, Timothy sobbing the while and telling us he was a genius. When we'd made it as far as the kitchen and dumped him on a stool by the breakfast bar, I had a look in the fridge. Today was the day for Mrs Stanley, our cleaner. She had obviously done her weekly sweep and binned everything that had fur on it. Usually it would also be Mum's day for whizzing round the supermarket, but when Frankie and I had fled here with Neil Young, we'd found a few scribbled lines on a pad on the hall-stand and a pound note: *Out for the count. Don't wake me. Dad's eating in town. If you don't fancy anything tinned, treat yourselves to fish and chips.* We hadn't fancied anything tinned and the nearest fish and chip shop was a bus ride away, so we'd filled up on salad-cream sandwiches. Later, we intended going back round to Francine's to share whatever her mom was keeping hot for her. I now took a tin down from the cupboard. Timothy was crying still, but the tide of madness had ebbed.

'How do Spam sandwiches grab you, Timmy?'

'I don't feel too good, man.'

'Food would help settle your stomach. You know what Dad always says.'

Timothy raised his eyes to the tin. Jellified pink meat gleamed back at him from the label. He turned his head away and sobbed heavily.

'Frankie, can you get him the Alka-Seltzer?'

'Where?'

'Bathroom cupboard.'

Relieved to be out of range of any projectile vomiting, she trotted back out of the kitchen and I heard her light feet tittupping up the creaky staircase. *D-o-o-o-nnngggggg.* The lugubrious lowing vibrated through us. The fridge door hummed.

'What in Christ's name is that racket?' enquired Timothy with sober irritation.

'Just Tarquin.'

'Tell him to put a sock in it, can't you? My head's killing me.'

'Where have you actually been?'

'Chess tournament. I won! Haven't you been listening *at all*?'

'No, I mean boozing. The pubs can't have been open.'

'Martin Butler's place. He's got a cache in his

66

bedroom. Cyprus sherry and that eggy stuff. Advocaat.'

'Bloody hell, Tim.'

'And a bottle of green chartreuse.'

'I bet the vomit was a fascinating colour.'

'Appropriate, I'd say, since I was sick down the back of his colour telly.'

'*Tim!* No wonder you never get invited anywhere.'

'Well! Serves him right for having a colour telly in his bedroom. How affectatious can you get? Ermintrude's pink, did you know?'

'Who's Ermintrude?'

'Josie, pull yourself together. The cow on *The Magic Roundabout!*'

'Oh. Right. Yes, I've seen it at Frankie's.'

'Though not afterwards, she wasn't – they all went sort of luminous green. Interesting Ph.D. thesis waiting there for someone, I'd say. Hey, Josie, did you hear about the prostitute in the leper colony?'

'Sorry?'

'She had to give it up because business was dropping off.'

By which I concluded that Timothy was on the mend. Francine was back, carrying a box stuffed with white discs like horse tablets. We heard her running a plastic mug under the tap, followed by a *plink* and a *hissssh*. There was never any point in looking for a glass in our house, they were invariably on one floor or another upside down with spiders under them. She handed the fizzing mug over to me with a little moue of distaste.

'Is he going to throw up any more?' She scrutinized her skinny jumper and zippered flares for contamination.

'He can answer for himself,' Timothy snapped back at her. 'He's pissed, not deaf and dumb.'

'Pretty dumb to get this pissed, if you ask me.'

'Nobody did.'

'If it was up to me, I wouldn't let you in the kitchen with sick dripping from your greasy hair.'

'Snotty little hypocrite! What about that time you were in here at midnight cleaning up before you went home to Mommy? Reeking of cider, and weeping and wailing about that folk singer who doesn't want you!'

'Timmy, that's enough!'

'At least I was in the *bathroom*, at least I wasn't polluting anybody's kitchen.'

'Snivelling over a bloke that wouldn't touch you with a twenty-foot pole.'

'Hark at Mr Sexy! What girl's ever going to touch you?'

' "Oh Jo, why can't I make him want me, Jo?" '

'Tim!'

' "Oh Jo, I love him so much." '

'At least I don't live in a haunted house with blood dripping down the walls and mad screams coming out of—'

A mad scream came out of mid air and hit us like another slamming door. Francine stopped in mid-contempt. Timothy jumped like a heap of rags tossed in the air by a pitchfork. The scream went on and on, howling some intolerable agony at us for immeasurable time before withering to a sob. Then it struck up again, an exact replica, like a recording.

'To hell with this!' shouted Timothy and stormed unsteadily out of the kitchen towards the staircase and Tarquin's studio. Francine and I stayed where we were, our ears straining to place the scream. It is notoriously difficult to locate sounds that are sustained at high pitch; we both knew this of old – we suffered a lot of sustained high-pitched sounds in this house.

'Sink,' decided Francine.

'I think you're right.'

We edged across the kitchen floor to the sink unit, a cheap stainless-steel addition to the house, replacing the beautiful stone basin that was in situ in the Richardsons' time, until fractured by (needless to say) Geoffrey. The cry was now replaced by a low laugh, gurgly and evil, like a stage Demon King hamming it up. This one was easy enough to place: it clearly emanated from the plughole.

'Laughing like a drain,' I pointed out. 'Clarence's idea of wit, perhaps. Frankie, I'm going to take a look under the sink. Dismantle the U-bend.'

'Oh *gross.*'

'Yes, I know, but . . .' I opened the door of the bottom cupboard. It was full of Domestos bottles and Vim. You'd think the house would be clean, from that cupboard. How easily would the U-bend come apart? I unscrewed the plastic ring. From above us, a different species of scream vibrated through the flaky plaster of the kitchen ceiling.

'SHUT UP, TARQUIN, YOU'RE DRIVING US ROUND THE TWIST, YOU'RE DRIVING US NUTS!'

Laughter glugged delightedly out of the pipes. I gave the plastic an experimental tug. *WHOOSH!* The U-bend toppled into a cardboard box of dusters, disgusting wet muck surging out with it. High above us, another door slammed. Not Tarquin's. The floor above that. Mum.

'*What the hell is going on?*' She was thundering down from the upper storey, the treads of the stairs creaking arthritically beneath her. Under the sink, a drenched and filthy duster swam out of the box, which promptly disintegrated. I shut the cupboard door.

'Have you no consideration whatsoever, any of you?'

'Look, Mum . . .' Timothy's voice sounded small. I straightened up.

'I've been working for thirty-six hours . . . !'

Francine and I crept from the kitchen.

'Is it too much to ask that I'm allowed some ordinary peace and quiet without my family screaming and hammering . . .'

Into the hall. To the front door.

Out.

8

The Switts were moving from Lossing Common because Francine's mother hated the place, had hated it since the day they came here. Her father didn't – he first stumbled on our patch of Essex one hot Whit week during a trip to the Ford Motor Company's UK headquarters at Warley; he found bluebell woods and hawthorn blossom, gardens full of flowering cherry trees, hedgerows frothing with cow parsley. Mr Switt was the sort of man who, having once seen bluebell woods in Lossing, would see them here for ever, their imagery overlaying less endearing visual impressions in a typically generous double exposure. Mr Switt was an Anglophile whose eyes lit up to hear a BBC voice intone the shipping forecast. I had once seen him leave a neighbour's garden in high summer reverently murmuring, 'Deadhead the petunias,' as though it were poetry.

His wife had different perceptions, and noticed only the scrubby verges, raw brick bungalows behind ranch-house fencing, plastic garden ornaments, houses exasperatingly named instead of numbered, the names themselves often built up from inappropriate bits of family appellation as though these were Lego bricks – Meldawn, Bevmandy, Glyn-vera-dan. She saw the glum post office, the unsavoury pub and our one dispirited local store, and everywhere she heard the moaning whine of Essex accents.

Of course, Mrs Switt had come over here to check things out before her husband signed the contract. They had flown in together one dark December day in 1967, and respectful estate agents, primed by Personnel at Ford and muffled against indoor cold, had led them through one house after another searching for power showers. Mrs Switt was presumably beguiled by her husband's enthusiasm; perhaps she foresaw a seasonal transformation of Lossing Common into the sort of English village that Americans are presented with in the movies. After all, December in Detroit wasn't so pretty either. But what we could never understand was how she'd failed to clock the radio tower.

Lossing Common's straggling bungalows gave out before they reached the Red House; between this and the Switts' four-bedroom residence with all mod. cons was an average-sized barley field beyond which loomed the tower, a hundred and fifty feet high, in an enclosure fenced with razor wire and behind a forest of official signs plastered with warnings in increasingly hysterical tones the closer you got. When we first moved here the tower was merely a lanky pole supported by guy-ropes and topped by a blinking red light. Locals used to joke that its purpose was to guide them home on dark nights from the further-flung public houses. And then, during our first months in Lossing, a metal tower began silently to build itself around the pole, girder by girder, day by day, erected by invisible workmen, a fearsome skeleton of grey criss-cross struts sprouting satellite dishes like enormous dustbin lids. An Eiffel Tower designed by Daleks. It squatted in its field on splayed metal legs, like a bitch straining at stool.

Objections by stunned residents were snubbed by an official blockade; journalists from the local press found their pieces slammed with D-notices. There was dark talk of early warning systems and top-secret burrowing beneath Lossing Common, a network pushing out like tumours from a bungalow in the woods at the back of the church. Bunkers. Nuclear fallout shelters. From the day the first girders went up, to live in Lossing was to be perpetually reminded that the government saw nuclear war as a real and imminent option.

Mrs Switt stood it for eighteen months, life in the shadow of our fizzing tower, before she lit out one day for London and came home with her arms full of glossy brochures. Regent's Park. The John Nash terraces in cream stucco, tiered like wedding cakes. It would be easy enough to commute, she declared, pooh-poohing her husband's insistence that nobody had *ever* attempted to live on Regent's Park and commute to rural Essex, that one week of it would kill him. Luckily, the project was stymied by the surveyor's report; apparently her chosen terrace was little more than a pretty face. Jerry-built. 'Mink coat and no knickers' was how the surveyor put it when Mrs Switt phoned to object that she'd read up her British history, these terraces were famous, an immortal monument to John Nash, architect to the Prince Regent. 'Exactly,' agreed the surveyor wearily. 'Another one who was all mouth and trousers. Two of a kind.'

As a concession to her husband's place of work, Mrs Switt expanded her search into the east side of London, but found only decaying back-to-backs and a young flurry of tower blocks. And black people. Mrs Switt – who had been in our country when Enoch Powell gave his 'Rivers of Blood' speech and could quote from it extensively, and who earlier had been in her own country when Martin Luther King gave his 'I have a dream' speech, and who had played absolute merry hell when Francine and I were striding up and down her kitchen reciting it – was particularly un-enthusiastic about this aspect of London once you strayed far outside the Circle Line.

Eventually they compromised; if Mrs Switt would lower her sights from the palatial, her husband would agree to a London apartment, in the vicinity of Regent's Park if she insisted, where he would join his wife and daughter on weekends. And he would swap the Lossing house for digs in Brentwood, in which to live Monday to Friday.

Francine's sole response to the family crisis had been to establish that Cecil Sharp House, Mecca to all the folk people, was just around the corner in Regent's Park Road; and that the folk clubs of Ilford and Hornchurch, where Florian could be found two nights a week, were accessible by public transport. On the other hand, unless Francine was to go along to these clubs on her own, the Starkey family had to achieve its own move to Harley Street.

The following Thursday. It was about a mile to St Andrew's Church with its recently built vicarage, a nasty oblong in yellow brick. Lossing had no pave-ments; you walked along the grass verges while speeding cars threw slush over you from the road. Tough humps of snow survived at the roadsides, pitting as they thawed. Behind the brooding silhouette of the church tower, the sky was turning an eerie crepuscular shade of green, so the scene was rather more Gothic than I would have chosen for a visit to a vicar to rake up the long dead who had presumably gasped their dying breath in my own home. By the gate, a sodden notice advertised 'Choir practice – Thursday evenings'. Tonight, then. Plus Lossing Common's only other forthcoming attraction, the Easter Monday Hard-of-Hearing Whist Drive.

'Excuse me.'

Choir practice had evidently finished; the choristers, coated and tweeded, stood about in conversational knots, among them Mrs Richardson, who saw me clatter in and smiled. And there was I, about to shop her to the vicar for selling us a haunted house. I felt the unwanted prickly heat of guilt. But where was he? Over everything lay the doughy smell of damp stone. Home from home, then. My voice seeped out nervously, to be mopped up by the air.

'Excuse me!'

'Yes? Are you looking for someone?' A large lady rocked towards me on a walking stick, stabbing at the flagstones as though it were a skiing pole.

'I wanted the vicar.'

'Mr Horne? Vicars don't attend choir practice, dear – they know the hymns already.' But her good-natured smile took the edge off the sarcasm. 'Try the vicarage.'

'Vestry,' put in another voice.

'Ah,' said the lady with the stick. 'There you are then. Vestry.'

I stood a moment longer, but that seemed to be it. Was this a place name? Or a condition, like AWOL or in purdah – the vicar can't see anyone, he's vestry? My big hands and feet seemed to swell with my embarrassment and confusion. But as I was dithering back the way I came, the stick lady saved me.

'No need to go all the way round, dear,' she called out. 'Use this door,' and gestured towards the altar.

He was in there, on his haunches locking a cupboard

and swishing a scarf round the collar of his winter coat.

'Yes?'

'I'm sorry to bother you. My name's Jo Starkey and I've come to ask for your help . . .'

'Starkey? The Red House. Both doctors.'

'My parents.'

'Atheists.'

He was upright now, facing me square on, a cavernous man, the flesh retreating from sharp cheekbones, pinkly veined skin, sleek silver hair in strands across a pinkish dome, eyes blue, a baby's colour scheme. Nothing babyish in the face, though, which had retained the creases from those hostile sibilants. Atheists.

'Humanists,' I countered. 'My father is a leading gynaecologist and my mother is Senior Surgical Registrar in A&E. She works—'

'Yes, yes, yes.' A waspish gesture of the hand. 'What is it you want?'

'Spiritual help.'

Yep, that stopped him – I thought I saw his nose twitch. I pressed home the advantage. 'I've come to you for guidance, Mr Horne, on a spiritual matter.'

He humphed a bit and went back to locking cupboards. Voices outside, and the crunch of gravel. Cars revving.

'Well,' he said eventually, straightening up, 'I suppose you had better come across to the vicarage. Can't deal with you here – we'll both catch pneumonia.'

He ushered me out and we left by the gate.

'Pity to see the church bare of flowers,' I chirped up. I'd seen church services on TV and had expected a sort of florist's shop. 'I suppose they're a bit expensive at this time of year.'

'We're in the middle of Lent, girl!'

So I shut up and followed him across the road.

76

*　　*　　*

Despite the limitations of the small house, the vicarage study was a scholarly room smelling of antiquarian books. I sat in a slippery leather chair polished by a thousand bottoms before mine, across from Mr Horne's desk with its inlay of old leather, deep red like the blood of horses. My eyes scanned the library now encasing me. Classicism, by the looks of things. Mr Horne had wrested an Oxbridge study from the 1960s utilitarianism of that ugly bungalow. I felt a pang that my school taught no history older than the plumbing in our bathroom, and in fact I wouldn't have trusted our teacher to know who came first, the Greeks or the Romans.

There was the occasional name I recognized but in another context: Pascal. Descartes. Euclid. I knew them as mathematicians, and although I didn't quite have Timothy's genius, maths was the love of my life. An anglepoise lamp cast light-pools and shadows in which formulae full of Greek letters sparkled in the air around the gilded and creased leather spines. Numbers cascaded from them, aglow with their certainties, their unambiguities, their universal truths.

I loved the crispness of mathematics, the sweet neatness of its inarguable logic in an otherwise unstable world. Maths can be looked at in several ways. For example, in schools it's mostly taught as a collection of recipes, ways of getting to an answer. When you go beyond the school curriculum the emphasis changes, and it's more like there's a great body of stuff out there, beautiful mathematical theorems waiting to be discovered. Or you can look at maths as problem-solving, which means a process, not a finished product at all. But the point is, whichever view you take, and whether you get to your solution by trial-and-error graft or flashes of inspiration, once you do get the correct answer you can prove that it's correct and can never be contradicted. Which isn't ever the case with the sciences. Two plus two will always equal four because that *defines* four; a (b + c) will always equal ab + ac because each defines the other . . . These things are true not because they are the latest theories by which to explain experimental evidence but because they represent a perfect internal logic, impossible to contradict. And supposing the Starkey philosophy were wrong and there really was a God? Well, He could turn the laws of physics upside down on a whim, but not those mathematical truths. They would be true for all time whether He liked it or not.

Seated behind the collegiate desk among his Greek geniuses, Mr Horne seemed the embodiment of wisdom, to whom all troubles could be unburdened. Presumably, frightened patients felt the same way in my father's consulting rooms, tearfully confiding their unwanted pregnancies as he reassured and arranged dates.

'Now then, child,' Mr Horne was saying to me, 'I run confirmation classes on Thursday evenings. Though in your own case, you would first need to be baptized into the Church of England. If it is Christian guidance that you're seeking.'

'Not really. At least, not here and now,' I amended tactfully. 'You see, I'm trying to cope with something I think is probably evil.'

His eyebrows rose and he cleared his throat. 'Ah,' he said. 'And is this a solo activity?'

I reran the question in my head. 'Solo?'

'Perhaps it's a matter you'd prefer to talk over with my wife. She's an experienced listener, you know. Girls uncertain of some aspects of their young maturing lives, they find great comfort in her advice.'

'I don't think so,' I said, still not understanding. 'It's about the afterlife.'

He gave me a cool look and then settled back in his chair, making a cat's cradle of his thin fingers. 'The afterlife. Is it now? Well, you'd better go on.'

'Yes,' I began and then stopped. My story, given permission at last to be told, threatened to bubble incontinently from me. I had to put a brake on myself for fear of crashing into incoherence.

'You see, we've lived in the Red House since January 1963, when I was seven. And for as long as I can remember, there have been goings-on, and I'm not sure that they can be explained by normal means.'

'I don't understand you.'

'No, you won't. I'm not sure anyone can. But you of all people understand about life after death, and the *ka* and so on.'

'What's that last word? Car?'

'You know, ancient Egypt; that part of us that survives the death of the body. "And Death Shall Have No Dominion", by Dylan Thomas.'

He blinked at me, lids briefly lowered over hooded eyes. 'I fear you may be labouring under some misapprehension. The fundamental tenet of Christian doctrine is that God's only son rose from the dead that all who follow Him might have eternal life.'

'Ex*act*ly!'

I got an unfathomable look from under the reptilian lids. 'Suppose you try to come to the point.'

'Well, you see, we've always had peculiar things happening but I can't remember when it started. 'Sixty-three was that terrible winter, you remember, so of course we were cold and the pipes froze up. But it was like the house never got properly warm again. And then the funny business started. Ghostly noises that might or might not have been my brother Tarquin's Theremin, but also other things more like practical jokes. We desperately need help, Mr Horne. It's like we're trapped. One brother's turned into a recluse and my twin is getting nearly as bad, shut in his bedroom with seventeen hamsters and Eric Clapton. Except for Tarquin, everybody in the family blames everybody else because, like you said – well you didn't, but still – they're all rationalists. Cutlery springs out of drawers when you open them, and in the unlikely event that Mum's home she just mutters about high spirits and puts plasters on the cuts and bruises. Bad cuts sometimes. I mean, whoever heard of a spoon wound?

'Tarquin's convinced it's a poltergeist; I expect you're having the same thought yourself. He's got that book, the *Rituale Romanum*, because he recited a chunk of it on one of the less heavy tracks of his latest album but I don't know how to do it properly, so I was wondering if you could come round and have a bash, sort of officially.' I took a deep breath and projected like an actor, '*Exorcizo te, immundissime spiritus, omnis incursio adversarii, omne phantasma . . .*'

'STOP THAT THIS INSTANT!' Mr Horne was out of his leather chair as though on a spring, looming across the desk, his face suffused. I thought he was going to slap me. 'What in God's name do you think you are playing at?'

'It's the words of the exorcism,' I told him. 'It's from—'

'I know what it is! And in all my born days I never thought to hear it from the mouth of a young girl in my own home! A Minister of the Church!'

'Mr Horne, I think our house is haunted.'

'Stop this!'

Light from the desk lamp cut his face into shadows and sharp planes, highlighting the threadwork of splintered veins across the surface of the cheeks and nose, raddled like gorgonzola. 'I know where that sort of rubbish emanates from – pop music! Filling teenagers' heads with ill-digested nonsense about spiritualism. Groups called Black Sabbath. The Beatles setting themselves up as idols and talking blasphemous twaddle about mysticism and Maharishis!'

'Actually,' I corrected the error unsteadily, getting to my feet, 'it was John Lennon who exposed that Maharishi as a fraud.'

'And then took Christ's name in vain in a pop song!' he retorted. 'Don't talk to me about John Lennon. Estranged from God and living with Yoko Ono!'

Mind you, that wasn't far off the view of Yoko held by a goodish proportion of the Western world.

'They're married now,' I said faintly. 'She's his wife.'

'Nonsense – the man has a wife already. Arrogance and sin and *this* is what comes of it!' Flinging a hand at me as though in demonstration, Exhibit A. Spittle frothed at the corners of the thin mouth.

'Please don't,' I urged him, close to tears, 'they've just lost their baby.'

'Good. Perhaps it will bring the pair of them to their senses.'

In the hall I caught sight of a woman, floury and pinafored, watching bewildered from the door of her kitchen. I stumbled home through the muddy slush, crying like a ten-year-old.

9

By Good Friday the snow had long gone, replaced by tangy rain, a general freckling of blossom, and daffodils left behind from March. Brentwood Folk Club met in a room off the saloon bar of the Castle pub – a modern, square, brick building, its function room just a function room, nothing to match the oak beams and candlelight of Stavering's slopy old pub. At the moment, the club secretary was introducing Florian:

'And now, everybody's favourite singer to be named after an Eye-tie boozer – Florian Smith!'

Applause and cat-calls. Francine sipped a glass of Babycham that several young men had fought for the privilege of buying her. The pale lacquered fingers trembled holding the glass.

He had a beautiful voice, I'd give him that. His songs of lost love and rent hearts lilted into the corners of the room and softened the texture of the air under the tungsten glare of the Castle's uncompromising electric light. I drank my lager and lime, and hoped to distract my mind from bodily ills; ever since I'd got out of the bath my toes had been stinging like hell; I seemed to have developed chilblains.

All the music was particularly good tonight; we were given a heartbreaking song about a West Indian cane strike, followed by Bert Jansch's 'Needle Of Death', then the shanty 'Sally Free And Easy' in which a sailor drowns himself for love, and finally a song set in a Victorian workhouse where the overseers murder a boy called Jimmy and serve him up for Christmas dinner. We all bubbled happily out to the bar at the beer break, which is when I recognized him. Mr Bailey – tutor from Timothy's first year at public school, who had once come round to the house to get our parents' approval for one of Tim's precocious exam sittings. Earlier this evening he had given us a couple of guitar instrumentals that nearly brought the house down. It was the guitar that had thrown me.

'Mr Bailey?'

There was a second or two before he even looked up, so I wondered whether he'd heard me. A deaf guitarist? Then he lifted his nose from his pint. 'I'm only Mr Bailey on school premises. While propping up a bar, I answer to Greg.'

'I'm Timothy Starkey's twin sister, Jo. You came to our house once when he started at the George the Sixth.'

'Oh yes, Tim. He was more interested in learning to decipher Egyptian hieroglyphs than doing any homework. I left there three years ago. How's he getting on?'

'Well, you know Tim. Wiping the floor with everybody else. He did learn hieroglyphics in the end.'

'I never doubted it.'

'We haven't seen you at the Castle before, have we?'

'Just moved to Brentwood.'

'Your rendition of "Angi" was absolutely brilliant.'

'True.'

That seemed to be it for conversation. 'Well, see you around then, Mr Bailey. Greg.'

'Looks like it.' He returned his gaze to his pint.

I looked round the bar for Francine.

'Jo! What a coincidence.'

Oh no. Stephanie Sandiman from school.

'Not much of a coincidence, Stephanie, as we've both been coming here every single Friday since about 1969.'

Might as well get in first. Stephanie used to be my best friend before Francine, and she hated me. Back inside the club room I found Francine herself among a returning crowd that had Florian at its centre. He had turned a chair round and was straddling it, his long arms resting across the back, long Levi legs sprawled. Very cowboy. Beneath a groovy grey suede jacket he wore a white shirt open to the throat, in fact open to the chest. His shoulder-length hair shone. You didn't have to ask what Frankie saw in him. As I arrived, he was apparently halfway through reciting one of his limericks.

> '. . . *Swept off her feet,*
> *By the whole whaling fleet,*
> *She got rather more Dick there than Moby.*'

Applause and raucous laughter, which Florian rode like a professional. I slipped between the seated rows and arrived beside Francine's chair.

'OK, so whose turn next?' He called the crowd to order, well timed before the laugh petered out.

Hands shot up. He did an *eenie-meenie-miney-mo* and came to a halt at a young woman in an Afghan coat. 'The lady on my left, who's brought her dead goat. Name please.'

'Sue Dunne from Fingest.'

'Fingers?'

She turned pink. 'Fingest! In the Chiltern hills. *Buckinghamshire?*'

She was wasting her time. This was Essex. You only went west of London to get to the States.

'You mean,' said Florian, 'there was a young lady from Bucks!'

More laughter, in which Mr Bailey, Greg, arrived at Florian's elbow with two halves of bitter.

Someone at the front piped up, 'I can't believe you people. Even *I* know the Chilterns and I'm a foreigner!'

'Bucks is too easy, Florian,' decided the club secretary. 'It's either Dunne or that village of wherever-she-said. Off you go – thirty seconds counting down *now*.' After twenty of them, he was on his feet like a ref at a boxing match: '*Ten! Nine! Eight!*' The crowd joined in. '. . . *Three! Two! One! Ding-ding!*'

Florian slumped sideways on his chair. Knock-out.

'Failed,' announced the club secretary, rubbing his hands. 'Only three out of four tonight. That's a pint you owe me.'

'Let's go for one more,' said Florian, glancing at his watch. 'How about the delectable American lady?'

My eyes went to Francine, but his didn't; I followed them to the foreigner who knew the Chilterns – pint-sized with black hair to her waist, dressed in a lot of fringed suede and a beaded headband. This was a year for conscience movies about America's Old West, and she was dressed exactly like the sort of extra who got massacred in them. Very pretty, too. As confirmed by Francine's expression.

'Just sock that accent to me one more time,' Florian was saying, his smile intimate as a double bed, 'and I'll have an orgasm while you tell me your name.'

She laughed. 'I'll bet you can't make a limerick out of me. Fasten your seat-belts, folks; it's Anna-Carlotta Campiani of Santa Monica, California!'

Everybody laughed, except Francine and me. The

club secretary got to his feet. 'Two in a row, Florian. You're losing your grip.'

'Not so fast, Mike. I can do the "Santa".'

'You mean that Father Christmas one *again*? We've passed twelfth night, you know – it's Good Friday!'

'It's good any day of the week,' called out a wit at the back and was raggedly cheered.

Florian waved an imaginary baton and all the regulars in the audience chanted it happily, except Francine and me.

> *There was a young fellow called Santa,*
> *Watching the revels and banter.*
> *"Oh golly," cried he,*
> *"We need balls for the tree!"*
> *And Rudolph broke into a canter.'*

Amid the subsequent applause, Florian turned quietly to Greg.

'Ready to go?'

'Certainly am.'

They drained their glasses. Then I watched with dismay as he turned again to Anna-Carlotta Campiani of Santa Monica, California.

'I'm taking this new-kid-in-town over to a friend's flat for a jam session. Want to come and listen?'

'I'm sorry. I'm meeting my sister here in a half-hour.'

Perhaps there was a God after all. I was dying to pipe up and say, 'Frankie and I would love to come and listen, wouldn't we, Frankie?' but at eleven o'clock Mr Switt would be waiting outside to take us home.

'Jo and I would love to come and listen,' said Francine in a strained voice, 'wouldn't we, Jo?'

'Well . . .'

'Yeah?' Florian responded. 'Great!' though he hardly glanced her way. And to the crowd, 'That's all, folks. Gotta split.'

The beer break was at a close so the four of us were struggling upstream. Florian tried to introduce Francine and me to Greg.

'He and I know each other already,' I explained. 'Greg taught maths to my twin brother.'

But Florian had stopped paying attention; he was turning round. He now pitched his voice to the back of the stalls: 'Hey, everyone!'

The singer, poised for the opening of his song, shut his mouth again and removed the finger from his right ear.

The club secretary gave a theatrical sigh. 'There's a rumour this is supposed to be a folk club!'

'I've got that other limerick.'

'And then you'll leave?'

'Never to return.'

'Can't say fairer than that. Go on.'

> *'There was a young lady called Dunne,*
> *Made errors of speech just for fun.*
> *For Miss Susan of Fingest,*
> *Had heard cunnilingus*
> *Was really a slip of the tongue.'*

The club room exploded with groans and calls of 'Shame!' and 'Resign!'

'Come on,' said Florian to the three of us. 'Let's get out of here before they realize the rhymes don't really work.'

'Just tell me,' said Greg, as we pushed open the pub door, 'the Moby Dick one. Who the hell was that for?'

'Didn't you see her? Japanese. Said she was from Kobe.'

'Thanks,' said Greg. 'I wouldn't have slept.'

Florian's car was parked down the road. The men strode ahead, Florian clutching his wildly flapping suede jacket that billowed like a cloak while Francine and I scurried behind them, jacket- and coatless, frozen; we hadn't expected to meet the night air for longer than it took to skip between the pub door and the muggy microclimate of Mr Switt's snazzy Granada, with its stereo tape-deck and automatic transmission.

'Don't you just love this sort of night?' Florian was shouting into the wind. 'Like the whole world is being swept clean! On a night like this, can't you just believe in Gaia?' As neither of us had ever heard of Gaia, we kept jogging. Passing Henderson's clock tower Francine addressed me out of the side of her mouth like a movie gangster. 'Have you gone crazy or what, saying you're Tim's twin in front of that guy! He'll know how old we are!'

'Frankie, he barely even remembers Tim. He would never have recognized me if I hadn't told him.'

'Well, thanks a bunch for telling him!'

Both sides of every road were cluttered with Friday-night cars jaundiced by the ochrous cast from the street lamps. When we eventually arrived at Florian's, which invariably looked newly washed and polished, he took an eternity stowing the guitars in the boot while Francine and I slipped, shivering, into the back, silently screaming at him to shut the door.

'Cigarette?' Greg asked us both, waving a packet of Rothmans over his shoulder.

'Yeah, thanks,' responded Francine, who didn't smoke. 'I don't think I've had a ciggie since my seventeenth birthday party.'

'Is this a special occasion then?' enquired Florian, slipping behind the wheel and slamming the door just in time before I actually burst into tears. 'Hear that, Greg? Looks like one of us might be in with a chance.'

Above the clicking lighter that Greg held out behind him for her cigarette, Francine suffered one of her drenching blushes. As Florian wriggled the car out from its parking space, she sucked her cigarette gingerly, like the gulps of some ornamental fish in a pond. The car pulled away, lumbering up Brentwood High Street. I had no idea where we were going.

'Starkey,' announced Greg suddenly. 'I don't think I ever asked – your family's no relation, I take it?'

'They most certainly are,' replied Florian brightly in his Tarquin voice. Francine shut her eyes. 'Jo's the great man's sister.'

'*You're Ringo Starr's sister?*'

Florian threw back his head and screamed with laughter. We swerved. A horn shrieked and headlights torched the interior. Francine's cigarette twitched, sending sparks onto the immaculate upholstery.

'Not Richard Starkey,' I explained, 'Tarquin Starkey.'

'Sorry, but I think his stuff's rubbish.'

'Well, thank Christ for that,' said Francine, which shut Florian up nicely. We drove quietly out of Brentwood. We passed Harold Wood and kept going. We passed Gidea Park and kept going. At eleven o'clock, Mr Switt would be outside the Castle, patiently waiting to give us a lift home.

After a while I took Francine's forgotten cigarette and smoked it myself; I knew the statistics and it seemed to me that one cigarette was unlikely to shorten my life. I decided that two wouldn't either, and accepted a second from Greg as we left Romford behind and headed on towards Ilford.

10

'Dad? It's Francine. Look, sorry about this, but we've gone round to a friend's for coffee and might be a bit late back to Brentwood. I'll give you a ring later when we know what time, OK?'

We were in a hallway. Behind one of the doors that led off it, the men were singing: '*And as for the weapons that hung by their side, / We took them and threw them far into the tide.*'

'We don't know yet. Say one o'clock? Half-past?'

' *"May the devil go with you," said Arthur McBride, / "For spoiling our walk in the morning!"*'

'Dad, how should *I* know? Somewhere in Ilford. A flat.'

Pause. Gentle quacking issued from the mouthpiece. Francine pulled faces at me, her free hand making impatient wind-it-up gestures in the air. 'But that's why I've phoned. So you weren't hanging around for two or three hours in Brentwood waiting!'

The quacking got louder. Beyond our hallway, some-one – Greg – launched into 'Angi'.

'Oh *Dad*. Look, we don't *know* the address.' She covered the mouthpiece and stage-whispered at me. 'He says he's going to come and get us. Here.'

'Why?'

'He says he needs me home!'

'Why?'

'God knows.'

'Well, ask him. Ask him what's happened.'

'Dad, has something happened?'

The voice at the other end talked quietly and steadily. Francine's face creased in puzzlement.

'Sunday? Why – Mom isn't dying of cancer or something, is she?'

Some more quiet responses from her father and Francine turned back to me once more: 'He says Mom's flying back to the States Sunday for a couple of weeks. To Miami, to see my aunt Janet who's got trouble. He says he'll explain when he picks us up. But how am I expected to tell him where to find us? I mean, what a drag!'

'Wait a sec.' I put down my glass of lager on a dirty table scattered with very old unopened mail. I blew the sticky dust off an envelope.

'Seventy-one Mayflower Crescent,' I read.

'Hear that, Dad? Number 71, Mayflower Crescent, Ilford. OK? Knock real loud so we can hear above the music. What? Oh, Jo says there's some bells. Ring the one marked "Pete Christie". OK, see you soon.'

She put the receiver down. 'This lousy phone rejected everything except a two-bob piece!'

'Ten new pence,' I corrected automatically as she fiddled with the coin-return lever. 'How's your dad ever going to find us with just that address?'

'He's Mr Navigation, my father. If you called him up from a camel market outside Timbuktu you'd hear a map crackling open and him asking which side of Yashmak Avenue you were calling from.'

There was something very un-Francine about this remark – I detected her mother's turn of phrase (and cultural misapprehensions) and guessed this was part of Switt family lore. We let ourselves back into Pete Christie's flat, past lurking bikes and a galley kitchen piled with sudded crockery, to the sitting room. Florian, Greg and Pete himself were well away, two guitars and electric violin, jamming an instrumental conceived in a Scottish reel. Pete was tiny, a gnome of a guy, the fiddle jutting from his chin like an outgrowth. The music skipped and swayed.

Tarquin said that most folk songs are actually an invention of the so-called collectors (by interacting, you bugger it up; the folk music clause of Heisenberg's Uncertainty Principle perhaps). But even so, he said we can trace a direct line backwards from folk music to ancient Egypt and Mesopotamia. We know about the 'folkish' modes they used, from Greek writings; we know the vocals were pungently nasal, like most of the songs I heard twice a week; in Egyptian friezes, the singers often had a finger in one ear, like most of the singers I heard twice a week. With the spread of Islam, this Near-Eastern style dominated the scene until the Renaissance when the new European music developed with its major and minor scales. But the old lingered on in poor and remote areas like the Celtic fringes.

And when its people fled to America, their modal music found a new home in the remote Appalachians, where it bred country music, and also in the rural Deep South where the music of the poor whites melded with the African legacy of the even poorer blacks, to influence the 'blues scale'. Or so Tarquin said.

He also said that because rock music exists only in recordings, one day our means of reproducing it will be obsolete, and future musicologists will be piecing together clues about how we sounded, exactly the way we have to guess at the music of the Ancients. According to Tarquin.

And in a parallel universe he would be here or somewhere like it, jamming with a bunch of friends on a Friday night – and back to a normal job on Monday.

Francine and I sank into beanbags. The reel was getting hotter, Pete's violin bow flying, everyone's fingers a blur.

'You're losing me!' cried Florian. 'Go it alone, you two!'

Laughing, he unstrung himself from the guitar. Smiled at Francine and sat by her on the floor, stretching his long length across the dirty, rippled carpet. Rested his head on Francine's beanbag. I watched her freeze. I watched her stop breathing.

'They're shit-hot, aren't they?' he was saying.

The only sound to come from Francine was a wheeze. Well, one of us had to say something, or he might decide he wasn't welcome and move.

'Frankie was just telling me,' I replied, 'how they're better than anyone she's ever seen back home in the United States, *weren't you, Frankie*?'

'Oh sure,' she responded eventually, very husky. 'The States. Yeah.'

Well, husky was good, at least. Florian turned his head towards her. 'Say something else,' he whispered. 'Just talk in that fabulous accent. Tell me a story.'

Go *on*, go *on*! What did Tarquin say about positive vibrations? Could I *think* the man into kissing her? Apparently I could. One long arm reached out languidly until it met Francine's hair. He slowly wound strands around his fingers. He lay back and gently pulled her face down towards his. Well, thank God I was the one wearing Francine's £28 wig tonight, I thought, scrambling to my feet to leave them to it, or the thing would have come away in his hands.

11

'*And as for the weapons that hung by their side—*'

'Sweetheart . . .'

'*We took them and threw them far into the tide. /
"May the devil go with you," said Arthur McBride . . .*'

'Sweetheart, I got to talk to you.'

'OK, Dad. Shoot.'

Francine was aglow in the passenger seat. Periodically she ran her fingers through her hair and twiddled a strand of it. Periodically she reshuffled herself into the car seat with a happy shrug and a humphing sigh. The car glided along the dark road, slowed at the roundabout, and Mr Switt checked his rear mirror. Which was when I caught a glimpse of his eyes. They looked sore.

'Mom's taking a plane to Miami Sunday morning, to be with Aunt Janet.'

'Yeah, you said. What's up?'

'It's Robert, sweetheart. He's coming home.'

'Yeah?' She gave her Florian-kissed locks another caress and then stopped. 'Oh, don't tell me they're sending him back wounded or a junkie! Are they?'

'No, baby, it's worse than that.'

But I knew. Sensitized by Arthur McBride's press gang, I knew from the moment I'd seen Mr Switt's eyes. And now, Arthur's spiritual descendants Country Joe and the Fish were singing it at me: *And it's one, two, three, what are we fighting for? / Don't ask me, I don't give a damn / Next stop is Viet—*

'Oh,' said Francine.

'Aunt Janet called while I was out giving you a ride to Brentwood. Your mom's devastated.' He addressed me in the seat behind him. 'Francine's cousin Robert, Jo. He was drafted eighteen months back.'

'I'm really sorry.'

'Thank you. Twenty years old. Robert and Francine were never real close, he was five years older and anyway the family moved to Florida, but her mom and Aunt Janet have always been very devoted sisters.'

'That's terrible, Mr Switt.'

And it's five, six, seven, open up the pearly gates. / Well there ain't no time to wonder why / Whoopee! We're all gonna—

'Maybe this will change your mind then, Dad.'

'Not now, baby.'

'They're not just numbers, you see, they're real young men and they're *dying*!'

'Honey, I always did know the boys were real, I've seen military action myself and I can envision it better than you can.'

'Well then . . .'

'But tonight I would be truly grateful if you didn't start in on this with your mom.'

'How could you vote for him? I just do not understand.'

'Will there be a big funeral, Mr Switt?' I interrupted quickly. 'Military honours, that sort of thing?'

'I believe so, Jo. The family wishes to have Robert

laid to rest in a marble shrine in the garden.'

'Oh *gross*, Dad.'

'I want you to promise me you won't talk this way in front of your mom.'

'Look, the politicians are *lying*. You've seen the photographs of napalmed children . . .'

'Why you should believe the misinformation put out by Hanoi instead of your own democratically elected—'

'Democratic? Like shooting unarmed student demonstrators at Kent State?'

'Francine, not tonight! Your mother's devastated!'

Well, I thought, Mr Switt might have understood that the young men were not just numbers, but I don't think I had. I'd never thought of Vietnam as anything other than our vehicle to the moral high ground. The idea that one of those deaths could bring tears to the eyes of nice people like Mr Switt had never crossed my mind. Robert was twenty. Two years younger than Tarquin. Tarquin dead for two years, lying in a shrine in the garden. *Be the first one on your block / To have your boy come home in a box.*

'Why is it,' mused Francine, staring out of the car window as the A118 slid past, 'that whenever something really groovy happens, you can just bet that something else grotsome and revolting will come right along to bugger it up?'

'Fran*cine*!'

'Sorry, Dad.'

'We are trying to raise you as a lady!'

But he should have heard my own head; Country Joe and the Fish were shouting at the crowd and the crowd was shouting back. The good old Fish Cheer:

'Give us an F!'

'F!'

'Give us a U!'

'U!'

'Give us a C . . .'

* * *

'One a.m., Francine! I should have you grounded!'

'Sorry, Mom, we went back to a friend's pad for coffee.'

'So how come your breath tells me beer and cigarettes? Bed – *now*!'

She was a long, tall, balletic sort of woman, her dancer's feet set in first position. All spoilt somewhat by the arms crossed tight below a heaving chest. For all her elegance, Mrs Switt always reminded me of the wife in the Andy Capp cartoons, curlers in hair and rolling pin at the ready.

'You I'm surprised at, Jo, I thought you had more common sense.'

'M-o-o-o-m!'

'Do *your* parents know where you are? Did you call them up?'

Silence.

'Then I suggest you get on home.'

'Yes, Mrs Switt. Goodnight. Goodnight, Mr Switt.'

'Sleep well, Jo.'

I gave a valedictory wave noticed by no-one and trudged the murky hundred yards home. The Switts' arguing voices wavered and dwindled and rose again until severed by the slam of the front door. Then I was left with nothing but Country Joe:

'And what's that spell?'

'Fuck!'

'And what's that spell?'

'Fuck!'

'And what's that spell?'

My mind's eye saw a seashore and its jetsam – the rusting muskets sucked and dragged by the waves, the soaked serge, the bloated white flesh and glassy bubbles that rose, stinking, from the watery lungs of Arthur McBride's press gang.

12

Saturday afternoon was spent painting my bedroom with the gallon of non-drip gloss I'd bought on Saturday morning and carried home from Brentwood on the bus. I'd decided that painting was a blameless occupation that would give Francine something to do that suited the oxymoron of dreaminess and grieving that she must be struggling to cope with.

We painted all afternoon, the windows firmly shut against fresh air, until by about six o'clock Francine's paint-fume headache had achieved the level where she was lying across the bed moaning, so we packed it in, threw open my bedroom windows and fled. As these didn't get opened very often, I had no feel for how the consequent draughts would affect the house. I did a quick recce and it was clear that we were freezing out every habitable room except the bathroom, so Francine and I shifted ourselves in there with the record player, lit a fire and locked the door on everybody else.

Despite our streaky brush marks and all the stiff

hairs that had stuck to the paint, they were beginning to look good, my bedroom walls, with broad shining waves executed freehand across the charcoal in something called Tuscan yellow gloss. This was the colour of sunflowers, or indeed the colour of 'Sunflowers', as these summery tones were recommended by Van Gogh for daubing liberally throughout one's interior décor. On the other hand, of course, he was mad.

In the vast, echoing bathroom, Francine had shaken off her headache and was now lying across our imported cushions. 'What do you think I should wear Monday – mini-caftan? Or hot pants?'

'Hot pants,' I told her. 'Definitely.'

'But he made that remark, remember, one night when I wore the caftan. About my boobs.'

'They were in his eyes, Frankie, because you were leaning over his beer glass. You could pull exactly the same trick in hot pants.'

I'd never been entirely happy with that caftan, which Francine and I made together, copying the design from a groovy colour advert and using her mother's Singer sewing machine. But we'd got bored doing the embroidery and stopped halfway round the back. Today Francine was in canvas flares and skinny blouse, embellished with one of the black armbands we'd made a year ago when the Beatles broke up.

'I just hope he'll be there!'

'Of course he'll be there, Frankie. He's always there. When has he ever missed a Monday at Stavering?'

'January eighteenth.'

'Well, but . . .'

'November twenty-third. September seventh.'

'He'll be there, Frankie! Lean over him in the teensy-weensy hot pants and give him an eyeful. Literally.'

Francine sighed with happy extravagance and placed another log on the fire. It was smothering the flames, so I hoiked it back out. Spread across our field of lino in the firelight, my album covers looked spectacular, all the gatefolds opened out and the inserts spilling – fabulous landscapes and starscapes and mythological animals. Wonderful worlds with no wars. And no unhappy families. I picked up an album in one hand and my rag in the other and started the long job of polishing out the scratches with Brasso.

'Let's bring the bedding in, Jo, and stay here for the night.'

'But your mom's flying to the States tomorrow. Won't she want you home?'

'I'll go back for breakfast. But she's being – you know. You know how she gets.'

'Did she keep on last night?'

'Something chronic. It was starting to evaporate, that lovely floaty feeling from the Babychams and lagers and everything. So when they weren't looking I had six aspirins and a glass of Dubonnet to bring some of it back.'

I was reminded of something. Oh yes. 'We haven't eaten, have we?' I pointed out.

'Haven't we? I had some lunch before I came round.'

'I had a bag of chips in Brentwood. Do you want anything tonight?'

We decided we couldn't be bothered and dragged the bedding through from my room across the wind-chilled landing, together with a Chinese screen that I'd carried home from Kensington Market on the tube and bus. It was for drawing across the loo, as and when necessary. I'd always had a practical turn of mind.

Tarquin's studio was relatively peaceful, just a looped tape of someone reciting the same line over and over: 'You're a better man than I am, Gunga Din'. At the other end of the windswept landing, I saw that Timothy had just nailed one of our long rugs onto the outside of his door to hang down as a draught excluder. Well, if Tim was shut in for the evening with his past papers for the Cambridge entrance exam, he might not emerge until Monday. Timothy had rigged up an electric tea-maker to heat soup and poach eggs. Of course, this deprived him of the actual tea-making so he converted a coffee percolator to brew tea. He also had a pop-up toaster modified to cook rashers of bacon, and a small grill appliance, which he simply plugged in and used for toast. Timothy might blow us all up, but he wouldn't starve.

It was Francine who raised the subject of Ouija. While I'd been downstairs fetching the kettle, she'd woken from her mooniness for long enough to collect the alphabet cards from my bedroom, along with pen and paper. She was now doodling on the pad, practising her signature. Her *F* and *S* were stolen from Florian, of course, but the other flamboyant letters were her own and getting better all the time. I wished I'd brought in my book of IQ tests. Last week I'd done one and scored only 110, but I kept on and on practising the same one and eventually got right up to 165, so thank heavens at least my IQ was soaring.

'I have good vibes about Clarence this evening,' Francine was saying.

'Yeah? I don't think I can cope with him tonight, Frankie. Clarence is such a drag.'

Though quick enough off the mark when it came to grossing out anyone who came to view the house, Clarence was never in a hurry to move the tooth mug across the lino when we asked him to. And then there was Cousin Robert, so recently departed; wasn't he the more likely of the two to haunt us tonight and send messages from beyond the grave? On the other hand, if I were Robert, I'd haunt Richard Nixon. Though admittedly there might be a queue.

Francine laid her biro down. 'Tonight's better, Jo. Mom's gonna come flying home from that funeral in

102

one of her clean-sweeping moods. I remember when Grandpa died. She'll have us out of Lossing even if we have to sleep on the benches in Regent's Park.' Francine raised her pad of paper. 'Have you ever noticed that my *w* looks like the back of a bare bum?' She doodled a potty underneath it.

I looked out at the last of the chilly dusk dwindling through the dirty windows. Light from a sooty wood fire gilded the Victorian tiles.

'Let's do it tomorrow,' I suggested.

'You said Geoff and Angela were here tomorrow. Easter Sunday.'

'Hell, I'd forgotten.' I had, too. You'd have thought the potty would have jogged my memory.

'You said you were coming round to mine as soon as Mom was out of the way. Let's get it over with.'

As I watched, a long furry tail flopped down over the cistern above our fabulous blue-flowered throne of a loo. This was burnished cast iron, seven feet up the wall and lidless for years, so Elvis must be propped up by the metal rim, his soft body sagging over the waterline. How could that possibly be comfortable? And however did he get up there in the first place?

'Where shall I set them out?' asked Francine.

She meant the letter cards. So I reluctantly sat myself down on the lino, and Francine dealt them clockwise into a broad circle, first squaring off the pack and snapping the backs like a card sharp. While I perked up the fire with the poker, she took the tooth mug from the shelf by the basin and placed it carefully in the centre. Sat down behind the letter *M*. Yes, I thought – handmade cardboard letters and a grubby old tooth mug. Sums up everything, really.

What might this house have been, I wondered, if some family other than the Starkeys had come into it? What if Clarence had never died here, or whatever it was

103

that compelled him to take it out on us, and drain and eviscerate our lives within these walls. What if some decent family had come in with a bit of money to spend and affection for its nooks, crannies and chippy plasterwork; for its hotchpotch of periods, and the aching voids of our rooms that cried out for some restoration and a shrubbery to look onto? What if a family had properly *lived* here, with a dining-room table groaning under bushels of vegetables, fragrant gravy boats, dishes of steaming meat, the clamour of voices and plates, a father carving, a mother with her sleeves rolled up – healthy family life in the living rooms of the house, instead of our own furtive existence in its peripheral spaces.

Then I thought of summer afternoons here in the bathroom, with badminton nets strung across from the dado rails, hot light twinkling over the glazed tiles, spangling on the shuttlecock as it hit the porcelain with a dry, ringing *tock!* Timmy and Francine had played with gusto, not cat and dog for once, Timothy's ruthless sense of competition shaken into good humour by the frantic energy with which Francine, all in white, the sweat glistening on her skin like icing sugar, was just failing to beat him. Their shouts of laughter had bounced and echoed in the swimming-bath acoustics of the enormous room.

But it wasn't just the once, was it? In my head I reran their laughter and swiping rackets, but I could see only one angle of the sun, Francine in one set of clothes, one distorted tape loop tripping happily through the door from Tarquin's studio. Just the once, then. One summer, one of my brothers and I had spent one normal, happy afternoon here.

As I settled on the floor, I expected to hear 'Gunga Din' seep into our quietness. I was shocked to hear instead Cliff Richard singing 'Bachelor Boy'. Oh gross! Well, if

Tarquin had got 'Bachelor Boy' on a loop, then I was putting James Taylor on, and if Clarence didn't like it, he could lump it.

'Come on,' ordered Francine. 'Fingers on the mug.'

Then Cliff melded into some other stuff, old stuff. Mr Switt's Elvis Presley. I had a feeling of déjà vu: I'd heard this same medley before. *West Side Story* was going to join in at some point. Come to think of it, when I'd last heard these songs I'd been here. In this bathroom. With my finger on the tooth mug.

The glass trembled. Francine jumped and her finger slipped.

'Blimey, that was quick!'

'It's just a lorry going past,' I said.

'It is not!'

It was, actually. I could hear the lorry.

'Come on, Jo, concentrate or we'll miss him!'

White to the cuticle, Francine's index finger pressed down on the upturned mug. I reached for the pen and paper.

'Get your finger on!' snapped Francine.

I did. The tooth mug nudged slowly across the lino towards the letter *T*.

I scribbled on the pad.

'Jo!'

It trundled back to the centre under our hands. Slightly more enthusiastic, I dug my own index finger harder into its sticky bottom.

'Clarence seems to have started,' I pointed out to Francine.

'Just keep concentrating!'

The mug shuddered to my left. Then back to the centre, home position, and out again. Then in again and out again, a fidgety, paranormal hokey-cokey. The music around us had now turned into 'Big Girls Don't Cry'. I remembered that from last time, too.

'Jo!' snapped Francine above the throbbing of the

song. 'You're not joining in properly. Press on the glass!'

'Sorry.'

Swhoosh. Towards me.

Swhoosh. Straight at Francine.

Obviously Clarence had woken up. The cat hadn't; he was still fast asleep on his cast-iron prop. I'd heard that animals are supposed to be sensitive to the supernatural; our Elvis would have slept through the masque of the Red Death.

Back and forth shunted the tooth mug, back and forth. As I scribbled the letters with one hand and held the first finger of the other tight on the glass, I vaguely registered that we were getting a lot of consonants. Now the mug snapped twice at the letter *K*. Francine was breathing heavily through her nose, short snorts of concentration – and a prickling apprehension. Always apprehension when we did Ouija. Dark forces. It was only Ouija that gave us the heebie-jeebs in the Red House. There was an *H* a bit further on, and then yet more consonants. A row of them. Clusters of consonants in an alphabet soup.

'Write them down, Jo!'

But I was looking at the paper.

'Put your finger back on the mug!'

Anger, not quite coherent, not quite directed at Francine, was percolating through the tissues of my mind like rising damp. This was no message; it was gobbledegook, rubbish.

'Jo . . .'

'No!' I scrambled to my feet. The mug, knocked by my hand, somersaulted neatly into the air and smashed against the tiles. 'No more!'

'*Jo!*'

'Look at it!' I waved the paper at her. 'Come on, this Ouija is your idea – look at it! What's it supposed to be – a communication?'

106

'Yeah, I know, but—'

'This is a poltergeist's message, is it, these letters? So what do they spell?'

'Well . . .'

'It's hogwash!'

'But it's the only clue he's gonna give us and maybe—'

'There's no such bloody thing as poltergeists, Frankie. You know that, too. This is just desperate wishful thinking! This is us pushing the glass and getting random twaddle!'

'And what's that spell?' sang Country Joe from the landing.

'Fuck!'

'And what's that spell?'

'Fuck!'

'And what's that spell?'

'Shut *up*, Tarquin!'

I hurled the paper at the door. Infuriatingly it went nowhere, just flitted to earth with balletic grace like a leaf caught in an air current.

Francine grabbed me, both her hands tight around both my wrists. 'OK, but calm down!'

'It *isn't* OK!' I yelled, pulling my hands free and lunging at the stupid broken mug, hurling a lethal slice across the bathroom. 'We'll never get out of this crumbling dump that's sapping the life out of us! It'll all get worse and worse, Mum never here and no-one to curb Dad's drinking and Timmy turning into another egghead recluse like Tarquin and—'

Fists hammered at the door. An adenoidal female voice: 'What the hell's going on in there? Come out! Open this door!'

Oh *no*.

'Do you hear me? I told you to open this door!'

'Now we've got bloody Angela!' I slumped against the lavatory, my head on the seat. Around us throbbed

107

the music of 'Telstar'. The cat still didn't wake up. I caught my reflection in the spotty old mirror suspended above the basin. Even the soft focus of its Victorian glass couldn't flatter my stevedore shoulders and Pinocchio nose. I wished, acutely, that I were dead.

'*Open up!*' shouted Angela.

'Look, Jo!'

'Now what?'

I raised my head from the hard mahogany. Poised inexplicably on the medicine cabinet, a pot of our Tuscan yellow gloss rocked precariously in the shock waves from the bathroom door. In the homely flicker of firelight, I watched it topple, and slosh down the wall in a violence of exclamation marks. Then the viscous liquid trickled illegibly along the ceramics and through the grouting, dripping onto the cold lino beneath. Francine unlocked the bathroom door and let in my sister-in-law. Below us a different door slammed, and my father's voice roared, incandescent, up the stairs to mingle with the recitation of 'You're a better man than I am, Gunga Din', which was playing out of Tarquin's studio, for all the world as though it had done so all evening.

13

Easter Sunday. It was easier for me just to get on with cooking lunch for everyone than to wear myself to a frazzle arguing with Angela about it. Frankie, to whom I'd spent an hour on the phone while her mom and dad went up to London airport, offered the services of their automatic dishwasher. By two o'clock, Timothy and I had finished our (separate) in-room dining with trays on our knees, and Geoff and Angela had left my curry to congeal in the pan while they dealt with the fire brigade.

It wasn't a fire, only Angus getting his head wedged up the disused chimney in the boxroom. He'd done this before, so no-one was really uptight about it and he clearly wasn't suffocating to death, as the screams were of such penetrative power that even Tarquin emerged from his studio.

Which meant that I'd got him. 'Tarquin!'

He was shaking his head in slow wonderment like a *Times* letter-writer hoping for the first cuckoo of spring. 'What *is* that?'

'Nothing,' I told him, 'just Angus with his head up the chimney. Tarquin . . .'

'Man, it's far out.'

'Yeah, wild. Tarquin. "Telstar".'

'Eh?'

'Did you have it on last night? I don't mean the satellite.'

He blinked, his eyes looking unnaturally pale in the daylight, like some nocturnal creature exposed to the sun. His hands were white and lifeless, like skin held too long underwater.

'Please, Tarquin.'

' "Telstar"?'

'Yes.'

'The Tornados.'

'I know. Were you playing it in the middle of your tape loop – you know, that Gunga Din thing?'

' "Telstar"?'

'Were you?'

' *"Telstar"?*'

This could go on for ever. Try a different line.

'Can you tell me about the record? Anything.'

'Clavioline electronic keyboard.'

'Thanks. What else?'

'Composed and produced by Joe Meek, released August 1962 on the Decca label. First British instrumental ever to top the US charts.'

I absorbed this. 'OK. Right.'

Tarquin gave me a vague smile and turned. I was losing him.

'Don't go!'

He hesitated at the door. 'Eh? What is it?'

What were the others in that damn medley? ' "Bachelor Boy"!' I blurted out. ' "Return To Sender". "America" from *West Side Story*. "Summer Holiday". "Big Girls Don't Cry".'

'What about them?'

110

'I don't know, Tarquin – is there a link? Not the composer, obviously. The record label? Studio?'

'Dates,' said Tarquin. 'Sort of. They're all late '62 into early '63. The soundtrack of *West Side Story* topped the British album charts eighteen times between summer '62 and the end of January, finally toppled by Cliff Richard's *Summer Holiday* soundtrack on the Columbia label. His "Bachelor Boy" was already released as a 45. It replaced Elvis Presley's "Return To Sender" as the British number one during Christmas week '62.'

It was my turn to stand there blinking. 'And "Big Girls Don't Cry"?'

'Huge seller here in January and February '63 after topping the US charts for five weeks at the end of '62. Knocked off mid-December in the States by "Telstar".' Tarquin's enormous hand was fiddling with the door handle. 'That it?' he asked cautiously.

'Thank you,' I told him. 'That's more than it.'

'Keep cool, Jo.' His door closed.

Thanks, Tarquin. You could always rely on his encyclopaedic knowledge. So, those songs would have been playing on the radio at the time we moved here. Or, put another way, at the time the Richardsons moved out. Who was playing them last night and why? Timothy? At the thought of trying to interrogate Timothy about 'Bachelor Boy', my heart sank. I retreated to my own room.

Luckily I had a new book to retreat into. This was Angela's, surprisingly, something called *Kiss Me, Deadly* by Mickey Spillane. She had been about to settle down with it when Angus started screaming; as Angela hurtled from the room like some overweight whippet out of the slips, I noticed a tatty bookmark at the start of the last chapter. Look, she wouldn't miss it, Angela was always too busy to be engrossed in a book! And anyway I'd long suspected that she kept half her

111

brain shut down, like a sleeping dolphin. But I was soon engrossed, I have to say. There was this detective called Mike Hammer, and on a lonely road a desperate blonde suddenly jumps out of nowhere into his headlights, and he has to rescue her because that's the sort of man Mike Hammer is, but then somebody follows them and pushes his car off a cliff! He calls his gun 'Betsy'. I decided I might finish this before I went back to reading Germaine Greer.

Francine came round to help me carry the dirty pan and three plates and forks along Stavering Road from our house to their dishwasher, dribbling quite a lot of curry onto the grass verge, which looked pretty disgusting. Stacking the machine, Francine looked down at my saffron-streaked crockery. 'Only three plates?'

'Yeah: me, Timmy and Tarquin ate ours; Ange, Geoff and Angus never quite got round to it. Mum was working.'

'And your dad?' Francine asked diffidently, her eyes on the dishwasher, the pans, anywhere except me.

'Oh,' I responded, just as offhand, 'gone to lunch with that barrister of his. You know, the one who helps him get off when the police do their breathalyser stuff.'

'Right.'

'When Dad drove away from the Golf Club last night he forgot to turn his lights on. The fuzz stopped him.'

'Oh.'

'And.'

'Right.'

Yes, the fuzz had stopped him, and – that said it all. When Dad stormed into the bathroom yelling about our noise, and was confronted by my apparent vandalism with the paint, Francine tactfully slipped away home. We never mentioned these things afterwards, Francine and I, never. Decent friends don't.

May 1967. A blue afternoon, all cherry blossom and

112

cut grass. Lossing's eleven-plus exam results had arrived that morning; our school had two passes other than Timmy and me: Stephanie Sandiman and a girl called Yvonne. Stephanie's parents were celebrating somewhere extravagant but Yvonne was the youngest of three and her mum and dad had seen it all before so we settled for bags of crisps and some tennis. My racket was in the conservatory. I scooted through the house to get it, trailing Yvonne.

Dad was slumped in an armchair, mouth open, spittle hanging like fangs, his snores dark and soggy. I pushed her back out, shoved her, closed the door, told her he was a surgeon and had been working all night long on emergencies. Though not before she'd seen his trousers, wet across the crotch and down one leg from wee. Yvonne never said anything. But after school broke up and she went to Brentwood High, I didn't stay in touch.

Anyway, last night I'd scraped and turpentined all I could, gouging the walls as I did so. The emaciated Tuscan yellow was now a pattern of splotches and dribbly ideograms, as though the opacity of our Ouija were reflected in the abiding script.

'Oh yeah,' said Francine, in the same throwaway tone as before, 'my dad got you an Easter egg. You know how he is. Thinks we're both little kids.'

I turned in the direction of her casually pointing hand and couldn't understand how I'd missed it on my way into the kitchen. Nearly a foot high, inside a holder full of proscenium arches and decorated side panels as delicate as a toy theatre, sat an enormous egg wrapped in gold foil and a fizzy mass of ribbon. And on the top left-hand corner, peeping over the edge with his head on one side, a yellow fluffy chick. Good old Mr Switt! Francine looked sideways at me.

'What was yours like?' I asked.

'Same.'

113

'Yeah?'

'I know. Hopeless, isn't he!'

'Thinks we're children.'

She slammed the door of the dishwasher. 'If you just unwrap a small bit of foil round the back and pick at the chocolate, the egg doesn't collapse till it's more than half-eaten.'

'Right. I'll try that.'

'I mean, we may as well make the most of the things since we're lumbered with them.' Francine straightened up. The dishwasher chugged efficiently in the corner. 'Do you want to stay and wait for Dad? I promised him we'd sort out the family photos when he gets back from the airport. Mom wants to make a sort of book of Robert's life.'

No, I didn't. First, Angela was drawing up a rota for showing people round the house. If this worked out, it would be real relief for me at last. Besides, strangely enough, Cousin Robert's necrology had even less appeal than an afternoon with Angela and Angus. Until now, death was something confined to psychokinetic manifestations in the dark corners of our old house. Death was Clarence. Even if it existed at all, which was by no means certain, it could eventually, with a little bit of luck and hard work, be expunged. I didn't think much of this other sort of death, that nullified twenty-year-olds and built shrines in the garden.

When I got home, Angela was still at the kitchen table, though most of her was obliterated by other flesh. The baby was sucking urgently at one sore-looking breast, in which a blue vein pulsed like a neon circle. Meanwhile, Angus writhed in her plump lap with his podgy hand in a tin-foil tray containing the sticky detritus of a takeaway. A milky smell hung in the air around them like white fug. Milk and something else, a generic dampness, the smell of intimate secretions and soggy clothes. Angus watched me, eyes like saucers following my progress past the kitchen with Mr Switt's gigantic egg.

'Oy, Josephine! You haven't seen that book of mine, have you? Mickey Spillane?'

'Sorry, Angela, got to go.'

'Hegg!' shouted Angus. Chewed lumps of sweet and sour pork shot from his mouth across the kitchen, *thock!* His mother jumped and the baby hiccuped. 'Hegg!' Angus threw out an arm to point at me. 'Hangus hegg!'

He'd learned how to pronounce his *G*s, then.

'Absolutely not,' I responded cheerfully and swept past, wagging the voluptuous ribbon with my finger in a puppetry 'bye-bye' wave.

As I got to the staircase I heard the slump of Angus's body sliding down his suckling milky mother. Then *splat!* as he landed, all lard and romper suit, on the quarry tiles.

'Hegg!'

I was up the stairs two at a time. Inside my room with the door closed. Home. Home amid my squiggly walls in mad Van Gogh yellow. Just seconds away from the soothing tones of James Taylor. I took him from his album jacket.

Thump! went Angus on the staircase.

I walked back to the door and turned the key in the lock.

Thump! Pause.

Thump! Pause.

Thump!

It was relentless, you couldn't close your mind to it. *Thump!* Each stair closer, nearer, more imminent. *Thump!* Rhythmicity and ruthlessness – the rationale behind the Chinese water torture.

Swearing vigorously, I unlocked my door and flung

it open. I faced him. Just yards from me now, Angus's Humpty Dumpty figure hoisted itself from one steep stair to the next, one fat little leg hauled itself up and over, one fat little arm heaved with its elbow as a pivot. *Thump!* Hoist-haul-heave.

'Angus,' I said, annoyed to hear that my voice wavered. 'Please stay away from my room. You've had your Easter eggs. This one's mine. Do you understand?'

'Hegg!' *Thump!* 'Hangus! Hegg!'

'No, *not* Hangus Hegg. Jo's hegg.'

His tongue protruded from the effort. With the lolling tongue and enormous hands and feet, he looked like a diagram in my parents' medical textbooks.

'*Hegg!*'

He was on the landing.

'NO, ANGUS!'

'*HEGG!*'

He swaggered through my bedroom door, then lowered his head like a rugby player in a scrum, slipping between my legs. I lunged at the egg and swept it clear. Elvis, who had been in a deep coma on my bedspread, rose like an uncoiling spring and clawed his way up the curtains to the pelmet. I was now holding the egg high above my head, far beyond the span of any two-year-old. I watched Angus drop to the carpet and sink his teeth into my right ankle.

After Angela had prised him out of my flesh, heaping anathemas on my 'unreasonable treatment of a small child', and after I'd done with dabbing Dettol into the wounds (human bites being among the worst of all animal bites for bacterial infection – something you know if your mother works at a busy Saturday-night-fight hospital in Essex), I eventually got round to picking up the books that had cascaded from my

116

shelves in the maelstrom. From inside a much-loved volume on Einstein's general relativity theory, a loose sheet of paper had fluttered across the carpet. I turned it over to discover a lined page covered with handwritten letters.

TDFVMYSKKKHAJRITTDFVMYSKKKHA
JLJGTDFVMLWVLUSG

I turned cold. Was it mine? The writing looked a bit like mine, though scribbled, which would make sense if it was from one of our Ouija sessions. It wasn't from last night. From last September, maybe: Francine and I in the bathroom, tediously noting down the letters indicated by the doddering movements of the tooth mug until I'd thrown a wobbly and refused to carry on with the game because we were getting nothing but rubbish. Not as violent as last night, though, when I'd screamed the place down. Supposing . . . ?

I couldn't remember what I'd done with yesterday evening's pad of paper. Had I picked it up? Well, no, probably not, with Angela yelling at us and Dad's whisky-breath barking at me about the mess of paint. Perhaps it was still in the bathroom.

Yes – on the lino by the scattered letter cards, slightly crumpled, a page of scrawled capitals.

TDFVMYSKKKHAJRITTDFVMYSKKK

Back in the bedroom, I moved slowly, collecting the things I'd need. Then across to the bathroom again, limping on my bitten ankle. I closed the door quietly behind me and leaned my back against it. The damaged wall looked even worse in daylight than it had at three in the morning, pockmarked and sliced with the edge of my scraper like ill-formed graffiti. I divided the pack of letter cards into two and took one half in each hand. I ran my thumbs across the edges of the split pack, like a conjurer at the start of a card trick; *bbrrrrrrrrrrrrrrrrrrrrrrrrrrrrrr!* The charivari echoed, sinister, in the tiled space and died away.

'Now you listen to me.' I raised my voice to the air. 'I don't know whether you're there or not. Half of me thinks you're just one more product of Tarquin's warped creative imagination. But if you are there, listen to this. We want something of one another, you and I. Give and take. So if you don't mess me about, I won't mess you about. Give that some thought. I can be out of this house the day I turn sixteen and you'll be left to negotiate with Angela, whose intelligence is on a par with one of Tarquin's clanging buckets, or up against the rationalist principles of my impervious parents. And when it comes to magic disappearing acts, believe me, they know a trick worth two of yours. Think about it.' I paused. The house paused with me. Silence.

'OK, then. Here's the deal. I don't want any more Ouija, I don't want any tooth mugs and messing about on the floor, and weird musical medleys and other showing off. Got that? Francine and I have left pads of paper for you before, and you've never touched them. But this time you'll do as I ask. See these? Paper? Pencil? When I next come in here, you'll have written out the rest of the letters. I've already got forty-four – up to *LUSG*. I want you to start with those again, so we know where we are. Start with *LUSG* and then take it from there.' I paused again. The house listened.

'I don't mind how long it goes on. Take all the time you need. Provided you just give it to me straight and no showing off.'

I walked slowly to the middle of the lino, carefully laid the paper pad on the floor with a pencil beside it, and left the room.

And credit where it's due, he did as I'd asked.

14

'I don't know why you've come to me,' said Mr Bailey. Greg. 'Your brother Timothy's the expert on codes.'

Stavering Folk Club; Greg was 'on the door' tonight, which meant that instead of lolling bored and morose at the bar, he was lolling bored and morose at a table on the landing at the top of the stairs, taking the entrance money. Through the closed oak door of the club room we could hear a plaintive voice singing about raggle-taggle gypsies-o. Next to it was the small anteroom that served as everyone's dumping ground.Guitars were angled against the furniture as randomly as pick-a-sticks, presenting the observer with every possible view of a guitar, as though rendering in flesh and blood (as it were) the fragmented images of a Cubist painting.

Your brother Timothy's the expert on codes.

In our kitchen in Ealing, with its hissing water-heater, Tim and Daddy used to conspire together at the breakfast bar, compiling and deciphering messages in numbers or letters or little dancing men straight out of

Sherlock Holmes. This wasn't a parental chore on Dad's part; numerical codes in particular fascinated him. In fact, numbers in general fascinated Dad, this being where Timothy and I got it from. Mum had problems adding up a milk bill. It wasn't until after the war, when Geoffrey was little, that our father abandoned maths for medicine, and then only because his own father bullied him into it. Family tradition. He might have withstood the pressure with support from Mum, but she was herself qualified by then, and working the wards with such missionary zeal that Geoffrey was born in a sluice room. Dad saw his first cadaver dissected in 1948. By 1950 he'd stopped throwing up, and by the end of 1955 he had four children and a houseman's salary. When he told Angela and Geoff that he and Mum had lived on tinned beans, he might have been glossing over the bad days.

Things began to improve not long after Timothy and I started school. First, Dad got his membership (Royal College of Surgeons), and almost immediately Granddad, with the perfect timing that had so eluded his horses over the years, was found dead in his Harley Street rooms. Together with a thriving surgical practice, these were seriously worth inheriting. There was nothing else. Grandma moved to a small flat and paid off the creditors – banks mostly, as bookmakers can't sue to recover their debts. The only other thing of value was the piano, and we already had that; Grandma had given it to us to prevent her husband selling it; he'd sold the Persian carpet literally from under her. Tarquin could still remember the removal van lumbering onto the pavement outside our front window one Saturday morning with its engine running, the vibrations throbbing through the house, and Mummy, pregnant with twins and the size of a whale, leaning wearily against the tailgate, demanding how we were expected to get a grand piano into a maisonette. (They managed somehow; Timothy and I spent much of our early years playing underneath it.) Anyway, Timothy's inheritance included our father's expertise with codes. But I wasn't going to tell Greg Bailey how Tim had reacted when I'd tried to start a conversation about deciphering messages from a poltergeist.

'It's something I'm cooking up as a surprise for him,' I improvised lamely, 'so I'd rather ask you for the low-down. Timothy used to say you were brilliant.'

I got a teacher's tutting sigh. 'Well, first off, you're using the word "code", but it's more likely a cipher. Codes are where you use whole words from a pre-agreed list. Say two people are arranging a secret assignation: "I'll meet you in Paris in the springtime" might actually mean eight o'clock behind the bike sheds.'

Now, I wouldn't have thought Mr Bailey's mind ran along those lines. So much for public schools.

'A cipher works at the level of letters instead of words and produces what looks like gibberish. In the simplest sort, you just move the alphabet forward by one, so that *a* becomes B, *b* becomes C and so on. That way, *Greg* would be,' he paused, 'HSFH. And *Bailey* would be . . .'

'CBJMFZ,' I said helpfully. From behind the door of the folk club, the plaintive voice had progressed from the raggle-taggle gypsies-o to the lily-white boys dressed up all in green-o.

Greg slogged on. 'You can generally crack any cipher by working out what are the most common letters in it, and then substituting the commonest ones in ordinary English. Fiddle around. Trial and error. It's called frequency analysis.'

'The commonest letter in English is *e*, isn't it?'

'Yes, but I don't know what order the rest are in, so you'll have to use a book.'

121

'Which book is that?'

'Any book.'

I stared blankly at him.

'Take a chapter of a novel, do a count of all twenty-six letters in it and calculate their frequencies!'

'Oh.' I don't know what I'd expected. To be handed some fancy formula perhaps, by which I could crack Clarence's message through my brilliant maths? The reality sounded like sheer hard slog. Greg pushed back his chair and reached out an arm for his guitar.

'Right,' he told me flatly, 'if that's the lot, I'll sort myself out; I'm on after the beer break.'

'Thanks,' I said and wandered back downstairs to find Francine.

She was fidgeting on a bar stool beside a bearded individual called Trevor, who was apparently attempting to woo her with technical anecdotes about his MG Midget.

'Jo,' she said flatly as I appeared. It was a voice without energy, just a statement of my name.

'Hasn't he arrived yet?'

'No.'

'It's still early, Frankie.'

'Yeah.'

'He's not often here before nine.'

'Yeah. Look, Jo, can't you go back up and keep an ear out? In case someone says something. You know – shame about Florian not being able to make it on account of his car breaking down. His auntie dropping dead. His house gutted by fire . . .'

'Yep, OK, Frankie. I'll go back up.'

I left her to Trevor and rustled obediently upstairs again in my floor-length gypsy dress in swirling scarlet paisleys. This was another one that I'd made with Frankie's help, and the seams weren't all they should be, but it seemed to me that swirling scarlet paisleys were a good way to reduce the impact of my large frame. Francine had borrowed my new wedge heels, so I was in her plimsolls. These weren't exactly comfortable, being two sizes smaller than mine and not lacing up properly where my ankle was swollen from Angus's assault, but with my long dress they looked rather fetching. By contrast, I'd felt that Francine herself wasn't looking her best tonight, shivering in hot pants. And her legs were bare, of course; with thick plastic false nails gummed to your finger ends, going to the loo is a nightmare even if you've only got your hot pants and knickers to put up a fight. If you also have to fight your tights, they shred like tissue paper.

Back upstairs, behind the oak door a female voice sang 'Let No Man Steal Your Thyme'. I slipped through to the anteroom and sat down wearily until everyone spilled out for the beer break. Over on the couch was a hillock of outdoor clothing with a tatty grey trench coat flowing over the top. As I sat quietly, it became inescapably evident that this heap was alive. A gently rumbling quake of slow, rhythmic movements was reshaping the contours of the ragbag, animating its multiple sleeves like the arms of a slow-dancing Indian god. From somewhere in its depths issued the sound of giggling.

'Hey!'

'So tell me you don't like it.'

'Of course I like it,' said an American voice. 'Do it again!'

'There was a young girl who said "Yes" . . .'

From beneath the trench coat protruded a lady's suede boot. Fringed.

Then absolute horror – I heard Francine coming upstairs. Her voice, edgy and irritable, gusted upwards accompanied by the imperturbable Trevor talking about carburettors.

Do something! Divert her! *How?*

The concluding bars of 'Let No Man Steal Your

Thyme' wafted from the club room, just yards away from where Miss Anna-Carlotta Campiani was apparently giving hers away by the handful. With a bit of luck, I thought, he's in his suede too and they're rubbing each other's nap off. I heard applause behind the oak door and the sound of the military-style manoeuvre required to get it open. Beer break. Francine's feet, flopping airily in my shoes, now clumped their way onto the landing. As soon as the outflowing crowd vacated it for the bar, Francine would get a grandstand view.

I stumbled from the anteroom and planted my painful plimsolls upstage between Francine and the trench coat in flagrante. There was nothing else for it but to sing. I didn't even know what song was going to come out. What did come out was something of Tarquin's from a previous musical life, an unpublished song about our conservatory with its Victorian stained glass. 'Sunlight The Colour Of Wine', he'd called it. The melody written in a folky mode fitted comfortably among the ancient oak beams and all the beards.

People who had been pouring down the stairs to the bar had now turned and were coming back *up* the stairs. To hear *me*. When my last verse died away, hands applauded me, patted me, tugged at my gypsy sleeves.

'Fan*tas*tic!'

'Wherever did you get that song?'

'Beautiful!'

'Your voice is shit-hot! We never knew you were a singer. Why haven't you sung here before?'

This one was Florian; he was on the landing, no-one with him, his slim, guitarist's hands holding my arms, his face close to mine. And of course, there was Francine standing in front of us. Her mouth hung open and her eyes stared at me, wide with the pain of my apparent and incomprehensible betrayal.

'Please, Tim.'

'I can't believe this. You. My sister. Talking about cracking codes from bloody ghosts.'

'Forget about the bloody ghosts. Just tell me what to do when frequency analysis gives me even worse claptrap than the original.'

I had done as instructed by Greg. Three hours of work on *The Female Eunuch* told me that in normal English the order of frequency of our letters is *e*, *t*, *a*, *o*, *i*, *n*, *s*, *h* . . . only that didn't help; no matter how I fiddled about substituting Clarence's letters, I still got double Dutch.

'Please, Tim.'

'Never.' He stopped short. 'Blimey, who's that?'

I spun around, half expecting to see Clarence himself stalking me from behind, but Timothy was pointing to an empty record sleeve leaning against my bedroom wall.

'What's up?' I demanded irritably. 'It's Joni Mitchell. The *Clouds* album.'

'Do you dig Joni Mitchell?'

'It's a lend.'

From Florian. Yesterday evening he had pushed it into my hands, saying that with my range and timbre I could make a wonderful job of 'Tin Angel', which I should therefore be compelled to learn immediately. I was supposed to put the record on tape.

Timothy picked up the sleeve. 'She's no oil painting, is she?'

I glanced again at the cover. It was an oil painting.

'Timothy, you are definitely developing into what Germaine Greer calls a "male chauvinist pig", do you know that?'

'Well, *look* at her!' he said.

'So what? Look at Mama Cass! Look at Janis Joplin!'

'Why do you give house room to all this transatlantic neo-folk rubbish anyway, when there's so much brilliant home-grown rock?'

Damn. Unknowingly, Timothy had lobbed a grenade over the wall. I had a deep, dark secret; this whole scene was Francine's influence, and in my heart of hearts I'd rather have listened to heavy stuff. Boys' stuff. When Tim put his music on, I generally turned mine off. I couldn't even make an intellectual case for my taste – I wasn't talking about the soft light and shade of prog rock with its virtuosity and classical borrowings, what I loved was electronic wah-wah, and throbbing riffs and drum solos that went on for twenty minutes. Unfortunately, this was anathema to every other girl in my class, and as a deviation from femininity it seemed to chime with my size, knuckly hands and Desperate Dan jaw line. It worried at my self-confidence like a terrier.

'Hey, Josie,' continued Timothy.

'*What?*'

'Did you hear about the prostitute who had her

126

appendix out? She told the surgeon, "Don't sew it up again; I can make a bit extra on the side." '

'Go!'

But he had already gone. I went back to Clarence's text. My right foot, now pounding like a rock riff, was propped on a chair; Mum had promised me antibiotics but then forgot. Angus's mouth bacteria were beyond the killing power of Dettol, unless I tried mainlining it. As I fiddled in a haphazard fashion with the letters of the code, someone thumped on the front door. It was Francine. She slouched in, swinging my wedge heels by their purple laces.

'How's it going?' she asked, nodding at the mangled alphabets.

'Nowhere. I did what Greg suggested, but it makes no more sense than the original.'

'Oh.'

'And Tim won't help.'

'Yeah?'

Francine sank onto the bed. It was a long time since I'd seen her this listless. She reminded me of a pot plant that needed watering.

'He must have slipped in early to avoid me, Jo.'

'Sorry?'

'Florian. You know he never gets to Stavering much before nine o'clock. He must have arrived real early to avoid me and crept straight up to the club room so I wouldn't be able to corner him.'

'Frankie, I'm sure it wasn't like that.'

No, it wasn't like that. Florian wasn't avoiding Francine, he hadn't given her a second thought since Mr Switt spirited her away from Ilford on Friday night. He'd arrived at Stavering with Miss Pocahontas at an unprecedented eight o'clock in order to get her tucked up under the nearest trench coat. I wondered how he'd got hold of her phone number.

'Look, he managed to crawl out from his hiding

place *to listen to you singing*. I must have done something wrong.'

'No!'

'He was all over me Friday and now he hates me. I had on that pink bra, you know, the padded one. Maybe he felt that through my skinny blouse and it put him off.'

'Oh Frankie!'

'And I hadn't used the spray. Oh God, perhaps that was it. Maybe I was, you know, when he was on top of me. Smelly. I disgusted him!'

'What spray, for God's sake?'

'You know. Intimate deodorant.'

'This is crazy. You hadn't even got your clothes off!'

'Yeah, but. We were a bit, you know, with his hand. I must have done *something* repulsive.'

Hating my knowledge, I wandered over to the window. The sunlight on the garden hardened and grew cold. For once, it was of little comfort.

'He slunk into Stavering and *hid*!' As Francine's voice slid up the octaves, her wild eye movements came to rest on Florian's Joni Mitchell album, dormant on my window sill. I'd been in the process of putting it away when second thoughts about the cipher had derailed me. I saw Francine's eyes widen in horror.

'*Jo!*'

Now what? She was off the bed, staring appalled at the sill.

'It's warped! You've gone and left it lying in the sun! Florian's record!'

A door slammed and Timothy stormed back into my bedroom.

'Will you please stop her shrieking!' he demanded. 'I'm trying to generate some ideas about Fermat's last theorem, and I can't hear myself think.'

Francine flailed at him with the album.

'*Look at it!*'

The flat surface bore a gentle undulation like that limerick lady's Chiltern hills.

'For God's sake,' snapped Timothy, 'it's just a deformity in the vinyl. Lay it back in the sun, and when the plastic starts to get warm it will flatten out again.'

'Of course it won't, it's ruined!' Tears streamed down Francine's face.

Timothy sighed. 'Look, I happen to know about thermoplastics . . .'

'Oh yeah, sure, like you know about poltergeists!'

'Fine.' He turned on his heels.

'Timmy!' He was striding out of my bedroom. I stepped in front of him. 'Do you really know how to straighten out records?'

'I've told you. Warm the disc until the warped edge softens, then lay it flat and Bob's your uncle. If I were you,' continued Timothy on his way out of the door, 'I'd float the record in a pan of water on the cooker ring. Give it about five minutes on a medium heat,' he went on, sounding like the recipe slot on the *Jimmy Young Show*, 'then elute the water from beneath it, preferably by siphon.'

Elute? Siphon? Lofty disdain was written across every pimple of my brother's face. Francine's teary features peered at him.

'Timmy, stay and help us,' I said, taking the album from Francine. 'Let's all go downstairs and watch you being a genius.'

Our enormous cast-iron frying pan was the trophy of one of Mum's rare incursions into housewifery. It was thick metal for slow simmering, its interior coated with state-of-the-art, guaranteed non-stick Teflon. At least, it used to be, before Francine and I fed it to the Switts' automatic dishwasher last Sunday, which managed to shred the Teflon from the underlying metal and coagulate it; congealed filaments dangled from the scuffed iron in evil black berries, like an illustration in my parents' textbooks of someone's armpit with bubonic plague. The pan had succeeded in getting its own back on the dishwasher; the sloshing remains of the curry silted up all the pipes, which in turn flooded the Switts' kitchen. Mr Switt arrived home from London airport to find sudded dishwater rippling across the hall carpet. To get Francine's attention, his yelling had to compete with Neil Young.

I limped heavily across the kitchen, carrying the cast iron in my road-mender's arms, and set it carefully on the cooker ring. Francine lowered Joni Mitchell's *Clouds* smoothly onto the wet surface. Plop! Droplets splashed playfully over her T-shirt. I turned on the ring.

'Right,' I addressed Timothy at his overlord position against the table. 'How long's this going to take?'

'Just keep an eye on the pan. Every couple of minutes, test the plastic. When it begins to soften, gently siphon out the water.'

'Timmy, I don't happen to carry a siphon in my handbag.'

'Take a straw from the cupboard,' explained Timothy patiently, 'and *suck*!'

I gave the plastic an experimental prod with my index finger. The water was pleasantly warm. The plastic was totally solid. After another couple of minutes I prodded again. The water was now pretty hot. The vinyl was still completely stiff.

'Suppose we miss the moment?' demanded Francine.

'There is no *moment*,' insisted Timothy. 'These materials deform extremely slowly. It's the property that makes them so useful for moulding.'

At that instant the record melted, turning into a black blob in the pan. Francine screamed. Elvis, who

130

had been watching us with his head on one side, now stood up and slowly left the kitchen.

'Fuck,' said Timothy. 'Look, get it out, can't you?'

I'd already grabbed the pan and was at the sink.

'Give it here!' Timothy wrestled the pan from me. Slammed it onto the Formica table. Scooped the album out by its edges. Unfortunately, only its edges came with him – Tim was drawing out the melted plastic like a floppy hat. Beneath the brand-hot metal of the pan, our Formica sizzled and bubbled. Francine burst noisily into tears.

'Straighten it!' said Timothy. 'Get the iron out.'

I was past arguing; I dragged our Morphy Richards from under the sink. Timothy was staring down at the black splodge of molten gunk. Francine sobbed against a cupboard. Slowly, methodically, I steam-pressed until once more we had an object that was record-shaped. The occasional groove was visible, winking in the light from the kitchen window. If Timothy would just invent a machine to follow its eccentric path with a stylus, no doubt we could have caught the occasional bar of 'Tin Angel' gamely crackling out from the mangled pandemonium of Timothy's thermoplastic.

Just then somebody knocked on the front door – a jaunty, optimistic knocking; a knocking that expected to be let in. Tim swore lavishly. Francine and I froze. We knew who it was. This was the Red House; human beings did not turn up uninvited, to knock at the front door. True, Geoffrey and Angela were always turning up invited, but they didn't knock and anyway they were barely human. Then it came again, a rat-a-tat-tat you could have sung 'Arthur McBride' to. Florian, of course. To collect his Joni Mitchell album.

131

16

'Well, fuck me!'

Florian gazed about him. His eyes took in our staircase first: the Venetian window giving onto sky and orchard, its light frosting the banisters carved with fruit and orange blossom. Then the plasterwork, the hotchpotch of periods across ceiling and coving – Robert Adam's twiddly little pendants dripping from great heavy scrolls of vine belonging to a less dandyish era. Dregs of old cobwebs dribbled from the whole lot, gritty with dust, swinging like hanged men. Our cleaner, Mrs Stanley, claimed a shoulder problem that meant she couldn't dust above eye level.

'This place is bloody *happening*!'

Francine hovered at the threshold of the kitchen. I heard a faint clatter, as of vinyl being skimmed across Formica. Then stepping out into the hall, she slapped backwards at the kitchen door to swing it shut and strode forward to meet Florian. 'Well, hi!'

'Hi,' he responded, eyes still focused on our plasterwork. 'I was on my way from Billericay to Brentwood, so I thought I'd stop by and pick up that Joni Mitchell.'

'Sure,' said Francine. 'Coffee?'

'Oh. Yeah, thanks.' He tore his attention from the walls and started towards Francine, which meant towards the kitchen.

'I'll make the coffee,' I told them hurriedly. 'Frankie, why don't you show Florian into the conservatory?'

I beamed a hostess's smile and slipped through into the kitchen. Timothy was still in there; he had picked up the LP from where Francine had slung it out of view and was examining the twisted contours with the air of one badly let down by his workforce.

'You missed the moment,' he told me with disgust and left by the back door into the garden.

In the conservatory, amid the stained glass with its saturated colours and motifs of mock-medieval heraldry; amid the undusted majolica pots, long, long empty of Mrs Richardson's starved cacti, sunlight the colour of wine illuminated Florian's shoulder-length locks so that he looked like a saint in a church window. He sipped at the mug of instant coffee while Francine's eyes followed his every move like a child watching a magic act. For some reason Florian wasn't in jeans but in suit trousers, and an undone tie was draped round the open collar of his shirt. The presence of a tie – anywhere about his person – should have made him look a complete jerk but surprisingly didn't.

'Well, fuck me!' he said again, unaware that this might be misconstrued. 'I had no idea you both lived in such an incredible pad.'

'Actually, Frankie lives along the road,' I corrected him. 'Different pad entirely.'

His face creased, puzzled at the reference to Francine. 'You and your brother,' he explained. 'Tarquin. I mean, no wonder he writes such wild

133

material – all this inspiration!' He gazed out onto the bitter grass of our untended garden.

Francine's smile looked strained. 'Hey, tell Jo that stuff you were saying in the hall.'

'Stuff?'

'About the plaster.'

'Oh yeah.' He turned to me. 'Your ceiling rose and coving. I'm confused. Most of it looks late Georgian to me, but other bits seem a lot earlier.'

'That's right. It's a mix of Robert Adam elegance and much earlier, heavier designs based on work by Christopher Wren's master woodcarver.'

How did I know? Another of Tarquin's songs was about lying on the floor of our hall, dreaming of cathedrals.

'Weird! How come?'

'The guy who built this house was a nutter, basically.'

'Yeah? And that staircase is shit-hot! It's called a Venetian or Palladian window, right?'

'Yes, but,' I said. There was a light in Florian's eye, a light suspiciously like fervour. Or, put another way, suspiciously like Tarquin's. In response, I seemed to be falling into some intellectualized version of my house-selling spiel. 'According to Tarquin, the name's a misnomer and the design wasn't down to Palladio at all, it was the work of his student Sebastiano Serlio.'

'*Yeah?* Hey, that's outta sight, I gotta remember that!'

My God, Florian was serious! And I'd always assumed that nobody but Tarquin either knew that fact or cared. *No*body. *Any*where.

Francine was coyly leaning forward. 'Gee,' she said predictably. 'How come you're into that stuff?'

'Brought up on it. Spent my childhood being dragged round galleries and churches while my mum sketched.'

'Why, precisely?' I asked, because I was actually interested. Neither of us knew anything about him; we'd never thought of Florian as having a mum, or a childhood, or any sentient existence outside the scope of the folk clubs and Francine's fantasy world. But he wasn't listening to us; his head was tilted and alert, as though on standby for something. For Tarquin.

'Florian?' I prompted him.

He turned his ears back to us. 'Mum used to be an art teacher until I came along. And my dad's one of the curators at the National Gallery.'

'Curating what, precisely?'

It was certainly beginning to make sense, why the man was so fascinated by my brother's music with all its foggy, recondite artistic allusions.

'Paintings.'

'Go on.'

'Old Masters. Belgium, Holland – Netherlandish paintings.'

'Wow, I just dig all that!' cried Francine, nearly knocking her coffee over. 'We don't have anything like it back home.'

'Yes, you do,' Florian corrected her. 'American galleries are full of the stuff.'

'You mean they hack them out of the caves?' cried Francine. 'That's gross!'

Florian's cup paused on its way to his lips. I spoke sideways at her.

'Netherlands, Frankie,' I said as quietly as I could. 'Not Neanderthal.'

Before anyone could digest this further, a gaggle of fat booming noises started up from Tarquin's studio. Florian's oddly tilted head twitched towards the source above us.

'The man himself?' he suggested. Then a thought unsettled him. 'Your brother has a Moog synthesizer and recording equipment *upstairs*?'

'And a grand piano. The floor had to be reinforced,' I admitted, while Francine's eyes flashed at me.

'Hey,' she started, 'you know "Electric Los Angeles Sunset"?'

'Why the Moog instead of one of the more pioneering synths?' asked Florian.

I shrugged. 'Because it's got a keyboard and he's a pianist?'

It was no use asking me to explain love at first sight, these things were better left to the poets. A couple of weeks after Woodstock, Tarquin heard a Moog concert and the rest is history. I remembered him directing its transportation through the upstairs window with instructions almost exclusively composed of the word fuck. I remembered my excitement when he said he was home for good. And then weeks of him shut away with a soldering iron and jack plugs.

Our piano had already been up there for years, no use to anybody else. It was a night shortly after we moved here: snowdrifts and an inadequate fire, and Daddy suggesting one of our sing-songs. In Ealing, Tarquin would often record us, and we'd play the tape back next time and try to keep up with it, Daddy pretending it was a race and playing faster and faster until his fingers were a blur and he was panting like a runaway horse and Timmy was hysterical. Only, this particular night Daddy opened the lid, essayed a flamboyant glissando and discovered that Tarquin had hammered nails between the strings, à la John Cage's 'prepared piano'. He took it very well, particularly considering it had belonged to his parents, who by now had both met tragic ends. So up went our piano to Tarquin's room and it was still there now, a Steinway boudoir grand worth about six hundred quid an octave. Except, not any more.

Florian had risen to his feet. As his height loomed

above us, the glass washed his hair with magenta and vermilion and gamboge.

'The loo's upstairs, is it?' he asked, already making for the door.

'Well . . .'

'I'll find it,' and he was gone.

His footsteps echoed as they retreated. I was now on my feet, too.

'Leave him,' whispered Francine, urgently.

'He's going after Tarquin!'

'Good. Let him think if he keeps coming round, he'll get inside that screwball studio. We'll have him here by the minute!'

'Not,' I pointed out, 'if Tarquin lays him out with a left hook.'

I was out of the conservatory dragging my poor infected foot across the echoing room, into the hall, up the staircase, past Sebastiano Serlio's bloody window. On the landing, Florian was already at Tarquin's door, wrestling with the handle.

'Please move away from there,' I shot at him, like a gallery guard catching the public pawing his father's Vermeers. 'The bathroom is this way.'

Florian turned to me with a sad smile. 'I won't disturb him if he's recording.'

He followed the direction of my pointing arm and I waited protectively on the landing while he shut the door and presumably made whatever sense he could of the scrubbed scrawl of gloss paint across the beautiful Victorian tiles of the bathroom.

17

At least he forgot about Joni Mitchell. By the time
Florian gave up on Tarquin and went away, Francine
was in a state of high excitement – first because
she was convinced that we could milk the Tarquin
business and keep Florian coming round, and sec-
ondly because on his way out of the door he had
thrown over his shoulder a question about whether we
were going to 'Dave's party on Friday'. There was no
elaboration and the folk clubs had more Daves than
you could shake a stick at, but Francine was back to
believing she was on a promise. This was the mood in
which she remembered that she still had Mrs
Richardson's back-door key.

'No,' I said.

'Yes. How about Thursday? She's out Thursday
evenings, Jo, you said. Choir practice.'

'And Mr Richardson?'

'He's never home early.'

'You're crazy.'

Besides, I was convinced that Amy Richardson

would have had the lock changed on the back door the minute she discovered the loss. Francine scoffed at this.

'People like her keep a spare key with a neighbour. She'll be using that and blaming herself for losing the other one.'

'Frankie – no!'

So come Thursday evening she did it on her own.

I got a phone call about a quarter to seven. 'Come round here, I'm finding amazingly horrible stuff!'

It was one of the few times in my life when I'd been truly frightened. I just about accepted Francine's insistence that if Mr Richardson came home we'd hear his car and have time to leg it out the back, but what if the neighbours saw us? (The miserable bat next door would be only too happy to shop me; she'd recently banned me from babysitting just because I accidentally left the gas tap turned on and didn't notice the smell building up all evening because of the cigarette smoke.) Or suppose Mrs Richardson came home early – she would be on foot. And my own foot, blue and solid, would not be a lot of use in a quick getaway.

Inside the kitchen, the surgically clean surfaces glittered in their readiness to record our fingerprints and forensic evidence of our footwear. Even the trim garden looked hostile through the window, its serried ranks of daffodils watching me with their ear trumpets twitching. I hovered by the door while Francine, looking disconcertingly professional in gloves, sifted through two piles of papers. She'd apparently carried out a sweep of every drawer in the house and dug these from the spare bedroom.

Birth certificates: *Algernon John, 19 December 1943. Letitia Anne, 30 April 1946.*

Letitia. Natasha? A muddled memory?

School reports: *Letitia is a bright child who applies*

herself well. She is a pleasure to have in school. So was I, once. Certificate for swimming twenty-five yards.

'Frankie, this isn't safe. Put them back, we're going home.'

'Rubbish, there's ages yet. Read these, I found them inside that family album. They'll break your heart and make you cry, but you've got to read them.'

Newspaper clippings – a sad, neat collection of yellowed, oddly cut paper shapes. As Francine opened up their sharp fold-lines I saw that the insides hadn't discoloured but were pallid and creased, like the palms of suntanned hands.

Missing girl.
A sixteen-year-old schoolgirl has been missing from her home in Lossing Common since Friday. Letitia Richardson, who lives with her parents and has an older brother in America, has not been seen since she alighted from the number 260 bus shortly after four o'clock at her usual stop and set off in the direction of home . . .

Lossing girl – appeal for witnesses.
The police have made an appeal on behalf of Mr and Mrs Richardson, whose sixteen-year-old daughter Letitia has been missing from home since Friday. Detective Inspector Cranley has asked that if anybody saw anything unusual in the vicinity of the Red House, Lossing Common, during the afternoon, or saw any person or vehicle nearby, they should come forward. Any information will be treated in the strictest confidence.

You'd be worried half to death, wouldn't you? Beyond my own anxiety and panic, I caught a glimpse of a woman waiting for news of a disappeared daughter. No sleep night after night. Desperately focused on the front door and the phone, and then it rings and all your nerves scream and you go half mad with hope, but it's only somebody else . . .

Letitia – Police seek man seen at house.

Police hunting the missing schoolgirl Letitia Richardson last night issued the Identikit picture of a man they wish to interview in connection with her disappearance. The man, thought to be in his mid-forties, was seen by two witnesses in the driveway of the Richardsons' home in Lossing Common last Friday afternoon. He is described as being of respectable appearance, slim build, clean-shaven, dressed in a City suit and bowler hat, carrying a briefcase. The police urge him to come forward so that he can be eliminated from their enquiries.

Letitia – Police dig up garden.

In an operation believed to be carried out with the full consent of the family, police have begun digging up the garden at the home of the missing schoolgirl Letitia Richardson. 'It is a huge and rambling garden,' explained Detective Inspector Cranley, in charge of the case. 'We cannot discount the possibility that if harm was done to Letitia, the perpetrator could have concealed the body somewhere in the grounds.'

A gent in a City suit and bowler hat? Wasn't it all a bit surreal – a bit Magritte and Monty Python? But the next one wasn't, it was harrowing: letter from Hanwell, Boyd and Christie, Solicitors. 11 July 1969.

Dear Mr and Mrs Richardson,

In re: Letitia Anne

It is our sad duty to inform you that, seven years having passed since the disappearance of your

141

*daughter and no evidence of her survival having
come to light, you are now entitled in law to assume
that she is deceased and to request the issue of a
certificate of death. Our understanding is that this is
Mr Richardson's wish. We therefore . . .*

A car pulled up in the drive.

Francine swept the papers together and flew upstairs.
I was frozen in the kitchen. Every brain cell wanted
me to high-tail it out the back and abandon Francine.
A key turned in the front door. I flattened myself
behind the open kitchen door and watched through
the gap between the hinges as Mr Richardson popped
his head inside the hall.

'Amy?'

Pause for two heartbeats, then he slipped out again.
As the front door shut behind him, Francine raced
back down the stairs and flew into the kitchen. We
caught the sound of Mr Richardson coming in again
just as Francine reached towards the back door. With
surprising gentleness she eased the handle round. The
door didn't budge; I'd relocked it behind myself in
case Mrs Richardson tried to come in the back way.
Her husband's voice now rose in the hall.

'Quick!' he was saying in throaty tones unrecogniz-
able from his shouted *Amy*. 'Quick, quick, quick . . .'

A girl's giggles interrupted him. 'Oooh, not *too*
quick!'

He gave a low laugh. 'Think of it as just a taster.'

'So when can I have my dinner?'

Now they both giggled. Wet kissing sounds floated
across to us in our frozen position by the kitchen door.
In defiance of the mad flapping gestures I was directing at her, Francine had crept across to the door and
was peering round it.

'Let's go upstairs, Teddy Bear. Please.'

'Can't, baby. We're a bit late this week – she'll be home in fifteen minutes.'

'But we can't do it *here*.'

'Well, I'm too big to do it in the car, sweetie.'

'But, Teddy Bear . . .'

I saw Francine's face. Stunned.

'Pretend we're in the woods. You *like* it in the woods. What's the difference? Come on, come to Daddy.'

Giggles. 'That stuff you put on your hair will smear all over her wallpaper!'

'So *you* lean on the wall, baby, and I'll . . .' The voices were muffled and lost.

I slunk across to Francine. Contrary to the sensible suggestion of a moment ago, Mr Richardson's large, tubby body was now slumped against the wall, trousers round ankles, his greying head rhythmically rubbing Brylcreem into his wife's floribunda wallpaper. The girl was half out of her clothes. Sixth-form uniform from Stebbing Comprehensive. Seventeen probably. She was on her knees. She was taking into her mouth . . . Bloody hell, I had three brothers but I had never seen . . . hooded, purplish; by the leaning light of the hall window, it had the rubbery gleam of wet fish heaped on the fishmonger's slab. As I started to retch, Francine grabbed my T-shirt and twisted me towards the kitchen door. She carried on twisting and pushing until I'd unlocked the door and she'd got us outside and back onto the road for home.

18

We found Dave's party by simply turning up at the Castle on Friday evening and following everyone else at chucking-out time. Our arrangements had already been cleared with Mr Switt (amazing what we could clear with Mr Switt while his wife was four thousand miles away) by telling him that Francine was spending the night with me and I'd organized a lift home. This also covered the contingency (in which Francine had more faith than I did) of her spending the night with Florian.

At least he had arrived at the Castle alone. He was friendly and flirty, but I still wasn't at all sure that he had any recollection of rolling about on the floor in Pete Christie's flat just a week ago, and the same thought must surely be haunting Francine. Anyway, by half-past eleven we were in a crowd somewhere in Romford, at somebody's front door, leaning on a row of bells.

It was a fabulous flat, lit softly orange from Moroccan pottery lamps, and full of elephants. On bare pine floorboards, fine-boned royalty rode decorated elephants across strewn Indian rugs. More elephants on the cushions, padded this time and spangled with tiny, winking slivers of mirror. And in reproductions of delicate Punjabi watercolours, elephants stood serenely by while a blue-painted Krishna snogged his girlfriend in public places in broad daylight.

I found Mr Bailey slumped alone in a bay window resembling a greenhouse; hanging baskets hung by their long tails, all at different heights like crotchets on a musical stave. He had a beer can tilted to his face. I left Francine with a cooing admirer and some guy who was flat out on an elephant rug reading Friedrich Engels's *The Origins of Family, Private Property and the State* by the sepia light of a Moroccan lamp. I sat myself down beside Greg, arranging the vast amplitude of my flares to hide my right foot. Over the last few days it had developed an elephantiasis to compete with anything on the rugs, and I was barefoot these days by necessity. Now, with dawning horror, I realized that something even more terrible had befallen my left eye. Its false eyelashes had disappeared. Well, two wrongs didn't make a right; no point in making *both* eyes look useless. I left the remaining one in place.

'Hi, Mr Bailey! Greg.'

He removed the can from his face, checked who I was and put it back.

'Look, sorry to bother you,' I began again, 'but I've run into an impasse.'

The beer can quivered a moment and then was still again.

'This cipher text. You see, I tried frequency analysis the way you explained it but . . .'

He slammed the can onto the floor. Beer dribbled onto the nearest trunk.

'This is a fucking party!' he barked at me.

145

'I only wanted . . .'

'I've come here to enjoy myself!'

And he got heavily to his feet. I watched him lurch irately through several spider plants to another corner, florets sticking in his hair like burrs.

Embarrassment stung my armpits and prickled along the hairs of my neck. My face burned. My bad foot throbbed like misery. I needed a drink and floundered off to the kitchen. Around me were dislocated pieces of party chatter.

'. . . perfectly *sweet* he was when we went to bed . . .'

'. . . about ten miles from Marrakech . . .'

'. . . then Merv turned up with his mandolin.'

The kitchen was packed, and by the time I realized Stephanie Sandiman was a yard away there was no escape. She was apparently engaged in one of those 'Is rock as good as classical?' arguments that cropped up recurrently in middle-class households, generally referred to as the 'Beatles versus Beethoven debate'. At the sight of me she began hectoring a bemused bystander about something completely pretentious as usual. This time it was apparently on the subject of jazzy polyrhythms in the music of King Crimson. It sounded stagy and contrived because it was, the whole thing directed at the deaf ear I was pretending to cock; her aim was to draw me in so she could start rubbishing Tarquin. Stephanie had never forgiven me for having a brother who became famous.

We went through primary school together, and then to the same Comprehensive because it was co-ed. Stephanie never much liked the Red House with its damp and sadness and the tendency for peculiar things to tumble out of cupboards, but she generously pretended to believe all my stories of imminent restoration, and in the absence of my own parents she lent me hers, who had a Bohemian warmth. Then in

146

1968 Tarquin recorded his first album in Toronto and was suddenly in the music papers. Some critics loved his stuff, some loathed it, but he was the nearest thing Brentwood had to a rock star. Stephanie's attitude to me had always been (to use a Sandiman expression) de haut en bas. Suddenly I was the haut, not the bas. Jealousy crackled from her like some demonic electrical static. At the mention of my brother's name, Stephanie exuded spite as uncontrollably as the discharge of a provoked squid.

And then my own popularity, my reflected glory as the local hero's sister, quietly changed into something else, something sinister. Other girls in our class suddenly knew about Dad. Cloistered knots of classmates stopped talking when I approached. There were jokes. Mrs Matlock trumped up some mysterious school medical at which a district nurse had me in tears asking about my bruises from the tennis courts. I was twelve, isolated, desolate. I could understand why it had hurt so much then. But the talk had long since settled down beneath the more pressing preoccupations of teenage life, so why did it still hurt so much now? Here in the kitchen at the party, I spun round and plunged back through the crowd, other people's drink slopping over my flares.

Francine needed rescuing, so she was glad to see me, thank God. The bloke beside her was telling a long, inebriated story about meeting Michael Caine: 'So I said to him, "Now look, Michael," I said . . .'

And thank God the Switt family was already over here when Stephanie fell out with me. One day, for General Studies, we all had to bring in a press cutting about issues worthy of our concern. Most people brought stuff about student demonstrators being teargassed in Paris; Francine and I turned up with the same one of a kitten up a tree. After school we went back to hers and played Leonard Cohen non-stop with the plastic arm cranked back, till her mother threatened to switch off the electricity at the mains.

Francine hadn't minded the Red House; she seemed to accept its discomfort and atmosphere of brooding November. Besides, Clarence didn't subject her to any of his tours de force until she and I knew each other well enough to cope with adversity as a team. Of course, Tarquin was still across the Atlantic when Francine and I first hit it off. I now bucked away from the thought like a horse refusing a fence.

'This is Jo,' she was saying to the Michael Caine man, still floundering inside the maze of his anecdote. 'I'm afraid we've got to go now and talk to a friend because he's trying to commit suicide.'

Cheerfully, she got to her feet. At this moment the inevitable happened: Florian walked in with his arm round Anna-Carlotta Campiani.

'Don't,' I was saying ineffectually.

'Vodka,' she decided, glugging colourless fluid into a pint beer glass. It smelled to me like petroleum spirit. 'Bottoms up.'

'Oh Frankie, he isn't worth it!'

I had the grace to wonder how many hundreds of thousands of times in human history, idiots like me had said things like that.

'Can I bum a cigarette?' Francine asked a couple necking by the cooker. The guy tapped the pocket of his velvet jacket and she dragged the carton out. He was shrugging the jacket off while she did this, onto the floor to join his girlfriend's blouse. At least Stephanie was no longer in the kitchen. We were spared that.

'Frankie, you don't smoke, you don't even like it and it's carcinogenic!'

She waved the pack under my own nose and I took

one without thinking. We lit up from a box of matches on the fridge.

'You chicks want some coke?' asked a passing beard, his eyes on Francine's hot pants. 'I'm selling.'

'*Coke?*' she scoffed at him, waving her pint of vodka. 'Do we look like schoolgirls?'

I managed to get her out of the kitchen before the phrase vodka-and-coke struck her fancy, but that brought us into the hall, where Florian was sitting on a stair with Anna-Carlotta on the one below, between his long legs, which he had wrapped tight around her in a devastating gesture of intimacy. Francine took a slug from her pint glass, followed by a conscientious drag from the cigarette dangling from her other hand. She coughed for a bit, then stalked back to the sitting room and across to the Friedrich Engels guy.

'Hey, man,' she said to him, 'you fancy coming upstairs with me?'

'No, Frankie!'

But he looked up from his book and gave her a sad smile. 'Sorry, babe, but I earned me a dose of gonorrhoea and the clinic says I ain't clear yet.'

'Oh!' Francine snapped upright like an offended vicar.

'Let's go home, eh, Frankie?' I suggested. 'Just you and me? Leave them all to it?'

She took another long draught of oily-looking liquor. 'Not on your life,' she enunciated carefully. 'I am going upstairs. Straight past Florian and that simpering little Minnehaha. And I'm doing it with a man on my arm.'

I was perfectly convinced that Florian wouldn't bat an eyelid if she went upstairs with ten men on her arm, but pointing this out wouldn't help. Francine was off again, as yet still steady on her feet, though with half a pint of neat vodka being steadily absorbed into her bloodstream time was running out.

149

'Hey, man,' she said again, this time to someone sunk so deep in a bean bag that I couldn't make head nor tail of him. 'How do you fancy coming upstairs with me?'

Her choice elbowed himself up. Oh God! Not a hairy. A skinhead! What the hell was a skinhead doing here? He wasn't a folk club man, a 'Beatles versus Beethoven' man, he was Doc Martens, drainpipes and Desmond Dekker and the Aces. They were all the same, skinheads: they'd 'Enoch Powell' you blue in the face, and then get it on, dancing to ska and reggae. Amid all our flowing hair, the tresses, beards and moustaches, this guy's head shone like a ping-pong ball. Francine hiccuped but pulled herself together.

'So let's go,' she said.

He hoiked himself up, flailing. Once his bovver boots were planted firm on the rug, he stood there adjusting the tight crotch of his jeans, plucking at his underpants round the back with a hooked finger. I whimpered. Francine, her eyes glassy, gazed aristo-cratically into the middle distance.

Halfway to the stairs, her vodka level achieved the liquid equivalent of flashover. She didn't stop, but flounced as best she could up to the bedrooms, casting looks of disdain at an unwatching Florian while her companion stumbled along behind, still making trouser adjustments.

'Look, she's drunk! This isn't . . .'

This wasn't what? Fair play? The act of a gentleman? Cricket?

'She's just a little tired,' he crooned, his head inside her skinny blouse. 'And I'm gonna make her feel much, much better.'

'She isn't even sixteen!'

'Oh, leave us alone, for fuck's sake!'

Then, tickled by the appropriateness of the words, he gave a snivelling laugh. Panic came at me in waves. Francine, her blouse now half on, half off, was barely conscious. He was trying to take down her hot pants. She was flapping ineffectually at his hands.

'She's only fifteen and you're breaking the law!'

'My, but someone sure is shaking her tail feathers.' Not the skinhead; the voice behind me was Mr Engels with his dose of the clap.

'Never mind my tail feathers,' I shot at him, crossly. 'My best friend's losing her virginity – she's too drunk to stop him, she's not protected and she isn't even sixteen!'

Francine's hot pants were not winning the fight. Her knickers were revealed, clean white cotton from Marks and Spencer's, conscientiously ironed by Mrs Switt's daily help. This shaven-headed thug must have his nostrils full of the linen-cupboard odour of fresh ironing.

'Pretty' was the comment from beside my right shoulder.

'*Pretty?*' I exploded. He put a hand across my mouth.

'Listen, babe,' he crooned, rolling a cigarette with the other hand. He ran a tongue along the edge of his Rizla paper and shreds of tobacco hung from his lips, dangling in the Zapata moustache. 'I heard what you said to her. "Let's go home, just you and me." We all know about you. Joe and Frank. You're jealous, sweetheart – jealous of his lucky, lucky tongue. D'you know Florian Smith? He's got a limerick about you.'

The hand dropped from my mouth and gave a definitive twirl to his cigarette end.

> *'There was a young lady called Frank,*
> *Had a friend who was built like a tank.*
> *Though she says, "Lesbe friends,"*

151

Frankie don't share her trends,
So she has to make do with . . .'

I hit out at him and threw myself in the direction of
the landing. As I toppled towards the stairs I heard the
unmistakable sounds of Francine throwing up across
the skinhead on the bed.

19

'She'll be OK now, there's nothing more to come.'

'Yeah, but . . .'

'Look, I'm an expert, right? My mother is senior reg in Casualty at Stebbing General and she deals with this sort of thing every Saturday night.'

And my father's a drunk but I'm not telling that to Trevor. Neither do I explain that drunks are well able to carry on being sick long, long after there's anything left to throw up, in defiance of all normal laws of influx and efflux. Not to mention their other unstable orifices, the outflow from which can do terrible damage to the upholstery of your MG Midget.

'Well, if you say so.'

Trevor reluctantly lowered Francine, sleeping heavily in his corduroy arms, into the only passenger seat. I clambered over the driver's seat, knocking my elbows and knees, and heaved my body painfully onto the ledge beneath the rear window.

'Look, I can't see out the back,' objected Trevor. 'I can't see to drive.'

'So? I've got my face pressed up against the window, haven't I? Just ask me and I'll tell you. I'll do a running bloody commentary all the way to Lossing if you want. Just get us home!'

'Yeah, but . . .'

'Francine's going to be really grateful, Trevor. I guarantee it. A knight in armour, I'll tell her.'

He cast a hopeless look around him and then sank into the driving seat. I felt the door slam.

Francine woke up somewhere around Brentwood and was sick once more out of the window, therefore down the side of the MG. Trevor, his teeth set, drove grimly onwards with his foot flat on the accelerator. By the time we got to Lossing Common the pain in my foot was so bad that I'd started sobbing aloud. I could just about walk, Francine could just about walk; we just about made it to the front door. Trevor revved off back in the direction we'd come – he lived in Romford, about a mile away from the party. As the car disappeared out of the drive I realized my remaining eyelashes had gone, too, presumably pulped under my enormous elbows and knees on the back ledge.

I eventually got Francine to sleep, though fully clothed and groaning with nausea and misery, on a pile of bedding in the bathroom. I positioned her next to the loo with a large mug of water and just hoped that she wouldn't mistake either of them for the other. Gently shutting the bathroom door I ran into Timothy on the landing.

'Don't,' I told him crossly before he could start one of his anti-Francine tirades.

'What do you mean – don't? I haven't done anything!'

I peered warily at him. He looked innocent enough, all stripy pyjamas and belted dressing gown. Actually, he looked like Christopher Robin off to say his prayers.

'Come downstairs and have a coffee, Sis.'

Sis?

'Let me put a jumper on,' I said.

It was cold indoors, colder than outside – a regular phenomenon of the Red House. I pulled on a previously unworn Fair Isle sweater, all chunky and sensible – but who cared? No-one who mattered was going to see me. Then I carried the electric fan heater down to the kitchen, tripping over Elvis asleep on a stair. Timothy was scalding the instant-coffee grounds with seething water from the kettle.

'Sugar?'

'Saccharine.'

'Why saccharine?'

Because I weighed myself last week and I'm terrified of getting fat.

'Look, Timmy, just a saccharine tablet and no bloody discussion, or I'm going back upstairs. My foot's killing me.'

We sat at the breakfast bar, a bodged construction of plywood and Contac, sipping fiercely at our supermarket coffee, tasteless and grey, mine smeared with saccharine scum. I wasn't surprised when Timothy said, 'The police brought Dad home again tonight. Breathalysed. Second time in a week.'

'Yeah? How bad was he?'

'Rolling.'

'Oh shit. Violent with them?'

'Worse. All hail-fellow-well-met. "Ho, ho, these fine gentlemen caught me being a bad boy. But good for them, say I, they've got their job to do."'

I groaned. I felt the stir of an old ache, cold and hateful, in my tummy. 'How did they react, the fuzz?'

'Called him sir and kept rolling their eyes. I mean, regardless of me being there. After they left, he slammed off to the bedroom with a bottle of twelve-year-old malt, swearing the air blue.'

'That barrister will get him off again.'

'Two charges, a week apart?'

'As long as it's a magistrate Dad will never have his licence taken away. Gynae surgeon. Harley Street.' I had no idea whether this was true or not, but there was no point in making things worse for Timothy.

'But, Josie, should he get off? Wouldn't it be better for him – for us – if for once in his over-privileged life somebody showed some fight? Disqualified him for a year; made him live here in the middle of Essex with nothing but public transport?'

'He commutes to town by train anyway. And once home he'd just run up a stupendous taxi bill and have some poor sod sitting in the Golf Club car park freezing all evening while he got paralytic. And then he'd finish by being very ill in the poor sod's back seat.' That much was certainly true. I drank the coffee. I'd ended up smoking quite a few cigarettes and they'd left me thirsty. Actually, I could have done with another one now. 'Tim, the only thing that will do any good is moving house, so he has more time with Mum.'

'Mum!'

'Yes, I know, but . . .'

'It was the last move, and Mum getting a new job with even worse hours than before, that started him boozing in the first place. Doing the same thing all over again wouldn't fix it. But a bloody good fright might do the trick. Hey, there's a word for what Mum is, heard it today. Workaholic. What irony, eh? How many *holics* can one family take?'

'No. "Workaholic" is an American word and they achieve something. They wouldn't still be doing the hours of a junior doctor in their mid-forties without a sniff of a proper consultant's job. Anyway, workaholics are in love with work. Mum's in love with martyrdom.'

It was ludicrous really, her stance on religion – our

mother was driven by a zealot's compulsion for self-sacrifice that most saints would have jibbed at. According to Tarquin, even having children was an act of humanitarianism: recognizing the fallacy of the view, currently fashionable, that large families were anti-social, our mother knew that an ageing society is a drain on healthcare, and so set about replenishing it from an intelligent genetic source. Poor old Dad. I gulped down another mouthful of the tepid coffee, wishing it were warm enough to ease my intestinal ache. It would not take much, I realized, to make me cry.

'I suppose things could have been worse,' said Timothy. 'She might have gone in for politics instead, and been on the telly all the time causing us maximum embarrassment ranting about homelessness and a minimum wage.'

It wasn't often that Timothy talked about Mum objectively, like this. The episode with Dad and the police must have shaken him pretty badly.

'Poor old Dad,' he continued, echoing my thoughts. 'When he married her, he probably assumed all those philanthropic urges would be redirected once she had a baby in her arms. Ha! And then he bought this crumbling heap with dreams of turning it into a show-place. Do you remember? It was a four-year plan, wasn't it? Within twelve months, they'd have saved enough cash to start work. Downstairs first, then landscape the garden, then finish upstairs – and by 1967 we'd have musicians playing in a minstrels' gallery and party-goers in fancy dress paying for entrance tickets. What a dreamer!'

'Shame though,' I said, determinedly objective myself – ignoring the sting of tears at my eyelids. 'It would have gone down well in the summer of love, musical parties in a setting like this. We'd have been raking in the money. I suppose Dad has the same eye for architecture as Tarquin. But unfortunately with his head in the same clouds.'

'I expect Mum was meant to supply the practical side,' said Timothy. 'He thought she'd turn into a home-maker.'

'And Tarquin says Dad underestimated the amount of work and the costs. Must have realized his mistake as soon as we moved in.'

'Yeah,' said Timothy.

I looked at him. He was exhausted. I decided to take a chance. 'I suppose that was the last straw.'

'Yeah,' said Timothy.

'That, and the place being haunted.'

'Yeah,' said Timothy again.

A thump came from somewhere above us. I jumped and coffee flew from the cup. Timothy froze. Then steady footsteps, heavy on the staircase, getting closer. Dad? Dad drunk and aggrieved? Timothy replaced his cup silently on the Formica and slipped towards the back door. I'd soaked my Fair Isle sleeves when the coffee spilled and consequently was slow getting myself together. As the door from the hall croaked open, Timothy was already out of the back. The pains clutched at my insides sickeningly. It was Tarquin.

'Oh, thank God! Tim, it's OK, it's only Tarquin.'

But he had already legged it round to the shed, which is where we kept the ladder. Timothy would be OK: we'd all of us climbed back in through the upstairs windows when we'd forgotten our keys; it's the one advantage of living in the sort of house where every lock has been broken since about 1925. I left Timothy to it.

20

'Shut that fucking door, Jo,' suggested Tarquin conversationally as he opened the cupboards and scanned the contents. 'Fancy a Spam sandwich?'

'I wouldn't mind.'

He dragged a wrapped, white sliced loaf from our crumby bread bin and gave an experimental tweak to the lid of the butter dish. The contents were runny but not rancid. He started buttering.

'Dad got busted by the pigs again, did you hear?'

'Tim said.'

'He actually tried to bribe one of them! Can you believe it? "Tell me, my good man, would twenty pounds in folding money go amiss? I can make it fifty if you'll accept a cheque." Man, it was as good as a comedy sketch!'

'I wish I shared your amusement, Tarquin.'

He gave a series of snorts that passed for a laugh and put the kettle on. No saccharine for Tarquin; he stood rock-like in the kitchen, a mountain of a man in a flapping white cotton garment that might have been an

159

Egyptian galabayya, spooning one sugar after another over the teabag in his mug.

'Dad's not the only one pissed tonight,' I informed him. 'Francine's in the bathroom, sleeping it off.'

'Yeah, I heard her. Who's Anna-Carlotta Campiani? Sounds like a Mafia gangster's moll.'

'Just a girl who got off with the bloke Frankie fancies.'

'That why you're uptight? Bad bad vibes coming off you, Jo.'

'No, that's not why.'

I had a think. You could never be certain with Tarquin. Generally he forgot absolutely everything straight away, but not invariably. After he'd made his tea I swilled the last of the kettle water into my coffee. Thick flakes of scale poured out with it.

'This skinhead was trying to get Frankie laid and some bastard told me I was jealous because I'm a lesbian.'

'Yeah?'

'And he said there was a limerick about me, along those lines. Apparently it starts *There was a young lady called Frank / Had a friend who was built like a tank.*'

'Right. Last rhyme's *wank*, then.'

'So I imagine. I didn't stick around for the last rhyme.'

'Lousy bit of writing. I mean, you can guess the punchline before you get to the couplet.'

'That wasn't precisely what I had against it, Tarquin.'

'Do you think it's true, then?'

I didn't respond.

'Is that a yes?'

'Oh sod it, I don't know! I keep thinking, there's Frankie gagging for it from Florian and I never have from anyone. No male has ever made me drink myself into a coma.'

The only guys I ever dreamed of while cuddling the pillow at night were James Taylor and Mike Hammer from *Kiss Me, Deadly*. And even James Taylor couldn't *really* be said to exist, leastways not the one who wrote 'Fire And Rain' about losing me because they forced him to stay away until I was sixteen and he changed the girl's name in it to protect me from all the publicity.

'Will it bug you if it's true?'

'It's not exactly bonzer, is it? A bad scene.'

'If it's the limerick stuff that bugs you, just screw the guy that wrote it. That'll change his mind. Who is he?'

'The bloke who Frankie's just drunk herself unconscious about.'

'Ah.' Tarquin munched on his thickly buttered Spam sandwich, then reopened it and reached for the salt cellar. Not healthy eating habits for a man who scarcely moved all day long. There was a lot of stuff in Mum and Dad's medical journals these days about the dangers of salt and fatty diets. And the benefits of jogging. I looked hard at Tarquin and regretfully decided not to mention the benefits of jogging unless he mentioned them first. He held out the plate of sandwiches for me and I took one.

'So are you gagging for it from any *chick*?'

'No!'

'Then maybe you don't swing either way, Jo. Maybe you're sexless. Frigid.'

'Oh thanks, that'll stop me fretting!'

'Ex*act*ly! Better a les, yeah? Any loving's good loving,' he mused, chewing. 'Anyway, it's easier for a gay girl than a gay guy. Gay guys get a real fuck-up of a deal from so-called liberated society.'

'But that isn't my alternative, is it – a gay girl or gay guy? The alternative's a straight girl, a normal girl, a

161

wife and mother.' That reminded me. 'Where is ours, by the way? Does she know about Dad?'

'She was already in bed by the time he came rolling home with the uniform branch.' Tarquin pondered a moment. 'I wonder whether Dad even knew who it was in his bed. When Tim tried to shush him about bribing the pigs, Dad went, "Who the fuck are you?" ' He delivered another of his snorty laughs.

'How do I check it out?' I asked.

'Whether you're a dyke?'

'Yeah.'

'Told you. Shag the balls off the guy that wrote the limerick. That'll settle it. Kill two birds with one stone.' He wiped his mouth on his white cotton sleeve and dropped the plate into the sink. Either I would have to wash that up or it would wait for Mrs Stanley next week. 'At least it would stop you doing your head in.'

'You haven't even asked whether he's attractive. The bloke could be a gorilla for all you know.'

'It's that folk singer. Very tall dude in suede, and hair like Lauren Bacall. He was trying to get in my studio Tuesday.'

Yes, you could never tell with Tarquin what he knew and would remember.

'I'd've said he's a good bet for your first lay. For a start, that hair will look pretty mean on a pillow.'

'Thanks. I'll sleep on the thought.'

He opened the fridge and scanned it. 'There is nothing in here that's edible,' he said admiringly. 'Nothing.'

He withdrew a hand with some cheese in it. 'Is this Danish blue?'

'No. Cheddar. It's gone off. Tarquin . . .'

'Have we got any tinned soup?'

'Top cupboard.'

As that seemed to be it for the discussion of my

sexual orientation, I considered what else was worth broaching while I'd got him here.

'You know our practical joker?'

'The poltergeist, you mean?'

'Yes, well. Frankie and I thought that if it *is* supernatural, maybe there was a murder behind it. They say that in an unsolved murder case, the ghost can't rest, don't they? Anyway, I got this message sort of by Ouija, only it's in code. My idea is that if I decipher it, we'll know who it is and what's eating them. And then we can get it sorted, and the poltergeist can rest its spirit.'

'And bugger off, you mean?'

Yes, that was what I meant. And then we could get the house sold and bugger off ourselves, but Tarquin would not be keen on that line, of course. He was pouring soup into a pan. The tangy aroma of Heinz cream of tomato spread across the kitchen like fog – a warm, ruddy smell, redolent of childhood and comfort and firelit wintry nights. Part of the shared experience of all British children, even those brought up in the Red House.

I remembered Tarquin at nineteen. His girlfriend had dumped him for the lead singer in an acid rock band with two stately homes and a heroin habit. Next thing we knew, he was announcing that he had a US visa and letters of introduction to every electronic music studio in the States and Canada.

'We'll *all* miss him, sweetheart,' my mother had said.

I was crying again, tears never far from the surface when you've eaten nothing for twenty-four hours. I was on hunger strike.

'He's grown up now,' she went on. 'Grown-up brothers do leave home. Like Geoff did.'

'Not thousands of miles!'

'But Tarquin isn't going for ever, baby. I bet he'll

163

be back before you've even had a chance to miss him.'

'It's *you* who won't miss him. You won't even notice! You're never here!'

By the sixth day I kept fainting and my breath smelled like nail-varnish remover. Dad dragged Tarquin from his room and made him stand before me and swear, on the lives of every surviving Mississippi delta bluesman and Andy Warhol, that if I would start eating again he would undertake to return home for a visit every few months. A gloating Timothy lost no time in informing me that money had changed hands in the transaction.

'You know the Richardsons?' I now said. 'We've discovered that they used to have a daughter and it looks like she died here. In this house. Perhaps if I can decipher the message I'll solve the mystery of her death.'

Tarquin stirred his soup. It was now bubbling, in contravention of the instructions on the tin. The regressive pleasure afforded by the Heinz aroma receded and all I could see was Clarence's bath of blood on the Sunday when that couple came to look over the house. I turned my head away.

'Why code?' Tarquin was asking.

'I don't know. Maybe it'll all make sense when I get the thing cracked.'

'Sorry, Jo, but it sounds pretty fishy to me. Tim's been into that stuff since he was a kid – if you get a message in code, then I reckon it's Tim's. Or conceivably Dad's. You're not telling me that in a house with two code experts in it, one of them professional, we get haunted by yet another one – and he sends his stuff to you instead of them? How'd you get this message, anyway?'

'I sort of asked him for it, and he put it in the bathroom.'

This earned me another nasal laugh.

'Tarquin, what did you mean, "one of them professional"?'

'Yeah, I got it from this cat I used to know in an electronics shop on Lisle Street. Old Polish guy. After we'd done the draggy Ringo Starr stuff about my name it turned out he knew Dad. Worked with him in the war – get a load of this – deciphering enemy codes at some place called Bletchley Park. Big secret even now, can you believe it? Our fascist government still busts anyone who blabs twenty-five years on. Those bastards just *kill* me.'

'Was Dad some sort of spy?' I asked, a glamorous hope leaping into my voice like a hiccup.

'Just a code-cracker. One of Churchill's grubbing minions in a makeshift army hut.'

'Oh.'

'Though you can bet he dug that more than clinical practice, poor sod. You must have guessed there was *some* big-deal-who-gives-a-fuck-anyway secret. Like when people ask Dad what he did in the war, and he says, "Kept my head down, mostly." I mean, that wasn't actually an option for an A1 fit dude who turned twenty the day war broke out.'

I'd never wondered, never given it a thought. It was a longish time since I'd heard strangers talking to our dad.

'And anyway,' Tarquin continued, 'we know who it is, who's haunting us.'

'We *know*?'

'Sure. It's one of those kids that went missing in the snow that winter we came here.'

'Tarquin, what are you talking about?'

'Who else? It's never a chick, is it? The Richardsons' girl, Letitia her name was, she'd never be into sabotaging toilets, she was a prissy little piece. Butter wouldn't melt. It's a schoolboy. Obvious. One of those three: Martin West, Tom Parsons and

Laurence someone. Briggs, Laurence Briggs.'

'How do you remember their names?'

'It was seriously bad shit, Jo, you were just too small to take it in. They're who I wrote the tone poem about, "Afternoons III". The one with Louis MacNeice's "Snow" backwards on voice synthesizer. Takes up side two of *Triangular Wednesdays*.'

Tarquin scraped a chair up to the breakfast bar and blew on his hot soup.

'How do you know Letitia was all butter-wouldn't-melt?'

'People said. She disappeared the summer before we got here. Mrs R wanted to stay on in case she came home again, but that drag of a husband forced her to sell up. Every time someone came to view the house she used to sit in here, in the kitchen, sobbing and wringing her hands. Seemed to put off everybody else except Mum and Dad, who presumably just swept in, patted her on the head and swept out again.'

'Right.' I digested this and drained my coffee. 'Frankie and I got into their place the other day. Illegal entry. Mrs Richardson was out at choir practice, but *he* came home with a sixth-former from Stebbing! They were actually at it in the hall.'

Disgust washed over me again at the remembered sight of him, the hooded prick like a spitting cobra. If I were a normal girl I wouldn't react like that to a naked prick, surely.

Tarquin shrugged. 'Yeah, he's got a thing about seventeen-year-olds. Charles Dickens did, too, not just his soppy little heroines, in real life as well. And Letty came home one night and found him with his head in the laundry basket, sniffing her knickers. Ken Richardson, not Charles Dickens.'

'Oh, gross me out!'

'Right on.'

I was about to ask him again how he knew all this,

but my energy was fading. It was always extraordinary just what Tarquin knew: I'd grown up with it.

'Mrs R thinks her daughter's the poltergeist, I'm sure,' I told him. She had certainly objected when Francine and I started bubbling about a ghostly presence in the house. Why does she stay with that terrible husband? I wondered. She must know about his seventeen-year-olds. But then where would she go, with no financial independence? I sighed for womankind.

'Anyway, those three boys weren't murdered, were they?' I reminded Tarquin. 'They fell through the ice on a pond and drowned.'

'They disappeared during a blizzard. The rest of the stuff was conjecture.'

'Are you sure? It's an awful lot of disappearances. This is Lossing Common, not the Deadly Bermuda Triangle!'

'Yeah, far out.'

He added his unrinsed soup plate to the unrinsed saucepan in the sink.

'But no more far out than that skulking metal tower with its so-called early warning systems. No more far out than a top-secret underground network and free speech gagged by the MoD.'

'Tarquin, you're not suggesting people disappear because they're abducted by the Ministry of Defence?'

'Ask yourself: what's really going on? Why this paranoia from the authorities? It's a labyrinth under here, Jo, and every labyrinth has its Minotaur.'

I considered the idea that our hauntings were due to children eaten by an underground monster.

'The afternoon Letty Richardson disappeared, all the neighbours saw some dude in pin-striped trousers and bowler hat coming up the path with a briefcase. That is not a mad axe murderer, Jo, it's the Man from the Ministry! I mean – why a *briefcase*?'

167

'For carrying his axe?' I mumbled.

'And if this network were nothing but a nuclear fall-out shelter, why arrest every journalist found within a half-mile radius? Why throttle the press with D notices slapped on any article that so much as mentions underground buildings? Instant threat of a jail sentence. Experimentation!' Tarquin continued, his voice rising. 'That's what's going on beneath our feet, as we speak. And think about this – nobody builds a real shelter next to an early warning system. It's stupid; any direct hit aimed at the shelter would nuke the warning system along with it.'

But it wouldn't matter by then, I thought. Its job would be over.

'And it's no good saying it wouldn't matter by then because its job would be over,' continued Tarquin. My head jerked up. 'A genuine early warning system would serve the country, not just a few miles of underground maze. No, they're located together because they operate together. Stands to reason.'

Operate how? I thought, but decided to leave it there. I had enough to contend with, God knows.

'I'm sure those boys drowned in an icy pond, Tarquin.'

'Yeah?' He scraped his chair back under the table, an uncharacteristic gesture of tidiness. 'Hope not. It wouldn't half fuck up my tone poem.'

I stared at him.

'I'm for the sack. You coming up?'

'In a little while.'

'See you around, then.'

'Yeah. Thanks, Tarquin.'

'Keep cool, Jo. If you're gay, you're gay; whatever turns you on. Oh yeah, did I tell you? Geoff and Ange are back tomorrow. Breakfast time.' And he left the kitchen, unthinkingly switching off the light as he did so. As I sat there in the dark, waving my good foot in the current from the fan heater, I heard Tarquin trip over Elvis on the stairs, followed by a dribble of music that leaked from somewhere around the fridge. 'I Enjoy Being A Girl'.

'Oh thank you, Clarence,' I said crossly and stumbled across the cold quarry tiles towards the light switch, the stairs and bed, seriously tripping over Elvis myself on the way.

21

Somehow I just didn't sleep, what with the unrelenting pain and my new-found realization that I was going to face life on the fringes of so-called liberated society. It was all very well, Tarquin saying that gay girls had it easier; I'd heard what the boys at school said about gay girls; I'd heard what apparently intelligent adults said about gay girls. For example, at the only cocktail party Dad had given at his Harley Street rooms, one Christmas. Another gynaecologist on his fourth gin and tonic: 'Fibroids and polyps, and she wasn't virgo intacta so I asked about her sexual partners and what were her plans for having children. She said, "Actually, I'm not the marrying kind, my lover's a woman." Afraid I lost my rag and refused to treat her. After all, if a girlie's that way inclined – happy to open her legs – it's the male of the species who's best designed for her purpose and I say we've a duty to close ranks!' The men around him had laughed a good deal and refilled their glasses.

In General Studies last month, we'd had a debate

about marriage; the class had voted that it was more important for girls to stay virgins until they married than boys, because a girl wouldn't really mind if she wasn't her husband's first, whereas you couldn't expect a man to marry some slapper who'd been to bed with another bloke. The point was, although I voted against the motion, I knew I wouldn't *really* have sex before marriage because I just wouldn't want to *do it*. If I was a lesbian, that would all fit, surely?

I was in the kitchen, reading *The Female Eunuch*, when Francine appeared round the door, her hot pants crumpled, her feet wedgeless and bare.

'Cup of tea?' I suggested.

'Suppose so.' Her voice sounded as though it were sand-papered.

I put the kettle on and she slunk miserably across to a kitchen stool.

'I've got a modelling job tomorrow,' she said drearily. 'Guess what for? A government advert about healthy drinking.'

'Ah.'

'Oh Jo, I wish I was dead.'

'Alka-Seltzer?'

'Not that sort of dead. Florian-dead. Anna-Carlotta Campiani dead. Now there's a thought!' she added, dropping onto the stool.

There wasn't a lot I could say to that, so I made two cups of tea. Elvis glared impatiently into the kitchen from an outside ledge, having chosen the only casement window in the house. Accustomed to sash windows that rose, Elvis had never got his mind around casement windows that opened outwards and knocked him flying down the garden. My brothers' attempts at training had failed to dent his confidence, meaning that the various concussions with which Elvis had scrambled, cross-eyed, back up the wall for a retry had failed to work as aversion therapy.

171

I now hauled up one of the sashes and pointed at it.

'I can't believe that I actually woke up this morning,' said Francine. 'I mean – why? Why does my heart go on beating . . .' She stopped, perhaps dimly aware that this was a song and not a very hip one. 'People do die of broken hearts, don't they?'

'Only really old people, I think. When they lose a spouse of fifty years, that sort of thing,' I added thoughtfully. Perhaps grief renders them susceptible to infection. It was pretty interesting, I thought, and felt a fresh wave of my own grief that in a family full of medics I had nobody in the world to discuss it with.

Francine sipped cautiously at her tea. 'I suppose I could kill myself. I could kill her first and then myself.'

'Yeah, you could,' I agreed absently.

There was a car turning into our drive. I heard the grating of gravel and suddenly remembered Tarquin telling me that Geoffrey and Angela were coming for breakfast.

'Hell!' I crossed the kitchen to the hall. Outside the front door were voices.

'I tell you I've *got* the bloody bag!'

'Not that one! Give it here, Geoffrey. You're as much use as a wet weekend.'

Oh damn, I'd left Angela's Mickey Spillane by the fridge. Hurriedly, I stuffed him up my jumper.

'That's Angela and Angus, isn't it?' Francine was off the stool, sloshing tea across the Formica. I watched her rosy feet and bare toes twinkle across the quarry tiles that I'd mopped this morning to give me something to do. I watched them twinkle right into the plate I'd put down afterwards. Elvis's cat food. Liver- and heart-flavoured.

Francine stopped as though she'd run into a door. She gave an experimental whimper and gingerly lifted one foot from the plate. Cat food like thick mud squeezed between her tiny toes – brown, gelatinous and very smelly. A thick lump of juice-covered offal slid from her instep to squelch onto the plate.

'I'm allowed back in the kitchen, then?'

Angela. Francine had eventually stopped whimpering after five rinses in our geriatric plastic washing-up bowl and I'd packed her off home to her dad, though heaven alone knew what he would make of her purblind hangover and the growl like Leonard Cohen. He'd tell her mom on the phone, that was for sure; he was a nice man, but a bit light on common sense. Meanwhile I'd hollered at Angela to keep out, though not before Angus had got an eyeful. 'Fankie in Welvis food!' he was shrieking as his mother dragged him from the kitchen.

Angela was putting on more weight, I was sure of it. Flower-sprigged and cushioned with fat, she had a lot in common with an overstuffed chintz sofa. You couldn't get pregnant again while still breast-feeding, could you?

'Oy, dream-boat! I'm talking to you, miss.'

'Yes, Angela?'

'That bowl off the Kenwood mixer – where is it?' She was on a wobbly stool, tippy-toe in her grotty brogues, peering myopically into the wrong cupboard.

'Why?'

'Because I want something properly clean to rinse the baby's bottle in, that's why!'

'Mrs Stanley smashed it,' I lied. '*This* bowl's clean, Angela.'

And I left the kitchen with Angela rinsing bottles in the geriatric washing-up bowl.

Timothy was in the bathroom – I'd seen him cross the landing in his dressing gown and now I could hear the plumbing shake and wheeze as he filled the tub. Well, let's hope it wasn't blood in the taps. I crept along the landing and into his room. In competition with the whirring hamsters, Soft Machine's *Third* wafted from Timothy's unattended stereo: more classically trained clever buggers with their jazzy polyrhythms – he should invite Stephanie round. Bookcase and shelves. Science fact and science fiction. Maths. A row of hard-backed exercise books with biro on the spines: *1967. 1968. 1969* . . . Then I found what I was looking for: *Cryptanalysis* by Helen Fouché Gaines. Herbert O. Yardley, *The American Black Chamber*: 'The Number One Bestseller on codes and codebreaking!' I grabbed them both and then evened out the volumes on either side of the vacancy to disguise the loss. I scooted out of Timothy's room and across the landing to my own.

An hour of riffling and I had what I needed. It really was a *Boy's Own* adventure, this code stuff – buried treasure, espionage, political intrigue! Anyway, in the sixteenth century a French clever clogs called Blaise de Vigenère invented a cipher that took his name. Basically, instead of using just one cipher alphabet, such as moving every letter forward so that *Greg Bailey* becomes HSFHCBJMFZ, you use several and keep skipping from one to another.

How do you generate them in the first place? You design them around a word of your choice. Say, for example, the word 'code' itself. Now draw up a table of four alphabets, based on 'code' (see Table 1).

(And you're supposed to write real English in lower case, and cipher gibberish in capitals, to avoid a total muddle and going blind and mad.)

Then we encipher our message letter by letter, using the four alphabets one after the other, round and round. *Josephine Starkey* comes out as LCVIRVLRGG-WETYHC. It's easy to see how this is hard to crack: suppose we encipher Timothy's name instead of mine – this time, when we start on *Starkey* we'll be up to the fourth alphabet whereas mine started with the second.

	a	b	c	d	e	f	g	h	i	j	k	l	m	n	o	p	q	r	s	t	u	v	w	x	y	z
1	C	D	E	F	G	H	I	J	K	L	M	N	O	P	Q	R	S	T	U	V	W	X	Y	Z	A	B
2	O	P	Q	R	S	T	U	V	W	X	Y	Z	A	B	C	D	E	F	G	H	I	J	K	L	M	N
3	D	E	F	G	H	I	J	K	L	M	N	O	P	Q	R	S	T	U	V	W	X	Y	Z	A	B	C
4	E	F	G	H	I	J	K	L	M	N	O	P	Q	R	S	T	U	V	W	X	Y	Z	A	B	C	D

Table 1. *A Vigenère cipher based on the key word 'code'*

His *Starkey* will come out as WVOUOGM whereas mine was GWETYHC.

Neat.

But not quick. Presumably, to *de*cipher you just do the same thing but backwards – *provided you know what the key word is.* I didn't even know how many letters might be in Clarence's; there was no rule that they should have four. I hadn't the foggiest idea where to start. Therefore when Angela screamed up the stairs, 'Your friend's been here ten minutes, Josephine. Aren't you ever coming down?' it was with less than my usual irritation that I slammed out of the bedroom.

If Francine had returned, why didn't she come straight up? But when I'd limped down the stairs and into the cavernous dining room that Angela always called the 'living room', though it was clearly designed for corpses, I found Florian Smith sitting in it, warming his hands around a mug of coffee.

22

I did a double-take. I'd spent so much of the previous black night silently screaming at Florian Smith that it took me a moment to appreciate that the man hadn't actually heard me, but had turned up here in ignorance of the opprobrium he'd earned for his bloody limerick. Oh, and for letting down my best friend. He had a wary eye on Angus, who was sitting at his feet and who, it was borne in on me, had a phenomenal cold. He slumped against Florian's chair, sniffing succulently, glugging on his sodden sinuses. A desultory fire burned in the grate, its flames pallid in a shaft of dusty, reluctant sunshine.

Florian got to his feet. 'Hi.'

I swung round in panic to check on Angela, thinking that she was probably breast-feeding the baby but for once she wasn't – her nylon blouse was damply milk-stained across the nipple area, but the buttons were done up to the collar.

'Your boyfriend has been telling me all about the folk clubs,' she said brightly. 'You see, Florian,

Josephine never lets her family in on her life outside these walls. Anyone would think she was ashamed of you!'

Florian gave me a strained smile. 'Your sister was explaining . . .'

'Sister-*in-law*!'

'. . . how your parents are hoping to move near Harley Street, and she's kindly come over to show potential buyers round the house.'

I looked at her.

'And I was saying how I'd buy this pad myself if only I had the cash.'

'Right.'

Conversation waned. I was still standing so Florian wasn't sure whether or not to remain on his feet.

'Your sister-in-law was also telling me,' he struggled on, 'that your father's an eminent surgeon and apparently he's meeting one of the country's top barristers. I said I trusted he wasn't up on a murder charge.'

'No. Drunk driving,' I said, to embarrass him and mortify Angela.

'Josephine! Take no notice, Florian, she has a very strange sense of humour. And while I've got you here, Josie, are you sure you haven't borrowed my Mickey Spillane? I've ransacked the house for it.'

'I don't read that stuff, Angela, I'm into Einstein's relativity and Germaine Greer.' I'd finished it at lunchtime and destroyed the evidence, thankfully. Dustbin.

'Oh yes – and what on earth has happened to the steam iron? There's some sort of black plastic melted over the surface.'

'I know.' I gave a weary shrug. 'Mrs Stanley gets worse.'

Florian was tentatively sitting back down in the chair when Angus gave a yell.

'*Welvis!*' shouted Angus.

177

Florian jumped. The cat had been slinking across the room. Now he silently vanished.

'No, dear, *El*vis,' corrected Angela.

Florian, who hadn't even seen a cat, turned to her perplexed. She beamed at him. In the hiatus that followed, I flopped into a chair to rest my bad foot. It had just occurred to me that I was still wearing that sensible sweater. Oh well, sod it.

'Do you live far from here?' perked up Angela in her hostess voice.

'Ilford,' Florian replied and then looked thoughtfully at me. '*Josephine*,' he said; he'd probably assumed I was a Joanna or Joanne. 'As in the Strawbs number? "Josephine For Better Or For Worse"?'

'Ooh, now that sounds serious!' Angela hauled her short, thick milky body out of the depths of the sofa. 'Well, Angus,' she said playfully. 'Let's leave these young people together, shall we?' And she smiled indulgently from Florian to me.

'Big Node,' said Angus, pointing a chubby finger at my face. Then he sneezed.

It took some time for his mother to mop up, but finally she carried Angus to the doorway, now flecking the walls with phlegm, cast one last bless-you-my-children smile at us and made a business of closing the door. The look she got from me should have impaled her on it.

'Look—' I started.

'It's all right,' interrupted Florian.

His eyes were on the unfinished mug of coffee; Angela's mopping hadn't reached that far. He turned his head away. 'Families can be guaranteed to say the wrong things.'

But I wasn't going to conspire with Florian, not even against Angela and Angus. Instead I faced him and asked loudly, 'How's Anna-Carlotta Campiani?'

178

'Carly? She's fine. Great.'

'You were with her last night at Dave's party.'

'Yes, we were there. We've got another one tonight, come to think of it.'

'Frankie was there, too.'

'Yeah?'

He was looking innocently puzzled at this turn in the conversation. I took stock. Was I really going to launch into an attack on Frankie's behalf? *You rolled about on the floor with my best friend and then ditched her.* She wouldn't thank me for that. Instead I found myself saying, 'I heard another of your limericks at the party. This one was about me.'

'I don't remember writing one about you. Was it good?'

'It started, "There was a young lady called Frank".'

He looked lost. 'Your name isn't Frank.'

'No. But there was a second line.'

'Yes?'

I stopped. I just couldn't. There was no way.

'Skip it,' I told him wearily. 'Anyway, what can I do for you? You didn't come round for a cup of Angela's coffee, with or without Angus sneezing in it.'

'No, I just thought I'd nip by and pick up *Clouds*. I promised to lend it to Carly. That's actually what I was doing with the record at Stavering, but then I heard you sing and it was shit-hot, so I lent it to you instead.'

'Oh?'

'So you could learn "Tin Angel".'

'Right.'

'Carly wasn't all that pleased. In fact it went down like a lead balloon. So here I am.'

'So you are.'

I turned an ear to the studio above, but there was nothing, not a sound. Florian's eyes followed mine.

'Is the great man working today?'

'Oh yes. Absolutely. Any minute.'

'Ah.'

From a distant room came the wailing of the baby and Geoffrey's voice shouting that he knew he'd brought the bloody thing, he remembered putting the bloody thing in the car boot.

'*Jodie!*' shouted Angus. '*Jodie Big Node!*'

'No, Angus! Geoff, don't let him – Josephine's snogging her boyfriend in there!'

Embarrassment scorched my face and chest. My armpits burned. Sweat trickled inside the heavy sweater. Then, worse, a convulsion exploding in my throat. Laughter, totally inappropriate, totally beyond control. I tried to turn it into a coughing fit, snuffling and snorting like Angus. Florian was now looking terribly uncomfortable. The laughter choked inside me and ran down my cheeks as tears.

'I'm s-sorry!' I stammered. 'I've had very little sleep and I can't cope with this gruesome family at the best of times.'

He smiled, less strained now. 'Families!' he said. 'Carly keeps asking why I don't take her home to meet my folks, as she calls them. I can't tell her the truth – that Mum would offer gentle advice about how to get rid of her American accent, and Dad would ask for her views on Jan van Eyck, who Carly wouldn't know from . . .' He paused.

'Dick Van Dyke?' I suggested.

'I was going to say Rip van Winkle.'

'Right.' I wiped my eyes and pulled myself together. From above us came a rumble. As though for the benefit of his admirer downstairs, Tarquin was patching up the sort of noise that serious critics called 'non-melodic sonic material' and which the rock journalist Lester Bangs had described as 'ear demolition for fuckwits'.

'Ah!' said Florian. 'The fat squelch of the Moog.'

But he was out of luck; after a few fuzzy, bloated

whoooeee noises, a genuine musical instrument took over. Acoustic guitar. Tarquin wasn't as good as Greg Bailey but he was better than Florian.

'He's better than me,' said Florian. 'Though I could give him a run for his money on piano.'

'*Really?*'

'Yeah, I was dropping out of the Royal College about the same time Tarquin was dropping out of the Royal Academy.' Florian pointed upwards. 'Know what that is?'

A pretty tune about to be massacred, no doubt.

'It's an English folk melody in mixolydian mode.'

'Fascinating,' I said in a voice deliberately sagging with boredom.

'Well, actually it *is*,' Florian responded cheerfully. 'Mixolydian mode is where folk music meets the blues. Hear it? You could just about sing either folk or blues to this. But if we just flattened the third, then it would start to sound like a blues scale proper.'

As he said this, the music coming through the ceiling turned into a blues scale proper.

'Well, there you go,' said Florian.

This precognition was so like Tarquin himself that I had to struggle to resent it. The music now metamorphosed into an actual song: Blind Lemon Jefferson's 'Hangman's Blues'. Oh good, that should cheer us all up. I opened my mouth to get in first before Florian started a lecture on the damn thing, but I was too late.

'He never has liked conventional major and minor scales, has he, your brother? That'll be the Marxism.'

'*What?*'

'Yeah, scales are about hierarchy, central and weaker chords. Very iffy stuff to a Marxist.'

'Tarquin isn't a Marxist, he's a Trotskyite.'

'Yeah, them too. Did he ever consider moving into folk?'

'No,' I said spitefully. 'He said he wouldn't be seen dead in any musical movement that contained Simon and Garfunkel.'

Florian lay back in our woebegone armchair and laughed until his chest heaved. As he sprawled there, uninhibited, ungrudgingly convulsed – vulnerable – I felt an odd rush of emotion. Of power. I also felt that this would be better left unanalysed.

'I love it!' he said eventually, blowing into a handkerchief. '*Got* to remember that one for Stavering! Which reminds me, tell me about the song you sang on Monday.'

I should have snubbed him again, but in the wake of that laughter – the word 'afterglow' rose unbidden – I found I couldn't.

'It was one of thirty,' I said.

'*Yeah?*'

'Yep. When Tarquin was churning out those bluesy songs that everybody knows he also wrote thirty others that he's never published, all of them inspired by this house. The one you heard in the Rose and Crown was about the stained glass in our conservatory.'

I pointed towards it, tagged onto this chilly and colourless room like some disreputable relative overdressed at a funeral. 'And he wrote another couple about the carvings in our hall. There was even a song inspired by this great echoing cavern that's meant to be a dining room.'

'He never published them? What a waste!' exclaimed Florian. 'Can you sing them to me?'

'I'd feel a bit of a twerp sitting here warbling, don't you think? Anyway, Angela would come back in asking silly questions.'

'True, we wouldn't want that.'

It occurred to me that I was no longer even paying lip service to my anger with him. Florian was asking, 'Did your brother move away from the song format because he foresaw that progressive music would go that way?'

'Nope. He moved away from songs because he said there aren't any left.'

'Sorry?'

'Tarquin believes there are no melodies left in the world. His last song about this house was literally the Last Song. And he's never actually played it. He's frightened to.'

Florian was just looking at me.

'I'm not making this up. Tarquin believes that the thirtieth song he composed about the Red House was actually the world's last unused melody. I've seen the manuscript – the lyric is about autumn in our orchard – but I can't read music very well and he's never shown it to anyone else. That's because he believes that if his last song is ever heard, then that's the last piece of music over.'

'But. Well.'

'And unfortunately, Tarquin also believes that once the last song has been played, all music will disappear from the world for ever. Modes, scales, all pitched music everywhere will cease to mean anything to us. The whole concept of tunes will vanish for all time. Like that Arthur C. Clarke story where the monks run through the nine billion names of God and then the stars go out.'

'Bloody hell.' Florian sat a moment, considering it. 'But people are writing new melody lines all the time,' he objected.

'According to Tarquin, they're not new at all, just cobbled-together chunks from old stuff.'

'But we'd know. People would sue.'

'We wouldn't even notice. We never recognize even the best-known tunes when they're under our noses. I can demonstrate. You know the song "Yes! We Have No Bananas"?'

'Of course.'

'Listen.' I sang the first four words at him. '*Yes! We have no.*' Then I did it a second time. '*Yes! We have no.*'

'Bloody hell,' said Florian again. 'It's the Hallelujah Chorus!'

'That's right. You can sing *HA-llelujah* to it. Now listen to the next line: *We have no bananas today.*'

He thought a moment and shook his head.

'No? It's the same notes as *O bring back my bonnie to me.*'

'Yeah! It's "My Bonnie Lies Over The Ocean". I never noticed.'

'No-one ever does. According to Tarquin, every new song is cobbled together from bits of other melodies. There's just a single original one left, Tarquin's the genius that found it, and he intends it to stay in his head.'

'Because when the last tune is played . . .'

'. . . we will have got to the end of music.'

'And the stars will go out.'

'So to speak.'

'Well, fuck me.'

'Absolutely.'

'That's totally bloody stunning.'

We sat, stunned, totally, in a silence that was rather pleasant. The flat light of an April afternoon reached us via the raucous conservatory glass. It was eerie but not unpleasant, almost an underwater light, strangely appropriate for a discussion about Tarquin. Meanwhile, my brother's interlude with Blind Lemon Jefferson had finished. Slow, rich organ chords oozed from the Moog to conjure a cathedral-like ambience, and then disappeared beneath a zizzing burst of radio static and *musique concrète*. There was no danger of trotting out the last melody by accident and exterminating music for all time, not if you never again in your life wrote anything that could be called a tune. Hence the sonic output of Tarquin Starkey.

Florian remembered his commitments. 'So, could you just get that Joni Mitchell then? Save me disappointing Carly.'

'Ah yes. Frankie's American too,' I reminded him loyally. 'Frankie, the Lucie Clayton model,' I added. 'Same accent.'

'Yeah?' He was on his feet.

'Look, Florian, the truth is I meant to buy you a new copy of *Clouds*. I just forgot.'

'Haven't you had a chance to tape it?'

'The truth is I left it in the sun and the record warped. Sorry.'

'Oh.' He bit his lip. One disappointed Carly coming up, then. 'How bad is it?'

'Well, it was a bit bad, but then my twin brother Timothy, he said he knew how to straighten out vinyl in water.'

'Water?'

'Yes, we sort of boiled it.'

'Right. How did that go?'

'Not well. So I ironed it.'

He blinked. 'That brother's not a genius, then.'

'Well, yes, as a matter of fact, but not in the field of thermoplastics.'

'What does it look like, the record?'

I shrugged. 'Like an LP that's been boiled and ironed.'

'Right,' he said again. 'I'll be going, then.'

'Sorry, Florian.'

'That's OK. I spend half my life in record shops. I'll pick up a copy tomorrow.'

'I'll pay you back.'

'Just buy me a pint at the Castle.'

'Well, thanks.'

In the kitchen, Angus's strangled cough reached a climax. Phlegm had a characteristic sound when it

185

originated from Angus. He was more than capable of taking aim and getting Florian on his way through the hall. 'There's a side door,' I said hurriedly.

'Good.'

Out of the room, we turned right in our dark passageway instead of left towards the hall. At the end was a wooden door, rain-swollen. I turned the handle, shoved, and then waited; waited while the man who was already knocked out by our crazy house, the man who liked to know his Serlio from his Palladio, copped a load of this lot.

23

'But *how*?' said Florian. 'How did it get here?'

We were in the courtyard with a rusty bicycle and an abandoned twin-tub washing machine. The floor was quarry-tiled like the kitchen, cambered towards the grill of a small soakaway clogged with mud. And the three external walls were tiled in a blue and white frieze, depicting the city of Lisbon in the eighteenth century: street scenes of a royal wedding; bewigged ladies and gentlemen in carriages, beggars, romping children, peeing dogs, against a panorama of the city.

Florian's eyes were wet with tears. 'It's totally far out! Like Voltaire's *Candide* come to life!'

'*All is for the best in the best of all possible worlds,*' I quoted, as taught me by Tarquin. 'It's actually a copy of a frieze in—'

'Bahia, Brazil. I backpacked there in '69. The scene is Lisbon before the 1755 earthquake.'

'Right,' I said, keeping my astonishment to myself. He wasn't keeping his: Florian just stood there, tearily shaking his head.

'*How?*' he asked again, waving a hand to encompass the entire Red House. 'How did the place get to be this way?'

'Long story,' I warned him.

And never my story, of course, but Tarquin's, which he was fervently researching in centrally heated libraries while the rest of us were freezing at home. Apparently, the Red House had been built at the end of the eighteenth century by a wealthy London wine merchant called Josiah Widgery, importer of port and sherry. Portugal and Spain. He had married a well-born Portuguese lady who was rather cultured and snooty – and unfortunately came to loathe her husband. Isabella Maria Theresa Widgery chose an odd, spiteful way of getting at him – Josiah being a particularly solid pillar of the Church of England, she would mock his religion. She sneered at the C of E. She used to say that to sit amid an English congregation with its vernacular hymns and doddering vicars was like being forced to watch a provincial opera company perform last season's failures from seats in the fleapit. Nice one. Josiah seemed to weather this with good humour until he built their country residence. Where he peppered the entire décor with allusions to his own Anglican Church overlaid with as much anti-Catholic symbolism as he could wangle with the craftsmen.

Those references to Christopher Wren's Protestant churches might have been harmless, but they were certainly weird – by this time, the country had gone Adam-brothers crazy, all twiddly little festoons, flutes and fans, so those heavy carvings were completely old hat. But the décor was also dotted with the insignia of rabidly anti-Papist bishops who had burned Catholics at the stake. In our drawing room (thankfully un-inhabitable from damp), the Adam cornice was decorated with little bonfires, flames and all – the stakes at which the martyrs were burned. And the fires had little figures in them.

In the pediment above the front-door casing was a bust of the Elizabethan spymaster Sir Francis Walsingham, the fanatic who chopped the head off every Catholic he could get his hands on. That was who greeted visitors at our front door. And as for the carvings across our banisters, they were oranges and orange blossom. William of Orange, naturally. King Billy. Been causing trouble for 300 years.

So Clarence wasn't the first malign presence here; the Red House was *born* out of spite. Such an obvious candidate for the vengeful spirit, Isabella Widgery; yet Francine and I just couldn't believe it was a high-born Portuguese lady who was Clarencing us, not with stink-bombs or tripe and onions.

I gave Florian an outline.

'Christ!' he said when I got to the bonfires. From nowhere, my bad foot gave a terrible twinge. It occurred to me that for all this time in Florian's company I'd managed to forget about it.

'But how do you know all the details?'

'Tarquin.'

'Right,' he said, nodding his head. 'Yeah, if this were my pad, I'd research it, too.' Then, 'You've really got figures burning to death in a Robert Adam frieze?'

' 'Fraid so.'

'Reminds me of something else in Bahia. There's a church where the carvings were done by black slaves. They got a bit of their own back. There are hundreds of carved cherubim and seraphim. Look closely, and you'll see that some have genitalia.'

Oh wow, that story was absolutely Tarquin. I could imagine Florian telling him. Those efforts of mine

189

were misplaced, weren't they – my efforts to keep him and Florian apart?

'But,' Florian was saying, 'even knowing what those oranges are supposed to mean, your staircase is still shit-hot, with that window and everything.'

'Another of Tarquin's songs is about exactly that – Serlio's sunlight purifying Widgery's ill-intentioned stairs. From hatred to Paradise. He called it "Stairway To Heaven".'

' "Stairway To Heaven",' repeated Florian thoughtfully. 'Nice title. But did she know? Widgery's wife, I mean.'

'Nope, not according to the stories.'

You picture her trotting through the new house, throwing out scathing remarks about her husband's beloved religion, and all around were emblems of persecution and triumphalism, and images of burning flesh.

And when she died, Josiah got the local C of E vicar, who'd also had a bellyful of her insults, to bury Isabella quietly round the corner at St Andrew's instead of in the Catholic cathedral. By the time her family turned up it was too late: the law doesn't like exhumation. And when Josiah died, they didn't dispatch him to St Andrew's but to the Norman church at Stavering. The earth in this part of Essex is clay; it would take a long time for Isabella Widgery to claw her way through four miles of it to get at him.

Florian was still standing with his mouth open. I resumed my potted architectural history.

'And then, about a century later, along came another philistine, who turned the Adam fireplaces into *inglenooks*, for God's sake, and clamped on bay windows, a conservatory and a new kitchen.'

'Your conservatory,' objected Florian, 'is fucking fantastic!'

Mmm. Well, the kitchen replaced a statue and a fountain. Now the nearest we got was Angus peeing in the sink.

'It's an insane treasure trove!' Florian was saying. 'These tiles alone must be worth a fortune.'

'That's what Geoffrey and Angela think, too. They insist it's Mum and Dad's duty to cough up enough cash so they can ruin their own turn-of-the-century terrace. Dad refuses, so if we don't get a buyer for the house, the pair of them are going to sell off all our tiling.'

'What?'

'You've seen the Victorian ones in the bathroom and conservatory – there's a decent market since *The Forsyte Saga* went on TV, so Angela intends hacking them out and dumping them on various antique shops for fifty quid a heap. These Portuguese ones she'll offload on specialists as picture chunks. The rest she'll chuck into the nearest skip.'

'That's obscene!'

'*All is for the best in the best of all possible worlds.*'

'But why would your parents allow it?'

'My parents aren't around much,' I admitted.

'And you think you might not get a buyer? Why not?'

But I wasn't going into that. 'Too big?' I suggested diffidently.

'I'd just love to show all this to Carly . . .' he started and then stopped. 'What did Tarquin compose for this courtyard?' he asked instead.

No, I thought, not Carly, who wouldn't know a van Eyck from a van Winkle. Any more than Francine would, I thought, and winced at myself.

'Tarquin? Two songs and an album track . . .'

'Album track!' Florian shouted. 'It's "Blue Reprise Six-O-Three", isn't it? Side one of *Metallic Ladybirds On Triangular Wednesdays!*'

191

I looked hard at him. His eyes continued to drink in the scenes of the fresco.

'Yes, it was "Blue Reprise Six-O-Three",' I confirmed. 'Well spotted, Florian.'

Then I drew him gently towards the door in the wall and out onto the weedy gravel of the garden path. I stayed outside for some time after he'd gone. And when I limped back into the house, it was as though every sound, every remark made by everybody, were filtered through Florian's voice. Even the sound of Angus.

24

The infection in my ankle eventually abated and with it the danger of septicaemia, but not until I'd spent two days in hospital. My mother, falling through the door of the ward with a bunch of daffs five minutes before the end of visiting time, insisted that all human bites have this potential, but privately I wondered whether I could sell Angus to bacteriologists at Porton Down. And then school began again.

Summer term. Our horrible serge was put away until September and replaced with dresses in horrible gingham (and the only way to hoik up the hemline was by stitching it, for which the penalties were harsh) plus *straw boaters*.

'Who designed these anyway?' grizzled Paula, trying to punch some flexibility into the brim of hers. 'I mean, what were they *on*?'

We were lying on the grass of the playing field, Barbara Paige reading *Naked Lunch*, Francine practising her new signature with an *F* and *S* no longer Florian's, me slogging away at Clarence's message. The sunlight was rather welcome, as our English teacher had kicked off the day with the direst passages she could dig up from Shakespeare: women psycho-killers and kings ranting till their eyes steamed – why the school governors allowed it, I could not imagine. Around us now were several hundred lazing figures. Most of the boys lay with their backs on the grass, knees in the air and their legs splayed, to spell out an ungainly M shape and display contours I'd rather not have had forced upon my conscious mind.

I turned back to Blaise de Vigenère.

```
TDFVMYSKKKHAJRITTDFVMYSKKKHA
JLJGTDFVMLWVLUSGLXBFVHRCRGGGZHB
VIHBPMQSVIHBREUHKMLHJVHSJYQR
TIGOPHWKGRWMVARDCVWWKMIWXIKI
PHUSFEQRUMAHAXZCREUHKM
LWQRHVWRGFGHDBFJRFVCSOTXLWK
SQSVLRIUEQRQRHVWRGFGHDBFJR
FVCWVTIHDCVWWKMVSXIQHGIQD
CVWWKMWKQLXBFVHRCRGSKKKHAILU
JXBGGZHBREUHKMLHYSWVQYVOPHQW
PIKIPHUSFEQRUMAHAWLLREUHKZL
WQRHHJSXGCRGSKKKHJYQRTIGOPH
WVKVWMPMQSREUHKMLWKMWVTI
HTQYU
```

That was Clarence's little missive in its entirety. Great fun. I no longer even had Timothy's books to work with; as soon as he'd realized I'd taken them, Tim had thrown a spectacular tantrum, a devouring paddy that might have defeated even his nephew.

'*You of all people!*' he kept spluttering at me, in the tones of a Tory father finding his daughter's Communist Party card. 'It will be fucking *horoscopes* next!'

So from then on I had nothing to work with but my wits.

*　*　*

Well now. Assuming this is one of Mr Vigenère's, how do you unpick it stitch by stitch?

If you're the intended recipient, it's easy. You already know the key word, so you draw up the table of alphabets exactly like the sender did, and plug away at your message letter by letter. Simple back-translation.

But if you've intercepted the message and want to crack it, you know none of this. You first have to find out how many alphabets you're working with, i.e., how many letters in the key word. As you can't literally find it out, you have to go by guesswork. Trial and error. Hours of fun. A passing fifth-year boy strode lankily by and a book slipped from his hand, bang! onto my head.

'Oh,' he said.

'Talk about butterfingers!' yelled Francine into his spotty face. 'You've nutted her!'

'Sorry.'

'Killed off some of her brain cells, probably!'

'Yeah, probably,' he agreed.

I picked up the book from where it had ricocheted off my bonce onto the grass. George Orwell's *Nineteen Eighty-Four*. Insult to injury.

'Look, what is it with boys and this book?' I demanded irritably.

'Wha'? 'Sgood.'

'Oh really? Big Brother? When I was five, one of my own brothers destroyed our TV by taking out the working innards so he could sit for hours with his head inside making announcements about the war with Oceania!'

The fifth-year goggled at me. 'Yeah?'

'And my biggest brother had a *rat* in a *box* and kept creeping into everybody's bedrooms and telling them they were in Room 101!'

The boy snuffled. 'Good stuff. Can I have it back, yeah?'

'No.'

'Wha'?'

'Watch.' I opened the paperback, tatty from use. I glanced at the page; Big Brother was watching them, apparently. I slowly tore the page out and into strips.

'No, Jo!' said Barbara.

'Bloody Nora!'

And he was on top of me, flailing. Paula and Francine threw themselves on top of him. Barbara Paige said quietly, 'Give it him, Jo. Give him his book back.'

By now, of course, I couldn't give anything to anybody, his arms and legs were in my eyes and nose and midriff. *Ooof!* Barbara walloped someone round the ears with *Naked Lunch*.

'Get off of her and she'll give it you back!'

He succeeded in rolling away from Paula and Francine, who appeared to be enjoying themselves, and snatched the book from me, which tore the cover away.

'You stupid . . . stupid . . .'

'Yes?' I prompted, pulling down the skirt of my dress and tossing him the remains of the novel like throwing fish out of a bucket to a performing seal.

'You stupid *wor*!' he shouted and stamped off, leaving the scattered remains of *Nineteen Eighty-Four* to blow around in the grass.

'Jo,' remonstrated Barbara, 'I happen to think it's a masterpiece myself. Anyway, you shouldn't destroy books. Hitler destroyed books.'

'You haven't got brothers.'

'Yeah, what was that about?' demanded Paula.

'Just her mad family,' responded Francine on my behalf. 'Don't ask.'

My mad family. Angela was apparently showing another couple round the house today. She had seen one yesterday too, but I'd had no feedback except for the clue that Angela was becoming noticeably less smug about it all. I returned my attention to the author of her difficulties.

I was absolutely *not* going to bugger about with trial and error over how many letters were in Clarence's key word. There must be a clue. For example, there were some bits of rubbish that kept recurring in the message; I had that early TDFVMYSKKKHAJ twice. There was also a EUHKML that kept cropping up. Actually, there were loads: DCVWWKM and SKKKH and . . . Look, suppose each was a real repeat of a real bit of English? Well, to get translated into the same gibberish, they must be separated by an exact number of alphabet cycles, i.e., an exact number of key words. So? Well, let's look at those EUHKMLs, etc.: they repeat themselves after how many letters? If five goes into the answer an exact number of times, then Clarence's key word has five letters. Or if six . . .

It was four. My recurring junk cropped up at intervals including 16, 60, 120, 96, 212, 76 . . . Five didn't go into all the numbers, neither did three or six. Only four. Clarence's key word was four letters long. So I then wasted a fair bit of time on the educated guess that it must be:

	a	b	c	d	e	f	g	h	i	j	k	l	m	n	o	p	q	r	s	t	u	v	w	x	y	z
F	G	H	I	J	K	L	M	N	O	P	Q	R	S	T	U	V	W	X	Y	Z	A	B	C	D	E
U	V	W	X	Y	Z	A	B	C	D	E	F	G	H	I	J	K	L	M	N	O	P	Q	R	S	T
C	D	E	F	G	H	I	J	K	L	M	N	O	P	Q	R	S	T	U	V	W	X	Y	Z	A	B
K	L	M	N	O	P	Q	R	S	T	U	V	W	X	Y	Z	A	B	C	D	E	F	G	H	I	J

Table 2. *A Vigenère code with a four-letter key word*

Unfortunately, this got me absolutely nowhere. It got me *yxhfrsu upejkolk dyxhf rsuu pejkofl qyxhfrfyf . . .*

Neither were the other two obvious words any use. Clarence might be puerile, but he was smarter than that.

'*Josephine Starkey!*'

I leaped about a foot in the air. Or I would have, but the desk didn't give me a foot of clearance – one knee cracked against the plastic. Much laughter. Jim Fräulein Schneider was upon me.

'*What* is *this*?'

We were not still lying across the playing fields with aromatic blades of grass up our noses and schoolboys' crotches thrust upon our collective vision. The afternoon bell had rung some time ago to summon Paula and Barbara to Geography, and Francine and me to German. My mistake had been to carry on tinkering with codes behind a vocabulary book.

'I am asking you what *is* it?'

'A mathematical puzzle. Sorry, Fräulein Schneider.'

She flicked through the paper, her small, mouse-like eyes scanning my pages. They crackled in her hands.

'We are taking this to Mrs Matlock,' she announced, and then to the class, 'Open your books to chapter seven! Be ready for testing when I am back!'

Francine, sitting next to me, had been going 'But, Fräulein Schneider . . .' throughout this exchange. Now she was snapped at.

'Francine Switt! When Josephine returns you will not any more sit next to her in my lessons. She is the bad influence.'

'Just *a* bad influence, Fräulein Schneider,' I corrected her. 'I'm only one of an entire *throng* of bad influences on Frankie.'

The class hooted with laughter. I glanced across at Torsten, who was leaning against the blackboard. I expected a conspiratorial smile. There wasn't one.

'Stand!'

And so I got to my feet, allowing Jim to march me across the school to the deputy head's office, my pages of cipher text and alphabet tables flapping in her hands.

'I'm really sorry, Mrs Matlock. You see, it's a mathematical puzzle . . .'

'Your apologies are due to Fräulein Schneider and your fellows in class, whose German lesson you have just disrupted. Not for the first time.'

Jim had said her bit and left me to it. Mrs Matlock had then read my pages rather carefully.

'Yes, Mrs Matlock. You see . . .'

'And don't interrupt me, either. You've forfeited the right to have your views heard.'

'I'm not allowed to get a word in?'

'I would say we've had all the words from you that we can stomach.'

She thrust at me the top sheet, the one I'd started work on during the lunch break. At first I saw only my grids of letters, neat mosaics in upper and lower case. Then I recognized my scribble across them. I saw 'SHIT' and then I saw . . . Oh God, my trial-and-error key words. All bloody three of them.

'A mathematical puzzle!' quoted Mrs Matlock scathingly.

I made some incoherent noise. She spoke across me.

'You are, of course, aware that you're a highly intelligent girl. Perhaps you believe that the corollary is that you are not required to work in lessons like the common herd. Allow me to disabuse you of this notion.'

'Mrs Matlock . . .'

'For once in your life, Josephine, pipe down and listen to what somebody else has to say. Quite apart from the harm you do yourself, your attitude causes disruption and dissent, and harms others. Most notably Francine Switt, who doesn't have your intellect and is not benefiting from the influence of your slovenly approach to work.'

Without meaning to, I swallowed. Sitting there, her words flicking at me like a wet towel, I felt an absurd desire to cry.

'I'm not even getting good reports about your maths. Apparently you spend your time on problems completely outside the curriculum. Whether they, too, are based on four-letter obscenities is a point on which I have no information.'

'But I can already do all the maths, Mrs Matlock. I could do it before I was twelve!'

'And that gives you licence to flaunt your indifference in front of pupils who actually have to knuckle down? Josephine, it seems to have escaped your attention that this is a *school*. To accommodate your precocious abilities and allow you to sit exams at unscheduled stages of your career requires considerable effort on our part. Yet your behaviour makes absolutely no concession to this.'

'Well, I'm sorry.'

'You will be. Because unless I hear better reports of your application in class, you will not be taking maths A level and Special papers in June. From this moment, consider yourself on probation.'

'That isn't fair!' It burst from me, the way a sneeze does.

Mrs Matlock took off her glasses and let them swing gently from her right hand.

'I'll tell you what isn't fair, Josephine. The hard, grinding work that most of your contemporaries are required to put in, in a conscientious struggle to lay a foundation for their adult lives, while watching you sneer at the system upon which they rely!'

It happened then. Tears seeped out.

'You will return to Fräulein Schneider's class. You will not sit with Francine Switt from now on, not in *any* lesson. I will be kept abreast of your progress. And don't entertain any doubts, Josephine – if you fail to buck your ideas up, you will not be sitting A levels this summer. You are now free to go.'

The expression 'buck your ideas up' sat oddly with the rest of Mrs Matlock's careful locution. Presumably it was de rigueur for teachers – fall down on your monthly quota for 'buck your ideas up' and you were expelled from the NUT. I walked out of her office, head held high, a matter of hydrostatics to stop the tears overflowing. And I carried on walking. I kept going until I'd covered the three miles to Brentwood and caught the bus home.

25

'Oh Jo, they'll really make a thing out of it now. It's hooky. Truant.'

'Let them. Sod them.'

'Yeah, but . . .'

'Forget it, Frankie. They can't stop me taking A level maths. I could pay privately and take the exams somewhere else.'

'Not this summer you couldn't, you're not registered with the exam board except at school.'

'Frankie, I said forget about it!'

She saw my face and shut up. Downstairs, Mrs Switt, newly returned from the States, was in the kitchen banging things about with Aunt Janet. I had known that she and Mrs Switt were sisters but not that they were twins. In fact, homozygous twins. I worked this out within a millisecond of Francine's front door being opened to me apparently by her mother gone ragged and vague, something like a blurred photograph of herself, in an outdated flower-power catsuit and shades. I could have done with the shades myself in order to face the catsuit. And she wasn't very communicative, at least not with me. This evening, motivated by a need to show I wasn't the supercilious creature described by Mrs Matlock, I'd expressed my sympathy for Aunt Janet in a tirade against the Nixon administration and the criminal pointlessness of the Vietnam war. Her responses were rather muted, so I supposed her at a loss for words.

All the clanking about in the kitchen was probably about jam. Since the death of her son, Aunt Janet had made jam. All the time. Now that they were on this side of the Atlantic, Mrs Switt would drive her to Brentwood, where she swept through Sainsbury's to empty the racks of fruit and mutter about stocking up against a world jam shortage.

But, happily, Aunt Janet's visit meant that the Switts' house move was delayed until the autumn – so the Vietnam war wasn't entirely bad after all.

'Hey, Jo,' said Francine. This was a form of address that I'd banned since 1966 when Jimi Hendrix released it. 'As it's not a bad evening, what say we go round to St Andrew's and check out the gravestones.'

'*What?*'

'Check up on the stuff Tarquin told you about those boys. If they did drown, they'll most likely be buried in St Andrew's.'

'Oh.'

'Leastways, if they are buried in St Andrew's we'll know for sure they're dead.'

'They are by now.'

'Not just disappeared, I mean.'

I didn't want to walk round to St Andrew's. I didn't want to do anything, or go anywhere, or stay here, or be with anyone, or be left on my own. But Francine was getting fed up with this and was now on her feet, so I ended up following her, though not with much grace; as we passed the Richardsons' house, I saw the glimmering doppelgängers of our reflections in their plate glass. I was lurching along behind Francine like a vampire's manservant.

It wasn't a bad evening, that much was true. The trees were in leaf, front gardens rich with spring flowers and the hopeful smell of grass. We walked the mile to St Andrew's, past the site of the lovely original vicarage that had been demolished and rebuilt in council-house style for Mr Horne. In through the gate of the church. Even I in my present despondency could recognize that it was extraordinarily pretty, the old church in stone and wood, its gravel path speckled with unplucked weeds but not rank with them as our own was. The bell-ringers were practising, their cheerful clamour remoulding the contours of the air. This had initially given me a fright.

'Are you sure we're allowed to be here?' I'd anxiously demanded of Francine.

'Of course we are. They're bell-ringers, not burglar alarms!'

It was an odd experience for me, reading headstones, I the daughter of humanists, staunch supporters of the crematorium approach, who considered that graves were an antisocial use of space. Dark anemones flopped daintily in display vases. Many of the stones were worn and mellowed – Isabella Maria Theresa Widgery was barely readable – while recent ones bore inscriptions that were really quite touching. *Loved by all who knew him*. And *Dearly beloved wife*. Then, on a gently lichened slab of marble, I came upon my favourite words in all the world:

> *But glad to have sat under*
> *Thunder and rain with you*
> *And grateful too*
> *For sunlight on the garden.*

My own Louis MacNeice! I'd found him in a book of Tarquin's when I was ten. That was spring, too; I could remember sitting under the arthritic old trees of our orchard, blossom tinkling down on me like confetti, trying to make a song of it the way Tarquin could. Strumming the white guitar with curved cutaways that I'd snaffled from his bedroom when he wasn't looking. I'd slipped away with it knowing that Tarquin never shouted at me (he shouted at everyone else), but if I got so much as a dirty finger mark on his pretty white guitar, he *cried*.

'Jo, get over here.' Francine was squatting on the grass. 'Come and read this.'

The grave she was examining was turfed over, an unmown but not unattractive contour. An inscription on polished marble:

Laurence Adam Briggs
14 September 1955 – 2 January 1963
Beloved son of Marjory and Peter
Now singing with the angelic choirs

'That was one of the names, wasn't it,' said Francine, 'that Tarquin told you?'

'Yes,' I agreed. 'The dates would fit, too. Our age, more or less, and he died that winter.'

It made me uncomfortable, a boy our age, who wasn't any longer. 'Let's look for the others.'

'I have – he's got Martin West living next door. Well, you know what I mean.'

This one was under an angel with a snotty expression:

Martin West
8 February 1956 – 2 January 1963
Beloved son of Yvonne and Gerald
Brother of Denise and Andrea
Suffer the little children to come unto me

'Can't find the third, he isn't here.'

'How can you be sure? I can't even read some of the stones.'

'All the newish ones you can. The crumbly green ones won't be 1963, will they?'

'True.'

'So Tarquin wasn't right. At least, not about these boys.'

'No.'

That was the trouble with having a brother who believed that our Ministry of Defence was secretly vivisecting schoolchildren. And that non-melodic sonic material was music.

'Come on, Frankie, let's split before the vicar turns up and recognizes me.'

'OK.'

We wandered homewards, a bit subdued. *14 September 1955 – 2 January 1963*. *8 February 1956 – 2 January 1963*. Francine was born on 25 November 1955, Timothy and I on 23 September. *They shall grow not old, as we that are left grow old*. I'd seen that on one of the gravestones. *Age shall not weary them, nor the years condemn*. Wild!

'Oh, Jo,' said Francine as we neared her house. 'Don't mention where we've been, will you? Not while we're round mine.'

'No.'

But I didn't understand why; Cousin Robert, never at the forefront of either of our minds, had been effaced from mine by the blameless graves of two boys who died less than a fortnight before we came to live at the Red House.

26

After that, I was kept in detention every night for a week and given silly punishment things to do. One of them was to 'copy out a page of a novel' so I borrowed Barbara's *Naked Lunch*. As a result I was kept in detention for another two nights. At the end of the last one I slogged home to find Angus with his head stuck up another chimney and the house full of firemen.

'But, Angela, why does he *want* his head up a chimney? Can't you buy him something you can undo yourself instead of calling out the fire brigade?'

'The little lamb hates anything round his head. He won't even wear the balaclava I knitted for him last winter.'

Well, that was a relief. At least I was spared Angus prowling round the place dressed as the Provisional IRA.

'If you're looking for something to do, Josephine . . .'

'I'm not.'

'. . . then you can brew the men a pot of tea.'

So I ended up in the kitchen trying to make small

talk with a huge uniformed fireman who was grumbling about being called here twice in a matter of weeks. Our portable TV was skulking in a corner of the kitchen and he was watching the early evening news. There had been a big fire somewhere and I could see envy written plain across his face. Just as the film crew were moving their cameras into the blaze, Elvis, who liked lying on the tops of TVs because they got hot, progressed into rapid-eye-movement sleep, so all his muscles went limp and his hairy tail flopped down across the screen.

'I was watching that!' grumbled the fireman.

'Come on, Elvis.' I nudged him slightly. One eye opened and he retracted the tail around his rear end.

'That's a habit of his,' I confided. 'He crept up there during the '66 World Cup Final. Nobody noticed until the nineteenth minute, when Bobby Moore passed the ball to Geoff Hurst. Swoosh! Down came the tail and we all missed it. My brothers kept throwing him off, but he just crept back up whenever they were too engrossed to notice. The tail came down a total of four times during the match – once for Martin Peters and a hat-trick for Hurst. By the end of extra time, my brother Geoffrey was weeping in complete hysteria.'

'I'd've had the bugger put down.'

'Bit harsh, don't you think? He'd just got engaged to Angela.'

'Sorry?'

'More tea?'

The fireman drained his mug and I made him another one.

'Quite a place you've got here,' he told me as I waited for the kettle.

'Yep.'

'Worth a few bob, I'd say.'

'Nope, can't sell it.'

'Really? Too big for the average family, I suppose.

And families are getting smaller all the time these days. I blame that birth control pill.'

Here we went.

'Then you also have to blame my father, I'm afraid, as he does a lot of prescribing. He's a gynaecologist.'

I had long ago learned that you can shut most men up with the word 'gynaecologist'. They make their excuses and disappear pretty sharpish. Not this one, it seemed.

'Gynaecologist, is he? He can help me then.'

'No,' I said with certainty.

'Well, not me exactly but my wife. You see . . .'

A terrible wail assaulted the air and I thought I heard the *plop!* of Angus's head emerging from the chimney.

'She had a baby five weeks ago,' continued the fireman with disconcerting timing. 'The thing is, they had to use the scissors on her, so afterwards she was stitched. There's a word for it.'

'Episiotomy,' I told him without enthusiasm.

'That's the word. Well, it's five weeks and she still can't. Meaning *I* can't. If you get my drift.'

'Unfortunately, my father . . .'

'And that can't be natural, can it? So I wondered, could you just ask . . .'

'Dad's not an obstetrician. It's a common mistake.'

'Yeah but it's his department. Fannies. Not to put too fine a point on it.'

'No, let's not put too fine a point on it,' I mumbled.

'Couldn't you just ask him?'

'He's not home, he's still . . .'

'Ring him, then? For his expert opinion. I'm climbing the walls. It was no-go for weeks before the baby even arrived. I'm going out of my mind.'

'Dad's in theatre,' I lied. 'He has a late list this afternoon. Look, is your wife worried?'

'Her? Well, it's her first time so she doesn't know

any better. Anyway *she* says she's got enough to think about with the new baby.'

'Then perhaps . . .'

'Can't hang on much longer, girl, your dad'll understand. Can't you—?'

'Truly, it's not a gynaecologist your wife needs. Has she discussed this with the district nurse?'

He swigged his mug of tea. 'District nurse!' he scoffed. 'Battleaxe. Told me to stop being selfish and give my wife some support. Well, I ask you! I reckon she's a dyke myself.'

Angus's wailing had been rising steadily in volume and pitch, a kind of Doppler effect. He now arrived in the kitchen, slumped in his mother's arms and sooted up like *The Black and White Minstrel Show*. Two harried-looking firemen tramped in behind. I left them all to it and went off to my cipher text.

I'd unpicked the message into four alphabets and counted up all the As, Bs, Cs et cetera in each. The most common letter in the first alphabet was M, in the second H, in the third also H and in the fourth K. So? Look, just suppose I was really lucky for once and each of them represented *e* in normal English. Then I only had to write the appropriate letters underneath *e* in the table and everything else would fall into place and I'd got all four alphabets! See Table 3.

Unfortunately, that meant Clarence's key word (under the letter a) was IDDG and his message translated into *lacpevpecheuboinlacpevpecheubigalacp* . . . Never mind, it was worth a try. Which is what I was doing in my bedroom when Angela tripped past, saying in a soupy salesman's tone, 'The bathroom is this way.'

I had known that the estate agent was sending some people round this evening and I'd intended to make myself scarce, but had been so focused on my deciphering that I'd forgotten.

a	b	c	d	e	f	g	h	i	j	k	l	m	n	o	p	q	r	s	t	u	v	w	x	y	z
I	J	K	L	**M**	N	O	P	Q	R	S	T	U	V	W	X	Y	Z	A	B	C	D	E	F	G	H
D	E	F	G	**H**	I	J	K	L	M	N	O	P	Q	R	S	T	U	V	W	X	Y	Z	A	B	C
D	E	F	G	**H**	I	J	K	L	M	N	O	P	Q	R	S	T	U	V	W	X	Y	Z	A	B	C
G	H	I	J	**K**	L	M	N	O	P	Q	R	S	T	U	V	W	X	Y	Z	A	B	C	D	E	F

Table 3. *A Vigenère code based on hard work with frequency analysis*

'Please excuse the unfinished paintwork,' I heard Angela say, presumably referring to the scrubbed Tuscan yellow gloss in the bathroom. Then **BANG!** The lights went out.

Thanks, Clarence. It was pitch without the lights – no street lamps closer than Brentwood. I kept candles in my room, not for emergencies but because candles were hip. As I started rummaging, the thought occurred to me that if Timothy needed proof that Tarquin wasn't responsible for our goings-on, then this was it – he might do many things, but sabotage the arterial supply to his Moog synthesizer, never. Then various people on the landing exclaimed, walked heavily into walls and finally, by the sound of it, fell down the stairs. Oh please, this was ridiculous! I fumbled for my door. Someone had apparently been leaning on it. He fell in on me.

'*Ooooff!*'

'Ouch! You're on my feet!'

'It's dark in here!'

'Then keep still until you get your bearings. Has somebody fallen down the stairs?'

A whimpering from the hall confirmed it.

'My wife!' said the bloke on my bedroom floor.

Someone was thudding around. Angela. She hovered towards us with a lighted candle.

'Nobody panic!' she advised, a bit bloody late in my opinion. 'It's just the electricity failing.'

'It didn't *fail*, Mrs Starkey,' corrected the voice on my carpet. In Angela's guttering light he resolved into a beanpole of a man, chinless and jerky. 'It blew up!'

'Surely not,' responded Angela, unconvincingly.

'Your main fuse has just exploded, Mrs Starkey,' he said stiffly, clambering to his feet. 'I had serious concerns about the wiring when my wife and I first entered these premises. Clearly my dubiety was fully justified.'

His language reminded me of someone. Several people – joke High Court judges and Mrs Matlock.

'Mabel?' he called down the stairs. 'Are you on your feet?'

'No, I'm jolly well not! You could come and give me a hand down here instead of standing about jawing. It's like a coal mine!'

'I'm just bringing the candle, Mrs Markham,' called the Lady with the Lamp.

'And the canary, Mrs Markham.'

'Josephine!'

The husband had now clawed his way out to the landing and stood sniffing the air.

'Dear God – that's fire, Mrs Starkey!'

'Just the candle, Mr Markham.'

'Nonsense! If this decrepit property is equipped with a telephone, I suggest you dial 999.'

'Just as soon as I have you and your lady wife on your feet.'

Another voice joined them. Timothy's. 'Look, you stupid bunch of tossers, the house is on fire!'

Above us was an angry glow. It flickered. Geoffrey's voice boomed from the kitchen.

'Have the lights gone off or something?'

'Listen, everyone, it isn't real,' I tried to explain above the shouting. 'It's just the poltergeist having some fun. As soon as this pair have gone, so will he.'

'The *poltergeist*?' sang Mr and Mrs Markham.

'Josie, for fuck's sake, there's a fire upstairs! Angela, GIVE ME THE SODDING CANDLE!'

I slammed back into my room and crossly rooted out my own sodding candle. The bedlam on our landing eventually retreated down the stairs. Then there was a tap at my door.

'Jo, what the fuck's going on? What's happened to the power?'

'Hold on a sec, Tarquin.' I finally got my candle lit. The flame-light illumined the great swirls of gloss paint across my walls, flamboyant as an arabesque. I must remember that effect and light candles more often.

'It's just your poltergeist,' I said again. 'I still haven't cracked his code, you see.'

'But he's never pulled a trick like this before – it's turned my Moog off!'

'He's got more adventurous since we put the house on the market, Tarquin. There was one couple . . .'

'Jo, I can see all this flickering light.'

'Yes, you would. Clarence has set the house on fire.'

'Sorry?'

'Look, it's only for *show*.'

Timothy came storming back up. 'Tarquin, she's insane, get her out of here!'

'But what about my studio?'

'Oh, what a fuss!' I slammed the door behind me and just made it down the stairs and out through the hall as the fire brigade returned, led by the man with the stitched wife.

* * *

213

'Ladies and gents – the culprit!'

He stood in the middle of the kitchen, helmet in one hand, squirrel in the other, black-charred and sodden.

'Hibernated up there, I expect. Come the spring he wakes up and gets chewing. Next thing you know, he's eaten through the cables and bingo! We've seen it all before.'

Wet flakes of scorched squirrel dribbled steadily from his hand onto the quarry tiles. He waved the corpse in his enthusiasm and the tail fell off.

'Welvis!' gurgled Angus happily.

The Red House had not burned to the ground; the firemen had ushered us all onto the drive, asked some fast, pertinent questions and promptly put the blaze out. It was the only time I'd ever seen Timothy impressed. The only trouble they'd had was with Tarquin, who they'd eventually prised out of his studio, lumbering under several priceless guitars plus a purring, uncooked cat, who'd apparently moved from our TV and gone to sleep on the Moog. This was a vision of my brother's studio I had never previously entertained: Elvis's tail flopping over the patch-leads, cat hair floating into the low-pass filter and clogging up the oscillators. Perhaps Tarquin thought it added something.

The saving of the Red House was not without its price, of course; water had poured through from the loft into our parents' room on the third storey. While my fireman friend was giving his lecture about char-grilled squirrels, two of his colleagues dragged the waterlogged mattress down the staircase to lay it in the garden. My parents' bed. We all trooped up to the top floor to do a recce; paper bulged from the walls and the carpet swam in a foul-smelling lake. With all the fuss we didn't hear my father's car. He, of course, had been greeted by the sight of a fire engine and a sodden mattress. As he slammed in through the front door, I heard my fireman friend say, 'The doctor?'

214

Angela looked surprised. 'How did you . . . ?'

Dad's baritone roared through the dark house. *'WHAT IN GOD'S NAME IS GOING ON?'*

I heard heavy boots crossing the flagstones of the hall.

'Good evening, sir. I understand you're a gynae-cologist.'

I've no idea how they all coped. I moved in with Francine.

27

'Jo! We'll be glad to have you!' said Mr Switt. 'How about the rest of your family? There's two spare bed-rooms, someone can have my den, and . . .'

'Jerry!' interrupted his wife. 'Now, Jo, it can only be for a short while. We're expecting Francine's cousin Patricia . . .'

'Robert's sister,' added Aunt Janet and excused her-self from the room.

'She's coming over for a visit.'

'Oh M-o-o-o-m, that isn't until July!'

'They may let her out of school early, Francine.'

'Honey, I'm sure all the girls will be happy sharing a couple of rooms,' promised Mr Switt, a man unfazed by the idea of having six females in residence in his home, one of them Angela.

'The rest of my family's fine, thank you, Mr Switt. They like our house the way it is; in fact, they prefer it.'

There was a comforting orderliness about the Switts' place, despite Aunt Janet floating around looking smudged and bleary, and trailing her Haight-Ashbury clothes in the cooking. Outside school hours, Francine and I did nothing much but watch their colour TV. One Saturday afternoon when her mom had taken Francine to another modelling job, Mr Switt and I spent a happy couple of hours watching the showjumping and spooning pineapple jam out of a jar with the curtains drawn tight to prevent the streaming May sunshine from bleaching out the TV screen.

I questioned Francine about this cousin, but she was dismissive.

'Patti's just a goof. A baby.'

'I thought she was sixteen.'

'Yeah, but you'd never know it – braces on her teeth, bangs, braids and bows. We'll just sit her in front of *Jackanory* and get on with our lives.'

In the meantime, trying to get on with my own life meant chipping away at the rock face of Clarence's message.

I was convinced there were four alphabets, so I fiddled. Just before our fire, I'd proved that the commonest letter in each alphabet couldn't represent *e* in all four cases. But perhaps one or two of them might, while the others could be *t*, *a* or *o*. Then I got a bit of a shock. If I drew up one table for every possibility and tried each of them for a couple of minutes, it would take me 5,040 hours of work. After throwing a major panic, I calmed myself down and tried to be intelligent again.

We knew that the most frequent letter of the fourth alphabet was K; well, it couldn't represent *o*; this was because I knew what the other most common letters were in that alphabet, and if K meant *o*, then a quickly scribbled table showed that its second most common letter, V, must translate as *z*. A real English *z*. I could believe many things of Clarence, but not that he'd completely zedded me up. Exactly the same applied to the third alphabet, where if its most frequent letter represented *o* then its second most frequent would translate as *z*. Similar reasoning eliminated a lot of other possibilities in all four alphabets.

It still wasn't quick. It took all of double physics, double maths and most of the night, so by the time I stumbled on the right answer, by the time I deciphered Clarence's message, I was punch drunk and nearly missed it. See Table 4.

	a	b	c	d	e	f	g	h	i	j	k	l	m	n	o	p	q	r	s	t	u	v	w	x	y	z
E	F	G	H	I	J	K	L	M	N	O	P	Q	R	S	T	U	V	W	X	Y	Z	A	B	C	D
D	E	F	G	H	I	J	K	L	M	N	O	P	Q	R	S	T	U	V	W	X	Y	Z	A	B	C
O	P	Q	R	S	T	U	V	W	X	Y	Z	A	B	C	D	E	F	G	H	I	J	K	L	M	N
C	D	E	F	G	H	I	J	K	L	M	N	O	P	Q	R	S	T	U	V	W	X	Y	Z	A	B

Table 4. *Clarence's Vigenère cipher*

The key word – EDOC – doesn't look promising until you notice that it's CODE backwards. And the text doesn't look very promising either: *partiveightyfourpartiveightyfivepart* . . . Double Dutch yet again, until you break it into words: *part iv eighty-four part iv eighty-five* . . . Which isn't very lucid, but it is English. I was so drained, I was nearly past caring; it was three o'clock in the morning and I'd never before realized that Frankie snored. But I made my dogged way through the enciphered message.

part iv eighty four part iv eighty five part iii three hundred and seventeen nineteen part iii three hundred and twenty two part iii five hundred and sixty two part ii ii one hundred and forty part iii one thousand one hundred and forty three part iii seventeen part iii two hundred and eighty eighty seven part iii two thousand nine hundred and sixty six part i vii one thousand eight hundred and thirty nine part iii iii three four.

Bloody hell, I'd done it! I hadn't the faintest idea what it meant but I'd deciphered Clarence's message into English. I crept down to Mrs Switt's kitchen. Jars of jam formed a pyramid on their pine table. I made myself a cup of tea, put my head on an unjammed corner of the table and cried for the rest of the night until Mr Switt discovered me there in the morning, after which I cried in his arms for another hour and made him desperately late for a meeting about the replacement for the Ford Cortina.

All the adult Switts diagnosed a case of overwork in preparation for my summer exams, even Aunt Janet adding her ten cents' worth from between a pineapple and three pounds of strawberries. I did nothing to dispel this sympathetic notion, though since Mrs Matlock's ultimatum I'd done not a stroke of work, spending my school hours in a swamp of misery and resentment, dreaming of selling up and moving out. And I no longer even had Francine to sit with. *But* I had now cleared the first hurdle of the obstacle course that led away from this hell – I had deciphered Clarence's text.

part iv eighty-four part iv eighty-five part iii three hundred and seventeen . . .

I could guess basically what this was about from those volumes I'd borrowed briefly from Timothy. A book cipher. First, choose a book and tell your friends. Then encode your messages to them letter by letter, by finding a word that starts with the one you need, and then doing a lot of counting. If I was right, Clarence's missive must mean: go to Part IV then count up to word number 84. Note down the letter it starts with. Then move on to the word next door (Part IV, word 85). And so on. Slow but sure. I reckoned there were twelve letters indicated in there. Well, that was enough to spell out a name, wasn't it? But not enough to name both a murderer and a victim. And more to the immediate point,

what was the book?

All those part threes and part fours suggested Shakespeare, so I spent every lesson with *Henrys IV* and *V* open across my knees, counting words. They were mystified teachers who put me into detention this time, for the surreptitious reading of Shakespearean histories under my desk. It was a baffled Mrs Matlock who scoured my word lists expecting a welter of filth, to find *perus'd* and *Plantagenet* and *liege* and *screech-owls*. But it didn't get me any further than it got Mrs Matlock. No murderer's name was spelled out by the initial letters, even though the text struck me as being appropriate to the task – Shakespeare seemed to stuff his plays to the teeth with aristocrats doing one another in. But the letters just spelled out tosh like *wnthpbiskqqc* and *dhppbjazwipc* and *thoiitgpokdb*.

It was late May when Mrs Matlock called me to her office.

'Well, Josephine.'

There was a buff folder on her desk. Across the top

was written *Josephine Starkey* in felt-tip pen. This shook me a bit.

'I understand from your teachers that you have handed in not a single assignment of homework for the last month. You appear to be conducting a campaign of dumb insolence against this school. It can therefore come as no surprise that this school will no longer make special efforts on your behalf. I have cancelled your registration with London University for A and Special level maths. I shall be writing to your parents. You may go.'

So I went. Unfortunately, this meant that I'd have to move back home; even *my* parents couldn't fail to respond to so grievous a dereliction. I'd need to intercept the letter and get Timothy to forge their signature on the acknowledgement slip, though I hardly relished Timothy's response either. And so I swapped the Switts' mod. cons for the builders' yard and campsite that the Red House had become. On Thursday of my first week back, I trudged home in a heatwave after another detention and a bus strike, to find Florian waiting for me in the kitchen.

28

I'd come from *school*. I was in *uniform*. I stumbled in through the front door in a bashed boater and gingham dress, not merely without false eyelashes but with all my mascara rubbed off. Even my legs – my only other decent feature – looked scrubby; on release from detention I'd peeled off my sticky tights and binned them, to hell with not having shaved since Tuesday.

Angela was smiling at Florian. 'Fancy you knowing something like that!' she was saying. 'Sebastian . . . ?'

'Sebasti*ano* Serlio,' he corrected. Then they both saw me.

'Josephine!' cried Angela. 'We were about to send out a search party, weren't we, Florian? Francine must have phoned for you five times.'

He rose from his kitchen stool and waved Joni Mitchell's *Clouds* at me as though it were a membership card guaranteeing admittance.

'I bought a copy for you,' he said, smiling. 'Thought you'd like to hear "Tin Angel" unmangled.'

'You could have given it to me at Stavering,' I said

without grace, dumping my school bag, which was close enough to a satchel to be a humiliation all on its own, onto the breakfast bar. 'Are you by yourself?'

I wouldn't have put it past him to have brought Carly, plus his father to check out our Robert Adam, followed by his mum with her sketchbook.

'Josephine!' objected Angela. 'I hope you're not going to have a lovers' tiff. Poor Florian's been waiting hours.'

The words *lovers' tiff* were too much for me; I strode across the kitchen, turned on the portable TV and plonked myself ostentatiously in front of it. Of course, the set was old and took time to warm up, so my gesture looked ridiculous. When the sound finally boomed at us I was gratified that it was livid with gunfire and military helicopters.

'Oy, madam! *Off!*' shouted Angela with a protective glance at Angus. Oh God, he was on his potty again, bare-bummed and everything, and in the kitchen! On the TV screen, a Vietcong village was being napalmed; blackened figures ran screaming from huts in the foliage. Right up Angus's street, in my opinion, but Angela yelled, '*Off!*' again.

'There's a child in here, Josephine, *if* you don't mind!'

She surged across the kitchen and threw herself over the TV set like a hero on a grenade, then tugged the plug out of the wall. The picture vanished into a hole in the middle of the screen.

'One day, madam, when you and Florian have children of your own, I hope you remember this as a lesson!'

'Look,' Florian intervened, 'Jo, why don't we leave your sister to her kitchen . . .'

'Sister-in-law!'

'. . . and take ourselves off to her conservatory?'

'*Thank* you, Florian,' agreed Angela without correcting

223

his possessive articles. 'Anyway, the baby will need feeding any minute and if it has to be a bottle again I'll leak all night.'

'Right,' said Florian hurriedly.

I found myself following his leggy strides out of the kitchen, across the hall and through the wintry living room to the conservatory.

'Don't forget to phone Francine!' Angela called after me.

From the direction of Tarquin's studio I recognized his prized 1930s recording of Robert Johnson's 'Cross Road Blues'. This was absolutely weird – Tarquin hadn't played any blues since the last time Florian was here.

'Look, this really isn't convenient,' I said.

Florian was standing at the window, staring out through the stained glass at a concrete mixer and a slice of cast iron that had mysteriously toppled off the workmen's umbrella roof.

'Oh.' He looked crestfallen. Well, tough!

'I have exams coming up – mock A levels,' I added hastily, remembering I was seventeen.

'Are you in the sixth form, then? I didn't think yours wore uniform.'

Ours didn't. Pity he knew that. There was no reply I could make.

'OK, I'll go. It's just that I was at a bit of a loose end.'

'Why?' I asked bluntly. 'What's happened to Carly?'

'Gone.'

I hadn't expected that. 'Gone where?'

'Tonight she's rejoining her sister in High Wycombe. But tomorrow . . . tomorrow they're both flying home.'

'Oh.'

'Yes,' he said, 'she . . . she left at four o'clock. I took her to the station. I put her on the train.'

The twelve-bar blues that drifted down the stairs painted Florian's words into a lyric. *I took her to the station / I put her on the train.* They conjured American trains with that haunting hooey whistle, and the evocative words of the West: *railroad* and *lonesome* and *blue.*

'But she'll be back, won't she?' I suggested, without thinking it through. 'To see you?'

'No. Carly's starting at UCLA in the fall, majoring in Business Studies. If I want to see her again I have to make plans to get to California.'

A direct quote if ever I heard one.

'Right.'

I sat down on a window ledge. Florian had sunk into our wicker sofa, a truncated curved couch of exploded Lloyd Loom. His long fingers tapped a dejected sort of rhythm. His eyes were pink-rimmed, I realized with an unwanted pang. I was looking at a man who had been crying.

'I'm feeling pretty lost, to tell you the truth,' he said.

Above us, Robert Johnson's raw guitar squealed and whinnied through the house, following his vocal lines like somebody answering back. Then somebody did answer back. Cream. Timothy must have come in; he'd put their version on his stereo system and was belting it out as competition. Bass-heavy and driving like a train, it boomed through the rafters.

'Ah,' said Florian. 'A late start but at the rate they're going they'll catch him up in no time.'

Robert Johnson crackled to an end, so Tarquin put it on again. And turned up the volume. Timothy, with warmongering zeal, turned up Cream. This really was all I needed.

'Look, Florian,' I said more gently, 'I don't mean to be rude, but I'd much rather you . . .'

But Florian hadn't heard me above my brothers' racket. He raised his own voice.

'Hey, I wish my house was surrounded by fields. If I tried this, the police would be round!'

And what made him think they wouldn't be round here? His voice was rough. It reminded me of Francine when she'd been weeping. Over Florian.

'Wonder who'll win,' he said.

Well, Cream's heavy electrical interpretation should have won hands down but it wouldn't; Tarquin was feeding his through a Marshall amp. I heard Timothy move his own speakers onto the landing.

I felt like bashing their puerile heads together. Why did this have to happen when Florian was here? The entire house thrummed like a washing machine on a spin cycle. As Cream's bass came helter-skeltering through the ceiling, our chandelier convulsed like a patient on ECT and then, apparently reaching its natural resonance frequency, started screaming like a brass band impaled on railings. A change in air texture suggested that Angela was charging up the staircase and shrieking. My brothers weren't having any of that. Tarquin turned up Robert Johnson. Timothy turned up Cream.

With deeply grudged admiration I decided Cream acquitted themselves rather well at ear-splitting volume – but of course I wasn't Tarquin, who would have to get in a comment about . . .

'White man's blues,' commented Florian. 'Genius musicians but they've ironed out the microtonal richness and rhythmic complexities.'

Oh God, it was Tarquin verbatim. In the broken sofa, Florian was sprawled. The long legs lay unconcernedly apart. I remembered him straddling a chair at the Castle. You didn't have to wonder what Francine saw in him, I'd thought then and suppressed it.

'Aren't you just so grateful?' Florian asked softly.

To hear, I had to lean over him. He smelled of suede and shampoo and maleness.

'Robert Johnson,' he said. 'Sold his soul to the devil at the crossroads, in exchange for the blues.'

The hollow beneath Florian's Adam's apple fluttered as he spoke, vulnerable as a fontanelle. His face wore a flush and a rumour of stubble – as if, I thought, my stomach tingling like electrical static, he were just waking up in bed. The shining red-brown hair that Tarquin had said would look mean on a pillow was now fanned back against our bracken-coloured wicker.

'Aren't we all just so grateful?' Florian closed his eyes and my heart thumped like Ginger Baker's drum kit. He had taken her to the station and put her on the train – and then, red-eyed and broken, Florian had made his way to Lossing to see *me*. I sank abruptly onto the window ledge. Onto Elvis, who stalked off, incensed.

'Blues is so erotic,' Florian was saying dreamily. 'It's the sound of a man's soul when there's a woman he wants so bad he *aches*. So bad he's ready to *beg*.'

He reopened his eyes and slowly smiled. I couldn't. My mouth was dry.

'You do look naughty in that uniform,' he said. He wasn't shouting now. He didn't need to. I could hear him through the warring output of two hi-fi systems and my own ringing ears. I would have heard him through a nuclear attack on our radio tower.

'All dishevelled, like a schoolgirl up to no good.'

There wasn't a word or a thought in my head – for the first time in all my life the running commentary of my brain had shut up. In the unwonted cortical still-ness, Florian reached out a hand for me. 'Come here, naughty schoolgirl.'

I slid onto him with the ease of the inevitable and he was on top of me, his long legs overspilling our silly, abridged, vibrating sofa. Florian kissed me, slow and deep. My brothers' insane decibels throbbed and swelled in an ineluctable blue tide and his hands were inside my dress, stroking me – inside my bra, inside my pants.

'You are *so* wet!' he whispered, laughing.

On and on and on – controlled and deliberate, the exercise of a guitarist's practised fingers. Disjointed concepts flared in my mind like shooting stars: to want someone so bad you could beg. Gagging for it. The plots of novels, the lyrics of torch songs, the sound of singers weeping into a mike. So it was all true, then – it sucked the power from you, flooded your brain. Eventually, something happened to me that bleached out even these thoughts, a long, creamy, tickly sensation that made my limbs shudder, something partly pleasant and partly not, totally outside my control. So it was all true, then. He laughed softly into my hair.

'Naughty schoolgirl,' he said again. 'Very bad girl.'

Some sense of time and place began to trickle back, and with it the realization that throughout Florian's attention to me I had done nothing but lie there. This thought jolted me with embarrassment and fear. He would think I was inexperienced! I murmured a frantic apology and moved my own hand down his beautiful chest, over the buckle of his belt to the front of his jeans. I'd never been in this situation with a man, but I expected something else when my fingers found him, something other than the stiffness of zipper and denim. Florian gently displaced my questing fingers and rolled over. He was no longer on top of me.

'Sweet,' he said and shuffled again until we were both upright. My own fingers had not been welcome.

I couldn't understand what had gone wrong. I grappled unhappily with the gingham skirt that was stuffed into an ungainly ruck under my bottom. I could now see my school regulation knickers sitting round my ankles in a puffball of navy blue, while Florian smiled down at them.

'Sweet,' he said again, watching me with that

indulgent smile while I wriggled. Around us, the house continued to shake. I cast about for something to say about Tarquin, anything to divert Florian's attention from my silly, clumsy fumblings and these childish clothes, to stop him noticing that my legs were shadowed with ugly stubble. I was close to tears.

I shouted above the din. 'Speaking of blues.'

A puzzled inflexion dented Florian's smile.

'We lived next to Ealing Broadway before we came here.'

'Yeah?'

'So Tarquin used to blag his way into the blues club. Nineteen sixty-two.'

'Nineteen sixty-two?' Florian repeated vaguely. 'Good year.'

Nineteen sixty-three was even better – the Rolling Stones were playing regular gigs there by April. Pity we moved in January.

'Tarquin wasn't a recluse in those days,' I added, rattled into indiscretion, but Florian just smiled vaguely at the garden. I tried a different line.

'And he's got a guitar like Eric Clapton's, a Gibson Les Paul. Plus a 1959 Flying V.'

Yep, that did it. Florian's patronizing smile was stamped out like one of Angus's snails.

'Your brother has a 1959 Flying V?'

'Certainly has. And a Les Paul, like I said.'

'So you did. What a wonderful conversationalist you are!' Florian was actually looking at me with admiration. I ran a hand through my hair and shook it across my shoulders. In the aquarium reflections of the conservatory glass, it looked rather sexy. Even my nose didn't look out of place for once, didn't look quite so much as though I'd evolved from an anteater.

'*And*,' I added, carefully offhand, 'also in factory condition, a 1956 Fender Stratocaster. Looks like it's never been—'

Florian was on his feet. 'No,' he said.

'Yes, he has, it's upstairs.'

'Nineteen *sixty*-six, perhaps . . .'

'I do not mean 1966!' I said crossly. I had three brothers, for heaven's sake, I was mechanically *and* musically literate. I wasn't Francine, who wouldn't know which of the Beatles was the bass player, and who once, when asked what car her father drove, Vice-President of the Ford Motor Company, said, 'A white one.'

'A '56 Stratocaster,' repeated Florian, unconsciously sketching the guitar in the air. All men can do this: there are two outlines they can all draw – impossibly breasted women and a Fender Strat. Florian's was a sort of Marilyn Monroe torso with horns on.

'He was buying them before they started being collectible,' I explained.

'I see.' Florian moved distractedly to the window, gave the cement mixer another stare and then turned back to me. 'Is it early 1956 or late?'

I looked suspiciously at him.

'You see, Fender changed the wood . . .'

'I'm sorry,' I said coldly, 'but I don't actually celebrate its birthday.'

'Well, what sort of grain has it got?'

Grain. My mood was deflating like a slashed tyre.

'A white one,' I said dismally and wriggled my feet back into the loathed school shoes. But Florian was reacting as though someone had thrown a firecracker through the window.

'White one! I'm in the same house as a factory-condition white-blond 1956 Fender Strat? Well, fuck me! Bloody hell. Jesus Christ. *Je*-sus Christ!'

This was clearly going to go on for some time. I stood up. Straightened the sun-bleached cushions on the sofa. Stroked Elvis, who had returned to the window ledge. Beyond the coloured glass a beautiful summer evening sparkled across the bricks and sand and bags of cement, a world away from the musical warfare going on upstairs. Beyond it all was the orchard in which I'd spent one afternoon, at the age of ten, strumming the '56 Fender Strat that I'd swiped from Tarquin's bedroom. I now realized I must have been sitting on ground the police dug up looking for Letitia.

Above us surged delta blues in one further deafening crescendo and then stopped. At the same moment, Cream's track finished. And didn't restart, so presumably Timothy interpreted Tarquin's silence as victory. Through our tinnitus we heard the studio door open. I didn't even see Florian take action: he was out of the conservatory, through the dining room, along the hall and up the staircase before I could do anything.

'*No, Florian!*'

As I reached the hall I heard his footfall clatter to an uncoordinated halt above me.

'You've got,' I heard him pant, 'a 1956 white-blond Strat.'

There was no response. I pictured Tarquin, solid and unhappy in the doorway. Trapped.

'Bakelite knobs and pick-up covers, not vinyl,' said Florian at him. Tarquin's hands would be clenching, his shoulders squaring, his chin up.

'Nitro-cellulose lacquer.'

'Yeah,' said my brother's voice. 'Well, they didn't change until CBS took over.'

'True. Ever try patching it through the Moog?'

'Now you mention it, yeah, but it's hard to control, needs some kind of pitch-to-voltage controller . . .'

I was halfway to the landing now, in time to watch the man who had just made a kind of love to me disappear into the studio I hadn't set foot inside since 1969.

* * *

Rejection, jealousy, they hit me like a wave, like some-one drowning, like someone tied into a sack and sunk. I stood on the staircase paralysed. Of course Florian and Tarquin belonged together, even I could see that; it was ridiculous to take Florian's sudden abandon-ment of me as a sexual slight. So how come my every brain cell screamed that it *was*, it *was*. I felt as though my viscera were flooded with black toxic waste. As I stood there fighting for the light, something even more bitter burst upon my thoughts – a realization that should have come earlier, that should have been clear even while I writhed beneath Florian's rhythmically stroking hand. There had been no reciprocal response from his own body because Florian had spent all day long in bed with Anna-Carlotta Campiani. All day long, right up until four o'clock, when, red-eyed with grief, he'd taken her to the station, put her on the train and driven over to Lossing to derive some comfort from the proximity of Tarquin Starkey's Moog synthesizer.

I sank onto the stairs. I heard hammering at the front door and out from the kitchen bustled Angela, whose presence I hadn't given a thought to since Florian drew me over to him on the sofa. She crossed the hall, muttering irately and wiping her hands on her pinny. She opened the door to Francine, who fell into the house.

'Jo!' called out Francine. 'Oh Jo, my cousin's here and she's driving me insane. I've been trying to get hold of you for hours!'

'And good evening to you too!' snapped Angela and stamped back to the kitchen, letting the front door slam.

I moved slowly, dreamlike, down the stairs.

'Oh Jo, it's absolute hell. I just cannot tell you.'

'Patti? The goof?'

Through the bay window, I could see a figure moving up our drive. I crossed to the door.

'*Don't!*' demanded Francine in panic. 'Don't open up!' but I already had.

Someone was sashaying up the drive, someone tall and shapely in tiny shorts, her skin suntanned to the colour of demerara. As the door opened she looked up. Mirrored sunglasses flashed insolently at me.

'Shi-i-it,' she said wonderingly as I stood inside the Georgian door casing, all white skin and gangling gingham. 'Talk about a falling-down dump! I mean, is this place haunted or what?'

29

Complete nightmare. Behind my left shoulder, Francine's agitation crackled in the air.

'Just shut her out, Jo.'

'I can't do that.'

Francine herself made a grab for the door to throw it closed while her cousin watched with gum-chewing scorn. No, not scorn, more like the half-interested glassy stare of someone bored at the zoo. As the old door swung achingly to a close, Geoffrey materialized in the hall beside us.

'Excuse me, ladies,' he said brightly through the echo of the slam, and dragged it open again. Which brought him face to face with Patti on the step.

'Ah!' he said and shuffled off down the drive towards the car.

Geoffrey was a man who always seemed to be on bad terms with the clothes he was wearing; his shirt, which he periodically stuffed back into his trousers in handfuls, was hanging out both sides like panniers on a donkey. He hauled at his belt as he walked. Patti watched him from behind her shuttered face with its insolent mirrors. She watched as Geoffrey tripped over his own feet and then, flailing to regain his equilibrium, boffed himself in the eye.

I suddenly realized that Francine was disappearing off in the direction of the conservatory. God, what would she find? Panicky images flickered through my imagination, of the sofa cushions eloquently indented with our body shapes, clearly mine and Florian's, like something from a Tom and Jerry cartoon. I imagined telltale scents in the air and 'Arthur McBride' percolating from Tarquin's studio on the Moog. I took off after her, abandoning both the front door and Patti, who therefore walked into the house.

'Frankie, don't go that way . . .'

But she was already in the conservatory, slumped on the very sofa. Elvis looked up as I came hurtling in. The silent witness. Well, Elvis wouldn't tell her, but it suddenly struck me to wonder where Angus had been at the time, because *he* certainly would.

'You didn't shut the front door,' pointed out Francine in a defeated voice.

I heard Patti's languorous progress through the house, sniffing at the damp air with its hovering dust. The front door slammed once more. Geoffrey coming back in. Then, just seconds later, he must have changed his mind and gone out again. His wife shouted at him from the kitchen.

'Where are you off to *now*? The tea's been on the table ten minutes with your cos going limp!'

Patti's lazy strides had brought her to the threshold of the conservatory. 'Hi,' she said to me. 'I'm Patti.'

'Yes,' I said.

'From Fort Lauderdale, Florida. And you are?'

'Jo.'

'Jo. Do you, you know, *live* here?'

'Only at present.' I hesitated. 'We're in the process of moving to London.'

'The process?'

This echolalia was terrible. 'I mean we're selling up.'

'You got a buyer?'

'Not yet, but . . .'

'Sure.'

I looked at her, that careless chewing, the complete and unanswerable contempt, so unlike the brand of insult for which I'd been trained at school all these years, the wordy quips of schoolboys: 'Nobody would climb over her tits to get at yours'; 'You're a two-paper-bag job – he'd need a bag over his head in case the bag over your head broke'; 'She's had more pricks in her than a pincushion'. The English way.

'When did you arrive?' I asked.

'Today.'

'So you spent last night on a plane! You must be really tired,' I suggested hopefully.

'I'm not tired. I told the air hostess my brother died in Vietnam and I was flying over to comfort my mom. She got the people round me to move seats so I had the row to myself. I slept eight hours. I mean, it happened. May as well use it or Robert got killed for nothing.'

Francine hadn't once looked round since her cousin entered the room. Her gaze was fixed on the window panes, staring through the medieval storyline of our stained glass to the sand heap and the cement mixer. As Florian had done.

'D'you want a coffee?' I asked Patti by a kind of reflex. I didn't want to make her coffee. I didn't even want to make Francine coffee.

'Ice tea?' she suggested instead. 'Or I drink juice. What do you have?'

'Orange?'

'Yeah, why not?'

Francine said without turning, 'Jo, it's a set-up: you bring her an orange squash and she starts screaming about Florida oranges and what sort of crap is this?'

'Lighten up, will you?' snapped her cousin. 'I *know* what you people drink, I had this before, OK?'

Music had been growing in the air for some minutes, but nothing that could identify Florian. I didn't know whether he might make a sudden appearance. I didn't know whether he'd leave Tarquin's studio for hours yet. I didn't know whether he would ever leave Tarquin's studio again.

'Look, Jo, I'm splitting.'

'Where to?' Francine had only just got here.

'Who *gives* a fuck?'

Patti's American influence, that Rhett Butler stress on 'gives'. I trailed after Francine, back down the passage to the hall, still in school uniform, a ridiculous figure, creased and damp, my legs unshaven. Where were we going? Nowhere, was the answer. As we slunk past the kitchen, Angela hollered, 'Oy, Josephine! Is Florian still in there with you or has he gone home?'

'It was nothing to do with me,' I said eventually and cleared my throat. 'He came for Tarquin. He's upstairs.'

'*Upstairs?*' repeated Angela, as though I'd suggested Florian was in her bed.

Francine just looked at me.

So did Patti. 'Florian,' she repeated flatly. 'Tarquin. What a place.'

'Well, is he staying for tea or what?' demanded Angela and then presumably clocked the fact that the three of us were half out of the door. 'And where are *you* going when your meal's ready?'

'He came for Tarquin,' I told Francine again, 'and managed to get into the studio.'

'Then we're staying,' she replied dully.

'We're staying,' I told Angela just as dully, and we trailed back to the conservatory in a blizzard of threats about wilting lettuce.

Florian did not emerge. Francine gave up around ten o'clock, Patti having already drifted away a couple of hours earlier in a cloud of unutterable boredom. I packed it in around one in the morning and went to bed where I lay sleepless and frozen with misery. I heard my mother come home and plod heavily up the stairs, followed later by my father. The old house sighed through its fire-broken windows. At breakfast I announced to Angela, who was sizzling cholesterol in a frying pan for Geoffrey, that I had been up all night with food poisoning and couldn't go to school, never mind whether she took that as an aspersion on her cooking. I promptly went back to my room where I stayed all day. But still there was no sign of life from Tarquin's studio.

30

On Saturday the temperature hit the nineties, which I noted from *The Times* was ten degrees hotter than anywhere in Patti's Florida. Workmen who had appeared only sporadically for most of the working week now piled into our house and garden to hammer, churn and saw through everybody's weekend. Tarquin emerged once in gargantuan flowered pants to scream incoherently into their faces, but retired again before I could collar him. No sign of Florian. Angus was apparently feeling the heat; bloody-eyed with hay fever, his skin deckled with hives and whitewashed by his mother's lotions, the child looked like something to frighten Clarence with.

'This place is a madhouse!' shouted Timothy and slammed out. Apparently his school had some kind of textbook sale today. Before departing he locked his bedroom door against all intruders, among whom he still numbered his sister.

When I could no longer bear the uproar, I wandered over to Francine's. It was lunchtime. There was a tiny

chance that everybody would be out except Mr Swit,
and we could shut ourselves in with some junk food
and the TV. No such luck. Indoors there was only Aunt
Janet and a bubbling vat into which sweat dribbled
liberally from her forehead, while outside were
Francine and Patti, sunbathing in bikinis. They
were obviously on better terms than when I last saw
them together, though maybe at a price – Francine
looked distinctly frazzled. A packet of American
cigarettes lay on the grass, testament to the unlikeli-
hood of Mr and Mrs Swit appearing. And to the
mental disarray of Patti's mother, of course.

Francine looked up from a copy of *Petticoat*. 'Hi,
Jo.'

Patti, by way of greeting, raised her eyebrows at me.
Her substantial bikini top was decorated with white
daisies. Her limbs glowed and she smelled of
Coppertone. By contrast, Francine's alabaster skin
wore the gentle blush of impending disaster. She was
not merely frazzled, she was griddled.

'I think you're starting to burn,' I suggested. 'This
sun's pretty strong.'

'Of course I'm not starting to burn,' Francine replied
irritably. 'I've only been out here a couple of hours.'

Patti's silence smiled its disparagement from behind
her mirrored shades.

A couple of hours. 'But, Frankie, you're supposed to
take it a very little at a time,' I said. 'Fair skin like
yours doesn't synthesize melanin at the same rate as
mine or Patti's.'

'Shi-i-i-t!' commented Patti. ' "Synthesize melanin"!
Who the hell talks like that?'

Her tobacco smoke wafted across my face. It smelled
really good.

'I know what I'm doing, Jo! I'll take it one day on,
one day off.'

'As soon as Mom moves out the kitchen, we're

gonna get the aluminum foil. You know – for reflecting the sun. Want to join us?'

'It's just to speed things up,' explained Francine.

I stared at them both. 'You don't mean you're intensifying the UV radiation? Frankie, you'll burn to a crisp! You'll develop malignant melanoma!'

'Oh Je-*sus*!' exploded Patti. 'Are you talking about sun cancers? Because you don't know *shit* about sun cancers! My friend Donna's father just died from one and he was *fif*ty and it took him all his life in the sun in *Flor*ida to get one! Frankie is not going to die from a sun cancer from one lousy day in a bikini in *Eng*land!'

'Yes but . . .'

'Mellow noma,' she repeated scornfully. 'What are you – a doctor?'

'I'm sorry my vocabulary offends you,' I snapped, 'but I've grown up with it. My father's a gynaecologist, my mother's a casualty specialist – and my oldest brother's training as a brain surgeon,' I added for effect, remembering too late that Patti had already encountered the brain surgeon, and the idea of our Geoffrey in charge of somebody's head and a scalpel tended to scare the hell out of people. But apparently she hadn't made the connection.

'Gross!' she said instead. 'There's something creepy about men delivering babies.'

Here we went again.

'Gynaecologists don't deliver babies,' I said wearily. Particularly not my father – on the contrary. Was that less creepy? I wasn't even sure what the abortion laws were like in the States. But Patti's attention was elsewhere.

'I hear Mom going upstairs!'

'I'll get the tinfoil.'

Francine scrambled to her feet and disappeared into the house. Well, sod it, I wasn't her keeper. My own skin tanned pretty well.

'I'll go home and change,' I told Francine's retreating back. The sight of her flaxen, vulnerable femininity, so unlike the figure I must have presented to Florian, was evoking emotions that didn't bear analysis. So I was determined they wouldn't get any. I'd go home for my bikini, but first, I decided, I would wander down to the post office and buy twenty Benson & Hedges. Plus a packet of menthol, and alternate between one and the other. There was an interesting definition of liberty in that, I decided – the freedom to choose your own carcinogens.

It was a pity that I had to go back into the Red House to change. As I crossed the building site that was formerly a forsaken garden, the old house looked as though it had turned in upon itself – as though it had been struck across the face. The noise that had earlier driven me out of here close to tears was now truly horrendous – electric drills screamed from the upper storey, boots clattered on the stairs, walls echoed with hammers slamming against nails. Nevertheless, it wasn't immediately clear why a racket should cause me such bubbling agitation – after all, I was Tarquin Starkey's sister. In the relative safety of my bedroom, I concluded that it wasn't the noise that was tearing me to pieces but the presence in my home of outsiders – strangers roaming at will. Witnesses to the way my family lived.

I tried to remind myself that this entire operation was about construction. Healing. That under those shrieking saws was good new wood, pliant and healthy. But imagination failed me, and the only coherent thought in my head was the desire to run.

Our ability to run was entirely up to me. This was not a time to sunbathe. I pulled a T-shirt over my bikini and settled down with Clarence's nutty message. This would also spare me from digging any deeper into my other discontent. Some words of Francine's sang in my head, about that evening in Pete Christie's flat: 'We were a bit, you know, with his hand.' I would clobber them into silence with Clarence's conundrum.

OK, apart from all those Shakespearean *Henry*s, what other books are divided into Part I, Part II, etc.? There must be thousands. Yes, but look – Clarence had given this to me, presumably confident that I had sufficient clues to point me in the right direction. So, let's look for some.

There was a serious oddity that I'd noticed before but had brushed aside: although most of the message made sense as a book cipher, i.e., gave clear instructions for locating the words once you'd identified the book, nevertheless there were some bits that made no sense at all. During my scouring of Shakespeare I'd just ignored them. For example, look at *two hundred and eighty eighty seven*. Had Clarence developed a stammer? I could understand the other type of repetition, *Part iii iii*, which must mean Part III Scene III (or Chapter III), but why *three hundred and seventeen nineteen*?

And then I knew what the book was; it was shouting at me, flashing from the page in neon. Look at the three oddities of the message: *three hundred and seventeen NINETEEN* and *two hundred and eighty EIGHTY seven* and *three FOUR*. Isolate those surplus words and what did they give you? George Orwell. Of *course*, of *course*, Clarence was a *boy*!

I nearly fell down the staircase. '*Angela!*'

She came bustling out of the kitchen with the baby over one shoulder.

'Angela, where's Geoffrey? It's urgent!'

'Why?' she demanded. 'What's happened?'

'I need a copy of *Nineteen Eighty-Four*, Timmy's

bedroom is locked, Geoff used to have a hardback, and some of his stuff is still—'

'A *hard*back?' exploded Angela in a creditable parody of Lady Bracknell. 'I thought something terrible had happened!'

'Where's Geoffrey?'

'He isn't here, you hysterical child! Geoffrey's taken the car to the garage to get the clutch fixed.'

Damn him, damn everything! Now what? Timothy's room! I could get into it via the ladder.

Except that it wasn't much better dealing with the workmen outside than dealing with Angela inside.

'Oy! Watch where you're swinging that bleeding ladder, love – you nearly had the carpenter's eye out!'

We didn't possess one of those new aluminium extensible ones; ours was wood and eighteen feet long. Horribly unwieldy. Carry it by the middle, there were still nine feet behind and in front. So let's think about this. If I spun right round on my heel, my ladder would swing through an entire circle of 360 degrees unless stopped by an obstacle. A carpenter, for example.

Look at it this way: suppose that when the carpenter's head put the kibosh on it, I'd spun for half a second through 90 degrees. This would mean I was rotating at a rate of pi divided by two radians per half-second. So the end of the ladder that hit him would be travelling at half a ladder times pi, which is 28.28 feet per second, nearly twenty miles per hour. A goodish speed for a ladder.

So what we need is $F_{average} = m \, (\Delta v / \Delta t)$, and with the weight of an eye about 7.5 grams and diameter 22 millimetres (it's easier in metric), then delta v is 0.0075 times 8.6 and delta t is 0.022/8.6 . . . Put this all together and it gives us $F = 0.0075*8.6/(0.022/8.6) = 25.21N$. Well, that's 2,521,000 dynes – which is *easily* enough to knock a carpenter's eye out, so the man was right.

'Sorry!' I called over my shoulder and hauled the thing up until it was positioned under Timothy's window.

It was uncomfortable, squeezing myself beneath the doddery sash and trying not to dwell on the analogy with guillotines and being sliced in half. The wood grazed every one of my vertebrae. I tumbled in.

God, it was filthy! I had landed on the grubby linen of Timothy's fuming bed. Seventeen hamsters whirred on their wheels in a haze of guano. Obviously, Mrs Stanley hadn't been allowed in here since the day I took his books on code and Timmy locked the door. One of his machines must have pebble-dashed the wall with splattered fat, including a framed copy of Lester Bangs's review from *Rolling Stone*:

> The stuff is weird shit. But hey, that ain't reason to hate the guy, there's a whole crock of weird shit I like. Electro-foodle-gunk? I got albums by Iannis Xenakis so far off the wall he's out the house and the other side of the goddam *bridge*. Compared to that, Starkey's nothing, just pretentious sludge. It's not even honest-to-God maniacal bedlam that frees your head. Judged as random-generated sonic art, he is sub-John Cage. As classical-background-into-rock experimentation he is sub-sub-sub-John Cale – but mostly I hate the guy because he's a fucking *traitor*.

Traitor to his blues and R&B roots. A common line from Tarquin's detractors. Nice of his little brother to frame it.

A sticky mug mouldered on a magazine, also sticky, of naked women with breasts like balloons. Oh *Tim*othy! Something suspicious had happened to his soup and egg machine, too, which had been adapted for some further purpose involving a broad pipe and a

245

sucking mechanism, but my initial assumption was probably unjustified as there was a jar of Nescafé next to the pipe.

I put both hands across my mouth and nose and scanned the bookcase above Timothy's festering bed. My eyes found the paperbacks.

Getting out again was even more uncomfortable than getting in. As I re-entered the house a new sort of din, like the clashing of cymbals, detonated above me.

31

I knew immediately that it was Florian, knew before I saw him or heard his voice or footsteps. I knew it was Florian from the air he displaced on the staircase above, from my own sensation of plummeting twenty floors in a lift. I took stock in a second – ever since Thursday night I'd kept myself fully made up, including false eyelashes, upper and lower. I'd even slept in them. And now I was in bikini bottoms plus T-shirt; not the worst gear for such an encounter.

Angela's voice piped up from the threshold of the kitchen. 'Florian, are you sure you know what you're doing with that? I'm worried for our wallpaper.'

Florian glanced around him, at the damp-stained paper shedding rotted petals of flock. He was lumbering up the stairs lugging something of brass. A sort of pylon, seven foot high at a guess, and hung about with bells. As he reached the turn of the stairs, Florian paused to wipe his forehead with one hand, and leaned the thing against the uprights of the Venetian window.

'Hi,' he said and smiled. 'I've brought you all a Jingling Johnny.'

God, he was good looking! I couldn't work out whether my heart soared or sank. The smile was friendly but there was no conspiracy in it. Had he forgotten our roll on the sofa? Like he forgot his roll on Pete Christie's floor with Francine? ('We were a bit, you know, with his hand.') My brain tingled.

'Percussion instrument,' Florian continued, 'used by Turkish military bands in the 1800s and later adopted by the Belgians.'

'Belgians?'

I could understand it better now, silhouetted against the cold light. The thing was brass on a wooden pole, all crescents and fluted hoods. As the house growled around us, its every dangly bit rang out in a sympathetic tinkle.

'You can bang it on the ground,' explained Florian, 'or shake it like a staff.' So he shook it. The noise was like an acre of dustbins hit by a bomb. I saw Elvis shoot across the landing and fly headlong up the stairs to the third storey.

'But isn't it heavy?' I asked, thinking of those Belgians.

'All in a day's work,' replied Florian cheerfully, and heaved the thing back over his shoulder. Stooped with its weight across his back, his long-haired figure reminded me vaguely of the stained glass in Mr Horne's church. Tarquin opened the studio door and the Jingling Johnny crashed its way inside. The door closed. I felt an unexpected stab of jealousy over Florian's access to Tarquin. I waited for several minutes, ears straining for a sound. Nothing. Oh well, I'd be hearing from them both when they banged the Jingling Johnny on the floor; we'd all look forward to that. I went back to my bedroom and at long last opened Timothy's scuffed paperback of *Nineteen Eighty-Four*.

There are three parts to the novel, and within each the chapters are headed with Roman numerals. Make a start. Go back to Clarence's message. *Part iv eighty-four*. Open the book to Part IV. It hasn't got a Part IV. No, Clarence must mean Part I, Chapter V. Slowly, slowly! This is a laborious job and prone to errors. Start counting words.

The text, exhaustively annotated by Timothy's margin notes, told of telescreens, proles, and The Party. Images from my early childhood wafted from the pages and stung. My brothers in a world of their own, their sister unwelcome. A story not of men and women but of men and *girls*. In which men were known mostly by their surnames and girls by their Christian names. The only female character to be fleshed out at all was his lover, Julia – and never mind all that energetic sex, even she wasn't dignified with any grown-up features like womanhood or a surname. This was the way my father talked, too. Eric Blair's generation. A meeting of the Royal College of Surgeons would be reported back to Mum as 'Ran into old Simmons at the dinner. Maynard-Cripps is retiring next year. Sally's lecturing in the States so she couldn't make it.' And of course every mention of Winston *Smith* put up my heart rate.

Then I scanned Clarence's message and foresaw a problem. *Part iii* could mean either Part I Chapter II or Part II Chapter I, and unfortunately there was no way of knowing which. I'd have to slog through both options and make a note of both possible letters. OK, don't panic, it just requires patience. Then Tarquin's studio door opened again.

I was out. Florian trotted across the landing, down the stairs and out of the front door, leaving it ajar. A minute later he was lugging a gong up the stairs. More than two feet across, bronze and dimpled like J. Arthur

Rank's. There was another limerick in there somewhere.

'Central Javanese,' he said brightly to me, 'see you
again in a tick,' and disappeared inside the studio with
it. I sat down on the stairs and waited.

'Boozaphone,' said Florian.

Yes, well, it had been an old broom until someone
nailed beer-bottle tops all over it. Florian's other hand
was waving a serrated stick about.

'Attributed to an Australian rabbit poisoner. You use
this as a bow,' he told me. 'Or you can bang it on the
floor.'

Oh good, another one.

'There are more sophisticated models that have
car reflector lights on top. But Tarquin's a bit of a
purist.'

'Right.'

He beamed another smile and melted away. The
image of that smile hovered on the landing like the
Cheshire Cat. Eventually I drifted back to my bedroom
and the methodical counting of words.

When I next raised my head I had: a letter *i* followed
by *w*, followed by either *t* or *a*, depending on whether
it was Part I Chapter II or the other way round. Having
set my heart on their spelling out a name, I would have
felt more comfortable with the rudiments of a Mike or
a Dave or a Peter. My confidence already ebbing, I
flicked over the pages and felt my spirits sink at the
prospect of all the counting: 1,143 and 1,839. There
was even a 2,966. Hell! I caught sight of Julia again,
this time gaily boasting to Winston Smith that at the
age of sixteen she had slept with a man of sixty. Oh
Orwell, honestly! Then the door to the studio opened
again.

* * *

But where were they *putting* it all? My brother's studio was all Moog, Steinway and a poster of Trotsky. As far as we knew, Tarquin slept standing up.

'This one's a bit different,' said Florian.

It certainly was. This one had a human being attached to it.

'Meet Mungo. Do you want to put it down for a minute, Mungo? It's best if we assemble everything here first.'

'But what is it?' I asked.

'Guitar machine.'

Mungo was small, gnarled and the colour of cold tea. He was screwing lengths of pipe together in a flurry of hands and elbows while Florian stood over him, smiling encouragement. On the floor was a contraption apparently made out of one normal guitar and the working bits of several others strapped above it with a lot of clunky piping.

'All controlled by the feet,' explained Florian. The feet he pointed at were bare, I saw now, and looked as though they'd been soled and heeled.

'Then there's the high-hat – two cymbals on a stand, one face up, one face down.' As Florian spoke, Mungo's assembly resolved into two cymbals on a stand, one face up, one face down. 'Totally original concept for bluegrass.'

'Bluegrass?' I repeated with misgivings.

Mungo had moved on; with the dexterity of a balloon sculptor fashioning poodles, he was creating a copper frame across which he rested a five-string banjo.

'He plays that one at lap level,' explained Florian enthusiastically. 'With his hands!' he added, as though this were a novelty.

'Bluegrass?' I said again.

Mungo's attention was now on a cuckoo clock, which he was nutting and bolting to the frame.

Finally, he gave a quick shake to some lengths of wood; they turned into a stool and he sat on them.

'But isn't bluegrass like country and western?'

'Take it away, Mungo!' said Florian.

Mungo flexed his meaty toes like the fingers of a concert pianist, and they felt their way across the floor. A dozen flapping pedals stuttered like a typewriter, wires tugged, metal capos whizzed along the guitars, strings were plucked; we had music.

'*I love my wife like I love my 'coon dog,*' sang Mungo. '*Daddy runs a still on the ole front porch.*'

The high-hat pumped up and down, *tchk, ch-ch tchk, ch-ch tchk*, and the caged apparatus juddered like H. G. Wells's doomed time machine. Such a pity Timothy was out – with a couple more wires and a three-pin plug, he could have got it to hoover the landing.

Cu-ckoo! Cu-ckoo! The traditional bird shot out on a wobbly spring, his eyes mad and feverish.

'*I like biled carrots with Mamma's biled possum,*' sang Mungo. '*Gonna shoot that hog in the huckleberry tree.*'

'But – isn't bluegrass like country and western?'

Mungo's left leg swung into the air, and with one barnacled foot he kicked the high-hat. *TCHEEEeee . . .*

'*Closed* high-hat,' noted Florian sagely. 'Mmmh.'

The studio door was opening. Mungo stopped instantly. Slumped. The machine shivered and died.

Tarquin was on the landing. 'Hi, Mungo. Good to see your skin condition's clearing up,' said my brother, who to my knowledge never left the house. 'Drag it from here, yeah?'

'But isn't bluegrass like country and western?' I asked again, forlornly.

The three of them shoved and hauled until the thing was across the threshold. I tried to squeeze behind them for a glimpse inside the studio but there wasn't room. Men and machine retreated. The door swung shut. Around us, all building work had stopped. Tea break. Silence. I crept towards the studio door and put an ear against it. Nothing.

'But bluegrass is like country and western!' I said to the empty landing.

Well, thank *God* none of my friends knew what I'd been listening to! I pictured the incredulity of my classmates, who'd always thought Tarquin was at least cool and trendy. Country and western! Too stunned for further jealousies, I slipped back to my bedroom to carry on counting words.

i, w, t or *a, p* or *f, u* or *r, i* or *y* or *k, t* or *b, d* or *t, f* or *a, n, s, t.*

That was it, in its entirety. None of the combinations spelled out a name in any conceivable language, I'd put money on it. Nevertheless, in contrast to my previous efforts with Shakespeare, I couldn't believe I'd just gone off down the wrong track. *Nineteen Eighty-Four* sort of *felt* right – there was a key somewhere in that novel.

I hid Timothy's paperback at the bottom of my underwear drawer, and locked my bedroom door on the way out. Poor Julia, only half a name and half a status, forever yoked to a rat-phobic wimp with five false teeth and a varicose ulcer – under a pile of my school regulation knickers.

32

It took three days for Francine's sunburn to subside from a state of continual screaming itch, so bad that she couldn't sleep, couldn't eat, could hardly speak for crying. It was bad all over: face, arms, legs, tummy, chest – all of it livid and on fire. But worst was her back. Francine would lie prone across the bed while Mrs Switt, or preferably Mr Switt when he was home, dribbled calamine lotion across her empurpled flesh – until the next spasm of raging irritation overtook her and she buried her face in a pillow and *shook* until the climax had passed. I was in the house the time she surrendered to the temptation to scratch, madly ripping her fingers across the expanse of her ruined back. There was a short, becalmed pause. Then Francine screamed the place down.

Mr Switt approached my mother as she was getting into the car. I don't suppose he'd spoken to either of my parents since about 1969. Now, they talked for a good quarter of an hour, which was a damn sight longer than she'd ever devoted to any illness of mine,

I resentfully noted. God knows what Mum prescribed, but by the time Francine woke up again, the inflammation had subsided and her skin was sloughing off. I'd had sunburn myself, of the rice paper variety, the ends curling gently away like lapping waves. Francine's skin hung off her like flaking plaster on a Red House wall.

There was one silver lining: for two weeks she was unable to go to either Stavering or the Castle. I'd done some thinking; if Francine did run into Florian in the Red House, he'd almost certainly be trotting up and down stairs, probably with half a dozen ukuleles and a Wurlitzer organ, and not much time for either of us. That I could cope with. But the folk clubs were different: they'd always been his domain and Francine's; they were the focal points of her passion for him. I dreaded, I *dreaded* being there now my status was transformed, gazing at Florian with Francine by my side. Any deferral was welcome. I was also loath to hear Florian's inevitable boasting to other singers about my brother, along the lines of that Michael Caine guy at Dave's party: 'So I said to him, "Now look, Tarquin," I said.'

I hadn't caught sight or sound of Mungo, but I had run into Florian on our staircase, shaking his head and smiling.

'Your brother,' he informed me, 'files his albums in alphabetical order based on the title of the second track on side two!' as though I might not know this, as though Tarquin were someone else's brother, somebody I'd once stood next to in a bus queue.

Did I *like* Florian? Not always, and never completely. Would I give five years of my life to lie underneath him once more while he kissed me and stroked me to another of those strange, pleasant-unpleasant tickly sensations? More than five years. I'd give ten.

The aberration I'd first noticed in April when Florian had left our tiled courtyard, the delirium in which I heard every thought in my head spoken by his voice, had reached a frenzy. I was losing my mind. My life had taken on an arithmetical rhythm – every third or fourth night I dreamed of him, the sensations less tickly and more explosive every time. My ears strained to hear his footfall on the stairs, on the landing, in the hall, in the flower beds, up the chimney. I listened for his voice even when I was at school. I listened for him on the television. I watched for him on the radio.

It was a Sunday at the end of June, while Francine was still housebound. Our own house was empty for once, at least on this side of Tarquin's studio door: Mum was at the hospital, Dad was at the Golf Club; Timothy wasn't out but he was locked away and didn't count; Angela, Geoff, Angus and the baby had gone home – not for good, life was never that kind to me, just to replenish their supplies of life-enriching print frocks, gents' slacks and romper suits. Enticed by the unwonted serenity and enervating heat, I finally gave in to the desires that nagged me. That screamed. I locked my bedroom door. I drew the curtains. Tugged off my clothes, dumped them, Indian cotton puddling on the carpet. I slipped into bed.

For nearly a month I'd put up a mental fight against letting Florian bring me to this. Now, from the moment I abandoned the battle, surrender was paradise. *God*, the sense of his presence was delicious. I could feel him and taste him. I luxuriated in the animality of it. I snuffled his hair, breathed the suede-scent of his skin, the skin-scent of his jacket. 'Naughty schoolgirl,' I heard in my head, with laughter in his voice. 'You are *so* wet!'

Yes, I thought bitterly, and have been ever bloody since, thanks very much. The world retreated; there was nothing but Robert Johnson selling his soul and Florian's weight on top of me, his voice, his slippery fingers—

The unaccustomed peace of the house was immediately rent by somebody thudding on the front door.

Typical! But so what? It wouldn't be for me. Ignore it.

Yet it wasn't easy to ignore. The intruder was rat-a-tat-tatting on the knocker. Florian had never thudded but he *had* rat-a-tat-tatted that first time he turned up here. My heart, already going twenty to the dozen, stammered and skipped a beat. Florian? – *and me here in an empty house*? I pulled some clothes back on and torpedoed down the stairs.

It was a bald-headed bloke with a paunch. 'Hello, love,' he said as I opened the door. 'I think you might be needing this.'

I goggled at him. He was handing me a hammer, the shaft a good seven inches long. At least an inch and a half thick. Shiny with use. My face blanched and then blazed.

'It's not our one, you see,' he explained. 'Picked the thing up by mistake. Somebody'll miss it.'

I didn't move.

'Aren't you going to take it, love?' he said.

Cornered, I lifted the hammer gingerly from his hand, careful to hold it only by the claw, but the metal slipped and my hand closed tight around the shaft. Mortified, I dropped the thing as though I were scalded. It clattered onto the floor.

'Careful, love,' he said, stooping to retrieve it.

I took the hammer more carefully this time. He left me looking clueless, and strolled off down the drive.

The house was peaceful for the rest of the day but I didn't go back to bed. The mood had passed.

* * *

'It's like this, Mrs Starkey,' said one of the builders – presumably the one who'd lost when they drew lots. He didn't look Angela in the face as he talked, I noticed. But then you wouldn't, would you? 'There's funny business going on.'

'Funny business?' repeated Angela in the tones of a seasoned fishwife.

'Things don't stay put where we've left 'em,' he told her, scratching his head. 'Like somebody is playing silly buggers. Pardon my French.'

Angela humphed. 'You lot aren't exactly the tidiest of men, are you?' she pointed out.

'Yes, but . . .'

'My little boy nearly tripped over a spirit level you'd left on top of the A-frame ladder!'

I saw a bewildered question form on the builder's lips, then he shook his head. 'That's not the sort of thing I'm talking about, Mrs Starkey.'

'You leave those buckets of yours for everybody to fall over and break their necks. Of *course* they get moved.'

'That's not the sort of thing I'm talking about, Mrs Starkey.'

'What then?'

'The dumper truck,' he said.

There was a pause.

'The cement mixer. Half a hundredweight of fired brick. The coping stones for the roof.'

'*Dumper* truck?'

'Six bags of cement,' continued the builder. 'Twenty scaff poles what were up by the gate. Low-level flush toilet unit for the en—'

'Moved where?'

'—suite bathroom.'

'Moved where, for heaven's sake?'

'All over the place. From one side of the garden to the other. Round behind the house. We found the truck back of that orchard. Harry was only gone ten minutes having a cup of tea. Come back, the bugger's gone. So Harry calls the police. The coppers turn up and George clocks it down there behind them trees. Coppers thought Harry was having a laugh.'

'There's a smart alec among you!' said Angela crossly.

'Two rolls of roofing felt. Seven ten-foot lengths of four-b'two. Ronnie's rope and pulley . . .'

'So what do you expect me to do about it?' demanded Angela.

'Me and the men was wondering, Mrs Starkey . . .'

'You've got a joker in the pack. Weed him out!'

'Yeah, but . . .'

'End of discussion!' She huffed back upstairs in a rustle of starch and indignation.

I gave the poor man a sympathetic look. 'What did you intend to ask her?'

He shook his head sadly. 'Whether she's had this sort of thing happen before.'

'Oh.'

'The neighbours've got stories. We 'eard the place was on the market, only you couldn't sell cos of kids playing practical jokes. One poor codger came to view, was taking a pee and a plastic snake went for his willie.'

I hadn't known about that one.

'We was thinking that if it don't stop,' he said, 'we're jacking it in.'

Right. 'Angela will insist that nothing like it has ever happened here before.' To outsiders she would. I pitied Timothy and Tarquin when she got her hands on them.

'Yeah,' he said. A pause. 'And has it?'

I did feel sorry for the man, but what could I do? 'We don't have things disappearing, not the way you've just described,' I told him.

259

'Yeah?' he said again. 'I never known a place so chilly neither,' he added, rubbing the gooseflesh of his bare arms. 'And it's July! How do you manage when it's bleedin' January?'

'We cope,' I assured him vaguely, and wandered off to the kitchen for a coffee.

Ever since the squirrel-fire put the lid on the house sale, Clarence had left the family pretty much alone. Rather clever of him to try to drive the builders away instead. Especially with this sort of prank. The case of the disappearing dumper truck. The sort of hoax that left you doubting your own sanity. Clever.

As for what did we do when it was January, I remembered our first winter. A euphoric Tarquin wandered from room to room in a giddy spin with a pad of music manuscript, and slept in his overcoat. Geoffrey lay in wait for Mum and Dad, and stalked them with a volume of Dickens in his hand. With his moon face muffled in scarves, he read them passages about Bob Cratchit. Geoff would stand outside the bathroom door while they went to the loo, follow them up to bed, loom from behind their cars of a morning.

Timothy had taken to his room and swotted, retreating from our intolerable present into the world of his intellect. Whenever I had to get up in the night and hurry on slippered feet across the frozen air of the landing to the bathroom, I would see a wedge of light under Timothy's door. When prised out of there, my brother would sulk and cry. We had cold sores, we had chilblains. The fact that we also had some kind of mysterious presence that set chairs on fire and made blood run out of the bathroom taps was somehow unsurprising in a dwelling more like a graveyard than a house. Nobody, in their heart of hearts, could begrudge Clarence the evanescent heat from any chair that he managed to set alight.

* * *

But my memories didn't make sense. My head was full of images of struggling firelight and drifting webs of snow – but these weren't unhappy, they were bound up with Daddy building snowmen on Saturday morning. And family music, too, our vast unfamiliar rooms cross-hatched with plashy piano, keening Theremin and Timothy strumming Tarquin's new electric guitar. That stuff with Geoff reading Dickens, he used to slam back into the house grumbling that it was warmer outside in the garden. And it was! So this must have been after the snow was over.

Well, the Big Freeze began to subside on 4 March, the date was famous. I could remember the melt, and Mummy and Daddy having a row about it in the kitchen. The voices batted back and forth across the ringing quarry tiles.

'. . . said you'd phone them yesterday . . .'

'How? I was out of here at half six, and didn't get home . . .'

'Then why in God's name did you say you'd do it? That's what drives me insane, woman, that's what makes me so angry I could bloody strangle you . . .'

'*Me?* I take the blame for most catastrophes that befall this ill-fated family but I'm not responsible for the British weather!'

'I've been warning you till I was blue in the face! "As soon as the thaw sets in," I kept saying, "as soon as it does . . ."'

I was sitting on the stairs, a book drooping in my small hand, an ache gnawing at my tummy. No worse, probably, than a thousand other households that March, with harried mothers and 'I told you so' men. But my tummy ache was already so familiar that I'd given it a name. Lossing pain. So when was the first?

And another chilly night. In his room upstairs, Tarquin was making a wobbling attempt to play Sibelius's *Valse Triste* on Theremin, its ghostly whistle shivering in dark echoes from half the house away. Daddy must have been in the bathroom. I heard a door thrown open, heard the smack as it slammed back against the wall. Now his voice barked across the cold air: 'WHAT THE HELL IS THAT?' Not parental end-of-tether yelling, but like he was scared. Rapid strides across the croaking floor of the landing. 'STOP THAT BLOODY WAILING! TARQUIN? *TARQUIN!*' He must have been at Tarquin's door. Fisting it. Shouting. I was at the bottom of the staircase. I'd come to hate the sight of the Venetian window whenever things were horrible with Daddy – eyeless and blank, it looked aggrieved and hating, like a face blinded by cruelty. Pains clawed my tummy, it was hard to stand straight. I knew I'd made a nasty smell. Upstairs was Tarquin's voice, but suffocated by my father's.

'. . . THAT WE'VE GOT TO LIVE IN THIS STINKING HOLE, WITHOUT HAVING A BLOODY LUNATIC FOR A SON! DO YOU HEAR ME?'

The splintering of wood, and exorbitant swearing. Daddy, having kicked a hole in a panel of Tarquin's door, was dragging his foot back through it. Furious, and half mad with pain, he stormed back down the staircase. He caught sight of me below. I suppose his concentration faltered. He missed his footing and slipped, bumping down to the turn of the stairs. I was whimpering. My father didn't get up, didn't move, he just sat there and cried. A big man in his mid-forties, crying on the stairs.

'DON'T, DADDY! I LOVE YOU, I LOVE YOU!' My mind reeled with unbearable chaos, terrified and revolted, desperate to stop him. His pouched, baggy, crying eyes looked rheumy and formless, the tears an unseemly bodily fluid dribbling onto his lips, into the corners of his mouth. He was swallowing it – swallowing it!

'DADDY!'

'Go up to your bedroom.'

'DON'T CRY, I LOVE YOU!'

'Didn't you hear what I said? GO UP TO YOUR BED-ROOM!'

Tarquin was waiting for me.

'It's all right, Jo. Dad doesn't mean it. He's just upset.'

But Tarquin was trembling. Not only his hands, his lips quivered. He led me along the landing. Closed my door. (Where was Timmy through all this? Shut in his room with his books, presumably.) Our cat Jefferson was on top of the wardrobe. My breathing hurt, my chest hiccuped when I tried to talk. I cried and cried.

'Can I sleep in your bed tonight, Tarquin? Please?'

When the reply didn't come instantly, I knew he was going to say no.

'*Please, Tarquin!*'

'No, Jo. I'm too big for that.'

'I won't wake you up in the morning, I promise!'

'Ask Timmy. It's better.'

'Timmy wets the bed! He's been doing it for ages!'

'Look, you'll have Jefferson. He'll come down in a minute. Come on, puss. Puss-puss.'

Mummy had got the cat for my eighth birthday. So this wasn't our first winter, it was our second, 1963–4. Exceptionally mild. Though not in the Red House.

And when did it begin? When did the happy firelit evenings that we imported from Ealing wane into the Red House's chilly misery?

Now, in our cold kitchen in a July heatwave, I put the kettle on. Angela must have cleaned the windows – for a second, I'd thought all the glass had fallen out! There were also bowls of greasy plastic fruit and an ornate hostess trolley with chariot wheels – a must for those dinner parties. They really were moving in, weren't they?

Upstairs, Timothy's voice was raised. '*Dumper* truck?' he was saying incredulously, followed by a volley of verbal ack-ack from Angela.

It was certainly a novelty, being able to see through the windows. And look who I could see. Florian! He must have come through the front door. *God*, he looked wonderful. One of the roofer's labourers stopped what he was doing and watched from the weedy gravel. The poor man was filthy from being in and out of our roof space all day long – and was now forced to confront Florian's crisp good looks, the tight jeans and frilled shirt, hair aglow in the sun. I watched as the labourer pursed his lips and wolf-whistled Florian out of the gate. Disgusted, I flounced off to the Switts', where Francine, fed up with shedding skin flakes like dandruff, was wrapping herself in most of a crackling roll of Sellotape and getting Patti to rip it off her.

33

I was increasingly depressed. My misery would have been easier to take had not everybody else seemed to be so bloody *happy*. Well, not Francine, of course, she never had, but school was full of it now that the O and A level exams were coming to a close and half the pupils were behaving like prisoners given time off for good behaviour.

Sixth-formers didn't wear uniform, so it was a ritual at the end of summer term for fifth-year girls (the year above ours) to have their gingham dresses slashed to pieces as they stood up in them. This was carried out by the fifth-year boys using scissors, bare hands and even (a few being truly intrepid) teeth. This rite of passage culminated in the spectacle of dozens of young women standing around at bus stops clad in tattered strips of cotton, hanging like November leaves. The severest efforts of Mrs Matlock had failed to curb the custom, and the good people of Brentwood shot off their annual incensed letters in vain.

Timothy sat his A level and Special papers in both

pure and applied maths, and then drove us all nuts reminding everybody that maths was the one subject – or in his case, two – where you could be marked higher than one hundred per cent by answering more questions than required. That his twin sister could have been in a similar position had her registration not been cruelly cancelled did nothing to restrain his swagger. I challenged him one morning.

'You were registered. You threw it away,' responded Timothy, swilling a cup of tea. 'Totally your own fault. Fuck, this tea's stewed,' he added, with slightly more interest.

The results of my fourth-year exams were, inevitably, grim. I had scarcely made the effort to write anything down. I brought home my report book for Timothy to forge our parents' signatures.

'Look, just sign, will you, Timmy?'

'Chemistry, thirty per cent,' he read, disbelieving. 'Physics, twenty-six per cent. *How?*'

'Because I couldn't be bothered.'

'Physics?'

'Just sign the bloody thing, Tim!'

The teachers' comments were no less of a shock for being entirely expected, and no less unfair for being thoroughly deserved. They lacerated me:

It is distressing to witness any bright pupil deliberately refusing to exercise their talents. In Josephine's case the refusal amounts to downright delinquency.

This result reflects Josephine's unwillingness to apply herself in class, hand in homework or take an intelligent interest in the questions on her exam paper.

Earlier this year, I was expecting to predict an A grade distinction from the summer's A level papers. Instead

266

I have to report that Josephine would probably fail to do justice to an eleven-plus exam.

Meanwhile, I had run into Florian in the Red House a few times, on a couple of which he lightly kissed me before disappearing to more urgent work, thereby managing with minimal effort to render me insanely in love with him and in increasingly desperate need of a claw hammer.

Louis MacNeice had a poem that talked about a flowery maze through which someone *had wandered deliciously till he stumbled / Suddenly, finally conscious of all he lacked / On a manhole under the hollyhocks*. It was called 'The Suicide'. Our medicine cabinet was invariably stocked with miscellaneous prescription drugs, some of which would surely be fatal in overdose. Brought up in the Red House, I was a stranger to flowery mazes, so, in front of the TV while our amiable weatherman stuck little cardboard suns on a map of the baking British Isles, I wrote a poem of my own.

> *I wish to inform the physics department*
> *That, in view of the weather,*
> *(Being Bert Ford's hottest week*
> *since the computer blew predicting sandstorms),*
> *And having failed my exam by a percentage error*
> *I blame on an Act of God,*
> *And then left my ambitions somewhere between*
> *The tensile stress and the tensile strain,*
> *I shall not*
>   *. . . be present*
>   *. . . tomorrow.*

Bloody brilliant, I decided! Just think what *that* would look like chiselled on a gravestone. I had to read it to Francine immediately, and from there we got onto other things until we'd whiled away a couple of hours, so by the time we finally got off the phone Angela was having a bath, her ablutions blocking my access to the medicine cabinet. Typical. So I copied my poem carefully into the exercise book in which I recorded my best work, and just prayed that the feeling would return before long. After all, a poem like that. Be criminal to waste it.

34

The shops in London's Oxford Street closed at lunchtime on Saturdays and didn't reopen until Monday morning, a simple piece of reality with which the rest of us had co-existed for most of my lifetime without complaint. Patti did the mad scene from *King Lear*.

'This is your *capital city* and it's *closed* on a *weekend*?'

'The shops stay open late on Thursdays.'

'*So?*'

This was pretty much the mood in which she boarded our train at Brentwood station, and then the Central Line tube at Stratford. By the time we rode the escalators up to street level at Oxford Circus, Francine and I badly needed a cup of coffee, and I would have killed for a cigarette. To make things even worse, my scalp itched. I'd washed my hair in egg, as recommended by *Petticoat*, and there was a lot still clogged in it. Luckily this was mostly at the back, and as the back of my hair didn't get brushed very often, at least I was spared the effort of tugging.

It was hot and airless in the street, and worse in the café, where a bald proprietor was wiping Formica tables. Steam hissed and gushed from the coffee machine; its heavy snorts laboured in the background like some fairytale huffing-puffing monster.

'Tea or coffee?' asked the bald guy.

'Cappuccino?' suggested Patti.

'I've heard they serve them things in Soho, love,' responded the proprietor levelly. 'In here it's tea or coffee, black or white.'

Patti gave a snort worthy of his machine. 'Regular coffee, white,' she told him.

With a *hisssh* he pumped dark fluid through a metal pipe into the customary translucent white cup. Then slopped milk into it from a foaming metal jug.

'So how much?' demanded Patti rudely. 'How many pounds, shillings and pence?'

'The country's gone decimal, love,' he replied with patience, plucking a mixture of new and pre-D-day coins from the hand she held disdainfully in front of her. At a rough calculation, I'd say she was clutching fifteen quid.

We shuffled onto the benches, their rust-coloured leatherette ripped and sticky. Steam condensed on our faces, glistening in beads that looked granular, like the cheap sugar. A radio played Frank Sinatra. Could things get worse?

Patti lit one of her American cigarettes. I was alternating between menthols and Benson & Hedges, but I'd lost track of where I was up to. Regretfully abandoning the option of lighting one of each, I put a match to a Benny. Patti's pack bore the legend *Warning: The Surgeon General Has Determined that Cigarette Smoking is Dangerous to Your Health*.

'Who's the Surgeon General?' I asked, for want of something better to say.

She shrugged. 'Some guy in the army. So now do we have a conversation about lung cancer?'

'Not necessarily,' I said pacifically, breathing deeply at my cigarette. There was no doubt two would have been very nice.

Patti had spent most of the journey conversing with an airmail letter from someone called Donna, and bemoaning everything she was missing back in Broward County. Britain dumbfounded Patti. We didn't have pizza – whatever that was – or quarter-pound hamburgers. There were no drive-in movies. And she was *appalled* to find just one solitary rock/pop station on the radio, and run by the state, too. I found this really galling, as not so long ago we'd had a profusion of pirate stations operating offshore until, in an act of petulance, the government closed them down. Interestingly, the politician who did it, Tony Benn, had previously been called Sir Anthony Wedgwood Benn, and it was only afterwards that bits of his name started to drop off, so perhaps there was a God after all.

Now, just to be pleasant, I asked what other news there was from Donna's side of the Atlantic.

She sipped her coffee. 'This really stinks,' she said in passing. 'Everybody at home is talking about a movie with some black guy, New York detective. Mind-blowing music. *All* my friends have seen it. Everybody in the United *States* has seen it!'

'Then I expect we'll get it here soon,' I said.

Patti rolled her eyes. 'You don't even get the movies till they're real old, I asked Uncle Jerry.'

Uncle Jerry? Oh yes, Uncle Jerry was Mr Switt.

'*And I'm a thousand fucking miles away!*'

I didn't correct her faulty quantification; it occurred to me for the first time that there was something in this resentment. Patti was a stunningly pretty teenager with a social circle that revolved around the beach and hot August nights of heavy petting in open-top American cars – and suddenly life had plunged her into an environment governed by a cousin with chronic melancholia and a mad jam-making mother. She had a nice dad, apparently, and he'd been left on his own, so she probably missed him, too. Oh, and of course her brother was dead. It was in more friendly tones that I asked, 'Does everyone in Florida smoke? I don't mean cigarettes,' I added, waving mine in the air. '*Real* smoking. Cannabis.'

She looked at me, uncomprehending.

'Cannabis,' I repeated. No response. 'Marijuana, dope, hashish . . .'

'Yeah, it's called marijuana. I never heard of any *cannabis.*'

'Well, that's its official name.'

'You mean it's *legal* here? Holy shit!'

'No, no, I only meant that's the name in the pharmacopoeia.'

'God – you people!' she snapped from behind her scathing glasses. 'You probably know what LSD stands for!'

'Lysergic acid diethylamide,' I told her without thinking.

Patti went mad. Pushing back her chair, she knocked the table. It tilted. Our coffees slopped across the Formica. 'It's like talking to a fucking encyclopaedia!'

My cup rolled, and smashed on the floor. Francine sprang away to protect her clothes.

'Now look what you've done!' I shouted. 'You stupid . . .'

'Best place for it, on the floor!' she screamed back. 'British coffee tastes like a toilet.'

'How do you know? Drink out of a lot of toilets in Broward County, do you?'

Amid the wrecked crockery, both my cigarette cartons swam in a foaming grey broth. I was just shouting about this injustice as an enormous hand slapped my shoulder and hauled me in the direction of the door.

'OUT, THE THREE OF YOU!'

I heard Francine yelp. He was holding her with his other hand. Patti ran at him.

'Get your mother-fucking hand off of . . .'

'YOU,' he told her, 'want to wash your mouth out. Dirty little Yank! Now get out of my caff before I call the coppers and have 'em arrest the bleeding lot of you! *Out!*'

Somehow we were on the pavement, colliding with a group of Hare Krishna people.

'Anti-American racist!' I screamed from the slew of saffron-coloured cotton and tinkling tambourines.

'You *dick*!' added Patti.

'Xenophobe! Bigot!'

The door closed definitively.

'Fascist!' we shouted in unison.

The Hare Krishna people had picked themselves up and looked as though they might suggest peace and love. Then they copped my expression and melted away. We scrambled up from the pavement, and grumbled along Oxford Street.

'We got guys like that in the States. They just hate young people.'

'It's jealousy.'

'He probably can't get it up, that's why he takes it out on girls.'

A hippie was selling copies of the *Socialist Worker*. 'Don't let the government turn you into a number!' he shouted. 'Be an individual! Join the twenty thousand marching on Whitehall!'

Wandering towards Bond Street, we found ourselves in front of one of Oxford Street's most notorious establishments – a boutique called Limelight, with a street-level window display but premises up a flight of stairs. They kept a rope across these stairs and made people queue. But the problem wasn't how to get up there, it was how to get out again once you were inside. Something in the window had caught Patti's eye.

'No, not Limelight,' Francine warned her. 'They're like wolves.'

'The assistants are on commission,' I explained.

'So? The gear looks pretty good.'

A cocky individual was holding the rope back and shouting like a fairground barker. 'No more than six, please, ladies! Six only!'

There was no-one queuing except us three. Upstairs, racks of clothes swishing on metal poles. Women with caked make-up pouncing. 'What are you looking for, girls?'

'When we need help, we'll ask you,' Patti told her.

'That's manners, is it, where you come from?'

To our surprise, Patti didn't start another fight. She was flicking efficiently through a rack of skirts. I'd found something really stunning, a hot-pants suit in seersucker with frilly ruched jacket and puff sleeves. Fuchsia pink.

'May I try this on, please?'

Patti cut in. 'Tell us you're kidding, Jo, and we'll all laugh.'

'What?'

'That's terrible for you.'

'Oh.'

The male assistant looked scandalized. 'That's one of our top ranges!'

'Look, Jo,' continued Patti, ignoring him. 'You gotta face up to it – you're kind of big. All these floaty clothes you wear, fussy patterns, paisleys, frills, they're not good for you.'

'How *rude*!' piped the assistant, hands on his hips.

'You know how they make you look? The truth now?

You look like a guy in drag.' She waved something in deep blue cord. 'This is better. Hot pants in a plain fabric. They're not baby-doll and they make the most of your legs. Jeans, leather, that kind of stuff is good. Or if you want a dress, go for slinky – black and slinky, that would be great on you.'

The assistant snorted. 'Leather and black slinky in the summer sales? You'll be lucky!'

Patti spun round. I decided I didn't want to be thrown out of two places in less than half an hour. 'Please,' I told the assistant, 'we'll be trying things on in a minute and we'll want your help then.'

He huffed off, making derogatory comments about Americans. I took the hanger from Patti and held the hot pants against my pelvis. They just about covered it. She was riffling through another packed rack, the hangers skewed, garments hanging half off them. She tugged out something long and purple.

'This one.'

I eyed it dubiously. Wrap-around with a halter neck.

'Hey!' called Patti at the assistant. 'Can you fix her up with the right size?' And to me, 'What are you, twelve?' which was quite flattering until I realized she was talking American sizes. I had no intention of shouting out 'Fourteen'; I flicked through the rack and found one for myself.

'And try these pants, they look about right.'

Hot pants, two pairs of trousers and a long halter-neck dress in deep purple cotton that wrapped tight round me and tied behind. Backless. Francine had bought a calf-length flowery skirt with lacey petticoat. (Patti had refused to let me take a similar one into the changing room.) She herself bought nothing, too busy tutting round me and staving off Limelight's commission-slavering assistants. When we fell into a carriage at Stratford station, I draped my purchases across the

275

tatty seat opposite, to scrutinize this new look without a single flounce or border print. I wasn't entirely convinced.

'How d'you get so much bread anyhow?' asked Patti. 'This is your dress allowance?'

I shrugged. We were neither of us going to admit that one reason our dress allowance went a long way was that sometimes we made our own.

'Mum and Dad earn quite a lot,' I told her. 'Mum's never been mean.'

'She means cheap,' translated Frankie.

'And I've got three and a half thousand quid in a building society account.'

'Nine thousand dollars,' translated Frankie.

'Though I can't get at that money until I'm sixteen. I babysit, too, sometimes.'

'If your folks are rich, how come you live in such a dump?'

How come indeed? Francine and I didn't enlighten her, and Patti was quiet a while. When the train rattled into Seven Kings, she stared disbelieving at the station sign. Earlier she'd choked at the names 'Barking' and 'Tooting' on a tube map.

'Frankie's got loads of dough, too,' she said, taking up where she'd left off. 'From her dad, and being a model and everything.'

There was a pause. 'So this *can*nabis stuff. Between you, you can afford enough for all three of us.'

Francine and I snapped to attention and looked hopelessly at each other. We had never in our lives.

'Aw, come on!' pleaded Patti. 'I'm dying for a joint, I've nothing except the change in my purse, and you know I can't get a cent out of *my* mom – she's on another planet!'

35

'Tarquin!'

He was on the landing, the studio door gaping open behind him. I stepped between his huge expanse and the banisters and tried to get a look inside, but he reached behind himself to slam it.

'Tarquin, where can I get hold of cannabis?'

'How much are you after?'

'Enough for three of us.' But how frequently did Patti expect to get high? 'To see us right through the summer.'

Tarquin sighed. 'Wait there.'

He reappeared a moment later with a brown envelope. 'That's all we can spare,' he told me.

That 'we' was presumably Florian. I experienced another of my stomach-twisting pangs, but was the jealousy directed at Tarquin for his proximity to Florian, or at Florian for his proximity to Tarquin? A bit of both, I decided, feeling a complete idiot.

I took the envelope into my own bedroom. There was something odd about it. I'd expected a kind of tobacco but the contents of Tarquin's envelope were solid and slid about. Inside was a stack of dark brown tiles. Eight of them. An ounce apiece, at a guess. A dull sheen softened their edges. The word *resin* clawed its way through my cortex. And just what did you do with resin? You baked cakes with it, as far as I knew, like Alice B. Toklas. Patti was no baker.

Back onto the landing. 'Tarquin? *Tarquin?*'

No response. For the first time, it occurred to me that Tarquin's sound-proofing wasn't to keep his cacophony in, it was to keep ours out. So I slipped the stuff into my handbag and took it down to Stavering on Monday evening.

Patti had never been to a folk club before. Casual in shorts and gleaming cleavage, she was surprised when Francine rustled out in her petticoat skirt, and stupefied when I trotted across to the bus stop in my new backless halter neck.

'You dress up for these clubs?' she asked.

'Oh don't worry,' I reassured her, 'you don't have to.'

'But that dress is for a party.'

'People wear all kinds of clothes – caftans, everything.'

'Yeah, but that is not a caftan.'

It certainly wasn't. There was no doubt about it, the dress did things for me. Made me look a good five years older for a start; rich purple against my suntan and sensuously wrapped across my bra-less breasts. And although, as the boys at school might have put it, nobody would have climbed over Patti's to get to mine, nevertheless the fabric and style made the best of what was down there. In fact, I decided, my brain fluttering at the thought, it wasn't a foregone conclusion that Florian, when he saw us, would find Francine more attractive than me.

We got to Stavering well before eight o'clock, and

too early for the club. It was another hot night. Stavering may have looked like England in the movies – all half-timbering and hollyhocks, thistledown and missel thrushes – but it wasn't. Motorbikes screamed and belched; cars tore through the narrow roads at fifty, sixty, seventy miles an hour, en route from some other place to some other place, splattering small animals across the tarmac at the edges of the fields. And tonight, those fields reeked of pig manure. We got Patti into the Rose and Crown in a hurry.

At the bar, she was astounded that you could get served without showing photo ID that a friend had bribed out of a twenty-one-year-old sister. Most of the drinks meant nothing to her; in the end she took a fancy to a passing glass of best bitter, ordered a half, took a swig and fled outside to spit it into the road. I went back to the bar and got her a lager.

'You look nice,' said the barman to me, the first time any stranger had ever said that in my life.

'Thanks.'

'Going somewhere?'

'Yes, the folk club upstairs.'

'Really? That will be ten new pence, love.'

In the club room, we settled on the floor. Having spent her life among uncompromising right angles, Patti was visibly unnerved by the Elizabethan geometry with its wavering walls and dippy floorboards. Also, as she was used to the aseptic atmosphere of air-conditioning, Patti was repeatedly disconcerted by the fact that British places smelled of things – in Stavering's case, beer, cider and cigarettes. I couldn't imagine the club without them; the music wouldn't sound right.

I had a kind of stage fright – the lining of my stomach zizzed like one of Timothy's electric appliances. The Florian-related tension alone was bad enough, with its exalting hope and swingeing guilt, but tonight these jostled with a brand new discomfort. Stavering Folk Club was so much a part of our lives, mine and Frankie's, that we had never considered how well its music would stand up to third-party scrutiny. And as scrutinizing third parties went, tonight we had a lulu. Greg, sitting moodily on a stair, would do us proud but otherwise there wasn't anyone much.

I leaned across to Patti. 'You have to understand,' I said sotto voce, 'that many of the regulars are on holiday. The standard drops.'

'Why are you apologizing for the place?' she asked, lighting a cigarette. 'They're your friends, aren't they? You seemed to know them pretty good when you said hello.'

'Hi, girls,' said one of the Mikes from Dave's party. And to me, 'You look nice. Are you going somewhere?'

Then my heart sank as he took the floor, stuck a finger in one ear and gave us 'She Moves Through The Fair' seriously off key.

After him was a visitor from Edinburgh. He sang 'Flower Of Scotland' and asked us all to join in, which we couldn't because we'd never heard of it. Even Trevor, he of the MG, had ratcheted up his courage. 'This is a tribute to my hero, Bert Jansch,' he informed the club. ' "Needle Of Death".'

'Do you know Bert Jansch?' I whispered across to Patti. 'Guitarist of absolute genius!'

'But this guy doesn't have a guitar.'

No, he didn't. He was terrible.

By the beer break I was sufficiently edgy to risk another snub from Greg.

'I was wondering . . .' Greg looked up and grunted. '. . . whether you'd be playing tonight. Be really great to hear "Angi".'

'No,' he told me.

Right. Damn and sod.

'Anyway, you're not staying, are you?' he asked.

'You look as if you're going on somewhere.'

Since Patti was downstairs queuing at the bar with Francine, this was an opportunity to ask a question to which a man of the world like Greg Bailey would know the answer.

'Can you possibly,' I began, 'tell me what one does with these?'

'With what?'

'These,' I repeated, fishing Tarquin's little tiles from my handbag. In the slow evening light through the ancient mullioned windows, they had lost their sheen and resembled nothing more exotic than a broken cow pat. Nevertheless he appeared to recognize them.

'Christ!' said Greg.

'You see, I've no idea . . .'

'Put it away!' he hissed at me. 'Before somebody sees me with you!'

Obediently, I slipped the stuff back inside my bag.

'I'm a teacher!' Greg was on his feet. 'Anyone catches me with a schoolgirl and a stash of illegal drugs I'll be unemployable. Where the hell did you get that much anyway? If the police bust you they'll assume you're dealing. You'll get a custodial.'

Well, no, I wouldn't actually, I was under age. I shrugged.

'From a friend,' I said.

'Then you can ask your bloody friend what to do with it!' he concluded, loudly enough for several people milling around the landing to stare at us. Then Greg steamed off towards the bar.

On his way downstairs he passed Patti and Francine on their way back up. From the flustered look of Francine I guessed that Florian had arrived. My heart was in my throat. Longing and guilt. Well, a folk club was as good a place for them as any; you could write me into half the songs on file at Cecil Sharp House.

'Jo!'

'Florian's here, yes?'

'On his way up now,' she whispered. 'Talk to me! Start a conversation. Look natural!'

Our anxiety was even infecting Patti – the three of us stood on tiptoe, peering and swivelling like a family of meerkats.

'For God's sake,' said Patti, suddenly coming out of it, 'he's just a guy. If you behave like you're crazy he'll *think* you're crazy.'

'What a fabulous accent,' said Florian, appearing at Patti's shoulder.

'Don't get too used to it,' she told him. 'I don't plan to stay long.'

'I guessed,' said Florian. 'You're all going on somewhere.' He smiled at me. 'Nice dress.'

'I mean, I don't plan to stay in England.'

'Yeah?' His smile irradiated the landing. 'Hey, do you know Santa Monica, California, at all? There's this girl . . .'

At that, I knew I had suffered enough. I left them, sought out the club secretary and asked him to add my name to tonight's singers.

I gave them Joni Mitchell's 'Tin Angel', or more accurately I gave it to Florian, followed by another of Tarquin's Red House songs, 'Before The Earthquake Came', written of course about our Portuguese courtyard. At the end of 'Tin Angel' the club room roared. After Tarquin's, everyone stood up. I'd never seen that before.

They said I had a better voice than Joni Mitchell. They said I should be singing in concert, filling the Dagenham Roundhouse.

'Your brother wrote that? He's Tarquin Starkey? You mean the *Night Train To New Orleans* Tarquin Starkey?'

They said, 'Are you sticking around? You look like you're going on somewhere.'

Florian sort of stood and beamed and nodded. It was the response of a party with vested interest. Possessive. This was unacceptable, of course; it was absolute audacity. Unfortunately, part of me gloried in it, basked, never wanted it to stop. Francine was not similarly divided: she absolutely bloody hated it, and could not understand why I'd opened my mouth in the first place.

'For Patti!' I told her. 'She hadn't heard a decent singer all night. Do you want her thinking the club's crap?'

'Bit conceited, aren't you, Jo?'

That might have stung were not the applause still echoing through my head.

'Anyway,' she objected, 'I thought they were all pretty good tonight,' and I had no way of knowing whether she was serious.

At the second beer break we couldn't get anywhere near Florian. He was in the room next door talking about work in progress, a tribute to Igor Stravinsky on gong and boozaphone. I caught one phrase: 'So I said to him, "Now look, Tarquin," I said . . .'

I stamped back down to the bar and ordered a double vodka and lime. When I'd finished that I ordered another one.

'So how do you smoke it? I mean as a joint,' I added hastily before Tarquin could direct me to a Turkish hookah and hubble-bubbling the stuff through crème de menthe.

'Roll a cigarette and leave it open, then heat the resin over a flame until it crumbles.'

'A flame? You mean I need a Bunsen burner?'

What *was* it with my brothers? No doubt I'd require a bloody Geiger counter into the bargain.

'Use a lighter, Jo.'

At that moment, Geoffrey's heavy tread vibrated through the staircase. The baby was in his arms. At the sight of Tarquin, it let out a shriek and tried to wriggle into its father's cardigan.

'Geoffrey!' A separate shriek carried up the staircase. 'Did you take the car back to the garage this afternoon?'

'No, Ange, I was carrying out a frontal lobotomy.'

Really? I thought. Was he meaning to?

'Tomorrow, Ange.'

Father and child receded to the third storey, so Angela started on Tarquin.

'Tarquin!' she hollered. 'Is Mungo ever going to finish with that soup tureen or what? And he's ruining my carving knife.'

'I'll bring them down, Ange.'

I stared at Tarquin. '*Mungo?*'

But he was moving on. 'Is that it, yeah?'

'No! I still don't know how much resin I crumble into a joint.'

'A couple of pinches.'

'Oh.'

Well, that would certainly explain Greg's surprise when I waved half a pound under his nose.

'OK now? Keep cool, Jo.'

Tarquin dematerialized back into his studio and Timothy appeared from the bathroom.

'Want me to lend you a Bunsen, Josie?'

'Oh very funny, thank you.'

'You're welcome,' drawled Timothy in a close imitation of Patti's voice, and then, unaccountably, blushed to the roots of his pimples. Before I could follow this up, Timothy was retreating into the seething mess of his terrible bedroom. From behind his door I heard the chugging of the tea, soup, egg and coffee machine. I dismissed my lingering suspicions about that and went down to make a coffee myself.

In the hall I found Angus sitting on the floor, chewing something.

'What have you got?' I asked suspiciously, in case it was mine.

'Welvis mouzer,' he told me and dribbled. Welvis mouzer? I lowered my face to his and peered.

'ANGELA COME HERE OH GOD ANGUS IS EATING A *MOUSE* HE'S EATING A *MOUSE* ANGELA!'

'Well, take it away from him, for heaven's sake!' Angela hurtled from the kitchen on stocking feet and skidded into the dado rail. From the side of Angus's mouth trickled a wet grey tail like some displaced handlebar moustache.

'HE'S SWALLOWING IT ANGELA OH GOD *GET IT FROM HIM*!'

I'd actually brought Geoffrey running, clumping back down the stairs, babyless and gormless. Angela was already on the floor. Angus, wild-eyed and starting to choke, thrashed at her with pudgy hands. His mother slammed a knee into his chest as an anchor and tugged at the disappearing tail, straining backwards like a Victorian tooth-puller.

Plop! A noise like a plumber's plunger slurping up from a drain. Angus let out an infuriated yodel. 'Welvis mouzer MINE!'

I had never seen *anything* move as fast as that mouse as it vanished out of our front door. I was next; I fled to the Switts'.

36

Tuesday night. The builders had restored my parents'
en suite, so everybody deserted our lovely old cast
iron for the spanking new low-level plastic in Avocado
Serenade. Which meant that Francine and I could do
our time-honoured trick of moving our stuff into the
main bathroom and locking everyone else out. This
time with Patti.

'Hey, this is some stash, Jo,' she commented, licking
her lighter flame around a tile. 'You must be a real pot
head!'

'Well, you know,' I said meaninglessly.

They had some news to impart, apparently.
Something pretty rotten, by the sound of it, as
Francine insisted we all get high before broaching the
subject. Patti licked and twizzled and we had a joint.

'Wanna start it up?'

'No, you do the honours,' I told her airily. 'It was
your hard work.'

'Know how to open wine?' she asked me, and
pushed across the lino a bottle that she'd sneaked out

of her uncle Jerry's den, and a corkscrew. No, I didn't – wine wasn't one of our drinks, so she did the honours with that, too, and glugged something called Montrachet, according to the label, into cracked Red House mugs. About the only operation I was comfortable with was putting a record on.

I'd brought along the Doors, out of respect for Jim Morrison. When his death was announced on Francine's transistor and she emerged from her bedroom weeping, Aunt Janet retired to hers and didn't emerge for two days, causing a Switt family row. Then Patti, who I would have expected to demonstrate more finely honed survival instincts, announced that she thought Le Père Lachaise sounded like a pretty groovy place to be buried and how far away was Paris anyhow? – until Mrs Switt bit her head off, which started an auxiliary row. It finally blew up so badly that neither of them was allowed to go to the James Taylor concert in Wolverhampton, so I didn't go either. Bloody Vietnam.

'Which Doors album do you want?' I now asked Patti. She was taking a drag and then sucking air through her nose. Then she breathed it out the same way, smoke streaming from her nostrils like tusks. OK, I could copy that.

'But we've been listening to the Doors for a month now,' she said. 'What else you got?'

What else I'd got was my latest discovery – Rachmaninov's second piano concerto.

'Do you know classical music at all?' I asked Patti. 'I listen to this sometimes when I'm stoned.'

Although this wasn't true, I felt that it should have been; Rachmaninov's long, honeyed melody lines were surely intended to flood across one's drug-heightened senses. So Rachmaninov it was.

I had assumed that if anything gave us away as

inexperienced, it would be Francine. I was wrong; she took to smoking pot with a panache that made me wonder whether they taught it at Lucie Clayton. By the time we were into the second joint, she and Patti were flat out on the lino, dreamily waving their arms at the concerto in a parody of conducting.

'You know,' mused Patti, 'I've heard this some place before.'

'Food for the soul,' said Francine surprisingly. 'Food for the head.'

I envied them this state of mind; my own seemed stubbornly unwilling to give way. Far from being soothed, my thoughts took on a paradoxical unease, nameless anxiety lowering at the edge of my senses like a baddie offstage in a pantomime.

'Jo,' called Francine, 'can you turn him up?'

'Turn him up while he turns us on,' said Patti.

I reached out to the volume control. The bathroom was full of mellifluous piano and florid strings. But the concerto was failing me, just like the pot and Mr Switt's wine (which wasn't much cop). I reached for a copy of the *British Medical Journal* from the pile by the loo but it was full of papers about risk factors for coronary disease: obesity, smoking, sedentary lifestyle, a diet rich in animal fats and salt . . . God, that was Tarquin. From there, my mind groped sideways and found Florian; I longed for him. Pain seeped into the evening light and blighted it. Rachmaninov took on the colour and timbre of his voice. Well, yes, I thought – if marijuana cured heartache, its street price would be exorbitant.

I'd managed to forget that the girls had news to impart. It was indeed bad. Mrs Switt had found an apartment in St John's Wood, not too far from Regent's Park. A date of Friday 1 October had been set for completion.

'Mom's twittering in and out with *Homes and*

Gardens, and swatches of material for the drapes. *Such* a drag.'

'She'll strip the house, Frankie,' put in Patti. 'You and Uncle Jerry will be left with one chair and a couple of light bulbs.'

'You're not moving with her, then?'

'Not until Christmas, so I don't change schools in mid-term. Then Dad can get his flat.'

The Ford people would fix up Mr Switt with accommodation (and as far as his wife was concerned, this need be nothing more than a cupboard space with running water) and then the Lossing house would go. I was conscious of having felt an unforgivable surge of hope. With Francine out of the way, I'd have had an easier conscience. And a clearer path to Florian.

What the hell was going on with me? If Francine went, I'd have no best friend, nor in fact a single trusted confidante in the whole wide world! My feelings were as twisted as bed springs. I felt so bad I wanted to cry.

'I'm getting hungry,' announced Francine unhurriedly.

She had never run into Florian here, it occurred to me, and therefore she didn't strain to hear his laughter or his breath on the air. And Francine didn't seem to mention him much any more, not outside the folk clubs. Or was this my own wishful thinking?

'Patti, wanna hear Jo's poems? She's really great.'

I'd brought them with me, intending to add new stuff. After all, mind-altering drugs did wonders for Coleridge.

'Sure. Sock it to me.'

Francine lay on her back and held out my slim volume (i.e. exercise book) at arm's length. My favourite was a sonnet about Basildon on a wet Saturday, though perhaps you had to know Basildon. Francine had chosen an anti-war poem.

' "The Dream",' she read.

> *I dreamed I stood in an empty street,*
> *Which dripped with death like a haemorrhage.*
> *Across my feet lay a boy called Peace.*
> *His raw wound bled into the gutter . . .'*

'Hey, Frankie,' said Patti quietly. 'No.'
'No?'
'I really don't think so.'
'How about this one?' She rustled through the pages.
' "The Nightmare".'

> *I dreamed the High Street shook with bombs,*
> *The pavings ran with blood.'*

'No,' said Patti.

'OK,' said Francine agreeably. She closed her eyes. 'You know what would go really good with this music? *Love Story*,' crooned Francine. 'The bit at the end when she dies. Is our copy here, Jo, or round mine?'

'Round yours.'

'Good,' said Patti.

Rachmaninov sluiced over my suffering, adding a further dimension, the sting of an imagined nostalgia. Francine was asking Patti whether it hurt, meaning whether *it* hurt, and Patti was saying no, not if you've ever worn Tampax. There was nothing there to hurt if you'd ever worn Tampax.

'Hey,' she then said, 'wouldn't this music be so great to make love to?'

Yes, wouldn't it? That was the dimension – the vicarious knowledge of another woman's joy. Anna-Carlotta Campiani's. From my brief encounter I could extrapolate to hers. Florian would want music. Yes, they must have had music; it had pulsed through her arterial blood while he was enveloping her, enfolding her, inside her; in the sway of his music, they had moved against each other's skin with the slippery elegance of ice dancers. Pain rang through my sinews, blotted out sound, blinded me. Any last vestige of belief in my own significance was blown away by the memory of Florian's red eyes in our conservatory. 'I took her to the station. I put her on the train.' His voice was all over my head like a song caught on the brain. 'Do you know Santa Monica, California, at all?' he'd asked Patti. 'There's this girl . . .' 'Blues is the sound of a man's soul when there's a woman he wants so bad he *aches*. So bad, he's ready to *beg*.' Images of a beautiful black-haired Carly formed on the inside of my eyelids. She wasn't just another quick grope to pass the time, like me. Like Francine. No, Carly was different – Florian was in love with her.

Now, through my head ran a chunk of imagery by a fellow poet. Shakespeare. *And with some sweet oblivious antidote, cleanse the stuff'd bosom of that perilous stuff which weighs upon the heart*. Well, my parents had a medicine cabinet that brimmed with it, only a few feet away. And Francine and Patti wouldn't stay all night.

Then somebody wrecked everything anyway by hammering on the bathroom door so hard that it shook the record player, sending the stylus leaping and bucking across the grooved plastic.

'Who's freaking out?' grumbled Patti and languidly raised herself upright to open the door.

It was Tarquin.

'Now look, Jo,' he said, striding through the drowsy air of the bathroom, straight past Patti and across Francine's supine form to where I was cradling my traumatized record player. 'I'm a tolerant dude, I'll put up with most stuff. But that fucking treacle is right out of order!'

291

At which he snatched the album from the turntable and slammed back out again with Rachmaninov, the Philadelphia Orchestra and Leopold Stokowski swinging from one enormous hand.

'Tarquin!' I shouted after him and scrambled to my feet. I felt my head spin. Then the room dissolved and I crumpled to the floor like a sabotaged deck chair.

37

Rain. I woke to it, a drum-roll on the plastic cement bags. A hectic stream poured from unmended guttering onto the dandelions and dock weeds below my window. Turbulent flow, I thought as I surfaced. Doesn't obey Poiseuille's law. Elvis had spent the night on my bed; in the grey rainlight I now saw his small body spasmodically heaving. Throwing up over my carpet. Fur balls probably. Worse still, Clarence had gone back to bugging us, and was wafting smells of sewage across the first storey. It was nothing to do with the plumbers; Mum and Dad's new en suite was fine and they hadn't touched the main bathroom.

Inadequately slept, I dragged myself downstairs to get a cup of tea and some food in my stomach before clearing up what had been expelled from Elvis's. In the kitchen I found Angela with the baby over one shoulder, slapping fried eggs about in a pan and eating a boiled egg sandwich. Little balls of rubbery eggwhite were exploding from it and bouncing all over the quarry tiles. Angus was at the table juicily sucking a bacon rasher. I wasn't hungry enough to share a table with Angus. If you look after animals you develop a kind of professional fortitude in the face of poo, widdle and vomit, but if you don't have younger siblings, nobody has ever dribbled in your breakfast.

'Josephine! Can you put the condiments on the table for me, please?'

I groaned and went for the salt and pepper.

'What was that about?' snapped Angela.

'It's just such an embarrassing word,' I complained. 'I mean – *condiments*. It sounds disgusting. Like . . . like cahoots,' I added, shuddering. 'Or vestibule. Or *plinth*!'

'You need your head examining,' said Angela.

I went back up to Elvis. By the time I'd carried out the necessary ministrations and returned to the kitchen for a second try, there had been a scene shift. Timothy was now at the table eating bacon and eggs. Angus was wedged under the hostess trolley, throwing plastic fruit so that the floor was strafed with flying bananas. His father walked up and down burping the baby. If I'd had a baby I certainly wouldn't have let Geoffrey do all this walking up and down with it. Babies probably wouldn't bounce on quarry tiles.

'What happened to Angela?' I asked the kitchen.

'She's right behind you, madam,' said Angela herself, taking off her pinny. 'While you're not doing anything useful, Geoffrey,' she said to him, 'you can go upstairs and check all the windows are closed against this rain.'

I scrambled some eggs in the pan and had them on toast, riffling through a copy of *Petticoat*.

'God,' exclaimed Timothy, 'is that what you've come to?' An unreasonable comment, I considered, from someone whose secret reading matter focused on women who'd require a block and tackle to stand them upright. Tim's exam results were due any minute, but today's post brought only the usual heap of mail addressed to Tarquin. This generally included at least one envelope seething with razor blades or something equally explicit, plus the bizarre output of his lunatic-fringe fan club, which today, by the looks of it, ran to a stamped and addressed bassoon.

'What have you got there?' I asked Timothy of his book.

'Schrödinger.'

'Borrow it after you?'

'Suppose so,' said Timothy, ungraciously.

'What's a Schrödinger when it's at home?' asked Angela, and was ignored.

A workman came in carrying a trestle table. 'We can't get on with papering the top bedroom, love,' he said. 'Something funny's happened to the wallpaper paste.'

'Funny?' we asked in unison.

'It's turned purple and solidified. Can't split the bugger with a hammer. Never seen nothing like it before in me life.'

'We have,' I told him sadly. It occurred to me that we might at last have found an application for all that pineapple jam of Aunt Janet's. When I tried to voice this, the mention of pineapple jam roused Timothy.

'You can't make jam out of pineapples,' he jeered. 'The fruit's fibrous. Its flesh would turn into black gunge when you boiled it up.'

'Oh, so pineapple jam doesn't exist either?' I shouted back at him. 'Like poltergeists don't exist?'

'That's enough of that!' said Angela. 'And I asked you both a question: what's a Schrödinger?'

'He's a man who invented an imaginary cat, Angela,' said Timothy.

'Don't you be so bloody cheeky!' she fired at him. 'You're not talking to your schoolfriends now, you know.'

'Actually,' I told her apologetically, 'he did invent an imaginary cat. It's quantum theory.' And to Timothy, 'You're getting really insufferable, Timmy, you know that?'

'So what's quantum theory?'

Timothy barked out a short laugh and got up to put the kettle on. The dregs of an earlier cup of tea sat on the table, streaked and peppered from a burst teabag like a fortune waiting to be told.

'I suppose I'm too thick to merit an answer, am I?'

I hurriedly forestalled any response from Timothy. 'It's physics, Angela. The thing is, if you're someone who thinks this is the most fascinating topic ever to engage the human mind, then you don't want to risk cocking up a quick explanation and making it sound like crap.'

'Mind your language in front of the baby, Josephine.'

'Yes, Angela.'

I slid Timothy's book across to me. *A neutron can be transformed into one proton plus one charged pion*, I read, *or alternatively* . . .

'But if this quantum thing of yours is the bee's knees,' said Angela, 'you should want other people to know about it.'

Timothy sat himself back down and swivelled his book away from me. 'I'm sure you'll find it child's play to explain, Josie,' he said across the steaming tea.

'*Thank* you, Timothy,' said Angela. And pulled up a chair at the table.

Yes, thank you, Timothy. And yet, the woman had a point; the world was full of spotty schoolkids of no more than average intelligence who'd never had the slightest problem with this stuff. You only needed to be a Timothy Starkey to understand it *at the age of seven*. He now opened his mouth for some further derogatory comment.

'It's about the basic particles that make up the universe,' I said loudly. Timothy subsided.

'Right,' said Angela comfortably.

'There are two entirely separate ways of describing what they're made of. For example, we can show that a beam of light consists of particles streaming along, we call them photons, and they're solid enough to knock atoms off a sheet of gold foil and splatter them on the wall behind. Unfortunately we can *also* show that light can't be made of particles because it's actually a wave – in any classroom you can demonstrate beams interacting in patterns just like ripples on a pond. Same thing with electrons in an atom: we can prove that they exist as particles whizzing round a nucleus, *or* that they're wrapped around the nucleus as a wave. Totally different things. It depends on which experiment we run.'

'That's impossible.'

'We know, but we're stuck with it. Incompatible and incomprehensible,' I added and then stopped. *Soundlessly collateral and incompatible*. That was from Louis MacNeice's snow poem. A feeling surged through my bones at that moment, coming out of nowhere. Not pain for once, but something good – a stealing warmth like a hot bath on a cold night. How weird. I also suspected that if I kept talking it would happen again.

'And where's this make-believe cat, then?'

'Make-believe cat. Right. Well. There's one school of thought that says: you run your experiment and it might tell you, yes, your electron is a wave or, no, it's a particle. But until that moment of truth you should consider that it's neither one nor the other, but in some halfway state. A *pave* perhaps, or a *warticle*.'

Timothy pretended to choke on his tea.

'Erwin Schrödinger was the man who said, "Now

look. Supposing you shut a cat inside a box with a vial of cyanide that might break or might not. Fifty–fifty chance. Until you open up the box, you won't know whether you've still got a cat or not. But nobody in their right mind would say the animal was both alive *and* dead just because you don't know which. Maybe he's fine, maybe he's snuffed it, but you can absolutely guarantee that you haven't got some undead zombie cat inside in suspended animation. And what's true for cats is also true for electrons – there's no such thing as a halfway state." That was Schrödinger.'

'Quite right, too,' said Angela.

'Quite right, too,' I confirmed. 'Though unfortunately it doesn't help us understand how things can be two ways at once. *World is crazier and more of it than we think,*' I quoted. '*Incorrigibly plural.*' My friend Louis again.

And then I knew the origin of my strange, surging happiness. If I'd been born into the wrong century or the wrong culture, I'd have had neither his poetry nor my quantum physics. *And*, and this was the crux, the same would be true if I'd been born *into the wrong family*. In some other family, without my brothers and their absorbing interests, I might never have been immersed in such glorious things. This was the first time since we moved to Lossing and fell apart that I had ever thought of other people's families as the wrong families. Here in this kitchen with Angela and my scowling twin brother, I would not have swapped my situation for anyone else's in the world.

'People always like a good puzzle,' said Angela. 'Look at Agatha Christie. She's just published her seventieth.'

'True,' I said happily.

'Well, thank you for that, Josephine.' And Angela left the kitchen, head held high.

'*Paves* and *warticles*?' scoffed Timothy. 'Schrödinger will haunt you!'

'Then he'll be erudite company for Tarquin's poltergeist,' I told him, scraping back the chair, and I was out of the kitchen and up the stairs.

38

When I got back to my room, my own cat wasn't looking much healthier than Schrödinger's. Elvis was curled motionless on the bed and hadn't touched his food, so I left him to himself and went to Francine's.

'Go round yours, can we?' she suggested immediately.

'Bad day. Angela's sticking her nose into everything.' I didn't much like the idea of Patti exposed to the smell of Clarence upstairs.

'Look, Patti wants a cigarette, and we can't go for a walk in this weather, can we?'

'If Angela catches us smoking, she'll kill me.'

'Look, Patti wants to ask you something, all right?'

With my reluctance to disturb Elvis's sickbed, we ended up back in the bathroom. We were wet and it was cold. In the shrinking light of the rainstorm, our Victorian china wore a woeful glimmer like the whites of the eyes of the dying.

'I'll have to open a window,' I told Patti as she lit up.

'Yeah?' she said unenthusiastically. 'Maybe it'll clear this stink.'

'It won't.' I threw the window open, then plonked myself down on the closed mahogany lid of our fancy loo. If Patti had something to ask me, she was in no hurry to come out with it.

'More boys' stuff!' she said scathingly on an intake of smoke. From Tarquin's direction, a synthetic violin was joined by a synthetic vocalist.

'It's called a Moog synthesizer,' I informed her.

'I was talking about the other stuff. I know what a Moog is. At home we got Moogs every Saturday night at every Taco Bell restaurant.'

'Oh, hardly,' I said with scorn.

'I think they do, actually, Jo,' said Francine, quickly. '*Restaurants?*'

'I think they do, actually, Jo.'

'I was *talking*,' said Patti, 'about the *other* stuff.'

The other stuff was Deep Purple's 'Black Night', which was woofing and tweeting from Timothy's room.

'Cock rock,' added Patti derisively.

'God, yeah!' put in Francine with a shrug. 'What's it good for? Air guitar and jacking off!'

I'd been on good terms with the world for all of half an hour – couldn't I be spared one of the few observations absolutely guaranteed to suck my self-confidence from under me like sand in a riptide? No, apparently I couldn't. I suddenly felt unutterably weary and irreducibly big-boned. I didn't hate boys' stuff, I adored it all, the louder the better – Deep Purple, Cream, Hendrix, I loved the thrust of it, the throb of it, the sheer sweat-soaked, testosterone-driven, kit-thumping *balls*. It made me feel alive.

My outsized frame dwarfed the pair of them, pretty little Patti, elfin Francine, filling my mind like despair. Had I ever really felt like a girl? Yes, for a few minutes in the conservatory with Florian, after which I'd entertained him with my knowledge of – *guitars*. Well, there could be no worse indictment; my heart sank irretrievably. I was never a lesbian, they were proper women; my case was something clinical. Look how I enjoyed maths and science and Tarquin's company with his suffocating male preoccupations. I might as well face it: I was transsexual, a boy in a girl's body. Never mind the Florian business – I was a boy who happened to be in love with Florian Smith.

God, I was dying for a cigarette. I grappled for a shred of self-respect.

'Did you ever hear about Schrödinger's cat?' I asked.

'Huh?' said Patti.

'What it is, you see, light can be either a wave or a particle . . .'

'Yeah, yeah. Hey, I just bet *you* like this kind of music,' she speculated. Schrödinger collapsed and misery swept through my veins like fever. 'You like most male stuff, Jo, it gives you a kick, yeah? You're the type that feels good just having guys round the place. You get a different look on your face – at that club on Monday you were glowing like a hurricane lamp. And I guess this heavy rock could feel like you got a sexy man in the room – from how those guys sing, anybody'd think they'd got the hard-on from hell and they're hung like a mule!'

'Jo!' interrupted Francine to rescue me. No, *please* don't rescue me! Not now!

'And pounding away like that, yeah, it could turn a girl on. Hey, I'm surprised you still haven't fallen real bad for some guy, I mean the whole number with—'

'Jo! Patti's got something to ask you. She knows about Clarence.'

My head whipped round.

'You *told* her?'

'Yeah,' said Patti flatly, 'she told me. Look, all I want

302

is this. My brother Robert, I want to give him a message. If this poltergeist of yours—'

'No,' I said.

'Well, why the fuck not? Clarence is dead, isn't he? Easier for him to talk to Robert than for us, for Chrissake.'

Why the fuck not? Because Clarence was a prankster – with a prankster's cruel sense of fun. He would have no respect whatsoever for the finer feelings of a girl who's obviously troubled. Ask Clarence to act as go-between for Robert and his sister, and his sister would be spending the next twenty years on a psychiatrist's couch.

'Patti,' I told her, 'we're dealing with somebody who has a very twisted mind. Even when there's something he *wants* us to know, instead of just telling us, he translates his message into something called a Vigenère cipher leading to a book code. I still haven't cracked the thing. Clarence is not somebody you ask favours of.'

'Yeah, but,' said Patti, 'he won't do *us* a favour but he might for Robert. One dead person for another, right?'

'Truly, you've got to forget it.'

'I can't fucking forget it!' She shrugged a cigarette from the pack and lit up. 'I did something bad. I was angry and wrote a lousy letter. And he *died*!'

'What was it?' I asked gently. 'What did you say?'

'I ain't telling *you*. I'll tell the ghost!'

I walked over to the window. In the driving rain, our overgrown laurels shook like wet dish mops; their musky scent mingled with the sewage smell of Clarence. I asked Patti for one of her American cigarettes. They had cardboard holders. Rather nice. It was a pity the babysitting had dried up before I took to smoking. As well as all that booze, the family always had a cache of cigarettes in a fancy onyx box; I could have kept myself stocked up from one Saturday to the next.

'What did you say to Robert?' I asked again, flicking Patti's lighter.

'He was dating a girl, right? Been seeing her a couple of months before he went away, saw her when he was home on leave, you know? I was going with this guy, Rick. Not a big deal, leastways not to him. He was my first. I wasn't his, well, OK. Then we had this fight. Robert's girl, Marguerite, had a party. We went and Rick got drunk and was horsing around. Party was by their pool, Marguerite's place. Rick pushed her in. She was wearing this short dress, real mini, and when it got wet you could see through it. He jumped in the pool after her. So later we had this fight and he said she was better looking than me and sexier and he got more horny just looking at her than he ever had in the sack with me. So I wrote Robert and told him I'd caught them doing it, having sex, and I said she sure wasn't gonna wait around without a guy just because Robert was in Vietnam – and then Robert *died*!'

Patti sobbed on the unwelcoming lino. It was strange to see her composure blown to the four winds, face burning and blotched. She suddenly looked like her cousin. I took the unsmoked cigarette from between her fingers; an inch of ash dropped onto the floor and scattered in the wet gust from the window. Francine, no stranger to a crying jag, looked rather lost at finding herself on the periphery. She tugged a long length from the loo roll and tucked it into Patti's hand.

I sat down and put my arms around her. 'Clarence isn't the answer,' I said. 'You need to speak to Robert directly.'

She gave an incoherent response.

'Write to him again, Patti. Sit down and write Robert a new letter telling him everything you've told us. Get the whole caboodle down on paper.'

'And then do something with it by Ouija?' suggested Francine.

'No,' I said. 'Nothing to do with Clarence, just a regular letter to her brother.'

Hiccuping, Patti tried to shout me down. 'That's. Fucking. Useless. He's. Dead.'

'It doesn't matter,' I said. 'It will still work for you.'

What did I mean? I meant that some psychological rituals are effective whether we believe in them or not. And how did I know this profundity? Had I read it in some psychiatric journal? No, Tarquin taught me when I was ten.

'Patti, try to believe me about this. It won't take all the pain away, but it will help.'

'Just shut the fuck up, will you?'

My first cat, Jefferson, was killed by a car. When he didn't come home, Tarquin went out to look, but didn't find him. I did, in a ditch by the fields. Blood had run from his nose and dried on his coat, and the fur had stiffened into spikes. I stumbled, howling, back to the Red House with his body cradled cold against my heart. I knew it wasn't fair to blame Tarquin for not getting to the ditch first and sparing me this. But I couldn't help it.

Mummy tucked the bedclothes around me as I soaked the pillow. 'Oh don't cry, little sweetheart. We'll be getting another cat.'

We had to have a cat. It was that or mice.

'I don't want another cat!'

She sat on the edge of my bed, running her fingers through my hair. Even this was wet. 'Time it was cut, too,' she said distractedly.

I snivelled into the bedlinen. The room was so much colder without Jefferson; there is *nothing*, nothing in the *world*, more comforting than slipping your hand against the silky warm tummy of a curled and sleeping cat. Mummy dabbed at me with a liquefying tissue.

'Sweetheart, I know it seems like the end of the world, but it isn't really.'

'Jefferson was *mine.*'

'I know, baby. Daddy and I would bring him back for you if we could. But try to see things in a wider context and you won't feel so weepy. Just last week I looked after another little girl called Josephine who'd been in an RTA and lost her brother. Consider how much worse that would be, darling. If you think like that, you won't feel quite so hopeless with things as they are.'

'It wasn't Jefferson's fault, not being someone's brother,' I'd cried out. 'Being a cat was all he'd got!'

When I was alone again, Tarquin crept into my room. I absolutely didn't want *him.*

'What we'll do, Jo,' he'd said, 'we'll write a song.'

I rolled over to the wall, turning my back on his tactlessness, so Tarquin just sat down on my bed and wrote it himself. I eventually joined in as the only means of evicting him. The song had verse after verse like some Homeric epic. It told the story of Jefferson's life, from his kittenhood to his premature conclusion in a sad ditch. And then we started on me, what I had felt when I came upon his poor little body and how I missed him. The tune wandered all over the place but Jefferson had his song and I would get some sleep.

Patti was now beside herself; a hard and increasingly rain-wet bathroom floor wasn't the place for her. Francine and I led her across the landing to my bedroom. I scooped Elvis off the bed, noting with dismay that he didn't move a muscle as I did so, and settled him on my Indian cushions just seconds before Patti collapsed onto the bed.

'Shall I get us all some coffee?' I suggested and slipped down to the kitchen.

Angela was feeding the baby. Angus, who was wearing the stigmata of his own recent tantrum, was communing with his potty again. Honestly, it was getting so that you never saw the child without that damn potty. I was reminded of his uncle and the Moog.

'Keep pushing,' Angela cooed at him helpfully. 'And push out a nice big one for Mummy.'

I made a lot of retching noises and three coffees, and was just looking for the tray when I noticed a jar of home-made jam on the draining board.

'Is this Aunt Janet's?' I asked, surprised.

'Who's Aunt Janet when she's at home? That's a present from Mrs Richardson.'

'Mrs Richardson?'

'What's the matter with you, Josephine? *Amy* Richardson. Amy and Kenneth.'

Sucking noises drew my attention to Angela's breast. I wished they hadn't. The baby unplugged itself and dribbled. She mopped up.

'But why would Mrs Richardson bring you a jar of jam?'

'Why shouldn't she? We're neighbours.'

Well, *we* are, I thought. You're not, actually, Angela.

'So when,' I continued, chipping away at this exchange as though at a coal face, 'did you run into her?'

'I've known Amy Richardson all my life – I come from Lossing, Josephine, remember? I wasn't always a housewife, you know. I wasn't born married to your brother.'

Angela came from Lossing. Of course she did.

'So you knew Letitia,' I pointed out.

'Yes, of course I knew Letitia, I was at school with her!'

'Right.' I thought back. Letitia was sixteen in 1962, when I was coming up to seven and Geoffrey was sixteen. And Angela, too, was sixteen and living here in Lossing Common. Going to school with Letitia Richardson.

'Letitia Richardson was a friend of yours,' I concluded.

'Why this sudden interest in Letty Richardson, for heaven's sake? *You* couldn't have known her – she'd been gone for months before your mum and dad came here.'

'Well, yes. Presumably, if she hadn't gone, Mum and Dad couldn't have come here because Ken Richardson would never have forced Amy into moving.'

'I don't know about that. Ken had been on at Amy for years to get rid of this huge great place because of the bills. He always did get his own way.'

Interesting. Was this just a front? If the poltergeist was making a nuisance of itself to Ken Richardson *before* Letitia was murdered, that certainly put paid to one theory.

'Right,' I said. 'And then he forced his wife to stick to that plan, even after the tragedy, when the poor woman wanted to stay put.'

'Who told you that?'

'I've heard people say. Amy used to sit in this kitchen and cry.'

'Well, not for long she didn't! Amy Richardson's all right, don't you worry – glad to get the Red House off her hands. She's the sort who's always a bit scared of change, that's all. Once in the new one she was happy as a sandbag. Everything neat as a new pin.'

'Oh, come off it! Your daughter disappears, her body's never found, you wouldn't want to leave her home. You'd cling to it.'

'Perhaps not everybody is as melodramatic as you, madam.'

'Melodramatic?' I repeated incredulously.

'Look, you don't know what happened, Josephine, you didn't even live here then, so this is one thing I know more about than you do.'

'Yes, Angela.'

'Things are not always what they seem.'

'What on earth does that mean?'

'Never you mind.'

I slapped the coffee mugs onto a tray and got out. *Things are not always what they seem*? God help us, it was like talking to some cliché-programmed robot. I was up the stairs. In my bedroom Patti still sobbed, her face lumpy and raw. I hoped no-one noticed that when I opened the door my first glance wasn't at her but at Elvis. He still hadn't moved. My bedroom smelled of cigarette smoke.

'Coffee,' I said unnecessarily.

Francine, who had been pawing at her cousin ineffectually like an unwanted dog, now turned to me with grateful camaraderie. Emotion welled up in me, and with it a clarity of thought that had been missing from the last weeks. How close we were, Francine and I. Two against the world! Why on earth was I keeping secrets from her? I felt as though a tight skin that had throttled my mind were splitting open. I was suffused with a sense of actual physical release, like drilling that hole in the head, that trepanning they kept going on about in *Oz* and *International Times*.

'Frankie!' I blurted out. 'Oh Frankie, there's something I've never told you! Look, you remember the Thursday evening when Patti arrived and you came rushing round here and I was on the staircase, all sort of—'

Patti's voice broke in. 'So what was that stuff about a letter?' she asked gracelessly. She was pulling herself upright on the bed and her voice was rough. 'A letter to Robert.'

It took a while for the name Robert to ring a bell. Eventually, I remembered what we were doing here.

'Look, just *tell* me, OK?'

'OK,' I began. 'It's like I said. Write the whole thing out. Explain to your brother what you did and why,

309

and then tell him what you've been through since he was killed.'

'And then what – *mail* it to him?'

That was acidic with sarcasm, but I gave the suggestion some thought. 'Yes,' I decided, 'in a post-box, in a properly stamped envelope. Not here in Lossing, in case the postman recognizes the surname and delivers it to the Switts. And not care of the US Armed Forces, or it'll get bounced back to the family.'

Both Patti and Francine looked at me. Patti's eyes were narrow with distrust.

'Post it in Brentwood,' I advised them. 'Addressed to Robert's full name, in Heaven,' was my final inspiration.

'You believe in that Heaven stuff? Like a little kid?'

With this, sympathy failed me. 'Then think up your own way of easing your feelings,' I said. 'You're the one with the dead brother and the guilty conscience.'

Patti launched into a convoluted American obscenity and took herself off. Francine looked wearily at me. 'Cheers, Jo. I've got to live with that,' she said and followed her. There was a parting shot.

'You people don't even have any damn poltergeist!' shouted Patti from the landing. 'This stink? You been using the tub in your mom's bathroom and haven't turned the faucets on down here. So all the water's dried out from the traps that catch back-up smells from the john. My dad's a plumber. We ain't fancy doctors, but we know toilet odours ain't a fucking ghost!'

I heard her clatter down the staircase. I sat on the bed in the crevasse left by Patti and looked across at Elvis. Both of us could do with some comfort. I plugged in the electric fire for him and drank all three coffees myself.

39

The weather continued bad the next day too. To be fair to the builders, they were unused to houses that fought back when you tried to fix holes in them, but they could have factored into their programme the possibility that it might, at some point in an English summer, rain. Our roof was tiled, coped, guttered and waterproof – all the workmen needed to do was ensure that the windows, the roof lights, were closed at night. But they didn't. Under one window, resting across the scaffold boards, was a roll of insulation waiting to be put between the joists. As rain drove in, the thickly wadded roll of porous thirsty foam drank it like a sponge. In the middle of Thursday morning the whole lot slithered between the scaff boards and crashed into my parents' room. This in turn soaked the unfinished plasterboard of the ceiling below, which disintegrated like wet blotting paper. So the entire caboodle fell right through the upper storey and crashed onto the landing, bringing most of our parents' bedroom with it.

Angela screamed bloody murder. Angus had been upstairs. Convinced that the child was now splattered across the landing, Angela rampaged through the filthy wet sea of disintegrated fibre, thereby spreading the catastrophe down the stairs and up the walls. Needless to say, Angus was untouched; he'd dragged his potty into the mayhem and sat contentedly in its upturned contents, stuffing cold soaked foam into his face by the handful. So Angela dialled 999 for an ambulance.

Unfortunately, our roof space had two windows. Under the other was an open bag of cement, into which rain had drizzled all night, followed, during the crash, by water from a couple of upturned buckets. We now had a bag of dry cement and slurry nicely laced with lumps of set concrete unevenly balanced on a makeshift floor. There was a terrible *crump*. As I watched from my bedroom doorway, the bag smashed through the house like a bomb, exploding onto the floor of the hall in a violent mushroom cloud, billowing back from the ceiling, splattering across the floor, piling up like some terrible mineral snowdrift against pelmets and ledges and Georgian door casings, and choking the air with chalk. Our wretched, long-suffering stair carpet was buried deep under crunching grit. And so, more or less, were Angela and Angus. The phone she was using to call the emergency services was in the hall, just feet away from the epicentre. Caught in the blizzard, mother and child were coated, crusted and stiff as Lot's wife. Though not, unfortunately, as quiet.

I just stood there, stunned. The landing swirled like a sandstorm. Blind and asphyxiated, I imagined Tarquin's beloved fruit-and-blossom banisters pulverized. In my mind I saw them spring apart under the plummeting weight, and in horrible slow motion topple to the hall below, followed by every other post in sequence, pop pop pop, springing from under their rails and tumbling through the cement-soaked air like fancy clubs from an incompetent juggler. Priceless eighteenth-century carving. Now, peering through a dust cloud like a muslin curtain, I saw that the Red House had spared us this one irredeemable catastrophe. The banisters were untouched. Landing on the floor below, the bomb must have missed the turn of the stairs by an inch. Speaking of Tarquin, where the hell was he? This was the *musique concrète* of a lifetime.

Once Angela and Angus had screamed out of Lossing Common in a fanfare of sirens, Timothy reclaimed the phone. He couldn't give a damn about the chaos; his exam results had arrived, since when he had been phoning Harley Street every five minutes trying to get hold of Dad, who seemed to have mysteriously disappeared. Timothy's was a brilliant achievement, as expected: an A grade in both A level papers and a distinction in both Special papers. Typical of the bloody Red House to upstage him by choosing today to collapse. I found my way gingerly downstairs, trotted off to the local shop, and then set to work on a celebratory chocolate layer cake.

Francine and Patti made no attempt to disguise their distaste.

'A *cake*? You mean like babies have for their birthdays?'

Apparently they had come round to impart some further bad news, but had abandoned theirs as soon as they clocked ours. 'Jesus,' said Patti, impressed. Men hauled buckets and trundled wheelbarrows up and down the staircase, the noise of which resounded through the house like Lester Bangs's maniacal bedlam.

'Timothy's got an A grade with distinction in both

pure and applied maths,' I explained, dribbling egg yolk from a spoon into the porcelain bowl of our Kenwood mixer.

'That's me,' piped up Timothy himself. 'The genius in residence.'

'Big deal,' said Francine.

Then Patti seemed to have an inspiration. 'Are you gonna add . . . you know?' She indicated the cake mix. It was clear that I didn't know, so she mouthed 'marijuana' at me.

'No, I'm not!' I told her, nettled. It might have occurred to her that if Timothy could achieve A grade distinctions he could probably lip-read four syllables. 'Look, I wouldn't even know how to go about it,' I said.

'Well, *I* would,' piped up Timothy. 'What you've got is resin. It's fat-soluble. Just stir up the stuff in a pan with melted butter, then add it to both the mix and the filling. Perfect chemistry.'

'Oh yeah, like your thermoplastics?' jeered Francine, predictably. But Patti cut across her.

'Right on,' she said to Timothy. 'The guy knows his shit. Come on, Jo,' she coaxed. 'Go get it and we'll have some fun.'

'Now look,' I told them. 'Much as I would love to dope Angela, she's a nursing mother and cannabis passes into breast milk . . .'

'Oh *gross*!'

'So we don't give any to Angela! We eat it in your room.'

'We can't get into my room. Half Mum and Dad's bedroom is blocking the door.'

'You managed to get out,' Timothy reminded me sweetly.

'Yes, but,' I said.

'What is it with girls?' asked Timothy of the world at large. 'Any marginally original idea gets the response "yes, but" as a kind of knee-jerk reflex. Does it come from social conditioning? Or is it programmed into the female psyche like premenstrual tension?'

I rounded on him, a Germaine Greer quote at the ready, but Patti was laughing admiringly. 'Hey, that's good!' she said, and reached out one long bronzed hand in a mock buffet. Timothy smirked. And then blushed. Misgivings flooded me. When Patti had lunged towards him, it was borne in on me that beneath the tight sweater she wasn't wearing a bra. Timothy cleared his throat. 'Two votes against one, so far,' he announced. 'If Francine is a veto, then I'll ask the builders to settle it.'

'Let's all get stoned,' decided Francine.

Deeply disturbed, I tramped upstairs behind a wheelbarrow, fought my way through the foaming sea of fibre and cement, and re-emerged in the kitchen with a dung-coloured slab of cannabis to spike a cake for the guy who apparently knew his shit.

The news that Francine and Patti had delayed imparting was truly terrible.

'Guess what,' announced Francine mournfully once we were in my bedroom. 'Mom wants me to start the new school at the beginning of term. September, before she even gets into the new apartment! I don't go back with you, Jo, I got to slog up there from *here*.'

'No!'

'Yes. She's got it all planned. Dad can give me a ride to Brentwood station each day, on his way into Warley. If we leave home at seven thirty, I can be at Regent's Park in time for school.'

'But your dad doesn't leave home at seven thirty.'

'He will do now,' said Francine grimly.

'That's not even a month,' I calculated. 'Three weeks and a day.'

Of course, it had been clear for ages that we had no chance of moving to Harley Street in time for the

Switts' house move, but I now felt the last faint hope being stamped out. Given the broiling chaos on the distal side of my bedroom door, I reckoned it would take more than Frankie's three weeks and a day to get the Red House back to the state it had been in yesterday afternoon.

'So what's this flat like?' asked Timothy. Patti had appointed him to take charge of the wine – two more bottles she'd filched from Mr Switt's rack.

'No-one's seen the place except Mom and Dad,' moaned Francine.

'All done behind our backs,' added Patti. 'Uncle Jerry I'm surprised at, he's usually such a good guy.'

They were all getting rapidly high – except me, of course, I bloody wasn't. Patti kept sighing heavily and stretching. Whenever she raised her arms above her head, which was frequently, the sweater would rise with them and flash her golden midriff. The contours of her breasts swelled against the tight material and subsided, Timothy's eyes following them like Elvis watching a tuna-fish sandwich. Then she would do it again.

'More cake?' I asked loudly.

'Hey,' responded Patti with lazy eroticism. 'Take it easy, Jo. Some things you gotta do slow. *Real* slow,' she repeated on an intake of breath, 'and del-ici-ously laid . . . back.' She snuggled down into her cushion. I was dismayed to see Timothy gnaw at his lip so hard he was drawing blood.

'So when are you leaving for the States?' I shot at her. 'Soon, presumably. You have to be back for school.'

'Well, maybe,' she said and held out the dregs of her wine towards Timothy. 'Maybe not. Hey, fill me up, will you, please?' Then she widened her eyes at the double entendre and giggled.

This was bad, this was very bad. Patti was not the

giggling sort, stoned or otherwise. What was she doing it for? I mean, it wasn't as though she could seriously have an eye on Timothy. I mean, not *Timothy*. Meanwhile, with his stare still focused on the bullseyes of her protuberant nipples, Timothy glugged more wine into the tooth mug and Patti made a succulent murmur out of the words 'thank you'. Bob Dylan's album *Blonde on Blonde* issued from the record player. Even his prematurely aged growl sounded sexually provocative in the sultry atmosphere emanating from Patti.

Perhaps Francine's eyesight was impaired by having pupils contracted to pinpricks, but anyway, she had rooted my candles out from a drawer. Patti reached for one, and with fingers as fluent as a harpist, she stroked one golden hand up and down the body of the candle like Faye Dunaway's chess-piece in *The Thomas Crown Affair*.

I was toxic with anger – black, painful and highly erotically charged. This was something I'd never experienced before. What was going on? Was my sexual arousal a vicarious response on behalf of my poor tormented twin, who looked as though he might whimper and was now trying to throw one of the cushions unobtrusively across his lap? Or was I responding to another woman's pleasure in the exercise of her sexual power? A sense of Florian was suddenly as intense as if he were holding me. It was bloody uncomfortable, I knew that much, and I wished to God that I could simply get stoned like everybody else and leave Timothy to cope with his own agonies.

It was now several hours since anyone had slammed the front door in this house, so it was long overdue when it came.

BANG!!!

The walls and Bob Dylan trembled and a voice carried from the hall. 'WHERE THE HELL ARE THE BUILDERS?'

'God, that woman can holler!' complained Timothy.

I jumped up, conscious of our cigarettes, and wrestled with the sash window. Rain bounced at the sill and dribbled down my painted walls into our warm nest of cigarette smoke and pot. Patti was lighting up again. I plucked the cigarette from her fingers.

'Hey, no sweat, the door's locked!'

'Angela has no respect for locks,' I reminded everyone. 'She'll use the baby as a battering ram if she has to.'

Francine helpfully slipped the ashtray into the nearest drawer, unfortunately the one with *Nineteen Eighty-Four* in it. And my underwear.

We heard Angela's progress up the stairs, together with furious expostulations.

'With a bit of luck she'll break her neck,' said Timothy, picturing the skiddy cement.

'JOSEPHINE? TIMOTHY?'

'Oh, for heaven's sake!' I opened the door just enough to pop my head around it. Angela was poised at the threshold, coated with grey and wet from the knees down. She had the baby rolled up under one arm, so I wasn't wrong.

'Where are the builders?'

'They went off to get some equipment, Angela,' I invented in the vain hope of a quiet life. They had decided on a tea break then idled back here after half an hour to take a fresh look at the task still ahead of them. In response to the fresh look, they vanished.

'Angus all right, is he?' I added out of politeness.

'No, he is *not* all right. The poor little lamb had to be dosed with paraffin.'

Paraffin? Gosh. And we'd put our cigarettes out too.

'They're keeping him in overnight until all the green

gunge works its way through.' A gagging sound behind me drew her irritated attention.

'Who's in there with you?' demanded Angela, pushing at my door, perhaps expecting that I'd smuggled the builders into bed with me while the Red House petrified beneath a cloak of solidifying concrete. Her right arm levered me sideways. She was in.

'Oh,' she said.

My companions offered a languid wave, unmistakably a portrait of stoned teenagers.

'Hello, Angela,' said Timothy smoothly. 'Don't worry about the mess in the hall – Dad will clear it out, it's what he's trained for. He'll stand on the front steps and work through the letterbox.'

'Timmy, that's a very old joke!' I grumbled, but Patti screamed with laughter, rolling onto the carpet. I watched Angela and Francine blink at him, baffled.

'Anyway, do come in,' he continued, waving a chipped mug. 'We're celebrating.' In the bow spray of Angela's fury, Timothy had apparently recovered his equilibrium. 'Celebrating my A level passes in pure and applied maths,' he enunciated carefully. 'Two A grades with distinction.'

'And the grown-ups don't get invited, I suppose.'

'There haven't been any grown-ups,' Timothy argued reasonably. Then grievance overtook him. 'Mum and Dad haven't even re*mem*bered,' he said. 'Geoff shot off without so much as wishing me good luck, *you* were out of here within half an hour of the post arriving . . .'

'In an ambulance!' objected Angela. 'Cradling a two-year-old at death's door!'

'Death's door!' responded Timothy, and I saw with horror that his eyes brimmed. 'None of you gives a stuff,' he continued with a quaver in his voice. 'Not even my own mother. Two A grades with distinction, for Chrissake – at *fifteen*!'

He probably hadn't intended to emphasize that 'fifteen' in front of Patti's breasts. Tears soaked Timothy's face. I wanted to cross the room and cuddle him, but that would only add to his humiliation. As I stood there dithering, Angela suddenly showed a side of herself that we didn't know.

'Right then,' she said with an air of rolling her sleeves up, 'shift along, you lot.' She lowered her large bottom onto the edge of Patti's cushion like a descending barrage balloon. The baby bounced in her arms as she landed. 'What are we drinking?' Angela grabbed Mr Switt's bottle. 'Mouton,' she read, 'Rothschild. Well, if one of you can get me a glass and a plate from downstairs, I'll be more than happy to celebrate Timothy's academic success.'

'Oh, do share *my* plate, Angela,' said Timothy, carving her a sizeable chunk of chocolate layer cake. He drained his own mug.

'By the way,' he continued, filling it to the brim for Angela, 'did you hear about the prostitute who bought a parrot . . . ?'

40

It was the alcohol, I decided, that would save the day – Angela wouldn't breastfeed after she'd been drinking. She was dressed in a print frock like a biddy just come from a milking shed, legs all over the place and suspiciously shiny round the chest. Having settled the baby on the bed in the lee of my pillows, she was waving a piece of cake about and talking with her mouth full. And because she'd missed her mouth once or twice, chocolate was generously painted across her nostrils. As an antidote to Patti's excruciating sexuality, Angela was an answer to prayer, though admittedly not to Timmy's. In the damp fug, Bob Dylan was singing 'Rainy Day Women Numbers 12 & 35', with its valuable insights into getting stoned.

Angela had launched herself upon some involved story about clandestine drinking of alcoholic beverages when she and Geoffrey were sweet sixteen. And suddenly I was extremely glad that my head was clear.

'Jolly sweet you were, too, at sixteen!' I interrupted

with such force that Angela jumped. 'Geoffrey was completely smitten.' I leaned back against the bed and tried to look expansive. Patti shot me an intelligent look. Francine blatted her eyes in surprise. Timothy, with open derision in his, drew back and stared.

'And to think that you'd just lost your friend Letitia,' I continued. 'I've found myself wondering whether you turned to Geoffrey as a kind of protector. In the grief of losing Letty Richardson.'

'You shouldn't believe everything you hear, Josephine,' said Angela with a complacent smile. 'Things are not always . . .'

'. . . what they seem,' I finished for her. 'No, so you said. But I mean, the complete disappearance of a teenager. The police flummoxed and her mother desolate . . .'

'Don't you worry about Letty's mum, she knows what's what.'

'Really?' I exclaimed in a pretence of astonishment. 'Oh, how *clever* of Mrs Richardson.'

'Clever is as clever does,' said Angela darkly. She'd polished off her first slab of cake and was tucking into a second. I poured more wine into her mug.

'Was Letty's mum in on it right from the start, then?'

'Ooooh no,' responded Angela happily. 'Not for *ages*. Nor Ken neither.'

'So they didn't know where their daughter had gone.'

'Skedaddled!' said Angela. 'Goody!' Then 'Shame!' she said immediately and shuddered. Shame? Her attention turned back to the cake; another minute and I'd lose her.

'That Ken Richardson,' I hazarded, tutting theatrically, 'with his young girls!'

'And why up there anyway?' Angela asked the assembled company. 'If they had to have sex, why couldn't they do it in the back of the car like anybody else?'

That slapped us all into silence. While her words twinkled in the indolent air, Angela picked cheerfully at the gloopy crumbs of her cake. For some time, Timothy, with his forehead rippled like a rucked rug, had shown signs of imminent explosion. Now he blew.

'What the hell is this about?'

I leaned backwards, smiling, and clamped a hand across his mouth.

'It's OK, Jo,' whispered Patti, 'I'll shut him up. Be glad to. It makes me so horny to see a guy can't take his eyes off of me! Timmy,' she said in a voice of velvet. 'Hey.'

I took my hand from his mouth. She clamped her own mouth where my hand had been. It crossed my mind to wonder whether she'd taken out her gum. I turned back to my interrogation of Angela.

'What *exactly* triggered Letty to skedaddle?' I asked.

She was smiling blankly.

'Angela, why did Letty go?'

'The MoD man.'

'MoD man?' I repeated tentatively. It crossed my mind that I'd seen episodes of *Lassie* in which the questioners had got a more lucid narrative out of the dog.

'What do you mean, Angela?'

'Oooh, you Starkeys do keep on!'

Then my bedroom door clicked shut. So who'd opened it? Timothy. He'd gone. So had Patti. I heard their conspiratorial laughter as they waded across the catastrophe of the landing. Timothy's bedroom door was opening. There was the sound of a yielding lock. There was a pause. There was a scream.

'G-*ross*!'

Timothy was trying to say something but Patti overrode him. 'Je-*sus*! This is filthy!' Then, 'Oh God oh God you got *rats*!'

323

'No, no, they're hamsters, they're pets! Look, we'll go downstairs if you want.' Timothy's voice was threaded with a coarse grain of panic. 'The whole house is empty.'

But Patti was kicking her way back through the pandemonium. 'Not for a million bucks,' she screamed. 'Let me out of this place!' We heard her sloshing down the stairs. Out the front door.

'What a lot of fuss somebody's making,' suggested Angela airily, before passing out. She rolled heavily from my Indian cushions onto the worn old carpet. Rain bounced off the peeling paint of the window sill and added its own insults to the milk-stained flowery print of her horrible frock.

41

I need not have worried about Angela's breast milk –
with the memory of nausea and vomiting living on in
her sprigged terylene, she needed little persuasion to
believe that she'd celebrated Timothy's success with a
heavy hand on the wine bottle, and should now refrain
from poisoning the baby with its after-effects.
Presumably Geoffrey had recognized the truth the
moment he came home and set eyes on her – a right
twit he might be but he *did* work with people's brains.
Still, he wasn't so much of a twit as to enlighten her.
Timothy hadn't responded well to Patti's rejection,
and was sulking in his room. I felt sorry for him, but
on the plus side I got to hear a lot of heavy rock at ear-
splitting volume.

Our air was full of cement dust for days; it dithered
in suspended skeins of pulverized stone, to settle with
quiet devastation in our hair and eyelids. But not on
our banisters. Tarquin was not taking any more
chances. A couple of specialist carpenters turned up
at the front door. Tarquin appeared from nowhere,

side-stepped a groggy Angela, and set them to dismantle our fabulously carved rails and balusters, which were duly removed for storage in a place that less resembled Edgar Allan Poe's toppling House of Usher. We now had one newel post and a lethal flight of unprotected stairs.

Elvis had still neither eaten nor moved, so I had to stop telling myself it was just fur balls. He was ill. I swept him up from the desolate vacuum of our sitting room – echoing once again with workmen returned to the Red House to clock up time-and-a-half on a Saturday – and got him to a vet in Brentwood.

Of course, there was no such thing as a cat basket in the Red House. In the end I borrowed a container from the Switts and was soon seated upstairs on the bus to Brentwood with Elvis curled like a cushion inside the delicate white tracery of Francine's Turkish birdcage.

I was worried half to death. The smell of the surgery was alien when I'd expected it to be familiar. A brisk receptionist established too quickly that my family had never graced these premises before and that my patient had been moribund for days before any of us had bothered to grace the premises now. I perched nervously on a sweating plastic chair while huge fanged dogs barked and snarled around us.

But the vet was kindness itself. As he lifted Elvis's soft body from the birdcage, he said, 'Well now, Tiger, what can we do for you?' Then he straightened up after the physical examination, and it was clear to me that the preliminary diagnosis was bleak.

'It's an ear infection,' said the vet, rubbing the bridge of his nose. 'Unfortunately,' he smiled sadly at me, 'in cats these are usually a sign of something growing in the ear that shouldn't be there.'

'Do you mean a malignancy?' I asked, and swallowed.

'Well, let's not jump to conclusions,' he advised me gently, running his hand through Elvis's coat. 'First, I need to syringe this ear, which will relieve the pressure and make him more comfortable. Then I'd like to keep him in and operate Monday morning. Take a look around.'

'Oh,' I said. Tears seeped from their ducts. The vet patted my shoulder and turned tactfully back to Elvis. 'Now then, little chap, this will be jolly unpleasant but we'll all be happier once it's done.'

The bus ride home was awful. The surgery didn't seem to need the birdcage, so I took it away with me and cradled it all the way home on the bus, uncaring that my eyes were blotched, that with my luck Florian was probably in the kitchen waiting for me. He wasn't. I went round to Francine's and spent a dismal evening in front of an illustrious estate agent's brochure with photographs of their new apartment. The rooms were vast, low-ceilinged, and unremittingly beige.

'It is a tumour,' the vet told me sadly on the Monday.

'Were you able to resect it?'

'Mostly. And I've sent biopsy tissue away for analysis. We'll get the results in five days.'

'Five days?' I repeated weakly.

'Then we'll know for certain.'

'If it is malignant,' I asked quietly, 'what is the prognosis?'

'Not good, my dear,' he told me, looking me in the eye.

I'd written a note for Mum, in response to which she had made out a blank cheque and left it for me in an envelope. I now filled in the details at reception while they put Elvis into a cardboard carrier. He was perkier now that his ear wasn't stuffed up, but one side of his head had been shaved for surgery and painted green, which made a poignant farce of his feline air of dignity.

At home again, Angus (himself thoroughly con-valesced, in fact fighting fit) was delighted to find a green-headed, semi-bald cat in the house. Intent on colouring in the rest, he stalked him, crayon in hand. I scooped up Elvis, took him to my bedroom and fled to the Switts'.

'So the vet says it is a tumour,' I told them, sobbing, 'and most likely malignant.'

I expected Patti to conclude that she'd heard enough from me about cancer to last her a lifetime, but apart from pursing her lovely mouth when I started on about the vet syringing pus from Elvis's ear (and to be fair, this reaction was shared by her uncle Jerry), she sat through the chronicle without a murmur.

'You did right to get him the best care, Jo,' said Mr Switt. 'I guess all we can do now is hope and pray.' These were platitudes, I knew, but he spoke them from a full heart. 'Hope for the best and prepare for the worst.'

I blew hard into his handkerchief and offered it back to him. Mr Switt courteously told me to keep it. His kindness made me cry again.

'So,' I said hurriedly, casting about for any topic, anything at all, 'what about your good news, then?'

'Mine?' queried Mr Switt, perplexed.

'The apartment in St John's Wood.' Francine and Patti had been up to see it yesterday.

'Ah. Yes, it's certainly an apartment in St John's Wood, Jo, nobody can deny it. Now, you come over whenever you want. Don't wait for your family to move to Harley Street.'

'It looks very impressive in the brochure. How lovely for you.'

'So they tell me, Jo.'

He sounded truly disheartened. Yet it wasn't nice, was it, to be away from his wife and daughter all the working week? Or from his daughter, anyway.

Mrs Switt was upstairs with Aunt Janet; they had been out buying new bedlinen. Decorated with pineapples. When eventually they came down, it was safe for us to go up. Francine clearly had something momentous to impart. Although she had cried when I told them about Elvis, there was a covert tendency to caress her hair and sigh. My heart raced and I felt sick. This was about Florian. She'd been with him somehow. All the stuff I'd thought about Carly was rot, what turned him on was simply the American accent . . .

'Jo!' announced Francine a millisecond after her bedroom door closed on us. 'Jo, I've met this guy!'

I sat down hard on the bed. 'Guy,' I repeated.

Francine turned to Patti, her eyes a-glitter. 'You tell her!'

'No, you tell her, he's your guy.'

'No, you tell her!'

'OK,' said Patti. 'Frankie's met this guy. He's nineteen, a student at the London School of Economics . . .'

'Oh, you're useless,' interrupted Francine. 'Let me tell her! His name's Joe. Isn't that just *the* most beautiful coincidence you ever heard of in your life? I mean, what a great omen! He lives with his family in one of those groovy flats nobody would let Mom have, on Regent's Park. His father's a dipsomaniac so he goes to Buckingham Palace a lot . . .'

'A diplomat,' amended Patti.

'Yeah, and Patti and me were going to Regent's Park Road so I could show her Cecil Sharp House, but then Joe just saw me the other side of the street and came over to say I looked like a model, and I told him I was! And it was love at first sight! So we dumped Patti and went to the zoo – isn't that just so romantic? – and he got off with me by the penguins. We've been on the phone practically every single minute since yesterday.

I have to pretend to Mom I'm talking to Paula and Barbara about how I won't be back next term. And we're going to the cinema Wednesday night to see *Soldier Blue*!'

This was one of the current wave of movies violently rewriting the old perceptions of the Wild West. Not a great choice. You'd have to be in a very deep snog indeed to keep going through the massacre of Sand Creek.

'So his dad's a foreign diplomat?' I said. 'Which country are they from?'

No response. There was a certain amount of fidgeting. I was about to rephrase the question when Francine and Patti both spoke. 'Kenya,' they told me in unison.

'Hey, far out! Frankie, that's terrific, you'll get to see equatorial Africa, you'll . . .' and then I stopped. 'Kenya,' I repeated.

'Look, Dad won't mind.'

'Uncle Jerry won't mind.'

'He won't, Jo.'

'Not Uncle Jerry.'

No, Uncle Jerry would scarcely bat an eyelid. But once his wife got a whiff of this, he might be very glad that he was living in Brentwood five days a week. Oh dear. Whatever would Francine do for a bolt hole?

After a while, Mrs Switt and Aunt Janet came back upstairs and we were in danger of getting roped into a discussion about linens, so we went back down to the kitchen. While Patti was in the loo, Francine whispered to me that I'd been right about that letter to Robert: Patti didn't feel quite so bad since the girls had posted it, addressing the envelope to

Robert D. Penrose,
c/o Jim Morrison,
Le Père Lachaise cemetery,
Paris,
France

Now why didn't I think of that?

While we were having another coffee, Mr Switt popped his head back into the kitchen.

'Girls,' he said in a stage whisper, 'the topic we discussed earlier. My view of things is just between the four of us, you understand.'

Patti smiled through the lazy chewing of her gum. 'Don't worry, Uncle Jerry, we won't give you away.'

'No,' I echoed, smiling, 'we won't denounce you.' Then my voice disappeared down my throat. Whatever was the matter with me? I was suddenly cold and frightened. Nothing to do with the Switts' house move, something worse. My own words had stabbed at me. *Denounce*. Children denouncing their parents – there was something in *Nineteen Eighty-Four*. Well, yes, there would be, wouldn't there? But it hardly explained this shaft of pain. No, not pain. Fear.

I continued to sit there, pretending to be part of the conversation. Jokes were parried about Mr Switt's weekday flat, how he'd probably end up sharing with students. Francine offered to get him a copy of *Night Train To New Orleans*, so they wouldn't think he was square.

I got up. The chair toppled.

'Jo?' Mr Switt rose too.

'I think I should go home. To check on Elvis.'

'Are you OK?'

'Yes,' I said unsteadily. 'I'm OK.'

But it wasn't true. I was quite terribly frightened in a way that I hadn't felt for years. The old Lossing pains dragged at my insides. I trudged out of the Switts'

house, along the road to ours, up the path. *Denounce,
denounce*, the syllables echoed with my steps in the
sepulchral hall. I needed to reach behind the word,
pull out the baggage to which it was attached, but
some protective instinct within me was putting up too
effective a fight and I couldn't get there. I plodded
upstairs to unearth *Nineteen Eighty-Four*. At the turn
of the staircase, an isolated newel post survived erect
amid the gap-toothed emptiness that had formerly
been our banisters. Florian's suede jacket was draped
over it. I froze. Florian himself was coming in through
the front door.

42

'It's a violin adapted for early sound recording,' he said, sliding his jacket from the carved wood. A splinter caught at the lapel. Florian didn't notice.

'Right,' I said. My voice squeaked as though unused for days. On the periphery of my fog of terror was a conviction that I would never in my life see Florian again.

'You point the big horn at the mike and the smaller horn at your own ear,' he continued.

Not much violin about it, as far as I could see: aluminium with two horns unfurling like some terrible fungal excrescence.

'Invented by a German in London ... Are you all right?'

No, I wasn't. Another word had been fired into my flesh with a barb: *invented*. Nothing to do with violins, another context. In which it carried intimations of unutterable horror. Florian gave a valedictory smile and turned from me, his right foot raised to take the next stair.

I looked from him to the jacketless newel post. It was phallic, I thought with a visceral pang. High time I did something about the visceral pangs. I drew on the courage of my despair. 'Florian!'

'What is it?' He looked surprised. I didn't usually address him in any way that might require a response.

'Would you be very kind?' I asked, placing a shaky hand on his arm.

The ubiquitous fine white cement dust had settled into the creases of his grey suede in a grubby smear. Settled on Florian? A thought became coherent before I could dismiss it: does dust fall on Florian like on ordinary mortals?

'Would you be very kind,' I began again, 'and make love to me?'

He blinked a couple of times, reminding me of Elvis. 'But, baby,' he said eventually with an uncertain half-smile, and then stopped.

'I won't keep you long from Tarquin,' I promised, my own smile ghastly, a mask. 'I know that you're busy with the Stravinsky thing.'

'Stravinsky's in the bag. We're reworking something I wrote for Carly when . . .'

'Florian, I would be really grateful if you'd make love to me.'

His tongue flickered across his lips. 'Baby,' he said again, 'I'm really flattered.'

'Good.'

'But. Are you even sixteen? Tarquin says you aren't.' Distractedly, he went to run a hand through his shining hair but that hand had the German inventor's violin in it, which he therefore whacked against his head. It was an odd situation – the thought flashed into my mind – asking a man to take me to bed who was bashing himself round the head with a horned violin.

'I'm very nearly sixteen, Florian,' I explained.

334

'September the twenty-third.'

He smiled again. 'How amazing,' he told me, 'to be sixteen on September the twenty-third.' He dropped a kiss onto my forehead. Then he gave the instrument another wild wave. 'Got to take my trophy into the studio. Tarquin's waiting for me.'

I watched him go. 'Goodbye, Florian.' My voice petered out. Those barbed words: *invented* and, strangely, *Tarquin*. I sank to the filthy carpet, steadying myself on the rail-less stairs. Now I knew which memory had been hoiked into the light of day, though not yet why it evoked terror. A scene from when I was very small, perhaps six years old. Tarquin incandescent, yelling at Timothy.

'You haven't *invented* it, you stupid kid!' he screamed. 'This isn't *invented*. It's bloody wrecked!'

'It's a telescreen,' fluted Timothy, his head inside it, the voice distant and muffled like a bad broadcast. 'I've invented it from our TV!'

Yes, he had. By ripping out the inner workings. He was very proud that the tube hadn't exploded. But Tarquin had; he'd raged up and down the stuffy room, all piano and gassy air. He clanged his fist against the metal of the fire.

'Mummy and Daddy will go mad!' he screamed. 'You've destroyed our television!'

'No!' said Timmy, struggling to lift the casing off his head. It was heavy, digging into his small shoulders. 'No, Tarquin, don't make Mummy cross with me!'

Not his beloved Mummy. Panic turned Timothy pale. He'd pushed up the casing over one side of his head, and it now crashed to the floor. The glass shattered. 'Not Mummy, Tarquin!'

'Don't make her cross?' screamed Tarquin, beside himself. 'What do we say then, you moron? What's she going to *think* happened – that it committed suicide? Like bloody Granddad?'

Timmy's lips were quivering. Tarquin shouldn't be doing this; he was thirteen, a solid great lad, all thighs and chest. His little brother was six and had recently been a baby. Timmy had little enough of his mother.

'Don't tell Mummy, not Mummy, don't don't don't . . .'

'I'll tell her NOW,' Tarquin had roared. 'I'll phone the bloody *hospital*!'

Timothy had collapsed into frank hysteria. Thank God Dad wasn't in, or we'd have had all three of the Starkey drama queens throwing a wobbly in one cramped space. An exasperated Geoffrey came striding out of his room, past Tarquin, picked up the howling child and carried him off to a place of greater safety.

Now, here on the staircase, my ears rang; a strange crackling ripped through them like a yawn. My heavy arms bristled with their black hair like the limbs on some hefty hod carrier up a Red House ladder. Timothy inside an Orwellian telescreen and Tarquin beyond the control of his own temper, shouting about Mummy. *Before* we moved here, *before* Clarence. Nothing to do with the Red House. But Tarquin often blew up at Timmy, for helping too hard, getting in the way, pleading with his doggy eyes. It never lasted long. So why was this memory damning?

Children denouncing their parents. Oh God, oh God, realization hit me like a deep hard punch to the stomach. He was a character in *Nineteen Eighty-Four*. He was Winston Smith's neighbour who was denounced to the Thought Police by his small daughter – they had the same name, him and the little boy who died on the ice during the winter we moved here. Not Laurence Briggs or Martin West, the other one, whose grave we couldn't find. Tom Parsons. He was Winston Smith's neighbour in *Nineteen Eighty-Four*.

Into my bedroom. I dug out the paperback, grubby now with the smelly debris of dog-ends that Francine had tossed into the drawer. Fumbling, my fingers made a hash of turning pages. Tom Parsons, I found him, his name already ringed with my own pencil because his were the letters T and P that I'd identified from Clarence's message. But of course Clarence's message *hadn't* called for the T and P, it did *not* use the initial letters of words from the novel, it used the actual words in full. Two of the words were Tom Parsons. *Nineteen Eighty-Four* was chosen for the book code *because the message was about a Tom Parsons*.

Thank God I had ringed all the words last time and there was no need to go through all that counting again. The first two were together. **I was**. Move on, move on. My hands shook like leaves in a wind. The next words were his name, that dreadful ringed print. **Tom** and then **Parsons**. So **I was Tom Parsons**.

On to the fifth word. It was **read**. Then **your**. Then **Brother's**. I knew the very essence of fear, a sort of whiting out of the senses. Stop! Breathe! Back to the text! And I had it.

I

was

Tom

Parsons

read

your

Brother's

diary

for

Nineteen

sixty

three

Terror running through me now. My brothers didn't keep diaries. Yes, one of them did. One of them had notebooks on his shelves, labelled in biro: *1969*, *1968*, *1967* ... Timothy. I saw that pitiful telescreen again, heard Tarquin screaming that he would tell Mummy. I was aware of a terrible falling into place of everything. I knew with whiplash certainty what Timothy had recorded in the pages of his diary for 1963 at the age of seven.

But how to get the diary? It would not be easy, not with Timothy holed up like a rat in a room full of rodents, day in day out, and not even Patti to entice him out now. And in the meantime, how would I cope? Could I live here in this house, with its grubby rooms linked by cold and malevolence – waiting to raid the locked chamber of my own twin? No, I couldn't. First thing next morning when Timothy emerged from his bedroom bound for the bath, I borrowed a chisel from the workmen and jemmied his door open.

43

It was an untidy job. The wood split.

'You are joking, love!' objected a plasterer in overalls as I shoved with one unfeminine shoulder and the door, splintering, gave way. He walked in behind me.

'Christ!' he said as the stench hit him.

Bookcase. Got it. *1963*. Riffle through the pages. It was startling to see calculus scribbled in a seven-year-old's hand. Early in the book some pages had been ripped out, leaving a soft beard at the centre. Damn! But as soon as I turned the next page I understood.

```
TDFVMLWKMLHGRSOTXLWKMLWGPHJGR
SOTXLWKILUJXKIPHUSFEQRPMQSVCICWV
SOTXLWKXZCVLRIUEQRPMQSJYQRTIGOPH
WKGRWMVLUSGTDFVMLLPMQSJYQR
TIGOPHICTXBGGZHBREUHKMLWXWL
LVCIWXISOTXLJKMLCPIWVQYVOPH
WKQLXBFVHRCRGHJMUHASQSREUH
KMYWHSXFJYQRTIGOPHQWPIWMVLU
SGTDFVMLWKMWVKVWMVLUSGTDFV
MLJKXZCJYQRTIGOPHWKGRWMREUHK
```

MYHYSWVQYVOPHWVTIHVWRGFGHDB
FWLLVCWKQTDFVMLWKZRBGTDFVMLWK
WLLJYQRTIGOPHQWPIWMHMYSREUHKML
HJVHSVLRIUEQRQRHVWRGFGHDBFJLTV
CICWVSOTXLWKXKFGIWVQYVOPHRBG
LXBFVHRCRGTKJWMHMYSREUHKMLHYS
SOTXLWXXKFGIWVQYVOPHDBFRLBGXBC
PISOTXLW

Code. Of course, of course! Tarquin in the kitchen the night I got home from Dave's party.

'Tim's been into that stuff since he was a kid – you get a message in code, then it's Tim's.'

Of course it was! That must be why Clarence's message was in code – it was the secret language Timothy invented for his childhood diaries; crack it and I could read them.

I grabbed what I needed. I fled the house running. There was a bus! Yes, at the stop – a Stavering bus! I flew across the road, car tyres screaming behind me, grabbed the pole just as the bus lurched away, panted up the shuddering stairs, paid my fare with hands that dropped their change. Sinking into a seat by the window in strobing sunlight, I sneezed and forgot myself, wiped my nose with my hand and my hand on the seat. The Lossing pains were so bad I was almost doubled over.

Our bus jerked through the country lanes, heaved to a halt at interminable bus stops. I knew I had to start work, trudge through Timothy's code, but I couldn't even begin, not in this state. I'd brought *Nineteen Eighty-Four* and an exercise book but the deciphering would take hours of careful, patient plodding – and a single mistake would throw the whole message out of kilter, lead me to the wrong word in that hateful book. I *must* get my head together.

Out of the bus at Stavering. Now where, where? The

vehicle moved off again, raking me with tiny stones thrown up from the road. Driven by some atavistic sense of sanctuary I made for the Norman church. The door was *locked*. It was *locked*. Turn down the crunching path skirting the cold grey walls and round to the churchyard. Graveyard. I sat on the grass. Still cramped with pains and ponging like a polecat, I drew up a table around EDOC, the way Timothy must have done all those years ago. I slogged through his diary exactly as I'd done with Clarence's message, drawing out my brother's terrible story, as slowly as chipping through ice. The story of a small boy called Tom Parsons.

> there is boy near us They say ingenious not my Class he go St Martin's he Junior me only seven one month

> all people say Tom Parsons brainy intellectual don't like it even my parents say he ingenious child at mathematical more than me

The desperate slowness of my task was almost too maddening to bear, but I was helped by all those margin notes of Timothy's, which often led me to his chosen words once I was on the right page. I should have recognized those scribbles for what they were weeks ago. Now I was aware of two parallel tracks in my brain, one decoding, the other screaming questions. *Why* this insanely complicated cipher in which it was nigh impossible to produce a proper sentence?

> want play happy again like when we got here from London playing in snow and with father and BIG BROTHER and sister they playing down stairs tonight but I don't want join in all gone doubleplus wrong

These weren't the imperfect linguistics of a child. Timothy's phrases, jerry-built from inappropriate borrowings from *Nineteen Eighty-Four*, were as clogged and jerky as the speech of some Martian.

> class today I told off not listen I reading book under desk she said is me being IGNORANCE but I said is too easy know all already she cross hit me on bottom I don't want my sister to tell my mother

> playground boys laugh about hit on bottom so I hit them but I'm not STRENGTH they STRENGTH and hit me back hurt horrid I cried

Why lumber himself with such needless graft? Having to ransack this novel for every word, and make do, skimp, use words that were close together to cut down on counting (capitalized slogans; *doubleplus*!), and then those punishing counts to define each word as Part X, Chapter Y, number Z . . . and then encipher *that* lot with a Vigenère table! What kind of obsessive would devise this – *and at the age of seven*?

> in Class Mrs FREEDOM keep talking me about Tom Parsons he don't even go school here he only live here why don't they all shut up

> And that is how my mother heard about Tom Parsons I think FREEDOM told her

God, this was agonizing, the very effort of making sense of Timothy's skewed text through my own frenzy, trying to deduce where sentences were meant to start and stop. 'Freedom' was Mrs Freeman, our first teacher here in Lossing Common, all cuddling plumpness and talcum powder. I had a sketchy memory of altercations with Timothy, who made no bones that he was cleverer than any mere primary school teacher – but taunting him about another child genius? No!

when we London my mother tell me I brainy mathematical and she tell neighbour now she don't

But if this work was gruelling for me, what had it been like for Timmy in that chilly bedroom in our draughty house? I remembered the light under his door in the small hours, and his cold sores and chilblains. I remembered his irritability and his tears. Did his mother remember? Or even notice? I ploughed on, my heart aching, and a shockingly lucid line took shape in the exercise book.

the whole place is nothing but pain and humiliation

To save on searching and counting, Timothy had lifted entire phrases from *Nineteen Eighty-Four* wherever he could. Their voice was not his own but Orwell's, their sudden fluency shocking – abrupt runs of inappropriate eloquence like short downhill bursts of a runaway train before once more careening off the rocks.

they used to say I am level of intelligence pretty smart for a nipper of seven always top of my Class more brainy than Brother's and sister but my mother says Tom Parsons capable of intricate calculations and staggering feats of memory and every mathematical problem Hate it

these boys I know school playground they live next house Tom I went DOWN WITH them his place met him

Tom never heard of me as ingenious his mother never heard of me too

344

my mother heard of him

The next stuff yielded nothing comprehensible. Timothy's counting must have gone wrong – it was top-hats, Capitalists and *unbellyfeel*. But what followed immediately afterwards made all too much sense.

two boys drowned fields in this neighbourhood playing on frozen water broke and boys sank in the depths

Oh God, Laurence Briggs and Martin West. 'Frozen water'? I gathered that Timothy couldn't find the word 'ice' anywhere in *Nineteen Eighty-Four*. And I realized, panic-stricken now, that for this particular story it was going to be a serious deficiency.

took Tom Parsons out went over fields to the edge of the wood I went day before too so knew where it was

told Tom was our secret game so he told his mother playing WITH boys by school I told mine playing end of our BIG garden it was a bright vilely cold day a draught was blowing the earth was like iron the water too everybody indoors so no-one WATCHING us

Tom Parsons sank in snow-drift face red and purple lips he cried wanted go home I say no got go field beyond

Tom stopped crying when him me playing new snow-drift game him happy reached the edge of the little wood and water frosted over but wouldn't break thick not melted I kept on WITH foot but not easy afraid frosted might crack and I drown too I'm not STRENGTH

made him go on another field he wanted home crying
again Hate him if we go home would tell his mother
about game and me making him go on frozen water she
would tell my parents I made him and then my mother
angry they might guess why what for

With each word hope retreated, my last helpless
emaciated hope that this story could turn around,
could twist itself into something innocent.

smashed frozen water my foot Tom Parsons crying so
he didn't see when it broke he sank in my leg slipped
got wet frozen but I got out

scared now cold wanted home but Tom would tell and
they guess

so had to do it finish it off

finish Tom off

push him in water like drowned boys

Like drowned boys. So finally he'd said it.

44

He'd said it. Getting to the point at long last was almost a relief, allowing my remaining heart-tearing hope to die away – my former wild panic steadying now to a kind of grief. Easier now to think.

Thought Tom Parsons will struggle no he went like dead straightaway

Easier to consider my own questions, too. Timothy must have realized immediately that his invented cipher was insanely cumbersome and restrictive, yet he stuck with its drudgery. To foil prospective code-crackers? God knew, it had foiled me for long enough.

he went heavy his face stopped looking like Tom no struggle all the fight went out of him I frightened

But why record it at all, this damning story nearly unbearable to read? Maybe you have to. You can't tell a soul, not your twin sister because she'll tell Mummy (and it is to disbar another child from winning the good opinion of your mummy that you've turned into a killer), and you can't even play any more with the brother you hero-worship because his intuitive understanding is on a level with ESP and he'll pick up the truth, he'll know. So perhaps you have to write it all out for a different somebody. Dear Diary.

> frightened wished someone come anyone I shouting nobody heard me all indoors

Those ripped pages will have been Timothy's initial record of hearing about the boy and meeting him, written innocently enough in lucid English. Later he had to destroy all references to Tom Parsons, and so rewrote the whole story in code. A code that used *Nineteen Eighty-Four* must have struck Timothy immediately because of the child's name and his own pre-existing fascination for Orwell's nightmare tale, a preoccupation he had brought with him from our old house. To this old house.

> his face eyes horrid I shouting help

Maybe the preposterous complexities of this lumbering system helped to distance the crime, to metamorphose the horror and shame into an intellectual exercise. Once you've clamped your narrative into the grotesque eccentricities of such a cipher, how much of your inner pandemonium survives onto the page?

> Why already dead? It too soon for Tom drown his clothes drenched fat in water Hate it shouted loud tried pull Tom out but I slipping in I'm not STRENGTH the weight of his body in the filthy water heavy not like when we carry girls in playground Tom like dead why?

348

Dry drowning. Oh God, that's what it must have been – the poor little boy dry-drowned. It's the cold that does it, I've read it in Mum and Dad's journals. Sudden fierce cold causes overactivity in the part of our brain that controls temperature. This spills over and in susceptible people triggers a massive outflow of impulses down the vagus nerve to the heart. And the heart stops. That's what happened to Tom Parsons, Timmy. Nothing to do with water in the lungs. When his poor body hit the terrible water, the electrical activity of his heart was stunned into silence, his healthy young ventricles ceased to beat, and they never beat again.

long time in field shouting crying but doublepluscold
Tom blue his forearms above his head I knew will not
come out I stopped shouting went home

It was cold home too

It was cold home too. I was beside myself now, shaking, tears splashing mucus-thick onto my T-shirt. But suppose the poor little boy had struggled, Timmy – what then? Could you have wrestled him back into the freezing pond? Of course you couldn't! The moment you saw what had happened, you panicked and tried to drag him out! So if Tom *hadn't* died instantly, he'd have struggled from that disgusting water to stomp home frightened and furious – and you, Timmy, would have been in such earth-shaking bloody trouble that your head would still have been spinning next Christmas! How could a child capable of such forethought, smart enough to recognize the potential of that earlier Lossing tragedy (and to formulate this devious cipher!), *how* could that child make such a blinding, moronic error of judgement? Because I'm seven, said the voice from the page. My maths genius

349

is all I have to win my mother's approval and suddenly here we are, living in the back of beyond, with someone else's child usurping my limelight. But, Timmy, no matter what the outcome for Tom Parsons, with every step you took towards that godforsaken pond, you were turning your life into utter nightmare! Maybe, said the diary, but I am already so wretchedly unhappy I cannot conceive that things could be made worse.

> told my mother I cold because played in our snow-white outside home my wet foot and leg frozen bad pain I crying

But the poor little boy didn't struggle, didn't clamber out of the pond, take a whack at you and hightail it back to civilization screaming attempted murder. You left his body in the water, walked home across the fields yourself and excused your own sopping wet clothes and raw skin by pretending that you'd slipped in snowdrifts while playing in our garden.

No mention anywhere that you'd considered the police, though God knew it wasn't for lack of the bloody word in *Nineteen Eighty-Four*. So weren't you afraid of being found out? I suppose enough snow fell later to obliterate the traces of Tom's companion, but you couldn't have foreseen this. No, judgement never entered into the thing, did it, Timmy? The very concept of investigation, of justice, *of somebody out there who cared enough to wonder how this happened* – never crossed the threshold of your warped, desperate universe. Your world was hollow at the heart – there was literally a hole in it, an absence: that of your adored, self-martyring mother.

'I was Tom Parsons. Read your brother's diary for nineteen sixty-three.' But if Tom Parsons was

Clarence, why didn't he just tell me the whole story? Why go through the code stuff at all? Because I would never have believed it. Not without this appalling document. And this appalling document would be incomprehensible until I'd learned how to break Timothy's ciphers. It was as simple as that.

Except it wasn't simple. Did I truly believe that the message was sent to me by the spirit of a poor dead child? Did I still believe in Clarence?

Terrified to think further, I pushed the diary away. A sob tore through my chest and convulsed my ribs with such searing pain I thought it was a heart attack. I was going to die, to drop dead in a graveyard among these snaggle-toothed headstones with a real-life murder story discarded on the grass beside my corpse.

Eventually the muscle spasm eased and I was still alive, trumpeting into Mr Switt's hanky and remembering that somewhere under one of these lichened, crumbling stones lay Josiah Widgery.

Not my class he goes St Martin's. It was a primary school, highly sought after. Roman Catholic. Which explained why Tom wasn't at our local school, where I would certainly have noticed when he died. And explained why he wasn't buried at St Andrew's. Did it also explain why for eight years he had rendered our drawing room uninhabitable by seeping damp all over Josiah Widgery's sick frieze of martyrs and bonfires?

I probably met him. In my own cold shock of moving to the Red House, one more boy would have been neither here nor there. No doubt Timothy's pathological sensitivity had exaggerated everybody's interest in this local wonder-child – Mrs Freeman's, Mum's and Dad's (our mother's interest would certainly have been minimal – in *any* child). Even so, they probably did say a lot of thoroughly tactless stuff about how Tom Parsons was a bigger genius than any

351

of us, and within my hearing. For me it had not held sufficient significance to carve out the faintest of trace memories. Timothy was my twin; our foetal limbs had entwined in the womb. But his mind took on the contours of obsession and mine didn't.

And later, when I overheard grown-ups talk about the boy's death, which they must have done – the third in a few weeks! – it meant nothing to me because I'd never noticed Tom Parsons, so I never gave him another thought. But I knew him now. I'd lived with Tom's boyish tricks and unhappiness for more than half my lifetime.

Or had I?

I hate live here worse now since I did that thing I want go home our last house or anywhere

trying to make house so bad they got leave got take us back home

my sister says I'm sad I'm not like before I never wet bed before I pretend she is stupid baby

And you went on pretending, Timmy. There was nothing more, no further diary entries until the summer, when the journal was downgraded to the ordinary schoolroom English of a gifted child, and the occasional slough of maths. But surely that silence was itself remarkable. If the friend whom you'd murdered had started to manifest himself in spirited antics round your house, wouldn't an obsessive diarist like you want to write about it? If you *didn't* write about it, either in code or otherwise, did it mean that the author of those antics was yourself?

My mind, reeling with shock and pain, quaked yet again. Yes, it was possible. The puerile tricks that had 'haunted' our new house could have been engineered by a brilliant and desperate child trying to drive his parents out of that woebegone village and back to an overcrowded maisonette in Ealing. The panic of those early days could have shifted later into darker compulsions, perhaps nothing more than the sheer frustrated wielding of power in an otherwise powerless state of isolation. That would explain 'Clarence's' desultory reappearances over more than eight years.

Yet even if I accepted this grotesque construction, the floor collapsed under it when I considered the recent surge of activity. When, after the best part of a decade, our parents finally did work up the energy to put the house on the market, to get away from Lossing, it made no sense for Timothy to frighten off the estate agent and prospective buyers. And anyway, who sent me the coded message?

Perhaps it did make sense, Timmy. Perhaps you just couldn't bear it any longer. You arrived in Lossing Common as a seven-year-old and scarred the village for ever. Perhaps you couldn't abandon the place without somebody, after all this time, knowing the truth. *Which* somebody? Not Tarquin, who by then you'd shunned for years – and anyway he might not even grace your story with a raised eyebrow, until the next thing you knew you were the subject of a concept album being reviewed in the *Melody Maker*. No, not Tarquin. Your clever sister. She was swallowing Tarquin's Clarence-theory. And she would, eventually, given access to the code books from your bedroom shelves, crack the message and read your diary. That depth of misery brewing in you as a small child and festering in silence through puberty to your teens – that might be motivation for a weird and twisted way to grass yourself up. It might be motivation for absolutely anything. When that sheet of paper with 'Clarence's code' fluttered from my bedroom shelves and I retrieved the other sheet from the bathroom, I hadn't recognized either as my own handwriting. I would never now be able to recall the true sequence of letters that Francine and I were 'given' by our Ouija. Did they match those scribbled sheets? Or did our Ouija produce the random rubbish of wishful thinking, whereas the retrieved sheets were plants? Yours, Timmy. Again, I remembered Tarquin in the kitchen:

'It sounds pretty fishy to me . . . How'd you get this message anyway?'

'I sort of asked him for it, and he put it in the bathroom.'

These last months, Timmy, I imagine you were floundering between resignation, relief and gut-churning panic. Handing me clues and tantrums by turns. Your shunned brother would call it existential angst.

Was this ridiculous? And was it less ridiculous than believing Tom Parsons had sent me messages from beyond the grave?

Either way, Timmy, you are going through hell right now. Coming out of the bathroom to find your door smashed at the lock, and your diary taken from the shelf. You already know I've got your copy of *Nineteen Eighty-Four*; it has been missing since June. Whatever the truth, you are going through torture today.

And now that I can confront you with the crime, presumably you can both rest, you and poor Tom; so now the tricks, the pranks, the jests, the evil . . . will all stop.

At this realization, my mind finally recoiled. Now that I knew Tom Parsons's story — his youth, his tragedy, *his genius with maths* . . . would I rather believe that it was he who had lived with us for so much of my life? And if he went away now, would I miss him?

* * *

354

Some time in the late afternoon I stumbled home, four miles, across the fields, along the roads, sobbing, my nose running unchecked, unshameable. None of the screaming cars even slowed down as they passed me. Beyond comfort, and sick with having eaten nothing all day, I turned into our gravel driveway. Between the builders' vehicles and cement mixer were parked a van and two removal lorries, into one of which the modules of Tarquin's Moog synthesizer were being loaded via a hydraulic lift, directed by Tarquin himself and Florian, in a welter of guitars and suitcases.

45

'Cool it, Jo!'

'This is *you*!' I screamed at Florian. 'It's *your* doing! Without you he would never have gone anywhere ever again – you've stolen him!'

Los Angeles, that's where they were off to.

'They won't let you into LA – your visa's run out!' I had objected, citing practical considerations, clutching at straws the way the drowning do, though not poor Tom Parsons, not him.

'It's all taken care of, Jo,' said Tarquin, holding down my thrashing arms. 'The visas were no sweat. We've got an American project about chess.'

'*Chess?*'

'Sonic material to play chess by. Think of Marcel Duchamp's exhibition match on the rooftop with the Velvets making music.'

My world was coming apart around my ears and Tarquin was talking about bloody chess.

'But the Velvet Underground are in New York!' I shouted in frightened exasperation.

Tarquin sighed and looked worriedly behind him. The hydraulic lift crunched across the gravel and whined up and down, to the shouting of male voices.

'We're working with Joe Byrd. You know him – used to have that band, the United States of America, pretty well the only prog rock outfit across the Atlantic. Great opportunity. He's classically trained like me and Florian, so the three of us . . .'

But my mind was racing beyond him. Los Angeles, California. Of *course*! Of *course*! I spun on Florian. 'This is about your bloody Carly!' I yelled at him. 'Using Tarquin is the only way you could ever get work on the West Coast! You're stealing my brother from me just to get to *her*!'

'Come on now,' said Tarquin, still restraining me, still gentle.

'He's hoodwinked you! There's this woman . . .'

'Jo, no guy does all this for a chick.'

No? Not even when he wants her so bad he aches? So bad he could beg? Tarquin was patiently shaking his head at me. He didn't see Florian colour and turn away.

'*See?*' I screamed. 'Look at him! Ask him! Her name's Anna-Carlotta Campiani and he's mad about her. She's—'

'You're taking this too hard, Jo, like it will be a drag with me gone. It will be a gas. Your life path is about to open. Just go with the flow and trust in the law of karma.'

This bloody karma stuff was even worse than his chess. I had to haul Tarquin back to reality. 'You've got a recording contract here! They'll sue you.'

'It's all negotiated. Now that Florian's finished working his notice period . . .'

'What notice period?'

'For his job,' said Tarquin, surprised.

I just stared.

'His job as a salesman, yeah? For EMI records. Selling to retail outlets across a territory covering most of this side of Essex,' explained Tarquin, in a startling plummet from his habitual vibes-in-the-cosmos style. 'Good bread, but he's tired of wearing a suit and tie.'

A salesman. Florian was a salesman. I'd never wondered, never thought about it, yet it explained so much. The good car, his perpetual comings and goings – and that ability to talk absolutely anybody into anything. Well, it had worked; Florian had everything now – his precious Tarquin and his precious Carly. And I? I had nothing left in the wide world.

Florian must have mentioned Carly to Tarquin. He couldn't stop himself; references to the woman slipped from him as haplessly as the secrets of an overexcited child. But Tarquin couldn't see that he was being manipulated; to him it was inconceivable that anything, ever, could mean more to a man than his music.

'Did you load the guitars?' Florian called over his shoulder.

'Sure.'

'Yeah? I didn't see the Strat.'

'They're all where they should be. The studio's empty, you can check.'

'That's OK, I just did.'

Tarquin, his hands loosening their grip on my wrists, bent over and kissed me gently on the forehead. 'There's a groove ahead for you, Jo. You just got to free your mind and listen to the call. The path is waiting. But you have to let me go now. I got to look after the Moog.'

When Tarquin released my arms I knew despair. I stood there, utterly wretched, not competent to move out of everyone's way. Vast men in overalls sidestepped me, hauling crates and anonymous boxes. The words 'air freight' and 'sea freight' and 'cargo' rang in the air around me. My grief howled into the masculine busyness. I no longer cared whom Timothy had killed or why – what Louis MacNeice called *the white light in the back of my mind to guide me* went out. Eventually the lorries backed away, down the drive. Then Florian picked up a leather suitcase from our front steps and, arranging it fussily in the back of the Bedford van, slammed the doors and slipped into the driving seat. He hadn't looked my way since I'd screamed in his face. He didn't now. I scarcely registered the fact.

Tarquin called across to me. 'Keep cool, Jo,' he said for the very last time. Then he opened the passenger door, got heavily in, and Florian drove away.

46

The studio was strewn with discarded packaging and seethed with electric cables like a snake pit, everything gone except the mutilated piano. The space looked impossibly small, as rooms do when people move out. I went for Tarquin's elderly desk, my shoes squeaking on bubble-wrap, its ruptured blisters squelching under my feet like burst pustules.

His desk drawers were stuffed with papers. Cupboards exploded as I opened them. I wrenched and ransacked. Addresses; Tarquin must have left a note of relevant addresses, the names of contacts, their phone numbers – he could not have achieved all this without leaving a trail.

Of course, the rest of the household wouldn't let me have the studio to myself. There was Angela, there was Timothy. The moment he'd clapped eyes on me, he'd known for certain.

'Jo-sie!'

'Go away, Timmy.'

'Tell me what you're going to do now. Who are you going to tell?'

'Leave me alone.'

'It's killing me, Josie, I've got to know what you're going to do!'

'I don't care if it kills you. I don't give a fuck. Go to hell.'

It was true, I didn't care. I'd had it with caring. My chaotic pity for Timothy had vanished when Tarquin deserted me.

Angela had found Tim's room exposed and gone into overdrive, stripping its bedding, its grimed furniture, its encrusted dust. Seventeen hamsters gnawed through cardboard boxes while she scraped at their cages with a kitchen knife. But she didn't do it mute. 'You could give me a hand, madam,' Angela shouted periodically into the studio, 'instead of mooning about in there!'

The house was also in another sort of disarray: a group of my father's patients had banded together to complain to the GMC of botched operations because he was drunk. Dad was on suspension pending an enquiry, and hadn't been to Harley Street for a month. He'd left the house each morning and whiled away the day in bars. That was why Timothy couldn't reach him when the exam results came through. I knew this because I'd been talking to Geoffrey in the kitchen.

Actually, I hadn't been talking as much as crying. All over him. I didn't say anything about Tom Parsons, of course, and anyway Geoffrey didn't ask questions, just let me sob in his arms while his wife's furious energy rattled the ceiling above us.

'Geoff,' I said eventually, when I was able to get out a coherent sentence. He'd made me a cup of tea. I kept hiccuping and scalding my lips. 'Do you know anything about Letitia Richardson?'

He frowned.

'Amy Richardson's daughter, and Ken's,' I spelled out for him. 'We bought this house from them.'

'Letty Richardson!' he said, working it out. That was reasonably speedy for Geoff. 'She was Ange's friend who did a runner. Before our time, but it was still big news hereabouts when we moved in.'

'Except the police didn't know she'd done a runner, Geoff, only that she'd disappeared. Neither did the Richardsons' solicitor, who pronounced her legally dead in July 1969.'

'Yes, well, it was very hush-hush. The girl took off without telling her mum and dad. Ange thinks she never would have told them either, but she phoned from London and Ange persuaded her.'

'Letitia phoned *Angela*?'

God, imagine escaping from Lossing Common and phoning *Angela*.

'Ange told her it was only fair, Amy had been distraught. Couldn't even pull herself together when people turned up to view the house.'

'But what was it all about? I know that that horrible Ken was playing around with her schoolfriends. But Angela said it was something to do with the MoD.'

'Letty came in from school one afternoon and found a civil servant in the house reading Kenneth the riot act. Well, the Official Secrets Act anyway. Her mum wasn't in, and it seems the men didn't notice her, but Letty heard all about it.'

'I don't understand.'

'Told him to pick somewhere else for his hanky-panky.'

Light flooded in on me. 'They were in the woods!' I said. 'The MoD's bit of the woods.'

Of course. Ken Richardson with his seventeen-year-olds. He must have been in the habit of taking them behind the church, unknowingly next to the entrance to Tarquin's fabled underground network.

'So the Ministry of Defence sent a man round to the house,' I faltered, '*this* house, of course. To warn Ken to do his shagging elsewhere. A man with a bowler hat and briefcase.'

There must have been a formal warning, and he was made to sign the Official Secrets Act. Only Letitia arrived home from school during this interview and . . . And then?

'And she ran off?'

'According to Ange, she was pretty sick of her dad anyway, making a laughing stock of her with girls at school. And sniffing round her underwear, apparently – the chap's a pretty unsavoury character, all in all. And Letty wasn't exactly generous about her mum putting up with him. Sixteen-year-old girls aren't the most tolerant of creatures,' he continued, forgetting that I was sixteen all but a month. 'I suppose Letty wanted to teach them both a lesson.'

'But eventually Angela did persuade her to get in touch?'

'Not long before we came here. Then we started courting, me and Ange. That's why I know so much about it.'

'So why wasn't that the end of the mystery? Letty's alive and well. Ken's had a bollocking from the Ministry of Defence for trespassing in their under-growth with half the local Guide pack and the Dagenham Girl Pipers; the CID ticks him off for wasting police time and then closes the missing persons file. All's well that ends well.'

'Apparently she'd been gone quite some time before she got in touch with Ange, even. She ran away in the summer. Must have been Christmas before she put Ken and Amy out of their misery.'

'So?'

Geoff poured himself another cup of tea. It was stewed black. He went to tip it down the sink, missed and drenched the draining board. 'Do you think there could be something genetic?' he said. 'Though I suppose it's unlikely to pass from father to daughter. I mean, the affected father would have it on the Y chromosome.'

'*Geoffrey!*'

'Sorry. Letty had that look, everyone says. Butter wouldn't melt in her mouth. It's a useful attribute, hides a multitude of sins.'

'Sorry?'

'Angela wasn't totally surprised, given Letitia and given London. The girl was raking it in. Schoolgirl, too. She'd kept the uniform.'

I must still have looked blank.

'Raking it in,' repeated Geoffrey. 'Dressed as a schoolgirl.'

Oh God. Butter wouldn't melt. I remembered what Tarquin had said – she gave the impression of being a prissy little piece. Perhaps that put the price up.

'Ange said it wasn't like most poor runaways, who get dragged down to prostitution because they're desperate. Letitia went into the classy stuff like it was a chosen career.'

'But – what about her mum and dad, and the police who were looking for her?'

'Ken was in no hurry to have her back, after what she'd witnessed. I mean it was one thing to be Jack the Lad with the girlies, and another to make a total prat of yourself, getting an official dressing-down in front of your teenage daughter. But it was actually Amy who put the tin lid on it. Churchgoer and everything. Women's Institute, jam-making, blue-eyed son in America – and her daughter on the game. She told Letty that they'd believed up to now that she was dead, so as far as Amy was concerned, the girl could stay dead. Ange was pretty shocked, but said it wasn't her business, it was a family matter. She washed her hands of it. I don't think she's ever told anybody but me. And I've never told anyone but you.'

I was stupefied. I remembered those press cuttings, carefully clipped from the newspapers, and then later stuffed inside a family album, and the whole lot shoved to the back of a drawer. I thought of all the parents whose children are genuinely never found; their own lives rotting, corroded by fear and grief and terrible endless hope. I thought of all the sympathy that must have been extended to the Richardsons on exactly that assumption, friends and neighbours breaking their hearts for Letitia's parents. I pictured Amy Richardson's round, girlish, soap-scrubbed face in the Lent austerity of Mr Horne's church. I wanted to slap her.

Obviously Ken hadn't put the police straight about the identity of the man in the bowler hat, but surely the MoD would tell them? Or didn't they co-operate even that much, these men with their male-bonding clubs and their secrecy rules? Well, they deserved one another, I decided. Ken, Amy, Letitia, the Ministry of Defence, the whole bloody lot deserved one another.

'Geoffrey,' I said now, because I couldn't put it off any longer. 'About Dad. What do you think . . . ?'

'Most complaints like this don't succeed against the medical profession.'

'I know.'

'They close ranks pretty solid.'

'So do you think it will be OK and everything?'

'I don't think so, Josie. Not this one. An investigation's in full swing and claims of malpractice seem to be multiplying like flies around a corpse. If you want the truth, I think he'll be struck off.'

'Oh,' I said. 'Oh.'

'And with the accusations being so serious . . .'

And then I knew what Geoff was going to say.

'It could be handed over to the police, even. There's

no way of knowing, not yet. We'll just have to wait.'

Yes, that seemed to sum up our time in Lossing Common – uncertainty shot through with half-hopes, and always a spectre just out of sight. Our lives in the Red House had been building to this, had been merely a prelude to the final torture of waiting for the final catastrophe.

'Sorry,' said Geoff. And then, 'You're too young to remember much about what it was like when we first came to live here. Big adventure, new life and so on. Stebbing General was crying out for vigorous young blood, Mum would get promotion, no problem, have time for a proper family life. And Dad with his dreamy, romantic streak, finding such a weird and wonderful house, lots of Georgian styles together, all that mathematical precision, what's-their-names, Adam brothers. In a couple of years there would be money enough to restore its former splendour. He talked about throwing the place open. Musical soirées. Fancy dress, with lights in the garden.

'Never really stood a chance. The consultants at Stebbing weren't going to admit a *woman* to their hallowed ranks, especially not one with a Mother Theresa complex, literally addicted to working eighteen-hour days. Which left Dad effectively a widower. I suppose another man could have rallied. He could have gone it alone, got on with his plans for the house with or without his wife. He could even have found himself some extramarital comfort into the bargain. But Dad doesn't come from strong stock, does he? The son of a compulsive gambler who committed suicide, and a mother who gave up eating and died of shame. Dad inherited the wrong genes, married the wrong woman, pursued the wrong career and set his heart on the wrong dream. Things were always going to turn out badly.' Geoffrey poured another cup of tea and looked quizzically across the table at me.

'No more for me, thanks.'

'It's likely to be pretty grim here, Josie,' he said. 'Afterwards, I mean. Mum will completely retreat into her work, I think, and stop coming home at all. If you can't stand it, just say the word. We're not spacious but there'd be no need to slum it by sleeping on the settee – we've got a put-you-up bed, and Ange wouldn't mind you sharing Angus's room.'

'I will have that cup of tea actually, Geoff,' I decided.

He got the milk from the fridge. Its white plastic racks, scrubbed clean of their drizzled egg yolk and rancid encrustations, were tight-packed with what Angela would probably call comestibles – bottles of milk spruce as ninepins, vacuum-packed bacon and crackling cellophane. Tupperware tubs. Upstairs, she was tearing the innards from Tim's room to create order from chaos, no doubt between bouts of maternal fussing and cooing at her children. A greater contrast with our own mother couldn't be imagined. I suddenly understood why Geoffrey had married her.

'That's a very generous offer,' I told him kindly. 'I appreciate the thought.'

'*Geoffrey!*' screamed a voice from above us. 'You're supposed to be helping me take this pelmet down!'

'I think I'm wanted,' said Geoff. He leaned over me, bear-like, and kissed the top of my head in a gesture unsettlingly like his departed brother. Then he padded on his enormous feet across the kitchen, across the hallway and up our creaking, and now forever banister-less, staircase. I remembered the bloke who had given a lift home to Francine and me, and his mention of a dead Natasha. I opened my mouth to ask Geoffrey. But he'd gone.

47

'Josie, who are you going to tell? Who?'

'Have you stopped doing it now?'

'Doing what?'

'You know what. Planting stink bombs, balancing buckets on doors, stuffing electrical gadgets up the chimney. Have you stopped now that I know the truth?'

Timothy had been crying all day. His wet-faced incoherence had driven Angela into a spitting fury. He was beyond answering questions about Clarence. About Tom. Timothy's haunting was at a level deeper than anything that had ever infested the Red House.

But the place *was* different. Not warm, its proportions wouldn't allow that, but the house no longer felt like a recently flooded cellar. Here in the studio I rummaged through tangled audiotape, nicotine-stained political tracts and tiny cables neatly coiled like a bakery tray of Danish pastries.

'All right, Timmy, you want to know what I'm going to do.' I sat back on my heels. It wasn't just that I had no pity left; I positively wanted to hurt. The desire to lash out, wound Timothy and watch him bleed overwhelmed me like infection and fever. And I made no attempt to fight it.

'I'm going to get out of here, Timmy,' I said, loud and clear. 'Tarquin's left you, now I'm leaving you. You're going to stew in whatever disgrace crashes down on the family. I'd say it's a pound to a penny that when Dad gets struck off you won't see our mother for dust, not even her usual brief appearances en route to bed. Geoff thinks there might be a criminal prosecution. You'll have the choice of staying here on your own to watch Dad drink himself to death before the police come to take him away, or moving in with Angela and Angus.'

From along the landing came the noise of an avalanche. Its cadences were familiar – this was how a bookcase sounded when every single precious volume came careening off the shelves to dismember itself on the floor beneath. I presumed that Angela had just toppled Timothy's.

'As for your diary,' I continued, 'I'm going to hang on to it. Always. If anything suspicious ever happens to anyone near you, *anything*, ever again, I won't ask questions, I'll just send the diary to the police with the Vigenère key and your copy of *Nineteen Eighty-Four* with the most damning words marked up inside.'

Timothy stared at me, not taking it in. 'Yeah, but are you going to tell Mum?'

I looked him in the eye. His face was growing to look less like my own these days, Timothy's jaw heavier, my features softening. We were no longer two peas in a pod. And with that thought, I knew why I was so desperate to hurt him. Through a glass darkly. Timothy, my twin, was my dark side. The desperate child of an uninterested mother, he was all my own anger and despair: he was what I might be if I stayed here, if I stopped fighting, gave up my endeavour to build a life behind my rickety front of maturity and intelligence. Lashing out at Timothy was an attempt to eradicate my own vulnerability. I wasn't Tarquin, who could wander at will in and out of a world of his own, or the imperturbable Geoffrey, who would probably have emerged unscathed from trench warfare. Reality touched me and hurt. Timothy was what I might be if ever I cracked. For the same reason, I could neither stay here to look after him nor take him with me; in the end, it wasn't the Red House that I had to escape from, it wasn't Dad's drinking, it wasn't even the continual heartbreak of those fleeting glimpses of our mother. It was Timothy.

And anyway, can we ever deal logically with our closest family?

But in Timmy's crumpled face, I could just about recognize Tarquin's little brother squealing with laughter at the garbled playback of those spliced tapes. With infinite weariness, I now reached out a hand, and Timothy sank onto Tarquin's litter-strewn floor and cried for an hour in my arms, as I'd cried in Geoffrey's.

I considered what to do. We had no other relatives; Mum was an only child whose parents had faded out of existence while she was at medical school. There was nobody on whom I could offload my twin brother and his hamsters. Then I remembered my words to him: 'You'll have the choice of staying here on your own . . . or moving in with Angela and Angus.' I'd contrived that out of careful cruelty, but suddenly I could see that of course that was where Timothy would go – and it wasn't like abandoning him to the wolves, it would do him the power of good! If what you craved was continual, clucking maternal fuss, Angela Starkey was just the ticket. Even the irritation would be therapeutic, would rattle Timothy out of his seclusion, shake some domestic normality into that cerebral retreat. And look how Angela had reacted to Florian as 'Josie's boyfriend': she'd probably make a crusade out of finding Timothy a girl.

I dug further into the possibilities. She and Geoffrey had known about Letitia all these years and never said a word to anyone. Suppose I told them about ... Suppose I presented to them the truth, the lot, finally shattering for all time this eight-year-long secret with its malignant life-force. Death-force. Would Angela fear for the safety of her darling little brood and drive Timothy away? No, I didn't think so. I would put it to Geoffrey.

Eventually, Timothy's raging grief subsided into exhaustion, his mind blank, that racing brain on hold, in hiatus. I gently disentangled my arms from his intransigent weight and quietly went back to Tarquin's papers, straightening them out one by one, scanning both sides for anything – a scribbled note, even – that might give me a lead and a contact.

48

'You *do* look as if you're going on an exciting journey!' said a woman in a flowery trouser suit and white floppy hat. I took my eyes from the track, which I'd been gazing at in a lazy daydream of *High Noon*. On the platform opposite, waiting passengers were wiped from my view as the Chelmsford train lurched to a halt. Amid all the fuming metal and din of slammed doors I wasn't certain that it was really me she was talking to, the woman in the hat, until I noticed her smile. A white-painted fingernail indicated my massed luggage.

'Yes,' I confirmed, smiling back. 'A *very* exciting journey.' My mind formed an image of flying railway lines watched through a train window, crossing and recrossing, writhing, mile after mile. I thought of the hooey whistle of American trains.

'I'm off to a wedding,' confided the woman. 'A funny sort of day to get married, Thursday, but at least they've got a lovely morning for it. And that's something you can't guarantee this late in the year, can you?'

'It's actually the first day of autumn,' I told her inviting smile.

'Really? I thought that was the twenty-first.'

'Astronomers would say it's today, because of the equinox. At precisely forty-four minutes and fifty-four seconds after five o'clock this afternoon, the sun will cross the celestial equator.'

The woman in the hat laughed delightedly. 'What a romantic fact to have at your fingertips! I'll pass that one on to the bride and groom.'

High on our left, up on the bridge, a low sun backlit the trundling buses as they heaved their way up Station Road. Light caught the dusty plane trees with what Tarquin, in a song lyric, had called 'a lively flavescence'. Encouraged by the reception that she'd afforded my equinox remark, I turned again to my fellow passenger.

'The vibrant gold of late September,' I said, indicating the glittering traffic. 'That same unearthly light as in Turner's "Fighting Temeraire".'

'Aha!' she cried. 'Now I've placed you. You're a poet!'

'Actually, I borrowed that imagery from a song.'

Her eyes lit on the guitar case at my feet. 'So I was nearly right. A musician.'

'Any day now,' I conceded, smiling back.

There was more metallic clatter and dirty exhaust, this time on our side of the railway line.

'Our train,' announced the woman happily. 'I'll give you a hand with your luggage. Smoking carriage or no?'

'I've given up, but if you prefer smoking I don't mind.'

'Not me,' she said, reaching out an arm for the beehive wicker basket and then laughing when she realized there was a cat inside. She peered closer. 'Oh, bless him! What's the matter with his poor head? He's got a short back and sides.'

Not a lot wrong with his poor head, if you wanted

my opinion; Elvis had been using it pretty effectively to headbutt the wire mesh of his nice new basket. The mesh now bulged like a sagging fence. He eyed the stranger suspiciously as she squatted down with her own head at a level that Elvis no doubt associated with Angus.

'He's all right,' I assured her, hauling open the carriage door. 'He had an operation and the vet was afraid it might be—' I stopped short, remembering that outside the Starkey household people didn't like the word cancer, and I was now – irrevocably – outside the Starkey household. 'The vet was afraid it might be serious,' I amended, 'but luckily it wasn't. Just a benign thing. Come on, Elvis.'

'*Elvis!*' she repeated, laughing again. Hers was a voice geared up for laughter. I found that I was delighted she was here.

My suitcase followed, then the leather portfolio I'd bought at the weekend. My new friend reached out a well-intentioned hand to the instrument case.

'It's OK,' I said hurriedly, 'I'll take that one.'

'Ah yes, your guitar.'

Then I hauled up the last of my bags and together we slammed the door. This was my erstwhile school bag, which now contained: a London *A–Z* map, a handful of addresses – including my bedsitter (cash in advance), the Switts' new apartment (they'd be moving in just over a week), and Joe's flat in Cumberland Terrace (great guy, loads of brothers and sisters, his mum was teaching me about Kenyan cooking!) – an airmail letter to Patti, my building society book (cancelled this morning after I'd withdrawn all the money – my birthday present to myself), and a beginner's guide to playing the guitar. I was making pretty impressive progress with this. Not all the Starkey genes were bad.

We sat ourselves down in the empty carriage that

was now strewn with the impedimenta of my new life, and the train lurched out of Brentwood station. It was lovely to have someone to travel with, though I had come prepared with a book – *The Road to Wigan Pier*. Barbara, being an Orwell admirer, had talked me into it. I had to admit, grudgingly, that it was pretty good stuff. I would never be able to pick up *Nineteen Eighty-Four* again, but I'd sort of made my peace with its author.

Now I peered happily through the smeary window at the vanishing small town. I'd always loved peering into houses from a train; not the fronts, they're for show, all stone cladding and Windolene, but the backs are the intimate clutter of other lives; ordinary hopes and heartbreaks. Unhaunted.

I'd tracked down the Catholic church where Tom Parsons was buried, and found out a little about him. He'd been one of five children, apparently – four boys and a girl, their father an actuary in the City. He was a clever and funny lad. Always playing practical jokes.

After Tom's death the family couldn't cope with Lossing and moved to the other side of Ongar, which was also nearer to the church. I caught several buses and bought a lot of flowers en route. I also took along a greetings card addressed *To Tom from a friend* which could cause no upset to the family when they tended his grave, and in which I'd written out a knotty problem in differential equations, followed by this really neat solution I'd found in a book.

Not a mossy green churchyard, this one, but modern, the headstones ranked like Marcel Duchamp's chessmen, Tom's own grave all black marble and chippings that glistened like bath salts.

Thomas Patrick Kevin Parsons
9 January 1956 – 25 February 1963
Beloved son and brother
Now at rest in the calm of the all-humouring sun

I knew the quotation: *Let me in the calm of the all-humouring sun / Also indulge my humour.* From the poem 'Spring Sunshine'. So thoroughly appropriate to a fun-loving little boy who died in such dismal cold so shortly before the end of winter. Louis MacNeice, of course. Tarquin had started reading him at exactly that time; it was Louis MacNeice whom he had used for the tone poem to the three dead boys that took up one entire side of his first album. When you cut away the barmy conspiracy theories and trusted to his intuition, it was extraordinary how much Tarquin knew that he'd never been told.

I'd come to terms with the fact that I would never be sure about Clarence; whether Tom's spirit had haunted us or the poltergeist tricks were Timothy's, conceived from various motives that mutated with the passing of time and his growing up.

And the nearly palpable misery that had pervaded our house like dry rot – was that Tom? Or did it emanate from that hole at its heart, the maternal indifference, with Timothy on one side and our father on the other, taking to the bottle and going down the drain. The Starkey family didn't need an avenging ghost to explain the bitter disappointment that surrounded us – we had enough pain of our own.

I had told Geoffrey the truth, everything. He was deeply shocked but he didn't doubt my story. 'Right,' he'd said eventually. 'We'd better get Ange onto this. She'll look after him.' And that was that. Looking back now on the conversation, I remembered that Geoff had cited case studies, psychiatric terminology. All my life I had paid attention to every medical fact I came across; presumably, I had been interested in that as a career. Now it seemed like part of a different life.

Beyond my carriage window, the houses gave way to a brief flash of autumn countryside – green belt. I thought again of Tarquin's song about the fields around the Red House, birds on telegraph wires, their patterns shifting like beads on an abacus. In the chaos of his leftovers I'd stumbled on all thirty songs at the back of a cupboard: lyrics, melody lines, guitar chords, cleanly arranged in a file and a surprisingly legible hand.

And I had found those names and numbers I was searching for. Every British producer Tarquin had ever worked with. I'd expected to slog patiently through barriers of secretaries and fobbings-off but in fact the very first one I phoned was extremely enthusiastic. I then made a tape for him, nothing fancy, just a tape recorder bought out of my accumulated dress allowance, on which I gave him a random sample of Tarquin's songs sung unaccompanied. Of course, I'd need parental agreement to sign his contract; sixteen might be old enough to leave home but not for that. Nevertheless, this was just a formality: things being as they were with Mum and Dad, they'd sign anything. And as for Tarquin's permission to use the songs, he'd left that for me inside the file, as a formal document. It wasn't just vibes-in-the-cosmos waffle, all his stuff about a path waiting for me if I followed the call. Tarquin had meant every word.

Anyway, the producer said he'd talk anybody round if need be; apparently he was a very powerful man in the music industry. Abbey Road studios, that's where he was. Which was truly fantastic, the very words had totemic significance. Besides, Abbey Road is in St John's Wood.

So that poem of mine, the one inspired by our TV weatherman, wasn't wasted after all; at the end of the day yesterday, I'd dropped it in to the school secretary, addressed to Mrs Matlock.

> *I shall not*
> *. . . be present*
> *. . . tomorrow.*

She will have read it by now. At the thought, I beamed and turned away from the carriage window, back to my companion.

'That's an impressive-looking guitar case,' she was saying approvingly.

It certainly was. Tarquin's parting gift wasn't confined to the songs. He had left me this, propped by my bed. The producer seemed to think it was a lovely touch, a sixteen-year-old girl with a 1956 white-blond Fender Strat. And of course, you didn't have to be an oil painting. Look at Joni Mitchell, Mama Cass, Janis Joplin. You only had to be able to sing.

That song about autumn fields was Tarquin's last. Not just his, of course – the world's last song. Everybody's. As I couldn't record that one for obvious reasons, I had twenty-nine in my initial repertoire, but that seemed to be OK with the producer guy. 'Twenty-nine of that calibre?' he had burst out on the phone. '*Twenty-nine!*'

I'd already decided what to do with the thirtieth song. One day, when the world lost Tarquin, that would be the time for it – my tribute to him: the day he died, I would give the last melody ever written its freedom to take to the air. And then music, having given us its swansong, would fall silent for ever, leaving humanity to cope with the jabbering soundscape of a songless, tone-deaf world. A most fitting requiem for the sonic material of Tarquin Starkey.

I'd thought the whole thing through carefully; even my worst fears for his unhealthy habits would have my brother survive into middle age. With a Californian lifestyle he might even toddle along a bit further. By then I wouldn't be young any more either, so I'd have a good innings before I brought music to an end for all time. Not until early in the next century, the next millennium in fact. *Ages* yet.

With my life now planned right down to that final detail, I sat back and prepared to make happy conversation as our train clattered along from rural to Romford, on a course that would obligingly veer away from any empty green spaces to head for the sooty echoes of Liverpool Street station and the metropolis.

THE END

ACKNOWLEDGEMENTS

There's a lot of people to thank: I'll start with Helen Porter for her invaluable insights into the literary capabilities of children, and thanks also to her mother, a.k.a. Dr Linda Barrow, for not charging me – and also for being the best colleague anyone, anywhere, has ever had. Next, there are all those who dug me out of a hole when I needed help with numbers or how to work the internet, and I insist that it's complete co-incidence that everyone competent in these disciplines was male: particular thanks to Peter Dunne, Dennis Chanter, Mark Porter, Gary Misson and Don Pitman. Also the architect John Hummerston for helping me to wreck the Red House, and the musician Paul Abrahams for tidying up my more outlandish musical solecisms.

My long-suffering mother put up with all kinds of lunatic enquiries, often phoned from the other side of the world at midnight when I'd misjudged the time difference, that went something like 'Mum, think back to Kelvedon Hatch in 1971. Now, you remember our ladder . . .' I'm also indebted to my late father for one scene, though it's taken me thirty years to realize that it might not have been a misunderstanding of thermoplastics that led him to persuade Karen and me to boil and iron *The Songs of Leonard Cohen*.

Eric Royer is the genius who invented the original of my guitar machine (except his isn't ludicrous). Simon Singh's *The Code Book* is an impeccably clear account of codes and code-breaking, and any errors in my own text are entirely mine, not Dr Singh's. There are a lot of great books out there about electronic music, of which *Analog Days* by Trevor Pinch and Frank Trocco is an enjoyable history of the Moog synthesizer.

Once the people above had written this novel for me, I had another lot to thank for getting it published. I'd be nowhere without my agent, friend, mentor and Samaritan Véronique Baxter; thanks also to Chloë Frayne for encouragement with every draft. Diana Beaumont is marvellous always, as is everyone else at Transworld including Deborah Adams and Prue Jeffreys.

Finally, a word about the location. The existence of underground bunkers inarguably identifies my village of 'Lossing Common' as Kelvedon Hatch, while Stavering is quite obviously Blackmore. (I seem to have left Brentwood intact.) However, anyone interested would find that other facts don't fit, the topography is all wrong, and, most particularly, if there ever existed a house remotely similar to my Red House then I never saw it, and it certainly never contained the grotesque characters I've landed mine with. Neither, I sincerely hope, has any other house . . .

PAINTING RUBY TUESDAY
Jane Yardley

'BRIGHT, ENGAGING AND VERY FUNNY' *Guardian*

It is the summer of 1965. Annie Cradock, the only child of
exacting parents who run the village school, is an imaginative
girl with a head full of the Beatles and the Rolling Stones.
Annie whiles away the school holiday with her friends:
Ollie the rag-and-bone man (and more importantly his
dog); the beautiful piano-playing Mrs Clitheroe who turns
Beethoven into boogie-woogie and Annie's best friend
Babette – streetwise, loyal, and Annie's one solid link with
common sense. But everything changes when the village is
rocked by a series of murders and the girls know
something they've no intention of telling the police.

In the present day, the adult Annie is a successful musician
and teacher in a stifling marriage. Her American husband
is an ambitious man uncomfortable with emotion and
impatient with his quirky wife. He's taking a job in New
York – but is she going with him? In a Greenwich Village
shop Annie discovers a photograph album from her past –
only then can she begin to lay her ghosts and come to
terms with the bizarre events of 1965.

'HIGHLY ORIGINAL . . . TOLD WITH HUMOUR AND
POIGNANCY BY A HUGELY LIKEABLE HEROINE . . . AN
ENTERTAINING AND COMPELLING READ FILLED WITH
ROUNDED, MEMORABLE CHARACTERS, AND BOTH
DARKLY FUNNY AND MOVING' *Time Out*

'*PAINTING RUBY TUESDAY* IS INDEED A COMIC NOVEL,
BUT ONE WHICH IS ELEVATED BY THE MUSIC WHICH
FLOWS THROUGH IT, AND THE UNUSUAL AND
ORIGINAL DESCRIPTIONS' *The Scotsman*

'I LOVED IT . . . I THOUGHT IT WAS WONDERFULLY
BLACKLY COMIC IN THAT UNIQUELY ENGLISH WAY . . .
INTERLACED WITH AN UNDERSTANDING OF HOW
FRAGILE MODERN RELATIONSHIPS CAN BE'
Isla Dewar, author of *Giving Up on Ordinary*

0 552 77101 5

BLACK SWAN

A SAUCERFUL OF SECRETS
Jane Yardley

It is 1969: London swings, men land on the moon, and thirteen-year-old Kim Tanner appears on Imogen's doorstep to announce she is her long-lost daughter.

Kim isn't the first to turn up; Imogen wrote a bestseller about the illegitimate baby she was bullied into giving away, so there have been many contenders, but Kim is special, and Imogen is convinced. Brought up by gritty, hard-working Peggy, she is bright, streetwise and will brook no nonsense. Now that Peggy has died, Kim moves in with the beautiful, bohemian Imogen, into her grubby house with the sponging boyfriend and hippie ideals. Exploding into Imogen's life, Kim and her huge woolly dog, Welly, proceed to bring order to chaos. Unfortunately, no sooner is she settled than along comes the pretty, appealing Sukie, also asserting she is Imogen's baby – and her claim is a strong one.

Kim is determined to prove she is Imogen's daughter but Peggy left no adoption papers to explain her background. And when kim starts digging she begins to unearth a very murky story . . .

A Saucerful of Secrets is a blackly funny, moving novel about relationships and identity – and with a stunning twist.

COMING SOON FROM DOUBLEDAY

0 385 60932 9

Doubleday